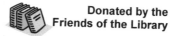

ALSO BY EDNA BUCHANAN

A DARK
AND LONELY
PLACE

EDNA BUCHANAN

SIMON & SCHUSTER
New York   London   Toronto   Sydney   New Delhi

Simon & Schuster
1230 Avenue of the Americas
New York, NY 10020

First Simon & Schuster hardcover edition November 2011

SIMON & SCHUSTER and colophon are registered trademarks
of Simon & Schuster, Inc.

For information about special discounts for bulk purchases,
please contact Simon & Schuster Special Sales at
1-866-506-1949 or business@simonandschuster.com.

The Simon & Schuster Speakers Bureau can bring authors
to your live event. For more information or to book an event,
contact the Simon & Schuster Speakers Bureau at
1-866-248-3049 or visit our website at www.simonspeakers.com.

Designed by Akasha Archer

Manufactured in the United States of America

10 9 8 7 6 5 4 3 2 1

Library of Congress Cataloging-in-Publication Data

Buchanan, Edna.

A dark and lonely place / Edna Buchanan. — 1st Simon & Schuster hardcover ed.
p.   cm.
1.   Outlaws—Fiction. 2.   Florida—Fiction. I.   Title.
PS3552.U324D37   2011
813'.54—dc22
2011017031

ISBN: 978-1-4391-5917-0
ISBN: 978-1-4391-6584-3 (ebook)

For T. Michael Smith, the best man I ever met

Those who cannot remember the past are condemned to repeat it.

—George Santayana

PREFACE

This is the novel I have yearned to write for half my life.

Dark stories whispered down generations about the notorious outlaw John Ashley and his sweetheart, Laura, haunted my dreams and stirred my soul from the moment I first heard their names.

The violent and gripping saga of outlaw lovers in wild frontier Florida hooked me instantly. But their voices were echoes, their faces ghostlike shadows, and I covered crime for the *Miami Herald*, lived for the moment, today's story, tomorrow's headline.

Until one late night long ago in the newspaper morgue, I stumbled upon an old photo, a handsome youth with a grin so infectious I couldn't help but smile back. The legend had become real! I was thrilled to see John Ashley's face for the first time.

How touching to see him, more than a hundred years later from my vantage point on the observation deck of history. He stood at the threshold of manhood, wearing a fresh haircut, a crisp white tropical suit, and a dark tie. His life stretched out before him like a promise. In his wildest dreams he could never have imagined how broken that promise would be or what his future held.

Nothing in his past or his family history hinted at the star-crossed love, turmoil, and turbulence in store, or suggested that he would become the most notorious and controversial character in Florida's violent and colorful history. That the governor would call him more dangerous than the Seminole Wars, in which thousands were killed. That the British would declare him an international pirate and send gunboats in his pursuit.

This year, 2011, is the centennial of the fatal shot that launched the legend. In 1911 young John Ashley, an outstanding marksman who could split the nose of a rattlesnake with a single shot from a .38 caliber pistol from twenty feet away, a hunter, fisherman, and the pride of a large and law-abiding pioneer family, was accused of murder.

Ashley swore he was innocent, vowed to clear his name, and surrendered, eager to be tried and exonerated. Instead, caught in a complex snarl of legalities, he was convicted and sentenced to hang.

His conviction set off a thirteen-year saga of jailbreaks, escapes, a bloody gun battle on the dusty streets of what is now downtown Miami, train and bank robberies, clamoring lynch mobs, rum-running, bootlegging, tragedy, and heartbreak.

To tough, hardworking, self-reliant Florida frontiersmen, John Ashley was a folk hero, a symbol of resistance to Yankee government, greedy bankers, and the law. To vindictive lawmen, he became a deadly obsession.

The initial murder charge against Ashley was eventually dropped. Too late.

No going back. Too many others had died.

I thought often of John and Laura on Miami's steamy streets as I covered the police beat, with its cocaine cowboys, Mariel boatlift, and deadly riots after the police beating death of motorcyclist Arthur McDuffie. When Metropolitan Miami became the nation's number one in homicide, gloomy New York writers called the city "Paradise Lost."

Wrong.

Miami was being itself, repeating history, over and over. The more things change, the more they remain the same.

It had to happen. One hot night on deadline a question occurred to me. *What if* the fictional descendants of the real John and Laura faced the same dangerous and desperate chain of events in Miami today? How would their story end?

Is it possible to change our own destiny? Can those of us with the outlaw imprint of violence and tragedy in our DNA break the cycle? Or is our fate indelibly programmed in our genes?

I knew then that one day I would write this book. *A Dark and Lonely Place* links their stories as they unfold and entwine a hundred years apart. The questions: How powerful is the pull of the past? Must desperate people in dangerous places always end the same way? Must fate, like history, always repeat itself? Real life and history can be dark and lonely places.

EDNA BUCHANAN

A DARK
AND LONELY
PLACE

PROLOGUE

Joe Ashley came home late, grim and smelling of whiskey. He woke his wife, Leugenia, and their nine children and told them to quickly pack up whatever they wanted to keep because they had to leave at once and would not be back.

"Was there gunplay?" his wife asked. Her eyes fearful in the lamplight, her voice trembled. "Is anybody dead?"

"No, but a man was shot. He'll live, but if we don't leave now, somebody will die."

She began to pack her best linens in a wooden chest.

The children, still half-asleep and in their nightclothes, began to gather their belongings, except for John, who was sixteen.

"Where are we going?" he asked his father.

"Get your things together, now, son."

John dressed quickly, carried his guitar and his banjo out onto the front porch, left them on the steps, and broke into a dead run down the dusty road. The dust, white in the moonlight, looked like silk.

His father stepped out and glared after him.

"It's that girl," he said bitterly, then moved to go after the boy.

His wife placed her small, worn hand on his forearm and raised her eyes to his. "He just wants to say goodbye, Joe," she said softly. "You remember how it was."

He nodded gruffly and caught her in his long arms.

"I got to get busy," she said after a moment, and gently extricated herself.

"You can't bring that sideboard," he said hoarsely, as she turned away. "It's too big."

It had belonged to her grandmother.

"We can fit it in the wagon, Joe. Bobby and two of the girls can ride up front with us."

He nodded and went to harness up the team.

Laura lived a mile and a half away. John arrived breathless, his lungs bursting. The place was dark. He stood beneath her window and whistled three times like a mourning dove, a signal they sometimes used. When there was no response, he found a feed bucket, carried it to her window, stood on it, and scratched the screen three times.

He heard her whisper in the dark. "John?"

"It's me, Laura . . ."

She was suddenly there, a swift shadow in the dark. He couldn't make out her face or what she wore but recognized her sweet scent, orange blossoms and roses. At that moment a mockingbird burst into a soaring, full-throated, heartbreaking song in the night. John knew he would never forget the sound or that moment.

"John, what are you—"

The front door burst open with a crash as though kicked by a mule. Laura's stepfather loped barefoot across the creaky porch in his long johns, brandishing his breech-loading, double-barreled shotgun.

"I got you now, boy!" he shouted. "Freeze right there! Caught you dead to rights climbing into my little girl's bedroom!"

John stood his ground, heart pounding. He felt no fear. He could die now, he thought, with no regret, outside her window.

"No, sir," he said boldly. "I did not try to climb into your daughter's room. I would never do that. I just tried to get her attention, to tell her something important."

Laura's mother, in nightclothes and a hairnet, materialized like an apparition on the porch. Laura's brother, Dewitt, trailed after her. "Mama, what's happening?"

"Hush, boy!" she told him. "Git yourself back to bed, right now."

"What could you have to tell our Laura at this time of the night?" her stepfather asked, then racked one into the chamber.

"Daddy," Laura cried. "Stop! Don't do anything! Please!"

John turned to her. "Don't worry, Laura," he said softly. "We're leaving tonight. I came to say goodbye. You are my girl, aren't you?"

"Goodbye? When are you coming back, John?"

He shrugged. "Don't know, Laura. But I will, I promise. Remember that. I'll be back!" Out the corner of his eye he saw her stepfather advance.

"Get down from there, you son of a bitch, now!"

"Are you my girl?"

"Yes, Johnny."

"Sorry, darlin'," he said. It was the first time he had called her that. He liked the sound of it as he stepped off the feed bucket.

"Git your skinny ass outta here. Now!"

"Yes, sir."

"You're damn lucky, boy. Last time I came this close to shooting somebody, I did it! Kilt me a Yankee. Git outta here now, afore I shoot you too!"

John stole a fleeting glance at her window then left the way he came. When he arrived home, heartsick and out of breath, the house was empty, his family gone. He and their dog, a bluetick hound that emerged from the woods behind the house, followed the wagon's tracks for two miles before they caught up with it. His father reached down and with a strong arm lifted both the boy and the dog into the wagon. His mother hugged his neck. "We worried about you, son."

"No need, Mama. We're together. Everything's all right." To cry in front of his mother would not be a manly thing to do.

Clouds drifted across the moon's face, darkening the trail ahead. Joe Ashley constantly searched the shadowy road behind them, to see if anyone was following.

John regretted all the things he didn't say to Laura. Too late now. With a ragged sigh he wrapped his arm around his little brother Bobby who was sitting up, sound asleep.

Is she asleep too? John wondered. Or awake and thinking of me? He knew he'd see her again. But how? And when?

PART ONE

Fate is the gunman all gunmen fear.
—Don Marquis

CHAPTER ONE

Gentle surf tumbled onto the sand beneath towering clouds adrift in a cobalt sky, a perfect day in paradise except for the crowded, noisy beach and the tinny radio that blared nearby.

Why am I here? John Ashley wondered. Why did I want to be here? What was I thinking?

He sat up to scowl at the radio's owner but was distracted by a leggy model in the shade behind the seawall. She posed in a short, sheer skirt and a crimson whisper of a blouse. He instantly recognized her but couldn't remember her name or where they met. The photographer snapped her from every angle, as a makeup man darted in between shots to blot and repowder her face and décolletage.

Two more models, a redhead and another dark-haired girl, appeared briefly in the doorway of a production trailer, its engine running, air conditioners blasting.

The girl beside him on the beach towel decided that he should lie facedown while she massaged his shoulders with coconut oil. Lulled by the scent and rhythm of the sea, he drifted into his recurring dream: dangerous times, violent men—and the woman. He couldn't quite see her face but would never forget her body. They were young and naked beside the river. What river? he wondered. Their feverish bodies entwined, mouths pressed together, he could taste her youthful passion on his lips.

He tried, as always, to focus on her face. He nearly glimpsed it this time, but a menacing growl shattered the dream. The hair rose on his arms and the back of his neck. His adrenaline surged and his eyes flew open as the predator's roar grew into earsplitting thunder. This was no dream. A high-powered speedboat rocketed toward South Beach. He raised his head, willed it to veer away. But it kept coming. Too fast. John Ashley, tall and long-limbed, sprang to his feet.

The speeding boat did not change course.

"John?" murmured the girl beside him. Her diamond ring flashed as she whisked beach sand off silky, sun-kissed knees. "John . . . ?"

He sprinted toward the pastel lifeguard station.

"Police!" he shouted. "Incoming! Clear the beach! Do it now! Now!"

The lifeguard lifted his binoculars, blasted his high-pitched whistle, then bellowed a belated warning. "Leave the beach!"

"Look out! Get your kids out of here!" John warned sunbathers. "Move it! Up there! Back behind the seawall. Now!"

Slow to react at first, people panicked as the howl of the engines grew louder and the boat loomed larger, closer, faster, its wake a streaming rooster tail across blue water.

French tourists fumbled for bikini tops. Half-naked, they scattered.

"He's not slowing down!" John shouted. Was anyone at the helm? He and his girl, tanned and graceful in her white bikini, snatched up toddlers, hustled the elderly, and yanked to their feet those too slow to move. The lifeguard joined them.

"Run! Go, go, go!" they shouted, as the blue and white speedboat barreled ashore. Throttle jammed, it flew like an arrow across a narrow strip of eroded beach, splintered a wooden fence, skimmed a swimming pool, and slammed with a thunderous crash into the back lobby wall of a small oceanfront hotel.

A man ejected on impact soared high and free, limbs as limp as a rag doll's. His flight ended with a sickening thud, his body grotesquely draped across a balcony railing.

John plucked a cell phone from the random possessions scattered like flotsam across the sand, summoned medics for the injured, cops for crowd control, and the medical examiner's office for the dead. He had no need for a homicide sergeant. He was already there.

He checked the beach and pool deck for life-threatening injuries, while Lucy, his fiancée, dashed to the car for his badge, gun, shirt, and trousers. He pulled the clothes on over his swim trunks, then followed screams to the hotel's second floor, trailed by a stunned assistant manager.

The screams came from the honeymoon suite. John suggested that the pudgy bride and skinny groom get dressed and pack up to change rooms, then stepped carefully onto the balcony. He glanced back at the photo shoot and stared. The dark-haired model kicked off her high heels and sprinted into the street to flag down an oncoming fire rescue van. He couldn't take his eyes off her. Look at that girl run! She always was fast.

She led paramedics to an elderly couple knocked to the ground during the mass exodus from the beach. He focused on the girl, the way she moved, her familiar gestures. She now wore tight, white jeans that exposed her navel. Who the hell is she?

He tore himself away to check the victim. He smelled the urine, the shattered bone, but where was his blood? Uh-oh. The flattened face looked familiar. So did the gold Presidential Rolex on the dead man's left wrist. It still worked perfectly, but time had run out for the man who wore it.

The soaring eagle tattoo on a fractured forearm confirmed John's suspicion. The speedboat's raw power made sense, now.

He made another call.

"It's a homicide. High-profile," he told homicide captain Armando Politano.

"How high?"

"Very."

"Who? You have a positive ID?"

"The Indian, Ron Jon Eagle."

"Crap. You shitting me?"

"Do I ever? You may want to give the chief a heads-up. He'll probably want to make some calls." Eagle, a high-profile lawyer, volatile litigator, dedicated playboy, and politically connected lobbyist for the tribe and its gambling casinos, had a long history of feuds, deals, and disputes with politicians, and police. John had stepped into one as a rookie and stayed clear ever since.

"You sure it's no accident?"

"Looks like bullet wounds to the back of the head."

One that exited the Indian's face had taken his left eye with it. John felt a painful throb in his own eye when he saw it. He never reacted physically to such sights. Too much sun and too little sleep, along with the trouble ahead must have triggered a headache.

"Oh, Lord." The captain groaned. "Another media event. Tell me you have a subject in custody."

"Nope."

"A suspect's name? Or description?"

"Nothing." Trouble clearly lay ahead.

The victim lived large, and big bucks complicate both life and death. When a man of moderate means is slain, good detectives usually know within hours who did it and why, then have to prove it. But the richer the victim, the more suspects there are. A writer once said the rich are different from you and me. John agreed. So many more people want them dead.

"The son of a bitch lived fast," the captain said, envy in his voice, "loved speed, kept the pedal to the metal."

"He's learned a lesson," John said.

"Which is?"

"Nothing's faster than a speeding bullet."

The captain snorted. "Too bad you can only learn that one once. Don't release his ID. Keep the press at bay till we get a handle on it." The last thing the department needed during the dog days of summer was a sensational homicide involving sex, scandal, and corruption in high places.

Eagle was no stranger to headlines and controversy. Winning was his lifestyle and he played as competitively as he worked. A champion powerboat racer, he lived the fast life on blue water with high rollers, grit, glitz, and danger. He raced Italian sports cars, piloted his own jet helicopter. The man had it all—fast boats, fast horses, and faster women. But today, John thought, boom, boom, bye-bye, all gone.

"I'll try," he told the captain, as he stared at the beach below. "But a TV sound truck with a satellite dish is rolling onto the sand right now. Looks like Channel Seven."

The captain cursed again. "I'll send PIO on a three-signal. What else you need?"

"My partner. Get J. J. out to Eagle's place, ASAP. On Star Island, I think. See who's there, who saw him last, where he was headed, and why. And advise the Coast Guard and Marine Patrol to appeal for information on their emergency channel and stop boaters in the general vicinity to find out what they saw."

"Any idea how many boats are out on a day like this?" the captain protested.

"Lots," John said. "Sound carries over water. On a day like today you can see and hear forever. They've all got binoculars, cell phones and cameras. Maybe we'll get lucky. Have choppers do a search for evidence and more victims in the water. Maybe the Indian wasn't alone."

The captain protested, "You know we're over budget with a freeze on overtime."

"Now or never," John warned. "Once this hits the headlines, how many witnesses you think will step forward? See if you can get the new recruit class to help."

The captain sighed. "Gotcha."

John returned to the chaos down on the beach. He had hotel employees use a catering tent and privacy screens to shield the name, *Screaming Eagle*, and the registration number of the splintered powerboat from the press. The photo crew were loading their trailer, the photographer packing his equipment into a padded, metal-sided suitcase.

"Finished for the day?" John asked.

"Just when the light's nearly perfect, all hell breaks loose," he griped. "That's Miami for you."

"Catch any of the action?"

"Not my bag." He smirked. "I'm high fashion only, no bleeding bodies or burning buildings. Been there, done that. My next shoot's in Barbados, then on to the Virgin Islands." He smiled smugly.

The dark-haired model emerged from the trailer. She'd changed into blue jeans and a T-shirt.

John caught his breath. The sunlight in her hair made him want to touch her. She looked as though she recognized him.

"Hey," he said.

She studied his face with bright blue eyes fringed by thick, dark lashes, as though trying to remember his name. She smiled, until her eyes dropped to the badge clipped to his waistband, then abruptly turned away.

For many women the badge is power and the gun a phallic symbol; for others, not so much.

"Wait . . . ," he said. But she slipped back into the trailer and firmly closed the metal door.

"Who is she?" he asked.

"Who?" The photographer looked up and frowned.

"That girl."

"Just a model. Forget it." The photog slammed the lid on a huge case of lighting equipment. "Listen. Girls like her shoot down a dozen guys a day. Even studs like you."

"I know her from somewhere."

"That's what they all say," said the makeup artist, who wore shiny black nail polish.

"The dark-haired girl. Who is she?" he asked the photographer again. The man didn't even look up.

"Okay." John flashed his badge. "You have a city permit for this shoot?"

"Of course," the man said indignantly.

"I'd like to see it now. I doubt it includes permission to park a trailer on county property. You may have a city permit, but this is a county park. When was this vehicle last inspected for illegal emissions? The engine ran all day, polluting a county park. Who is it registered to? What's with that out-of-state inspection sticker? May I see your driver's license, registration, and proof of insurance?"

John paused to sniff the air. "Is that weed I smell? Are you holding? Is that a Baggie in your pocket? Do you mind if I—"

"Summer," the photographer said. "Her name's Summer Smith."

That rang no bell.

Lucy trotted up at the wrong moment, hair tied back, now in jeans, sneakers, and an MPD T-shirt. Fire rescue and lifeguards were treating two apparent heart attacks, she said, a woman in premature labor, and more than a dozen injuries, none life-threatening.

By the time she filled him in, the photographer's trailer had lumbered out of the park and merged into congested southbound traffic on Ocean Drive. Summer Smith was gone with it. How will I find her? he wondered.

Uniforms kept the public and unruly press at bay on the far side of the street. The growing crowd bristled with cameras. News photographers and paparazzi focused through zoom lenses. Tourists clicked away with cell phones, with digital and disposable cameras. Small children rode above the crowd, hoisted high on the shoulders of adults for better views of the carnage. What's wrong with them? John wondered. Would this become a cherished childhood memory, along with the circus, the carnival, and the county fair? People never used to do that. Or did they? he wondered. His head throbbed. How did he let her get away?

Miami homicide detective J. J. Rivers trudged unhappily across hot sand an hour later. He looked as pale as a prison inmate or an aging cop who'd worked the midnight shift too long, which he had. "The hell we doing here, John?" he demanded. "What are you? Volunteer of the year? You coulda rolled up your blanket and crept to your car, nobody the wiser. You don't like the damn beach. You're no tourist! You hate crowds! What the hell were you doing here and what did you get us into?" He responded to angry cries from the press, confined by crime scene tape across the street, with a sullen stare.

"Don't agitate 'em," John warned. "You know how they get."

"They think my attitude stinks, they should smell my underwear," J. J. said.

John sighed. "Anything at Eagle's house?"

"Ha! Should see it. Gloria Estefan's a neighbor. Housekeeper speaks a few words of English. The victim entertained several young ladies yesterday. One, two, or more spent the night in his room. The girls were up and out before the housekeeper came downstairs at six a.m. Eagle ate breakfast and left alone, about ten, on the *Screaming Eagle*.

"The girls'll be back if they don't see the news. Left their luggage. What girl leaves behind her Jimmy Choo four-inch heels and Victoria's Secret thongs? Left my card so the girls can give me a jingle and impressed the urgency of my request upon the housekeeper, who is minus her green card, by the way. Promised to give us a buzz at the girls' first sighting.

"Not that I don't trust her, but I also left a rookie in an unmarked behind the island's guard house. He's watching for 'em."

"Good," John said. "You find next of kin?"

"A couple ex-wives. No problems with 'em lately, the housekeeper says. Parents deceased. His office manager'll know. Left a message; Eagle's law office is closed for the weekend."

"That buys a little time," John said. "If we can't inform next of kin, we can't confirm Eagle's ID to the media."

After the body was bagged, tagged, and en route to the morgue, both returned to headquarters.

John shook the sand out of his shoes. As he wondered where he left his socks and where Summer Smith was staying, Eagle's housekeeper called. The three young women had returned.

"Keep 'em there. We're on the way," J. J. said, then paused. "What?" He clamped his hand over the mouthpiece. "They just left!" he shouted. "What the hell? Sez they changed clothes and took off!"

"What about the rookie watching for 'em?"

"If he ain't dead in the bushes, he'll soon wish he was."

Two of the women, the housekeeper said, drove off in one of Eagle's cars, a yellow Lamborghini, a two-seater.

"No two high-maintenance broads ever got dressed that fast to go out on Saturday night," J. J. said, grimly. "They know something. They're running."

The third girl left in a Yellow Cab with her luggage.

They found the rookie staked out to watch for the girls' return alive, well, and texting a friend. He had missed their return to Eagle's home but had seen the sunshine yellow Lamborghini depart. Its sleek design so dazzled him that he had failed to notice the occupants.

"A bright yellow Lamborghini can't be that tough to find," John said.

"Right. We can rule out my driveway for a start," J. J. said.

Yellow Cab reported that the fare picked up at Eagle's place went to the departures level at the United Airlines terminal at Miami International Airport.

Pressed for descriptions of Eagle's young female houseguests, the Guatemalan housekeeper suddenly forgot what little English she knew. Questioned by a Spanish-speaking detective, she seemed to have forgotten Spanish as well.

A BOLO, Be On the LookOut, paid off after midnight. The Lamborghini lit up the night, parked in plain sight on the street outside Sky, a Miami nightspot just south of the Design District.

The doorman clearly remembered the car and the two women who arrived in it. Clearly unaccustomed to waiting behind velvet ropes for admittance, they brushed by the line and strolled inside, too hot to be challenged.

But that was hours ago and they no longer seemed to be there.

The detectives even checked the restrooms, both men's and women's.

John and his partner sat in the manager's office with the doorman to watch the video surveillance tape.

"There they are!" The doorman pointed as two shadowy figures entered the frame. "That's them! They're hot!"

John blinked at the grainy tape. "I don't believe this!" He rocked back in his chair, hungry, thirsty, tired, and elated. His head ached, his eyes stung, but no doubt about it.

"They're models! They were working at a photo shoot on South Beach today when it all went down."

"Yesterday." J. J. glumly checked his watch.

John stared at the tape, and Summer Smith, her familiar walk, the way she tossed her head back and laughed.

"I know that girl," he said with certainty, "just can't remember where we met."

"That's a first," J. J. said. "You never forget a face."

"Her name's Summer Smith, got it from the photographer. Didn't ring a bell, must be an AKA. Wonder if she has a rap sheet." Perplexed, he squinted at the screen. Had he seen that face on a wanted poster?

Now she has to talk to me, he thought. He looked forward to it. Couldn't wait, in fact.

They took the tapes to view back at the station. Hopefully they'd reveal who the girls met at the club, who they'd left with, and when. Why leave an exotic $400,000 car behind? When no one returned for it by four a.m., with rain threatening, the police had it towed for processing.

An hour before dawn, a call went out: a charred body in a still-smoking Dumpster a mile north of Sky.

Not their case, but John decided to swing by the scene. J. J. argued against it. "I'm running on empty," he complained. "Let's call it a night. I hate it when you do this. I need sleep and something to eat. We can start fresh in the morning."

"Just this one stop," John said, as they waited at a railroad crossing for a passing train. "Let's see what they've got."

J. J. bitched, moaned, and complained. But John loved watching the Southeast Railway train roar through the city, gates lowering, lights flashing, the train stopping traffic as it raced through the night like a wild animal. It reminded him of something intimately familiar yet impossible to remember.

Unmistakable odors—smoke, gasoline, and burned flesh—hung in the air. The rain hadn't come. A security guard on his way home had spotted the flames and called it in. Firefighters were unaware until they doused the blaze that it had been set to cremate a corpse along with any physical evidence.

Like most such attempts, it wasn't successful. Something always remains. Even professional gas-fired cremations need hours of twenty-four-hundred-degree heat to consume a body.

A woman's purse, the contents scattered, was found two blocks away. No ID, but car keys with a distinctive emblem lay in the gutter and fit the Lamborghini.

The victim was burned so badly that only a medical examiner could determine the sex. But a small silver ring fell from a charred finger bone as the remains were carefully removed from the Dumpster. Cleaned up at the morgue, the ring was a woman's size five with the initials *S.L.S.* engraved inside.

John would never see her again. Ever. Why did that hit him so hard? Summer Smith was a stranger. Or was she? Weariness overtook him. He agreed with J. J. They'd quit, catch a few hours sleep, then restart, refreshed, in midmorning.

Lucy had let herself into his apartment to leave a meal he could reheat in the microwave, and a note to call her if he wanted company, no matter how late. He didn't. He couldn't eat or sleep but dozed after daylight. In the recurring dream she was warm, vibrant, and she loved him, despite the danger around them, but this dream was different. He finally saw her face.

He awoke with a start, realizing he had finally found the girl, the woman who had haunted him both day and night since childhood. But too late. She now slept in the morgue, a charred corpse.

CHAPTER TWO

The knock at his door was familiar—three sharp raps. John didn't want company but Lucy had her own key and wouldn't hesitate to use it, kick out a window, or smash in a door. A positive trait for an ambitious, aggressive young cop. For one's sweet young fiancée, not so much.

"Miami Police! Open up! Now!"

He surrendered.

"Hey!" Detective Tracy Luisita Dominguez stepped inside, a spectacular sight in her starched, tailored, sharply creased dark blue uniform. She was so perky it made his head hurt. Her dazzling Latina smile hurt his eyes. But he followed the aroma as she took over his kitchen. She had brought strong Cuban coffee and warm, fresh-baked guava pastries.

"You look terrible," she chirped. "Tell me every gruesome detail. You know you should switch to days. Midnights kill our social life."

She didn't understand, never would. Dangerous predators roamed Miami's wilderness after midnight, and he was the hunter. He popped the lid off a steamy-hot coffee, then bit into a pastry. He knew it was sweet and flaky, but it tasted bitter, the way he felt.

"They posted the date for the next promotional exam," Lucy said. "Are you taking the lieutenant's test?"

They'd discussed it before. "No. Promotion would mean a transfer out of Homicide. I like what I do." Except today. Except now, he thought. "It's what I do best."

"But"—she straddled a kitchen chair, a supersexy position for a woman, especially one wearing a gun, a uniform, and lots of leather. "You could climb the ladder, fatten your pension, then land a chief's job in some small town, stay long enough for a second pension, and we retire in style. Chief Ashley. I like it." She licked her bright red lips suggestively.

"If I retire, I won't go into policework somewhere else. It's too political. You know I don't play well with others."

He didn't tell her the real reason. How could he, when he didn't understand it himself? All he knew was that he was never more alive than when on Miami's darkest streets. The first time he'd felt the city's pulse beat, he knew it was where his destiny lay. Several times he'd thought the moment had come, but realized later it was not the challenge he was born for, waited for.

"You need to be a team player. Think about it, *querido*."

She shoved the chair aside, balanced daintily on the steel-tipped toes of her safety shoes, and kissed his mouth. She was hot but not the woman on his mind.

"We're working Eagle hard," he said gruffly. "Gotta go."

"You okay?" She rested her palm on his forehead.

"Just tired. The case . . ."

"Developments?"

"Nothing good," he said. "A second victim."

Her dark eyebrows rose. "Who?"

"Just a girl he knew," he said bleakly. He hated how that sounded.

"Probably a hooker," she said casually, opened his fridge, and gasped. "You didn't eat the meat loaf? Not even the mac and cheese?" She turned, shocked, hands on her hips. "You didn't call either! I wanted to hear all about your case."

"Came home and crashed," he muttered.

He was grateful his phone rang.

"What do you know?" J. J. crowed.

John heard the traffic around him.

"The other broad made it through the night. Called to report the Lamborghini stolen this morning. Used Eagle's address. Said she was a houseguest using his car until it disappeared from the street in front of Sky—"

"Good, she coming in?"

"Hell, no. I'm not taking any chances. I'm picking this one up myself. See ya at the station."

* * *

John's desk phone rang as he walked in the door. Eagle's office manager, Gil Lonstein, returning J. J.'s call.

"We need to talk," John said.

"It's about my boss, isn't it?" He sounded young, a slight tremor in his voice.

"Why do you say that?"

"A speedboat just like his ran aground and crashed yesterday on South Beach. I saw the TV news. The reporter said the only person aboard was killed. I immediately tried to reach my boss but couldn't. His housekeeper said he left in the morning and a detective showed up that afternoon to ask about his next of kin. You don't have to be a rocket scientist to put two and two together."

"Right," John told him. "And we need your help."

Lonstein arrived twenty minutes later. A young-looking thirty, with a fox-sharp face and intelligent, deep-set brown eyes set a tad too close together. His glasses were rimless, his shirt button-down, and he wore a jacket on the summer's steamiest Sunday.

"He's dead, isn't he?" Gil Lonstein greeted him.

John nodded. "He is."

"He was a daredevil, full of bluster and bravado." Lonstein's voice shook, as J. J. joined them and pulled up a chair. "But he was also smart, careful, always used a checklist."

The man who expected bad news seemed shocked to hear it. ". . . was a championship boat racer. Flew a jet helicopter . . ."

The detectives winced, imagining the scene had Eagle crashed a big jet chopper instead of a powerboat on the crowded beach. "Thank God for small favors," J. J. muttered.

"How could this happen?" Lonstein's brow furrowed. "A stroke? Heart attack? I had an uncle, age forty-four. He passed his annual physical with flying colors. Fell dead in the street the next day. An aneurism, they said."

"Was Eagle in poor health?" John asked.

"No." Lonstein waved the question off as preposterous. "The man's an animal. Never late to court. Never missed a day of work in spite of . . . all his other activities."

"Enemies?"

The young man's jaw dropped. "You don't suspect . . . ?"

John nodded. "No heart attack, no stroke, no accident."

"Deliberate?" Lonstein looked aghast. "You think somebody tampered with his boat?"

"Let's just say the circumstances are suspicious. He was dead before the crash."

Lonstein fell back in his chair, bit his lip, and studied the ceiling. His eyes were shiny when they refocused on the detectives. "Not a good time to job hunt." He sniffed and wiped his face with a monogrammed handkerchief. "I'll need a new resume . . ."

"I'm sure you'll be asked to stay with the firm."

"What's to stay with?" He laughed ironically.

Eagle worked alone, he said, no partners, no associates—just a staff of bright, young, good-looking female paralegals. "He liked women," Lonstein said, his face serious. "Said they work harder."

"I'm sure they do," J. J. said.

"How'd you fit into the picture with all those females?" John asked.

"I have a partner." Lonstein's back straightened. "We've been together for eight years. He's an architect. I was no threat to my boss when it came to women and he liked—he loved—my work. You see, I was born to organize, cut expenses, and run a tight ship. Eagle loved women, but he *trusted* me." He smiled proudly. "Gave me my first pay raise after only two weeks on the job."

"He ever mention a model by the name of Summer Smith?"

Lonstein shook his head and lifted his shoulders. "Don't think so, but that doesn't mean a thing. He knew lots of models."

"How 'bout his will?" John asked. "Who profits? Who were his enemies? Any recent threats?"

Lonstein knew of no will, he said, on file anywhere.

"Man's a lawyer, a topflight litigator," John said impatiently. "Must have a will."

"Not necessarily." Lonstein cocked his head, his brown eyes earnest. "You know how the shoemaker's kids go barefoot?"

"Gotcha," J. J. said instantly. "My son-in-law's a professional photographer, but the only baby pictures of his kids"—he jabbed his chest—"my grandbabies, are the ones I snapped with my digital."

"Typical." Lonstein nodded. "Human nature. People like Ron Jon, despite their risk taking, never expect sudden death."

"We're the only ones who do," J. J. said. "We always expect it, especially on our days off. And sure enough, it never fails . . ."

John frowned. "What risk taking?" He hoped Lonstein's list was short but knew in his heart that it wouldn't be.

"Racing, flying, deepwater diving, high-speed cars, boats, and motorcycles, Jet Skis, jet planes, and choppers. Loved competition—in the air, the water, on the ground, and in the courtroom. Had to win, always. The risks he enjoyed most were with people. He loved to piss people off."

John leaned back in his chair. "Who? What people?"

Lonstein sighed, threw one knee over the other, and began to enumerate them. He quickly ran out of fingers, and started over. "Legal adversaries, politicians, judges, gaming kingpins, scary mob types, union thugs, shady characters, regulatory groups, and cops, including you, Sergeant, if I remember correctly." He smiled slyly at John. "I never forget a name." He continued: "Big people, little people, his best friends, worst enemies, neighbors, and strangers. Even when it wasn't important, he had to win."

"Such as . . . ," John prompted, ignoring J. J.'s muffled groan.

"Well"—Lonstein blinked, sucked his lower lip, then scratched his nose—"to start with, he sued every neighbor he ever had—and always won."

"Sued 'em? Fah what?" J. J. demanded.

"Oh"—the wave of Lonstein's hand indicated that the answers were infinite—"over property lines, trees that dropped fronds, fruit, flowers, branches, berries, pine needles, or leaves. Landscaping that grew too tall, too thick, too thin, or obstructed a view. To silence barking dogs, howling cats, potbellied pigs, parrots, parties, loud music, and burglar alarms. Had a thing about odors he found offensive. Sued neighbors who barbecued, left garbage cans out, grew smelly flowers, or used insecticide, fertilizer, compost, or mulch, especially red mulch.

"And"—Lonstein sighed soulfully—"he loved to seduce the wives of his friends, colleagues, and adversaries. Always had to make sure the husbands knew, of course. He'd throw a big dinner party, invite a dozen couples, then brag that he'd had every woman in the room."

J. J.'s eyes narrowed into a murderous heavy-lidded expression, as the suspect pool grew more and more crowded.

"Recent threats?"

"None he took seriously." Eagle was controversial, Lonstein said, criticized by judges, journalists, and the public. Threats, angry letters, and obscene phone calls came in regularly. Eagle laughed at them. His staff had a less cavalier attitude. They carefully filed the letters, voice tapes, and threats. Lonstein agreed to open the office so the detectives could sift through what Eagle had jokingly referred to as "the crank file."

Lonstein seemed to bask in the detectives' attention. They even took notes. Proud that he had guessed the truth before hearing the bad news, he bragged about how he always knew the climax before the first commercial of *Law & Order.*

"Read all of Sherlock Holmes when I was twelve," he said. "Sir Arthur Conan Doyle helped develop my powers of deduction. Always thought I'd be an excellent investigator. For the FBI, or in a job like yours."

John nodded. "Maybe you can help us with one more thing."

"Of course." A smug smile played around Lonstein's lips.

"Normally we ask a relative, but we haven't found one. Since you worked for the man for years, you knew him well enough to positively identify him. It's just a formality."

"You mean, go to the morgue?" Lonstein's eyes grew wider.

"If you don't mind."

"Glad to be of help," he said, jaw clenched, shoulders square.

"Good."

John took J. J. aside. "Where's the witness?"

"In interview room one. She was ready to split. When I pull up, she's doing a full-tilt boogie out Eagle's front door with her little suitcase. Had a taxi waiting."

"Who is she?"

"Skinny, smart-ass little bitch. The type that woulda pissed off Mother Teresa."

"Can she wait till we make an ID?"

"No problem. She ain't the talkative type anyway."

"Sure you're okay with this?" John asked at the morgue. "He's pretty banged up."

"No problem." Lonstein said jauntily. "I'm fine."

Only Eagle's face and upper torso were exposed, enough to reveal his tattoo.

"Is this Ron Jon Eagle?" the morgue's investigator asked, her pen poised.

Lonstein looked pale.

"Is he all right?" she asked the detectives.

"Sure he is," J. J. said.

"I'm fine," Lonstein said weakly. "That's him, but . . . where's his jaw? What happened to his eye?"

"You're sure he's okay?" she asked again.

"I'm fine," he murmured.

"No, he isn't." John caught him just before he hit the floor.

"They always say they're fine," she complained, "just before they pass out. Why do they do that?"

Dr. Nelson, the chief medical examiner, met with the detectives while Lonstein waited in a chair outside, his head between his knees.

Framed photos of the doctor's pretty wife and children stood on his desk, along with a number of suspicious specimens in labeled jars and plastic containers.

Eagle was dead prior to the crash, which explained the lack of bleeding, he said. He'd been in good health, until he was shot in the back of the head, apparently by a nine-millimeter weapon. Ballistics would be run on Monday. Toxicological results would be back in ten days.

"The victim in the Dumpster was female, early to mid twenties. Two bullet wounds, to the heart and brain."

John swallowed. The radiant girl he let get away had been reduced to a paragraph on a sheet of paper.

"Dead before the fire?"

"Unfortunately, no," Dr. Nelson said. "The soot in her airway showed she was still breathing. We'll need dental records to make a positive ID."

Still embarrassed by what happened in the morgue, Lonstein was red-faced as they left.

"It's okay," John told him, "happens to police rookies all the time."

Lonstein looked relieved, as though he might land a career in law

enforcement after all. At Eagle's office, photos of the lawyer with prominent politicians and millionaires, sports and entertainment celebrities,
covered two walls, along with cheek to jowl awards and proclamations.

Lonstein rolled two legal-sized boxes full of files, letters, tapes, and
transcripts into a glass-enclosed conference room. "Here's the one," he
declared feeling better and back into amateur detective mode. "I'd say
he's your man, the person of interest, your prime suspect." He presented
a fat file folder marked Baker, Keith/Karen.

Most of the letters came from Keith Baker, although his sisters,
in-laws, and a family lawyer wrote as well. Their polite letters asking
straightforward questions evolved over months into passionate, unan-
swered pleas and eventually into furious diatribes.

Baker's wife, Karen, the twenty-seven-year-old mother of their three
small children, had visited a popular Indian gambling casino with her
sisters, Celia, twenty-five, and Morgan, twenty-two, The young women
played bingo and poker, ate dinner, and watched a nightclub show. The
event was a threefold celebration: Celia's birthday, Morgan's graduation
from the University of Florida, and, belatedly, the birth of Karen's third
child. At midnight she called Keith to say they'd be home soon. They left
the casino with Karen, a nondrinking, nursing mother, at the wheel of
her Toyota Camry.

They were never seen alive again.

Baker tried to call his wife, and then her sisters, at 1:30 a.m. None
answered. His in-laws were asleep and had heard nothing. He checked
police and emergency rooms. Nothing. At 3:30 a.m., he called police
to report them missing. The officer said the girls were probably still
partying or had stopped for breakfast. They were adults, he said, so
no missing persons report could be filed for forty-eight hours. When
Baker protested, he was told to call again if he had no word from them
by 9 a.m.

He called at nine, and insisted on filing a report. Family members
searched, prayed, and printed posters. Twenty-seven hours later, his
telephone rang. The caller, a clerk from the county medical examiner's
office, asked him which mortuary he wanted to have pick up the bodies
of his wife and her sisters.

Minutes after they'd left the casino, a Dodge truck traveling east at
a high rate of speed in the westbound lane of a dark and lonely road had

slammed head-on into their Camry. In the Dodge were several Indian men from the local tribe. Treated for minor injuries, they were released that night. All three women in the Camry were killed.

Tribal police were at the scene first and waved off Florida Highway Patrol officers as they arrived. The crash occurred in their jurisdiction, they said, and they'd handle it.

The accident had actually taken place on a state road.

Even after the missing persons report was filed, the tribal police never notified next of kin. Motorists who'd stopped at the crash scene later told reporters that whiskey bottles were scattered in and around the Dodge, the smell of alcohol was strong, the men were clearly drunk, and that only they were receiving first aid.

The medical examiner's report stated that prompt medical attention might have saved two of the women and that Karen Baker had neither drugs nor alcohol in her system.

The victims' family and state and county police had been denied all access to information about the crash, even the identities of the Dodge's driver, passengers, or registered owner. The family turned to the media for help, but the accident report, crash photos, witness statements, and follow ups, if any, were also withheld from the press.

"How did they get away with that?" J. J. demanded. "It's all public record."

"Oh, no, it isn't." Lonstein shook his head and wagged his finger. "The tribe is a sovereign nation, which gives them the right to withhold documents, photos, and information."

"He's right." John nodded.

"It's the law," Lonstein added righteously. "And R. J. Eagle, may he rest in peace, would defend tribal law to the death."

"Maybe he just did," J. J. said.

The Indian system, based in part on tradition and ancient customs, was closed to outsiders. The judge ruled that the women were responsible for the crash. No explanation was given and no one else was charged.

Tribal judges need not be lawyers, there are usually no prosecutors, the accused can elect to have the entire proceeding conducted in his native tongue, and the tribe will pay for the defense. Indians found guilty of alcohol- or drug-related offenses are not jailed. They attend rehab instead, on the reservation.

"I've met people who had legal cases," John said, "but the tribe simply ignores personal injury suits filed by people hurt at their casinos."

"How can they?" J. J. said.

"The tribes never signed treaties with the US government after the Indian wars," John said. "They declared themselves sovereign nations and made their own laws. I never sat in court myself to see how they handle cases like this."

"And you never will, Sarge. That's the point," Lonstein said passionately, "the beauty of *tribal* law.

"Now listen." He played for them a call received two weeks earlier from a man who identified himself as Keith Baker. When a receptionist told him that Eagle was still too busy to speak to him, Baker responded, in a ragged voice. "Tell that sorry son of a bitch you work for to stop ignoring my letters and dodging my phone calls. If I have to come down to his office, I will. And Mr. Eagle will live to regret it."

"There's your man, detectives," Lonstein announced. "Hear the anger in his voice? How it quivers? Here, I'll play it again." He nodded in cadence with the words as he listened smugly, eyes half-closed.

"Did you, or the receptionist, tell Baker that he was being recorded?" John asked.

"No."

"Then it's inadmissible in court. That's *Florida* law."

"But we've identified your suspect." Lonstein's eyes glittered, his voice dropped to a whisper. "He probably doesn't know it's inadmissible. If that's the case, you can confront him, make him confess. You have your ways, your own techniques, of making that happen."

"Yeah, we could waterboard 'im," J. J. said. "Or attach electrical wires to his—"

"Let's go," John said abruptly.

"Wouldn't it be nice if it was all that simple," J. J. said, as they hit the street.

"Let's go see Lonstein's 'prime suspect,'" John said.

"Think anybody still lives here?" J. J. asked. He squinted at the modest home. "The lawn's a mess. It looks like mine."

Weeds, vines, and parched dry patches had taken over.

The doorbell didn't work, so they knocked, repeatedly.

The man who answered wore a week's worth of stubble, a dirty dish towel over one shoulder, a stained T-shirt, rumpled shorts, and flip-flops. Keith Baker's eyes were bloodshot. His hair needed a trim.

A barefoot girl of five sat on the living room floor behind him. She wore a striped T-shirt and bleach-stained shorts and squinted through eyeglasses at *SpongeBob SquarePants*, a box of juice and a bowl of Froot Loops beside her. The TV, at full volume, nearly drowned out the screaming baby in the kitchen.

Her father's tired eyes lit up.

"Police?" He stepped back and opened the door wide. "You found out who killed my wife?"

"No." John saw the disappointment in his eyes. "I'm sorry."

"I'm sorry about the mess." Baker looked around, hopelessly aware of how the place must look to strangers as they followed him into the kitchen.

Keith Jr., age three, in training pants and one small tennis shoe, gripped a small yellow dog as the animal yelped and struggled to escape.

"No! Let that dog go!" His father tried to control the struggling tot, as nearby the howling baby flung fists full of creamed peas from her high chair. The sticky, puke-green food was smeared all over her face and arms, in her hair, nose, and ears as she screamed at the top of her lungs.

Baker rushed to snatch a pan off the burner as rice boiled over onto the stove top. He picked up his son, let the dog out, then led the detectives to the Florida room, apologizing again as they passed the bathroom. "Sorry about the smell. I'm trying to potty train my son. He's my kid, my namesake, but I can't get him to pee in the toilet. He'd been doing fine, but when his mother . . . he keeps screaming that he wants Mommy in there with him, not me.

"Here," he told the boy. "Stay where I can see you."

The baby still howled in the kitchen. SpongeBob whined down the hall.

Baker studied the strangers for a long moment. "You probably know that my wife was killed early this year."

John nodded. "Has to be tough on you and the kids."

Baker blinked. "But that's not why you're here. I still want to know what happened, who's responsible. Sometimes I'm sure I am. I'm the one who let her and her sisters drive away. I could have objected, but she'd had a bout with postpartum depression after the baby." His eyes roved toward the cries from the kitchen. "And she was happy, really looked forward to a night out with her sisters. They hadn't spent much time together lately. Morgan was away at college. Celia lived two hundred miles away and was engaged. That night was a big deal. I thought it would be good." He teared up. "Karen's an excellent driver, never had a ticket, doesn't drink, the car was in perfect shape. I felt good about babysitting the kids. For the night." His eyes teared up again. "But it's never ended."

Baker had taken time off from work and was now worried about his job. The little girl, still barefoot, slipped into the room and climbed up onto the couch beside her father. He kissed the top of her head. "She's a huge help to me." As she snuggled closer, he looked around the room. "How could I live here for five years and not be able to find a thing? I'm still trying to figure out which pan to use on the stove and how much bleach to put in the wash. And we haven't had a decent meal since my mom went home to take care of my dad."

"Can your in-laws give you some help?" John asked.

"Maybe. Someday," Baker said. "Right now, they have trouble getting out of bed in the morning. Imagine, losing all three kids, gone, just like that. I want to fall apart too, when I see 'em. But I don't have time. If you didn't come to help us find justice," he said bleakly, "why are you here?"

"Ron Jon Eagle," John said.

"That SOB!" The anger in his voice startled his little girl, who gazed up at him in alarm.

"You wrote some letters, made some calls," John said.

"Yeah! I sure did. He helped cover up what happened to my wife and the girls. The police and the tribe stonewalled, said to call their lawyer. Him! He didn't even reply to a lawyer I paid to contact him. Eagle has a responsibility; he's an officer of the court. Now that arrogant son of a bitch has complained to police about me trying to reach him? That coward, that poor excuse for a man. I wish I could put a bullet in his head!"

The detectives exchanged startled glances as Baker's eyes leaked tears of frustration.

"All I want is the truth." His voice cracked. "For our family, our kids. Why won't he, or somebody, help me?"

"Eagle's dead," John said. "Somebody did put a bullet in his head. It's why we're here."

Baker stared in disbelief.

"Where were you yesterday around noon?"

"Is this a bad joke?"

"No," John said. "We have to talk to a lot of people."

Baker sprang to his feet, as his little daughter watched from the sofa. "Are you saying *I'm* a suspect? You're suggesting that with all of this—" He gazed at the chaos around him: SpongeBob in the hall, the baby crying in the kitchen, the dog barking at the door, and the two tots staring wide-eyed at him. "Even if I had the time to track down that son of a bitch, you think I'd blow him away and leave my kids orphans? Are you crazy? Has the whole world gone crazy?"

"No," John said. "I don't think you did any such thing. But for your protection, we have to check it out. Where were you?"

"Right here! Where I've been since that night!"

John sighed.

"My next-door neighbors, God bless 'em, invited us for a barbecue and a swim in their pool. Half the neighborhood was there. Ask them!"

"We will," John said.

Baker followed them to the door. "I'm not sorry he's dead. I applaud whoever did it! When you find him, give him my thanks. The man was rude, crude, and insulting, never offered one word of condolence, explanation, or apology. I'm glad he's not sucking up any more oxygen on my planet."

"You ain't the only one," J. J. said.

"Was it a quick death?" Baker asked.

"I think so," John said.

"Then he was lucky. Luckier than me."

They left Baker in the doorway, his tiny son clinging to his leg, his little daughter holding his hand.

His alibi was solid, from eleven a.m. to three p.m. The neighbors even had photos, group shots that included Baker, his eyes haunted, and his children.

"Poor bastard. How's he gonna raise those kids alone?" John said.

"Not our problem," J. J. said. "We have plenty of our own."

CHAPTER THREE

Good luck, Sarge." J. J. opened the door to the interview room with a flourish. The witness had a bad attitude before; how ugly would it be now, after waiting for hours?

John stepped inside and reacted as though he'd been sucker punched.

She wore blue, the same deep color of her eyes.

"Hey," he said, barely able to speak.

She looked startled, then smiled warmly.

"You two know each other?" J. J.'s expectant expression screwed into a frown.

John closed the door without taking his eyes off hers. "I thought you were dead," he finally said, and took a seat across from her.

Her eyelashes dropped like a curtain, then rose again. "Whatever gave you that idea? Reports of my death have been greatly exaggerated."

"Mark Twain," he said.

"Samuel Clemens," she said.

Both laughed, more in relief than humor.

"I'm Sergeant Ashley. Call me John."

"Hello, John."

He recognized the way she drawled his name.

"I know you," he said.

She gave a slight nod. "I recognized you on the beach yesterday. I knew I'd see you again."

Her voice resonated, like an echo. He remembered it, and the quick, unconscious way she pushed her silky black hair behind her ear.

"Did you go to Miami High?"

She shook her head. She'd grown up in northwest Florida.

"I never forget a face," he said, half-serious. "Did I ever arrest you?"

She laughed as though he were hilarious.

He loved the sound; it warmed the room. He'd waited so long to hear it again. "So I wasn't your prom date," he said. "Did we ever have sex?"

She laughed again. "You wouldn't have to ask, John. You'd remember." Her laughter was contagious. He joined in, full of joy and relief. He watched her fold her hands and raise her eyes to his, the way she always had.

"Who are you?" he asked.

Detective "Dick" Tracy Luisita Dominguez, hair tightly pulled back, her uniform crisp, found J. J. at his desk. "John doesn't answer his cell," she complained.

"He's busy, interviewing a witness."

She gasped. "Can I watch?" she asked eagerly. "I'd love to observe his interview technique. I learn so much from him."

"I'm sure." J. J. got heavily to his feet and steered her to the interview room's one-way window.

Laughter came from within.

"Must be losing my charm." J. J. stared. "Bitch wouldn't tell me shit."

Their body language was unmistakable. John and the witness leaned toward each other across the small table, eyes locked, faces close. Their words tumbled out so quickly, their voices so low and intimate, that those outside could not hear them. Their faces glowed, as though bathed in a flashbulb moment.

"Who is *she*?" Lucy asked quietly. "Is that his usual interview technique with females?"

J. J. snorted and rolled his eyes.

"Who is she?" she asked again. "Do they *know* each other?"

J. J. squinted thoughtfully. "Looks that way, doesn't it?"

John pushed back his chair, still grinning. "Cream and sugar?"

She nodded. "You know how I like it."

I do? he thought. He hesitated, then closed the door behind him. Mood changed, headache gone, he felt like a new man, energized and enthusiastic.

He nearly collided with J. J. and Lucy.

"Who is she?" Lucy asked.

"Her?"

They turned in unison to stare at the witness. She now sat alone, hands to her lips, her face aglow.

John couldn't take his eyes off her.

"Sure isn't bummed by the loss of her dead boyfriend and best gal pal. Was laughing her ass off," J. J. said.

"She barely knew Eagle." John lowered his voice. "She doesn't know about the murders."

"Doesn't know? You're not buying that?" J. J. stared in disbelief. "She's tooling around Miami with victim number two, in a sports car that belonged to victim number one. If she's gonna lie, she should get better at it. Don't let 'er snow you, John."

"Never happen, J. J."

"Who the hell is she?" Lucy asked again.

"Her name is Laura," John said.

CHAPTER FOUR

The car wasn't stolen." Laura sipped her coffee. "So what's the problem?"

"We need to talk," John said.

She sighed. "I told Summer not to park it on the street. But we were late, and Eagle asked her not to valet it."

"Summer," he said thoughtfully. "She was the other dark-haired model with you at the photo shoot. You two went to Sky last night?"

She nodded. "She and Eagle are old friends. She'd driven the car before. He trusts her. I'd never met him."

"Exactly when did you last see Summer?"

"I saw him toss her the keys. She had his permission. I can vouch for that. She's in no trouble, is she?"

"No," he said truthfully. Summer was beyond all trouble now.

They'd met at an Atlanta fashion shoot, she said. Summer mentioned the Miami job and that they needed another model. Laura contacted her agent and was hired.

"How'd you happen to stay at Eagle's place?"

"Summer has an open invitation when she's in Miami and she invited us. His place is great, close to the job, and free. And he's a good host . . . up to a point."

"What point is that?"

She blinked and looked away. "They're a faster crowd than I'm used to. I didn't realize it until I got here."

"Eagle wanted you to spend the night in his room?"

She nodded. "I declined, but the other girls joined him."

"Summer and Cheryl. The redhead?"

"You don't miss much, do you, John?"

The way she spoke his name touched him, and he felt an unexpected surge of jealous rage at a dead man. "Did Eagle pressure you?"

"Not really." She folded her hands in her lap. "When I said the job was early and I needed my beauty sleep, he looked surprised but okay with it. I braced a chair under the doorknob before I went to bed, just in case."

"Good girl."

She grinned. "The photographer wanted to start at dawn. Cheryl was tired and moody, complained that Eagle had a friend join the party, which turned into an all-nighter with cocaine and kinky sex. Bondage, I think. Cheryl didn't like it, said she didn't know the invitation had strings attached. Neither did I.

"I expected him to be a playboy," she said, "but thought it would be more like a pajama party with Summer and the housekeeper as chaperones. I assumed there was safety in numbers. How naive."

"Welcome to Miami."

She nodded solemnly, then brightened. "But the energy level here is amazing. I'm crazy about the city, always wanted to see it."

"I was lucky," John said. "We moved here when I was in third grade. What did you say that other guy looked like?"

"Didn't see him." She shook her head. "He showed up late."

"So, exactly when did you see Summer last?"

"John, what *is* all this about?" She waited for an answer.

He leaned back, watching her. "That was Ron Jon Eagle's boat that crashed ashore. That was him hanging off the hotel balcony. He's dead."

She gasped, eyes wide. "That's not true! It can't be! He's alive! He telephoned last night! The girls were to meet him at Sky and go to dinner. But Cheryl decided to leave town early and Summer asked me to come along instead. I was starved, hadn't eaten solid food since I arrived. You know how the cameras add pounds."

He wondered what she was talking about. She looked as sleek as a racehorse.

"But Eagle didn't show up at Sky, he sent someone else. Summer knew him." She paused. "She didn't say as much, but I thought he must be the other man from the night before. He kept insisting she call Cheryl. Then his phone rang. He said it was Eagle who was running late and would meet us at the restaurant."

"By then Eagle had been dead for six hours," John said. A stranger taking two beautiful girls to meet a dead man insists that a third girl come along. Did Laura's skin crawl too?

"I don't believe it!" she said.

He got to his feet. "Okay. We can go to the morgue now. You can take a good look at what's left of him."

"Oh, my God. You are serious." She shrank back in her chair, eyes flooding. "It's true!"

He nodded. "What happened after you left Sky?"

"I said we'd follow him." Her voice was thin. "But he insisted we go together and come back for the Lamborghini later. I didn't like the way he looked at us. The man gave me chills. There was something about him . . .

"Summer knew Cheryl went to the airport, but she simply told him the girl had other plans. He demanded to know where she was, and who she was with. When Summer said she didn't know, he punched the steering wheel hard. I knew then that I didn't belong there. I always follow my gut instinct."

"Attagirl." Did she know how close she came to the fire? "How'd you get away?"

"He drove a black Escalade, blew several red lights like he owned the road. When traffic finally forced him to stop, I just opened the door and stepped out. I could see Summer didn't want to be alone with him and held the door for her. But she didn't make a move, so I said, 'See ya later,' and walked away.

"He jumped out after me, but the light changed and the horn-happy Miami drivers behind us, God bless 'em, made such a racket that he jumped back into the Caddy and drove. I'da kicked off my heels and run like a rabbit if he'd turned around. He creeped me out that much. I ran track in high school, I'm fast on my feet. I'da cut through those dark, narrow alleys."

"I'm glad you didn't have to."

"Me too." Their eyes locked. "Had no idea how to get back to Eagle's for my things. But we country girls have a good sense of direction. I walked east to the Boulevard, turned south till I saw a taxi outside a restaurant. Had the driver take me past Sky. The Lamborghini was still there. Then he took me back to Eagle's. It was spooky. Nobody home. Oh, God, he was already dead, wasn't he?" She gazed up guiltily, eyes watery. "I raided his refrigerator, ate some stone crabs and key lime pie, locked my door, and went to bed with my cell phone."

He wished he'd been there.

"I never heard Summer or Eagle come in. They didn't. Hoped to see the big yellow machine in the driveway at dawn. It wasn't. Summer didn't pick up her cell. Hated to leave that expensive car on a downtown street, so I hired another cab. We passed Sky and the Lamborghini was gone. When it wasn't back at the house either, I called the police to report it missing, and another taxi to take me to the airport. But your friend J. J. pulled up with questions about the car and I've been here ever since."

"For good reason, Laura." Her name sounded so right, so familiar on his tongue. He'd never felt so instantly attracted to a woman. He studied the curve of her chin, the shadows of her throat, then struggled to refocus on business.

"We hoped the girls who stayed at Eagle's place could help us with a time line. I didn't know you were one of them until I saw you on Sky's surveillance tapes. The first time I saw you at the beach, I asked the photographer who you were. He must have misunderstood. He gave me Summer's name instead."

"You asked who I was?" Her wet eyes focused fondly on him.

"Right." He sighed. "Do you remember what I said when I first walked in here? I thought you were dead."

Her smiled faded.

He nodded. "Summer was killed last night."

"No! It can't be! How?"

He described the burning Dumpster in detail.

Her eyes grew wetter, wider, tears spilled over. When he said the charred corpse was unrecognizable, her fists clenched.

"Then how can you say it's her? It could be anyone!"

He described her ring, her purse, the car keys, and his own certainty that dental records would confirm her identity. If her shock was not genuine, he thought, she deserved an Oscar.

The tiny lace square she dug from her handbag was soon crumpled and sodden. He hated to see her cry and groped for a man-sized hand-kerchief, which she gratefully accepted.

He needed to know more about Summer.

"Said she grew up in South Carolina, Charleston," she gulped, wiping her eyes with his handkerchief. "Her mother's name was Lucinda. I remembered, because that's my cousin's name."

He hit pay dirt on the Internet, a Parks and Lucinda Smith in Charleston. Their only child, Summer Lark Smith, debuted at a debutante cotillion at age seventeen. She was crowned Magnolia Queen at eighteen, which qualified her for the Miss South Carolina pageant, a Miss USA preliminary. She was first runner-up. Her parents sent her to Sweet Briar College in Virginia. But Summer had tasted glamour, knew cameras loved her, and loved them back with a reckless passion. She dropped out of school to chase fame and fortune as a model and actress. Played a trampy vamp on a daytime soap, her career high. But her character was quickly killed off, and in the decade since, DUI and cocaine charges had punctuated her sporadic modeling career.

"Would you recognize the man Summer left with?"

"Of course. I'll never forget his face or those pale, ice-blue eyes. In fact, I saw him again this morning."

John did a double take. "When?"

"After your partner decided to bring me here and chased off my cab. As we drove out the guard gate, I saw the Escalade. He had a passenger. They both turned to look. They saw me."

Damn, John thought. J. J. had arrived like the cavalry, just in time. "Did you point them out to J. J.?"

"No." The word had a hostile edge. "Didn't seem important. And though I hate to say it, your partner, bless his heart, is rude and heavy-handed, a typical law enforcement officer."

"You see me as a typical law enforcement officer?"

"No." She did not hesitate. "I feel I know you."

"I know you too, girl. You trust me, Laura?"

She smiled wanly. "My gram warned me about men who ask you to trust 'em, but I do, John. I trust you."

He felt a rush when she said that. Had he lost his mind? He'd just met the girl. He had to focus.

"We have to locate Cheryl," he said, briskly. "What's the name of the guy in the Escalade? What did Summer call him?"

"Manny. Cheryl said that the second man in Eagle's room that night wore a gun. When I saw Manny wearing a shoulder holster last night, I wished I was packing myself."

He lifted his eyebrows.

"I own guns," she said with a shrug. "Have a concealed weapons permit. But local law differs everywhere, and it's too much of a hassle to take a gun on a plane, so I don't."

"You know how to shoot?"

"Sure. My granddad taught me on an old muzzle-loader."

He smiled and checked his watch. "We have to get to work, and I need to find you a safe place to stay."

"Why?" she said softly.

"You're a witness in two homicides. You could be at risk."

"But I don't know anything more than I've told you."

"Maybe you don't know what you know. But somebody might think you do."

The mysterious Manny, who claimed to receive a call from the dead, was a mere shadow on the nightclub video. Dark hair and clothes, face turned away. Lucky? Or savvy enough to evade the cameras?

Cheryl Sutter had flown home to Silver Spring, just outside Washington, D.C. Her cool, seductive, recorded voice answered her phone. John pictured her red hair and attitude as he left a message to call him ASAP.

He asked Laura to work with a forensic artist to create a sketch of Manny. She was eager to try, but hadn't eaten all day, so he offered to take her to a Cuban restaurant first.

They were about to leave when he had a return call from Silver Spring. "Hold on," he told Laura. "I think it's Cheryl."

It wasn't.

"You called Cheryl Sutter?"

The ring of authority in the man's voice made John's heart sink. He sounds like me, he thought, a man who asks a lot of questions and expects answers.

"That's right, is she there?"

"Who are you?" he asked brusquely.

"Who are you?" John asked back.

"Sergeant Danny Sandler, Montgomery County Police."

"Detective?" John asked.

"Right."

"Homicide?"

"Right again. You?"

"Homicide sergeant John Ashley, Miami PD. Tell me she's alive."

"Sorry. Can't do that."

John turned so Laura couldn't see his face. "What happened?"

"Tell me why you called her first."

"Look, pal," he kept his voice down, "this is no game. It's serious god-damn shit. She's a witness in two Miami homicide cases and I need to talk to her."

"Well, it ain't gonna happen." His voice rose. "I knew it! You Miami guys piss me off. Why don'tcha keep your mess down there insteada sending your garbage up here. We got enough problems of our own!"

John saw the forensic artist arrive early, step off the elevator, and hail J. J., who introduced him to Laura. He'd hoped to sit across from her, watch her, and listen to her talk. Instead she and the artist settled down in a cubicle.

The cop at the other end of the line continued to bellow in his ear. What's his problem? John wondered. He didn't like or trust most other cops, particularly his own colleagues. In Miami it was a common sight to see handcuffed police officers and politicians do the perp walk. Cor-ruption was a way of life. The only cop he trusted was himself, along with two of his brothers who also wore badges. All they wanted was what good cops always want and almost never find—true justice.

"What happened to Cheryl Sutter?" he asked.

"It's ugly," the Montgomery County detective said. "The ugliest I've seen and I've worked homicide for fifteen years."

"You tell me the circumstances and maybe I can tell you if it's related to our cases."

"Wasn't robbery or burglary, doesn't appear random, and isn't your typical sex crime either—though there is nasty sex involved. What

I *do* know is I had tickets, hard-to-come-by tickets, for me and my thirteen-year-old kid for the Nationals-Marlins game today. But guess what? I ain't there, because you guys spread your mess all over the entire goddamn eastern seaboard!" His voice rose again. "So my kid's skinny ass is in my seat at the game, alongside my ex-wife's new boyfriend insteada me!"

"You're lucky," John said. "You wouldn't like it. Be glad you're not there to see the fish torpedo your team."

"Whadaya crazy? We got the league's best pitcher."

"That overpaid, snot-nosed kid who skips like a girl every time he throws a pitch?" John laughed.

"You can't be serious!" Sandler sounded apoplectic.

John looked up and frowned. J. J. had interfered with Laura's session with the artist. The artist was packing his gear.

Laura's eyes, wide and questioning, caught his.

"What's going on?" he mouthed to J. J.

"Say buh-bye." J. J. gave Laura a little wave.

"What?" John clamped his hand over the mouthpiece.

"The county's on the way to pick 'er up." J. J. approached John's desk. "Your new girlfriend here is a material witness in a long-term investigation by a federal-county task force, which supersedes our investigation." He shrugged, smirked at Laura, and said, "Buh-bye."

"No way. Whose authority?" John asked.

J. J. shrugged. "The chief wants her released to county detectives who are en route."

"They can't interfere with our investigation!"

John told the Montgomery County detective, "Have to call you back. Stuff's hitting the fan here."

"Been down that road myself," Detective Sandler said. "My sympathies, buddy. Call when you can. I'll give you what we got."

Laura insisted she knew nothing about any county-federal probe. She'd just arrived in Miami for the first time. Had no priors, not even a speeding ticket. Did have a permit to carry a concealed weapon, no small thing. Applicants pass tests on the gun laws, prove their marksmanship at firing ranges, undergo background checks, are fingerprinted, photographed, and pay a fee.

"Did you get the names of those county cops, J. J.?"

The detective pulled a crumpled scrap of paper from his pocket. "Miami-Dade deputies Donald Woodbury and Angela Haskell."

"Who?" John said. "I need to see the paperwork, their IDs, and talk to their supervisor."

"I want to leave. Now!" Laura demanded. "Am I free to go? I'm not charged with any crime." She glared at J. J., her eyes narrowed. "You tricked me. I was flying home this morning. What right did you have to stop me? I want a lawyer. Now. I refuse to be handed over to another agency—especially a county sheriff."

John saw her shiver. "Don't worry," he said. "You won't be."

He called the Miami-Dade County shift commander, who took his name and badge number, then dodged his simple question: *Does your department employ two deputies named Donald Woodbury and Angela Haskell?* Legally, that information should be available to anyone. The commander stalled and promised to get back to him.

John called a longtime friend in Miami-Dade communications. "Hell, yeah," he said. "Woodbury's a veteran deputy. Donnie's a neighbor of mine, in fact."

"What does he look like? And what's he working on that involves snatching one of our homicide witnesses?"

"Whatcha talking about, John? Sure you got the right guy? Donnie's in his fifties, balding. Worked missing persons for the last twenty years. Had a heart attack on the job, nearly bought it, less than a year from retirement. The docs still don't know when, or if, he'll ever be back to work."

"And Angela Haskell?" John's voice was unnaturally calm.

"Heard she was on maternity leave, let me check the roster."

John waited. The county's 3,034 officers worked out of eight districts scattered across more than two thousand square miles.

"Right," he said. "She's not expected back for two months."

"What's she look like?"

"Good-looking, black, great smile, nine months pregnant. Worked vice undercover, the john squad. Being pregnant didn't slow her down at all. In fact it made her more effective. Who knew we had so many sickos itching to hook up with a pregnant prostitute?"

The other line rang, the county shift commander, as promised. He could only divulge, he said, that both individuals he'd mentioned were indeed Miami-Dade deputies.

John thanked him for his courtesy.

"They're here," J. J. sang out. He wagged his phone at John.

John took it. "Should I send 'em up?" asked the officer at the front desk. A wounded rookie, on light duty, he had walked into a fast-food joint for coffee during an armed robbery. The gunman saw his uniform, panicked, and fired a shot, which struck the patrolman's right big toe. On crutches, he was manning the front desk on a slow Sunday night.

"No," John said. "Keep them where they are. They are male and female, correct?"

"Yes, sir."

"Race?"

"Caucasian."

"Both?"

"Affirmative, sir."

"Can you describe the female without them hearing you?"

"Yes, sir." He dropped his voice. "Five feet seven, a hundred forty-five, brown, and dirty blond."

"And the male?"

"Late twenties, six foot, two twenty, brown and black, a mustache, wedding ring."

"Keep them there. We need to arrest them for impersonating police officers and attempted kidnapping."

"Should I request backup, sir?" he whispered.

"Are they armed?"

"Affirmative."

"Use caution. I'll be right down." John heard shouts in the background. "What's going on?"

"Civilians in a dispute, sir."

"Shit!"

"A homeless individual, sir, came in to report an assault. Two tourists just arrived to report her purse stolen and recognized the homeless . . . uh, urban outdoorsman, as the offender who took it. He denies it, says they assaulted him without provocation."

"Hang tight."

John snatched up his radio. "Stay," he told Laura. "Keep working with the artist."

Her eyebrows lifted.

"I'll be back." He tossed her his handcuffs, which she caught gracefully on the fly. "If anybody tries to take you out of here, for any reason, cuff yourself to that desk and scream like a banshee for me and Joel Hirschhorn, your lawyer."

The mere mention of Hirschhorn, a high-profile criminal defense lawyer, gave most cops and prosecutors pause for thought.

"Can you do that?"

"Joel Hirschhorn," she repeated. The defiance in her eyes moved him. He'd seen that look before. *Who the hell is she?*

He hit the button, saw the elevator was in the damn lobby, and radioed for all available officers in the building, relatively deserted on weekends, to respond to the lobby on a 3-15, assist an officer.

Two sharp reports rang out seconds later. They weren't backfires from the nearby I-95 overpass. He hit the stairwell running.

CHAPTER FIVE

H e heard seven more gunshots as he hurtled down the stairs, fol-lowed by the dreamlike echo of the dispatcher's cool voice. *"Shots fired in the station lobby."*

He took a deep breath, slid the Glock from his shoulder holster, and burst out of the stairwell.

The rookie lay sprawled behind the front desk bleeding from the head, gun belt empty, weapon gone, his crutches at odd angles beside him.

A civilian couple had taken cover, crouched nearby. The pair John wanted had fled.

A gap-toothed, whiskered derelict, face bloodied, hands in the air, his shoes duct-taped to his feet, shuffled toward John as he ran toward the doors that opened onto the parking lot.

"Leon!"

"Hi, ya, Johnny."

A habitué of Bayfront Park, Leon was a CI of John's, a man who saw everything and forgot nothing. "Wasn't me!" he cried. "I didn't do it!"

"I know that, Leon. Where'd they go?"

"Thataway." He jerked his thumb toward the parking lot.

"Their car?"

"White, four-door, yellow county plates. Said they wuz cops! First time I ever seen cops shoot at each other on purpose!"

John heard him over his shoulder. Already out the door, he saw the car lurch across a sidewalk at the far end of the lot and bump down a curb to escape.

"That's them!" Leon shouted. "Get 'em, Johnny!"

John radioed as he ran. "Shots fired. Officer down! In the station lobby. The subjects' 2009 white Ford Crown Vic, with county plates, is southbound on Northwest Second Avenue. Occupied by a white male driver in his twenties and white female passenger. Use caution. Both are armed police impersonators."

He tried to read the tag number as the car fishtailed into a sharp turn, then he took cover as the passenger side window slid down. He saw the muzzle flashes. Two rapid shots. One flew over his head; the other pinged off the bumper of an SUV two slots away. He returned fire twice as the car accelerated almost out of range. Both shots hit the rear window. Tires squealed. The car swerved hard to the right. The driver fought for control and won. The big engine whined as he floored it and they were gone.

John radioed the direction of travel, then walked back to the station lobby, not even breathing hard. In combat, pursuits, and dangerous encounters, time slowed, the world looked brighter, and everything became crystal clear. It had always been that way for him.

The first thing he saw, despite the chaos in the lobby, was the memorial plaque for the thirty-six Miami police officers killed in the line of duty. It now hung at an odd angle. A stray bullet had slammed into it just beneath the name of the city's first fallen officer, J. R. Riblet, shot June 2, 1915, in a bloody gun battle on a dusty street just blocks from where the station now stood.

John stood, eyes riveted to the name of the long-dead hero. He felt the heat of that day so long ago, heard the shots, and then the screams. He blinked, turned, and breathed a sigh of relief.

The rookie was sitting up. He'd looked bad at first, sprawled out and bleeding from the ear, but was now complaining loudly, a good sign. The bullet had nicked his earlobe, which bled profusely, then it slammed into the City of Miami crest on the wall behind him.

No new name would be added to the list of fallen officers—at least not tonight.

PART TWO

CHAPTER SIX

He first saw her at the little wooden schoolhouse in the clearing. John was seven and Laura five. Four of his siblings were sisters, so he was convinced he knew everything about girls. But she was not like them. She confounded him, ignored him. But when he'd give up and stop seeking her attention, she'd cut her bright blue eyes at him, flash a smile, then turn, or run away quickly.

Rain or shine, Miss Helen Peters, the sweet-faced schoolmistress, would ring the big brass bell that signaled the start and the close of the school day. The desks of her twenty-four students, ages five to sixteen years old, faced her and a blackboard at the front of the room.

The children were as wild as young hawks, most of them the progeny of pioneers who'd lost everything in the Civil War and migrated to Florida to start over. Some parents were outlaws on the run from the law. Others were restless souls seeking new experiences, challenges, and frontiers.

Life was difficult.

World powers—Spain, France, England, and the United States—had all tried and failed to tame Florida's wild frontier. Its rugged, brawling pioneers relied on their marksmanship, their fishing and trapping skills—and their will—to survive. Most raised large families. So who could blame Miss Peters when her gold-rimmed spectacles skidded down her nose in the moist heat and classroom chaos and she occasionally called a student by the name of a sibling or a cousin, nephew, or uncle.

She never mistook John Ashley for anyone else. One didn't need a teaching certificate to recognize a leader. Everyone knew his name. Like his siblings, he was well behaved, kind, and respectful to elders. Quick and gregarious, high-spirited and mischievous, he was, above all, loyal to his family and friends.

Little black-haired, blue-eyed Laura Upthegrove ran fast, played hard, and competed fiercely with bigger, older peers. She never whined, shed a tear, or fussed about a scraped knee, torn dress, or muddy shoes. Her sole, secret embarrassment was that, sometimes, under pressure, she'd hiccup.

She ignored John each morning when the children surrounded the iceman's horse-drawn wagon. The children begged for chips as the man hacked ten pounds of ice off a two-hundred-pound block. Laura shared hers with his horse as the boys competed to carry the ten-pound chunk of ice to the water cooler and communal cup at the back of the room.

At recess, their game of choice was crack the whip. It was exciting, dangerous, and best of all, forbidden. Adults hated the game. So while Miss Peters graded papers at her desk, a big boy would seize another's hand and the whip would swiftly assemble. The boys raced to form a line, like boxcars behind a locomotive. The last one was the caboose, usually a slower, slightly built small boy who tried not to look terrified as the leader took off at a dead run.

The boys sprinted behind him, dragging each other along the zigzag course set by the leader. Their speed accelerated. Hands tightened. Arm sockets strained until a sudden hairpin turn cracked the whip. Boys flew through the air, feet lifted off the ground. Some slammed into trees, poles, or the wooden fence, resulting in broken teeth, smashed noses, and torn clothes. The runner at the tail end bore the brunt of it all.

One scorching day during John and Laura's second school year, a whip formed like a sudden storm. Duncan Moody, an oversized thirteen-year-old with wild red hair and a mean streak, was the leader. John Ashley landed the solid third position behind him despite his tender age.

His adrenaline soared, until he spotted the hapless soul in last place. Laura, then six, was the caboose.

"Wait!" John shouted. "There's a little girl at the end!"

"She wants to do it," other boys protested. "Not our fault."

"Nobody forced her." Duncan grinned wickedly.

Laura, in a blue dress, had taken the hand of an eight-year-old, who was clearly relieved to be last no longer.

"It's not right!" John relinquished his coveted spot, broke the chain, and trotted indignantly to the end of the line. Boys hooted and hollered as he passed.

"Let go, Laura," he said quietly. "You might get hurt."

"I am *not* a little girl. I can do this." The fear in her eyes betrayed her words.

"No. You can't!" he said. "You're a girl. You're too little. You're only six."

"Almost seven!" she blurted. Her face flushed, she aimed a kick at his ankle, but he jumped back.

"No, you're not! You just had a birthday." Why, he wondered, is she so stubborn?

Duncan pawed the ground like a maddened bull about to charge.

She gritted her teeth. "Get away from me, John Ashley."

She knows my name, he thought, taken by surprise.

He reached for her hand to take the tail-end position himself, but she evaded his grasp.

"What's wrong with you?" he muttered.

"Don't touch me, John!"

She had said it again. He was elated. She knew who he was after all.

He scowled darkly at the boy beside her. The youngster's eyes widened. He quickly shook Laura off and took John's hand.

A gaggle of girls shrieked from the sidelines as Laura reached for John's free hand, which he snatched away,

Duncan took off, and the whip lurched forward.

John glanced back at Laura, a mistake. She smiled. He was yanked into a sprint as he smiled back. "God help me," he murmured, echoing words his mother often uttered.

It's not so bad, he thought, an instant before the whip cracked and he hurtled face first into the sharp corner of the outhouse.

Everyone crowded around him, except Duncan, who strutted like a rooster.

Dazed and bleeding from the nose and a deep gash above his right eye, John tried to look nonchalant and scrambled to his feet. His arm throbbed painfully.

Laura pushed her way through the others and took his hand. Tears glistened in her bright blue eyes. "Does it hurt?" she whispered woefully.

"No." He glanced about jauntily, his vision blurred by the bleeding.

"Let's get some ice," she said, and led him to the schoolhouse door.

Miss Peters glanced up from her desk, pushed up her spectacles, and jumped to her feet. "Mercy! What happened to you, John?"

His shirt and trousers were bloodied. So was Laura's dress, but she didn't seem upset. She's not like other girls, John thought.

"He played crack the whip," Laura said mournfully, her sad eyes downcast. "I told him to stop, ma'am." She shook her head. "He wouldn't listen."

"Boys never do," the teacher said sharply.

John's startled glance at Laura splashed blood onto the pine floor.

She smiled sympathetically.

The teacher had him lie on the floor, his head back as Laura applied cold compresses to his injuries, none of which seemed serious.

Her patience tried, Miss Peters sent a note home with him. He had failed to listen to her, behaved recklessly, and ignored warnings from a concerned fellow student. "John" she wrote, "is clearly capable of better."

Leugenia, his mother, wept. Joe Ashley vowed to march his son out to the woodshed and whup him with his belt, then winked at John, as the boy's mother turned away in despair. He'd been injured by his own bad behavior, his father said, which was punishment enough.

Miss Peters disagreed. She kept John after school for weeks to clean erasers, empty wastebaskets, and tidy up. Laura chose to stay and help as well. The teacher was pleased. That girl's positive influence would surely keep John Ashley out of future trouble.

From then on, when he had no pressing chores or afterschool errands—and even when he did—John and Laura would meet on the bank of the Caloosahatchee River.

By age nine, he could play a spirited version of "Dixie" on his older brother's banjo. He focused on his finger work and his singing. But she'd distract him. She danced with such abandon, skirt swirling, shoes pounding the damp riverbank, that she'd eventually collapse, panting on the ground in front of him.

She was difficult to ignore.

Sometimes he cut them each a pole with his double-bladed pocket-knife. The rolling river teemed with jumping, silver-finned fish. Unlike other girls, Laura was not afraid to bait her own hook. Worms didn't scare her.

"Who are they?" she asked, as they fished from a small wooden skiff one golden winter afternoon. Two strangers waved repeatedly from the riverbank. She took off her sun hat and waved back.

John shrugged. "They look citified, not from here. What are they doing?" He shaded his eyes with his hand. The men had set up some odd-looking equipment down by the water. "Stop waving, Laura. You don't know who they are."

"Maybe they're lost," she said.

"Could be surveyors." John squinted at a contraption on thin legs.

He dug the oars deep and turned slowly toward the bank, close enough to hear the strangers but not too close.

"A moment of your time, son," called one, coaxing them closer.

They look alike, John thought, balding men with bristly mustaches, dark city suits, vests, ties, and pocket watches. They had an odd-looking little dog with them.

"If they try anything," John muttered under his breath, "I'll knock the closest one down with a paddle. Then you run as fast as you can."

"Oh, John!" Laura fanned herself with her hat and glared in exasperation. "Don't you dare! Look how elegant they are."

He frowned. "Do what I say, Laura." He squinted suspiciously at the strangers. Up close they looked even more alike.

"I'd like to introduce myself," sang out the man who'd beckoned them. "I'm Charles Homer, and this"—he gestured with a flourish—"is my brother Winslow. Winslow Homer, the great American artist."

John stared blankly. Laura blinked in the brilliant sunlight and looked thoughtful.

"And this is Sam." Winslow imitated his brother's flourish and introduced the dog, whose ears perked up at the sound of his name.

Laura smiled at the pup, who wagged his tail furiously.

"What kind of dog is that?" John asked.

"Sam's a fox terrier." Winslow clapped his hands and laughed heartily at their keen interest in the dog, not the artist.

"We planned to do a bit of fishing," Charles explained, "but my brother is quite overwhelmed by the beauty of the Caloosahatchee at this spot . . ."

"It's only the river." Perplexed, Laura wrinkled her nose and peered over her shoulder at the familiar bright green water.

". . . and has an idea that the image of you two there in your little boat . . . He's already done a few sketches . . ."

"He's drawing our picture?" Laura's face lit up and her shoulders straightened.

"Yes." Winslow smiled. "We hoped you wouldn't disappear around that bend before I finish. I'd like to keep you in sight a bit longer, unless, of course, you have a prior engagement."

"What should we do?" Laura adjusted her bonnet.

"Exactly what you were doing before we hailed you. Pretend you don't see us. Forget we're here."

"Can we, John?" She turned to him eagerly.

"If you want to, Laura." He sounded doubtful.

"So you are John and Laura." Charles jotted their names in a small notebook.

At their direction, John paddled back out onto the shimmering gold and green river.

"It is beautiful here, Laura," he said.

"Sit up straight, John," she said primly, her small chin firm. "That man is painting your picture."

When it came time to go home for supper, Winslow Homer asked them to return the next day so he could continue his work.

"I'll ask my father," John said.

"We'll be back," Laura confidently assured them.

Charles handed them little blue cloth bags of shiny nickels, for their time.

Laura was ecstatic. "Don't tell your father, John. He might say no."

John gave his nickels to his parents and told them everything.

"Homer?" Joe's brow furrowed. "Winslow Homer? I know the name. If he's the same one, he traveled with the Army of the Potomac to illustrate the war."

"A Yankee?" John asked in dismay.

"No, he reported on the war, drew sketches of the battles for magazines and newspapers. My uncle John, the man you're named after, met him in Virginia during the prisoner exchange. Maybe I'll go down to the river with you tomorrow."

"What were you doing on the river with little Laura Upthegrove?" his mother asked.

"Rowing." John's face colored. "And fishing."

"You go fishing with little girls?" It was Joe Ashley's turn to look dismayed.

"No, sir. Only her. Mr. Homer said the river is beautiful."

"He's right, son."

Joe Ashley met Charles and Winslow Homer the next day, another cool and golden afternoon. John watched them, keenly aware for the first time of the difference between the well-tailored city gentlemen and his father, in overalls and a simple work shirt. He and Laura understood little of the conversation, but the men heartily shook hands at the end.

Winslow Homer painted Laura wading in the river, then beside it as a storm threatened, her long hair loose, skirts swirling, as tree limbs groaned in the wind. On another day, he painted John swimming in the mirror-bright water beside the boat, as Laura sat inside, her face shadowed by trees and overhanging vines.

They shared the brothers' picnic lunches, played with Sam, and listened to the artist tell tales of his travels. He had just come from the Bahamas, had been to Key West, seen the Gulf Stream and the island of Cuba, had even been to England and seen castles. They were swept up by the artist's enthusiasm for Florida's light, sky, and water. He said they were unlike any he'd seen before. The children began to look at the familiar sights around them in a different way.

John understood. He often heard the river call his name. For as long as he could remember, he'd been drawn to its peaceful, green-walled waters and the wilderness around them. Before he met the artist, he believed that only he felt that way.

After ten days, the brothers packed up their easels and said they hoped to see John and Laura again one day. Then they and Sam, the fox terrier, were gone. Laura was crushed; it was as though she somehow expected them to stay on, to continue to chronicle her life and John's in pictures.

John tried to comfort her. "Everything ends," he told her. "Nothing lasts forever, Laura."

"Some things do," she stubbornly insisted. Her deep blue eyes never left his. "Like it says in the Bible, 'forever and ever, amen.'"

Homer had left them a few black-and-white sketches on scraps of paper. John kept one of Laura. He admired how Homer had captured her spirit and posture in just a few spare lines.

The river now held a new fascination for them both.

They met there, alone, as often as possible. By the time John was fourteen and Laura twelve, he'd learned to play the guitar. No matter how stealthily she approached, she never did succeed in surprising him. He never looked up, just grinned and played: *Yes, we'll gather at the river, the beautiful, beautiful river* . . .

They sang hymns, "Amazing Grace" and "The Old Rugged Cross." His favorite folk songs were laments, involving disaster and heartbreak. "The Wreck of the Old '97," "Sometimes I Feel Like a Motherless Child," and "Oh Shenandoah" moved Laura to tears. She'd sing along, in a clear, high voice so sweet that he'd stop to listen. *Oh Shenandoah, I long to see you.* He said she had the saddest voice he ever heard.

Some afternoons she set up melons and bottles as targets so he could practice with his pistol and Winchester rifle. His father, a well-known marksman, had taught him and the boy was already a crack shot. His brothers were good as well, but John's aim was truest. He could fire from thirty feet away at the mouth of a bottle on its side atop a fence post and blow out the bottom without even scratching the small opening through which the bullet passed.

A patient teacher like his father, John taught Laura how to shoot.

When he was sixteen and she was fourteen, Laura's mother forbid her daughter to spend time alone with any member of the opposite sex, especially John Ashley. The woman soon became put out that Leugenia, John's mother, made little effort to help enforce the ban.

John and Laura still found ways to be alone together.

One steamy summer afternoon they sat and dangled their feet in the clear, cool water at the river's shady edge. He'd brought his guitar but felt too lethargic to play.

"I'd love to take a swim right now," he said in his slow, easy drawl.

"Wish we could." Her voice sounded husky in the heat.

A fine mist filled the air as waterbirds called amorously to each other.

"We can," he said.

"What if somebody saw us?"

"Nobody else ever comes here." He clasped Laura's warm, responsive hand in his.

"We'd burn in hell," she murmured.

"Then we'll burn together. But it's no sin, only a swim. Go on. Undress behind that big live oak. I won't look. I promise."

"But there's manatees in the water," she protested.

"They don't mind. Sea cows are harmless. They love company."

"Mama warned me. You *are* the devil." She pushed him down on his back and straddled him, her long hair falling like a veil around his face, tickling his cheeks and ears. He smelled her skin, her hair, and the warm, fertile earth beneath them.

"All right," she said, and rose slowly to her feet. "But remember, you promised not to look."

"Nothing I ain't seen before." He sounded bored, but his heart pounded.

"Oh really," she teased from behind the oak tree. "You ain't seen nothing."

"I live with four sisters and my mother."

He looked, of course. Saw her cotton skirt drop in a graceful circle around her tanned bare feet. She was nothing like his mother or sisters.

He closed his eyes until he heard her splash into the river, then sprang to his feet, peeled off his clothes and followed.

She watched him from gleaming waist-deep water, her arms shielding her breasts.

"Hey," he protested. "You weren't 'sposed to look either."

"I never promised." She laughed and swam off, eluding him among a dozen sausage-shaped manatees, some with their calves. They played together and with the gentle, giant creatures so homely that they were beautiful.

He watched her tread water, nose to snout with a huge flat-tailed, bewhiskered sea cow that rolled over so Laura, her hair streaming in the current, could scratch its belly. He could almost see the creature smile. A great blue heron, at least four feet tall, squawked, croaked, and watched from shore as dozens of pelicans flew overhead in formation, their distorted reflections skimming across the water. John ached to paint like Winslow Homer, so he could preserve the moment forever.

They finally clambered ashore, laughing and out of breath. She eluded him again and snatched up her skirt to wrap around her before they embraced. Then he kissed her, really kissed her, for the first time.

She wrapped her warm, naked arms around his neck and drew his face down to hers as the skirt slipped to the ground. They followed it. Her breath came in little gasps as he kissed her forehead, her eyelids, her mouth, chin, and the hollow of her throat. Her wet skin was smooth, slippery, and soft, and her eyes took on the color of the river.

"We can't," she finally said.

"I know. But can we just—"

"No," she said firmly, and disengaged, then began to gather up her clothes.

He lay on his back staring in bleak frustration at the sky. "You're killing me, Laura."

"You'll be fine; take deep breaths," she said, serenely content to lie beside him without touching.

He sighed and closed his eyes until frogs began to croak in the reeds. The sun was nearly gone, yet the air seemed even warmer and more moist than ever. Their swim had not cooled him off at all.

Sharing the water with the gentle river creatures as birds darkened the sky above brought one of the Bible stories his mother read aloud after supper vividly to life for the first time. This, he thought, is how it was for Adam and Eve in the Garden.

He gazed at the girl beside him and knew he would always remember the brightness of her body, the water's reflection in her eyes, and would forever think of her and the river together.

Both caught hell from their parents for coming home late that night. John felt the imprint of her lips on his for days and was sure everyone could see it.

For weeks they found it difficult to be alone together. John's brothers, sisters, and friends clamored for his company, while Laura's watchful mother, vigilant siblings, and protective half brother surrounded her.

John and his brothers often played music for dances and church socials. He had adamantly rejected Laura's offers to teach him to dance until he watched her do the two-step and the Virginia reel with Duncan Moody. Later that night he demanded that his favorite sister, Daisy, teach him immediately. They practiced every day for weeks.

He and Laura danced together for the first time at the next church social, the night their lives changed forever.

That was the night Joe Ashley arrived home late, grim and smelling of whiskey. He woke Leugenia and their nine children, told them to quickly pack up whatever they wanted to keep because they were leaving now and wouldn't be back.

"Was there gunplay?" his wife asked, her eyes fearful in the lamplight, a tremor in her voice. "Is anybody dead?"

"No, but a man was shot. He'll live, but he has a big family. We best leave now, or somebody will die."

She began to pack her best linens in a wooden chest.

The children, still sleepy and in their nightclothes, dutifully gathered their belongings, except for John.

"Where are we going?" he persistently asked his father. "When will we be back?"

"No time to talk, son. We got to go! Get your things together, now."

John dressed quickly, carried his banjo and guitar out onto the front porch, left them on the steps, then broke into a dead run down the dusty road. The dust, white in the moonlight, looked like silk.

His father stepped out and glared after him.

"It's that girl," he said bitterly, and moved to go after the boy.

His wife placed her small, worn hand on his forearm and raised her eyes to his. "He just wants to say goodbye, Joe," she said softly. "You remember how it was."

He nodded gruffly and caught her in his long arms.

"I got to get busy," she said after a moment, touched his stubbly cheek, and gently extricated herself.

"You can't bring that sideboard," he said hoarsely, as she turned away. "It's too big. We don't have room for it."

It had belonged to her grandmother.

"We can fit it in the wagon, Joe. Bobby and two of the girls can ride up front with us."

He nodded and went to harness up the team.

The Upthegrove house was a mile and a half away. John arrived breathless, lungs bursting. The place was dark. He stood beneath Laura's window and whistled like a mourning dove, a signal they used. No response. Again. Nothing. He carried a feed bucket to her window, stood on it, and scratched the screen.

He heard her whisper in the dark. "John?"

"It's me, Laura . . ."

She was suddenly there, a swift shadow in the dark. Eyes straining, he couldn't see her face or what she wore but recognized her sweet scent, orange blossoms and roses. At that moment a mockingbird burst into a soaring, full-throated, heartbreaking song in the night. John would never forget the sound or that moment. They would remain with him, in his memory, forever.

"John, what are you—"

The front door burst open with a crash as though kicked by a mule. Laura's stepfather loped barefoot across the creaky porch in his long johns, brandishing his breech-loading, double-barreled, .44 caliber shotgun.

"I got you now, boy!" he shouted. "Freeze right there! Caught you dead to rights climbing into my little girl's bedroom!"

John stood his ground, heart pounding. To his surprise, he felt no fear. In fact, he thought, he could die now, without regret, outside her window.

"No, sir," he answered boldly. "I was not climbing into your daughter's room. I wouldn't do that. I just wanted to tell her something important."

Laura's mother, in nightclothes and a hairnet, materialized like an apparition on the porch. Laura's brother, Dewitt, trailed after her. "Mama, what's happening?"

"Hush, boy!" she told him. "Git yourself back to bed, right now."

"What could you possibly have to tell our Laura that's so important at this time of night?" her stepfather asked, as he racked one into the chamber.

"Daddy," Laura cried. "Stop! Don't do anything! Please!"

John turned to her. "Don't worry, Laura," he said softly. "We're leaving tonight. My whole family. I came to say goodbye. You're my girl, aren't you?"

"Goodbye? When are you coming back, John?"

He shrugged. "Don't know, Laura. But I will, I promise. Remember that. I'll be back!" Out the corner of his eye he saw her stepfather advance.

"Get down from there, you son of a bitch, now!"

"Are you my girl?"

"Yes, Johnny."

"Sorry, darlin'," he said. It came naturally. It was the first time he'd called her that. He liked the sound of it as he stepped off the feed bucket.

"Git your skinny ass out of here. Now!"

"Yes, sir."

"You're damn lucky, boy. Last time I came this close to shooting somebody, I did it! Killed me a Yankee. Git outta here now, afore I shoot you too!"

John stole a fleeting glance at her window but still couldn't see her. He turned and left the way he'd come. When he arrived home, heartsick and out of breath, the house was empty, his family gone. He and their dog, a bluetick hound that emerged from the woods behind the house, followed the wagon's tracks for a good two miles before they caught up with it. His father reached down with a strong arm and pulled them both into the wagon. His mother hugged his neck. "We worried about you, son."

"No need, Mama. We're all together. Everything's all right." He would never cry in front of his mother. That would not be a manly thing to do.

Clouds drifted across the moon's face, darkening the trail ahead. Joe Ashley constantly searched the shadowy road behind them, relieved to see no one else following. John regretted all the things he did not say to Laura, and her stepfather. With a ragged sigh, he put his arm around his youngest brother, Bobby, who leaned against him, sitting up, sound asleep.

Is Laura asleep? John wondered. Or awake and thinking of me? He promised himself he'd see her again. He'd be back. But how and when?

CHAPTER SEVEN

POMPANO, FLORIDA

The lure of work, adventure, and exploration led Joe and Leugenia Ashley and their nine children across the state by horse-drawn wagon to booming southeast Florida.

Aging empire builder Henry Flagler was making history. He needed every strong back he could find to help build and maintain his railroad. His crews relentlessly slashed south through a steamy, mosquito-infested wilderness toward the tiny outposts of Miami and Key West. Flagler had never intended to extend his railroad so far south, but Julia Tuttle, a Miami pioneer who urged him to do so, had changed his mind by sending him fresh Florida orange blossoms during a particularly bitter northern winter.

His new vision, referred to by doubters as "Flagler's Folly," was to link civilization and the semitropical jungle along Biscayne Bay for the first time.

Joe Ashley and several of his sons hired on as woodchoppers. Wood was the fuel that produced the steam to feed the hungry engines of Flagler's huge "iron horses."

Music, laughter, and new friends quickly filled the family's modest new home in Pompano, between Miami and Palm Beach.

John worked briefly at a packing house, but chose instead to hunt, fish, and trap. He explored the South Florida wilderness, an outdoorsman at home in every wild and lonely place. He was instantly drawn to the Everglades. The solitude and the green-gold light of the great swamp fascinated him, despite its physical discomforts.

The 'Glades offered no shade or shelter, only razor-sharp sawgrass and hip-deep black Everglades muck. Wading through it was like trying to walk through quicksand. Flat terrain, ruled by alligators, snakes, and scorpions, stretched out forever beneath mountainous white clouds that drifted so low, he felt he could touch them.

There were flying ants with red-hot stinging feet. Clouds of yellow gnats swarmed into the eyes, ears, throats, and noses of visitors. Vicious, biting horseflies grew bigger than bumblebees. Deerflies bored into their victims' skin to lay eggs, and there were millions and millions of huge, bloodthirsty Everglades mosquitoes.

Most people felt as though they were being smothered by warm, wet wool blankets and found it difficult to breathe in the hot, thick, moist air. Yet John felt oddly at peace in the eerie silence, broken only by bird cries, crashing thunder, and the bellows of alligators.

He roamed south, all the way down to Miami, the city by the sea. Excited by its tourist attractions and the enthusiasm generated by real estate developers, he decided it was the perfect place to stake out a homestead and raise a family. He wished Laura were there with him to see all its amazing modern conveniences.

He met a girl at a church social in Pompano. He heard her before he saw her or knew her name. A sudden high-pitched laugh built into an ear-splitting screech that reminded him of the sounds made by wild animals as they did nasty things to each other in the swamp.

When he turned to look, she caught his eye, stepped forward, and waited expectantly.

"Hello," he managed, after an awkward silence.

He blinked as her laughter escalated into another screech. What's so damn funny? he wondered.

"Not very imaginative," she said smartly, and cocked her head. "But I 'spose a man has to start somewhere." Still amused, she asked him to fetch her a cup of punch.

Small in stature, Lucy was voluptuous in figure. Freckled, with straw-colored hair, she loved to gossip and flirt. As they sipped the lemony drink, she entertained and startled him with naughty, even salacious gossip about others present.

Relieved when his brothers Bill and Frank arrived, John introduced them to Lucy and escaped into the quiet night.

But the damage was done.

Bill was smitten. Though Lucy continued a teasing one-sided flirtation with John, she accepted Bill's marriage proposal.

John secretly hoped the romance would fail. But each time he returned from a hunting or fishing trip, the wedding plans had taken a giant stride forward. The close-knit Ashleys warmly welcomed the local girl into their family.

In the barn, John built a handsome sideboard, his wedding gift to the happy couple. Joe Ashley, an expert carpenter, had taught his sons the art of woodworking at early ages. On the eve of the wedding, as John applied the final coat of clear varnish, Lucy cornered him in the barn. The gift was to be a surprise, John feared her laugh might spook the horses, and he felt uneasy alone with her, so he steered her outside.

"But I just love the smell of fresh hay," she objected.

Safely out in the open, under a moonlit sky, his soon-to-be sister-in-law took his arm.

"I am glad it's you standing up for us, John." She paused, her lips moist and slightly parted, her eyes bold. "You *are* the best man, you know." She winked. "Just say the word, Johnny, and this wedding can be postponed, unless you and Billy agree to trade places in the weddin' party."

Speechless, he groped for words strong enough to convey his dismay.

She mistook his pause for interest, unbuttoned her snug shirtwaist, and with her full breasts free, reached for his hand to lead him toward the shadowy grove behind the barn.

John's jaw dropped.

"Don't pretend to be surprised, Johnny." She stared at him confidently, one hand on her hip. "You've known from the start that you're the man I want. I just took up with Bill to stay close to you."

"You're not close to me, Lucy. I've told you before, I'm committed to another girl."

Her freckled breasts were still exposed and impossible to ignore.

"For God's sake, woman, cover yourself up. Then grow up. What if somebody came out here? My brother plans to marry you, and you're damn lucky to find a man like him."

"*You* grow up!" Her gray eyes darkened. She stepped closer and got in his face. "And when did you last set eyes on *your* girl? She probably doesn't even remember your name. Think she's waiting on you, Johnny? What a pipe dream! Maybe she doesn't even exist. Maybe," she said slyly, "you don't like real women at all. Is that what ails you, boy?"

"Laura remembers my name," he said. He stared at Lucy standing in front of him on tiptoe, her nipples exposed, her wet lips challenging him to prove his manhood.

Then he laughed, loud and long.

She dropped to a flat-footed stance, her face red, nostrils flared, jaw clenched. Fingers shaking, she quickly rebuttoned her shirtwaist.

"You just lost your chance," she whispered bitterly. "And you will regret it."

"You ever hurt my brother, Lucy, and you'll be the one with regrets."

She drew her right hand back to slap him, but he roughly caught her wrist.

"Bill deserves a good wife," John said. "If you marry him tomorrow, you damn well better be one."

She wrenched away and angrily stomped back to the house.

He watched her go and wondered why in God's name he had ever introduced them. Who knew? He wanted to tell Bill, to level with him, right there and then, before it was too late. But his brother was crazy about the girl. And both families had happily planned the event for weeks. The ball had rolled too far to stop now.

The union that joined two popular families was reported in flowery prose on the social page of the local weekly newspaper.

John stood up for his brother and wished him good luck. The beauty of the simple ceremony—its music, vows, and his mother's happy tears—touched his heart. More than ever, he needed Laura beside him. She and the Caloosahatchee River haunted his dreams both awake and sleeping. He'd only written her twice, had promised to come for her as soon as he could support a family. He couldn't be sure she'd received his letters, since his father had warned him against using a return address for the same reason they'd departed.

Now, after nearly four years, he'd accumulated the resources to properly court Laura. He had scouted Miami sites suitable for a homestead. The time had come, at last. He announced his plans at a family supper on a summer Sunday.

"Oh, John. I'm so sorry." Lucy sat directly across the table, fanning herself. "Bless your heart. Didn't you hear, honey? My west coast cousins in Fort Myers wrote me weeks ago that Laura Upthegrove died in that yellow fever epidemic last spring." Stunned silence followed. Yellow fever had killed scores across the state, even wiped out entire families.

"Are you sure?" John asked, his voice grave.

Her shoulders lifted toward her ears and she rolled her eyes. "Well, I wasn't there, was I, sugar? But I was told by kin who were. Would they lie?"

John rose to his feet so abruptly that his wooden chair toppled to the floor with a crash. He left the room without another word.

Every eye at the table was fixed on Lucy.

Face flushed, she slowly spread sweet butter on a warm biscuit and took a dainty bite. "Well." She lifted her chin, smacked her shiny lips together, and pouted. "Don't you all be giving me that look. How was I to know he'd take it so hard? Wasn't me killed that girl, I just gave him the news. He'da heard it sooner or later. Bobby, dear, would you please pass the chicken?"

His mother, Leugenia, followed John into the kitchen and touched his arm.

"Did you know?" he asked, anguish in his eyes and a lump in his throat.

She shook her head. "No, son. I heard it when you did, just now."

"Think it's true?"

She pondered the question, brow furrowed.

"Lucy wouldn't have no reason to lie, would she?" She looked him square in the eye. "Lots of people died in that epidemic, but maybe somebody mistook her name . . ."

He slumped into a chair and rocked, as though in pain, hands tightly clasped. "It can't be true."

"You haven't seen that girl for a long time, son. Only way to know for sure is to go on over there, see her parents, her friends. If the news is bad, I know you'll take it like the man you are and pay your proper respects." She touched his face gently. "I'm so sorry, son." She hugged him close.

His heart filled with love for the tiny, worn woman in his arms. It always had. He'd hoped to pattern the life he intended to build with Laura after the one his parents shared.

"You're right, Mama. I have to go. But if it's true, I'll doubt myself for the rest of my life. I always had a way of knowing things, always have, Mama, you know that. I swear, if Laura was gone, I'd know it. I'da sensed it. I'da seen it in my dreams."

She nodded. This boy, the golden child among all her children, had a gift, a sixth sense, an innate way of knowing the truth.

How could he sleep? He left that night. His mother packed up some food and gave him her Bible to carry with him.

"Remember, son, Jesus is our rock in a weary land."

He could not imagine Laura's strong life force and spirit gone forever, cut down by illness in the bloom of youth. If she had left this earth, he would know it, feel it. He had never doubted that she'd be there when he returned. How could he live in a world without her in it? She can't be dead, he told himself over and over during his five-day journey through wet and windy weather. A river flooded, a bridge washed out, constant rain, mud everywhere: the weather matched his mood.

He stopped at a stream about a mile from her stepfather's house to shave, change into his good suit, and put on his tie. The weather had cleared, a good omen.

His heart pounded as he approached. The house looked occupied. Wash fluttered from a clothesline. Chickens pecked in the side yard. Thank God, he thought. They're here. If she's alive, I might see her now.

A scrawny yellow dog charged down off the porch and barked.

John ignored the animal and was halfway up the front steps when the door swung open and a woman stepped out. Laura's mother, a bit heavier, a little older since he'd last seen her.

Her hands flew to her throat. "Good God! It's John Ashley all filled out and growed up. Look at 'im now!" She looked sallow and washed-out in the harsh afternoon sun.

"Whatcha want here, Ashley?" Laura's stepfather stomped out behind his wife. He wore boots and overalls and waved the same damn shotgun.

"Laura," John said, her name a prayer on his lips. "I came back for Laura."

"Oh, Jesus, he doesn't know," the woman murmured.

"She ain't here, son," the man said. "Laura's gone."

A wound opened in John's heart. He felt it bleed.

He swallowed, fought to catch his breath. "Was it the yellow fever?" His voice broke.

The couple on the porch stood transfixed for a long moment. The man cut his eyes at his wife. "That's right," he said slowly. "The yellow fever. It was the yellow fever."

The woman reacted, as though startled, then turned to John. "I'm sorry. Laura always spoke so highly of you, son."

"You got no business here now, boy." Her stepfather glared, then stepped back inside. His wife followed, after a brief, mournful glance over her shoulder.

John knew the cemetery. There was still enough light left to find her.

He stumbled, searching through the headstones, read and reread the words, familiar names, so many from his childhood.

He found a headstone inscribed with the words "Beloved Teacher." He had never known Miss Peters's first name was Helen. But where was Laura? Did she lie here too, beneath the weeds? He couldn't find her. Which fresh, unmarked grave, still adorned with wilted flowers, was hers? He knelt beside a new grave, a lonely gash in the earth. Is she here? Head in his hands, he tried to pray but forgot the words. He longed to touch her, hear her voice, see her face.

If she is here, I can't find her, he thought, then got to his feet and left.

Numb, eyes wet, paying scant attention, he ran a buggy wheel off the road and broke the axle. He trudged three miles to the blacksmith shop, paused outside, wiped his eyes, took a deep breath, and walked in.

"Glad you didn't quit early, Pete."

"Well, if it ain't young Ashley. Good to see you again, John. Look like you just lost your best friend. What's the problem?"

John sighed. "Without bad luck, I'd have no luck at all. Where's Randy?" The shop was empty except for a lone customer in the back. Pete's son, Randy, had worked for his father and planned to one day take over the family business.

"Moved down to Palm Beach to look for work." The burly middle-aged blacksmith spoke gruffly. "Thanks to *Mister* Henry Ford." He angrily spat out the name.

John looked puzzled.

"Ain'tcha heard? Accordin' to *Mister* Ford, every man with a job'll be able to afford onea his Model T automobiles, putting men like me outta business."

"It'll never happen." The other customer spoke up as he approached. "Horses won't never go outta style, Pete."

"Damn right," John agreed. The tall, sandy-haired fellow looked faintly familiar.

"How can they call it progress when it puts people outta work?" the blacksmith asked plaintively.

"You're John Ashley." The sandy-haired fellow reached out to shake his hand. "Remember me? Your old friend, Edgar Tillman."

John had a vague recollection. They had never been close. Tillman's family, from New York, had been somewhat shunned as Yankees. Most Floridians had fought for the Confederacy or had kin who did. John remembered Tillman as neither scholastically nor athletically gifted, not even a fair rifle shot. More follower than leader, he was otherwise inoffensive, despite being a Yankee. He carried a bit of a paunch for a man his age.

Tillman's face colored. "Got myself a wife a few years ago, John. Didn't waste no time. Two little ones now, a boy and a girl." His prideful smile revealed good teeth but too much of his pink gums.

After John described his axle problem to Pete, Tillman spoke up again. "Pete can't get to it till mornin', so why not come on home with me for a good home-cooked meal? You look worn out, John. You can stay a day or two till you're back on the road."

Grateful for the generous offer from an old acquaintance he barely remembered, John agreed.

They rode out to Tillman's place on the outskirts of Fort Myers. John stepped out of the buggy and stretched. The small, well-kept house had a front porch that faced east and a flower-fringed vegetable garden. A red-gold sun was slowly sinking beneath the horizon.

"I'll put up the horse," Edgar said. "Tell the missus I'll be right in."

John nodded and watched him walk away. He seemed far more comfortable in his own skin now than he'd been as a boy. Edgar had found his way into manhood, most likely through marriage and family life. Some men never grow up, he thought wistfully, until they settle down with a good woman. That's what his mother always said.

Rows of cheerful pink periwinkles bordered the path. John wearily climbed the five plank steps and crossed the porch to the front door. He turned to look; Edgar was unhitching the horse by the barn. John knocked, then again with three sharp raps.

"Who's there?" A woman's voice came from behind the door.

"John Ashley, ma'am. A friend. Your husband is putting up the horse."

The door flew open.

Eyes alight, lips parted in surprise, she looked graceful, blossomed, and beautiful, in a blue dress with three tiny pearl buttons at her throat. The raven hair had been chastely pulled back, but unruly tendrils had fought free in the moist warmth of her kitchen and curled around her face.

He stared, as though in a dream. She's tall now, he thought in disbelief, almost as tall as I am. Memories flooded as he drowned in the scents of rose water and orange blossoms and the aroma from a bubbling pot on the woodstove behind her. His heart stuttered, then pounded quick and hard. He felt as though he'd seen a ghost. He *was* seeing a ghost.

Her eyes misted. She blinked rapidly and focused somewhere over his shoulder.

"Did you bring your wife with you, John?" Her voice trembled.

He found it difficult to speak; when he did, his voice was husky. "I can't believe it's you, Laura." He moved toward her.

She shook her head and stepped back. "Your wife?"

"Thank God, Laura!" Emotion deepened his voice even more. "I thought you were dead."

"Your wife!" she demanded. Her voice rose, along with her stubborn chin.

"Wife?" He frowned impatiently as though she'd spoken in some foreign tongue. "What wife? I have no wife. I came back for you. They said you died of the yellow fever."

She bit her lip, eyes wide. "Margie Haggert's cousin wrote her from Pompano that John, one of the Ashley boys, had married. I saw the letter myself."

"Maybe she meant Bill. He married a Pompano girl. Didn't you get my letters?"

"No." She wilted.

"Bill's wife, Lucy, told me last Sunday that you had died of yellow fever. Today your stepfather told me it was true." He recalled the shifty-eyed stare of the man on the porch.

They moved into each other's arms and fit perfectly, as though they had never been apart. She felt soft, warm, and alive.

"John," she murmured into his sleeve. "I waited so long."

"Wasn't all that long," he said, "before you took up with a Yankee."

She pushed him away and struck him hard across the chest with her fist.

Catching him by surprise, his guard down, the blow left him gasping. She always was the strongest girl he knew. That was one reason he loved her.

He caught his breath and laughed aloud. "That the best you can do, girl? Come on, hit me again, hard as you can, Laura. Give it all you got, little girl. Right here."

He stuck his chin out with a giddy grin and tapped it twice with his index finger. "Make me see stars. Then I'll know it's true—we're alive and we're together."

She shuddered, fists clenched, her eyes leveled at him like loaded weapons.

"Okay!" he said. "Better yet, go get a gun. Come on, girl! Shoot me!" He slapped his right hand to his chest. "Shoot me! Right here. Now!" He felt the beat of his thundering heart. "I'll die happy."

"Be careful what you wish for! Damn you, John Ashley! Why didn't you come back? Why?" Her eyes darted to a shotgun that stood next to the door.

"Laura?" His grin faded. He raised his hands like a prisoner. "Don't kill me now, river girl. Not yet. Don't make me bleed all over your clean floor before I get to kiss you."

She took a deep breath and opened her mouth at the sound of boots on the porch. The door creaked open and Edgar stepped inside. He wore the look of a road-weary man happy to be home at last. He did a double take. "You two know each other?"

A shout ended the silence that followed.

"Daddy!" A tiny girl, with her mother's black hair staggered across the room on chubby, unsteady legs. Edgar swept her up, hoisted her high, then higher, as she laughed and squealed, then lowered her to his broad chest and held her close. Over her tiny shoulder, Edgar's questioning eyes refocused on his wife and John Ashley.

"There's beef stew for supper," Laura announced.

John cut his eyes at her, then addressed his host. "I met Laura when she was five. We went to school together."

"Small world." Edgar chewed his lip, eyes speculative. The little girl squirmed in his arms. He set her down, as a wail came from another room.

"I'll get the baby," Laura said.

Edgar watched John stare after her. She returned moments later carrying a chubby-cheeked boy with sandy ringlets and a healthy howl. His father smiled, and the infant stopped crying.

"How is my little man?" Edgar gazed fondly at his son. Laura's eyes caught John's, her expression resigned.

They dined at a rough pine table after Laura removed the kerosene-soaked rags tied to each leg to repel crawling insects.

John had eaten little since that Sunday supper but only picked at the savory beef stew with potatoes, onions, carrots, and peas. To him it tasted like sawdust and felt as difficult to swallow. Laura ate sparingly as well, while she and John politely discussed old schoolmates, neighbors, and friends. She inquired about his sisters, especially Daisy, everyone's favorite. The air between them felt thick with tension, but Edgar, focused on his meal, didn't seem to notice, though at one point he did stop chewing and asked, "What brings you back to your old hometown, John?"

"I was looking for someone," John said.

"Find 'im?" Edgar asked.

John shook his head. "A day late and a dollar short."

"Is the coffee ready?" Edgar asked his wife.

Laura's hand brushed John's as she served coffee and homemade arrowroot cake. He fought an urge to kiss the inside of her wrist, her palm, and each fingertip. Lips dry, he gazed into her eyes and knew she read his thoughts.

She whisked the children off to bed as the men laughed, sipped whiskey, and talked like old friends about fishing, hunting, and home-steading. Edgar poured them each another drink, loosened his belt, and relaxed at the head of the table. His eyes proudly roved the modest room, as though he were lord and master of the manor.

He is, John thought wistfully. He has everything. He has it all.

"So, you fancied my wife when she was a girl," his host finally said, as though reading his thoughts.

John hesitated only a moment. "I won't sit at your table and lie to you, Edgar. Laura and me . . . we were childhood friends." He paused to toss down his whiskey neat, aware of his gross understatement, then took a deep breath and swallowed to ease the burn. "But"—he licked his lips—"when she was in her teens, all I ever thought about was her."

Edgar smiled. "I know the feeling."

"That's when my father moved us away." Confession concluded, John scraped back his chair and shrugged on his jacket. "I'll be moving on tonight, Edgar. I understand. Thank you for your hospitality, and your wife for the fine meal."

"Sit down!" Edgar gestured impatiently and raised his glass. "Half the men in this county felt the same way about Laura at one time or another. I invited you here and I'm a man of my word. My door is always open to you, John. We didn't have the chance to spend time together years ago, but I heard the stories about you and your family. I know your reputation. We have no problem. After all," he said, "I'm the one who got the girl." His wide smile exposed his teeth and pink gums.

John nodded, an odd ringing in his ears. "When I accepted your invite, Edgar, I swear I didn't know she was your wife."

Wife? The word felt foreign on his tongue. Laura? Someone else's wife? He hated Edgar for a moment and wished him dead, but he realized as they talked and drank that he would probably like the man—if he had only married some other woman.

Laura flounced into the room, her face flushed.

Edgar announced that John was staying and asked her to make up the daybed on the side porch.

After a quick, startled glance at John, Laura took some time to fetch the linens and a pillow. Edgar continued to drink.

*   *   *

Laura draped mosquito netting above the bed on the shadowy, covered sleeping porch and patted the pillow. "Hope you'll be comfortable, John. How nice to see you again." Her words sounded sweet, sad, and rehearsed.

He said nothing as she firmly closed the door behind her, the way he was now closed out of her life.

He sat on the hard, narrow bed, head in his hands, then stretched out and tried to sleep. The entire day seemed unreal. Hope at dawn. Grief in the afternoon. Then joy followed by a different sort of despair.

He listened to the angry, high-pitched whine of mosquitoes that hungered for his blood and thought about what he hungered for more than life itself. If he could only go back in time, to the moment he saw her bright body naked in the river, the sky and the water the same color as her eyes.

She's a woman now, he thought, and I am the goddamn fool who waited too long and lost everything.

How could he sleep with her so close, in another man's arms?

He crept out of bed, yanked his clothes on, and stepped quietly out the creaky porch door, which protested loudly in the silent night.

The entire house was dark. An old dog rose stiffly from the stoop, stretched, and padded across the yard at his side. Each found comfort in the other's company. Neither moon nor stars shone in a somber, overcast sky. John felt alone under a shroud of darkness. "I lost her," he said bleakly. The dog gazed up at him, eyes watery, as though he understood.

John decided he couldn't stay, went back to the porch, and let himself inside. He smelled orange blossoms and rose water and heard her breathing softly in the shadows just inside the door.

"I was afraid you left," she whispered, relief in her words.

"I couldn't sleep," he said.

"Me either." She paced the room, graceful in a white nightdress, shaking out her long, loose hair as she rubbed the back of her neck.

He sat down on the bed, afraid to touch her. "Where's Edgar?" His voice sounded hollow.

"Sleeping like a baby. He drank too much."

"Is he good to you, Laura?"

"Yes," she said softly. "He is a plain, boring, and decent man." She covered her eyes with her hand in the shadows. "Why didn't you come back sooner?"

"I was putting enough money together to build us a home down in Miami. Found us a nice piece of property on the river."

He heard her swift intake of breath, then a hiccup.

She slumped down next to him and rested her head on his shoulder.

"I'll always love you, Laura," he said miserably, scarcely breathing, fearing what might happen if he touched her. "Do you still love me?"

"Always have, always will." Her words were low, sweet, and mournful.

When he turned to face her, her mouth melted into his with the taste of passion and regret.

He kissed her again and again. "If I don't die of a heart attack now, I never will," he whispered. Their youthful explorations of each other's bodies were the gropes of innocent children compared to the passion that now overwhelmed them.

They writhed on his bed in a deep embrace.

"I can't." He pulled away, voice pained. "Not here, under your husband's roof. It's not right. You're killing me, Laura."

"He will probably kill us both," she said.

"Edgar's crazy"—John struggled to catch his breath—"to let me stay here. We can't do this."

She caught his hand and placed it to her breast. He could feel her heart pound. "Oh, Johnny, it's like we never were apart. It's like it always was, but better."

"If Edgar doesn't kill me, your stepfather will. He waved that shotgun at me again today."

"I'll hunt you down and kill you myself, if you ever leave me again, John," she said, her voice steady.

He knew she meant what she said and nodded. "Sounds fair, darlin'."

She laughed. The sound was clear and sweet, the laughter of the river girl he remembered.

He held her close. "We belong together," he said.

"Yes," she whispered fervently in his ear. "We do."

CHAPTER EIGHT

Edgar's head throbbed as he pulled on his overalls, then plodded out to feed the livestock in the morning. His painful hangover drove him back to the house sooner than usual.

As he stepped into the kitchen, the smells of ham, hot biscuits, and coffee turned his stomach. So did the sight of his wife and John Ashley.

Rosy-cheeked and radiant, Laura stood at the wood-burning stove, a long wooden spoon in her hand. Ashley stood behind her, his arms around her waist. Her laughter was a singular sound.

He'd never heard his wife laugh like that. He blinked and rethought what Ashley had said about their childhood friendship. Pale and melancholy yesterday, he looked like a new man now. Edgar frowned, then blinked again. That shirt he's wearing—is it mine? He cleared his throat. Neither had the decency to react with embarrassment, guilt, or surprise. They remained focused on each other.

He stood, ignored, in his own doorway. Can they see me? Am I still asleep? he wondered. Is this just a bad dream?

Despite the dull pain behind his eyes, he mustered up enough swagger to stride into that kitchen as big as life, as though he owned it, which he damn well did.

"Mornin', Ashley," he said. "'Bout time for us to ride out to the smithy's shop. If your axle's fixed, you can be on your way. If not, you can wait on it there."

No reaction, so he took a deep breath and the direct approach.

"You've overstayed your welcome, John."

"Sorry, Edgar." John tore himself away from his murmured dialogue with Laura. His smile faded. "I didn't mean . . ."

For the first time, Edgar noted, the silver-tongued houseguest from hell groped for words.

John and Laura exchanged a glance so tender that Edgar decided to forgo breakfast. He'd have Laura fix him a plate later, when he came home. Alone. His stomach should be settled by then.

"Let's go." He emphasized the final word.

"Let's talk," John solemnly countered.

"No, unless you'd rather walk than ride."

"Edgar . . ." Laura dried her hands on her apron. She looked concerned.

About time, he thought. "Stay outta this, Laura. I'll deal with you later."

John took offense. "Hold on," he said.

Laura touched his arm. Their eyes locked, then she turned and left the room without a word.

John stared after her, dismayed. What did that look mean? He could take nothing for granted, even after last night. Sure, they had expressed their love and agreed they belonged together. But they hadn't hammered out a plan. What if, in the light of day, she'd changed her mind? That she had married still had him reeling. In a fit of passion he'd promised to never leave her again. But what exactly did that mean? He frowned. Did she expect him to stay here? With her, Edgar, and the children?

Fearless in the wild, an unrivaled marksman with an unfailing inner compass, he now felt bewildered. Laura was so different from the other women he knew best, his mother and sisters. And thank God, he thought, she's not at all like Lucy.

He weighed the pros and cons from Laura's point of view, ignoring Edgar's impatient glare. He and Laura had a shared history. But so did she and Edgar. The man was her husband, the father of her children. This house, his house, was her home.

Edgar fidgeted, his fuse growing shorter.

He wants me gone, John thought. But if I go, how and when will I see her again? Are she and the children safe with him now? He needed time to figure it out.

"Ready?" Edgar marched to the door, his bloodshot eyes narrowed, increasingly obsessed by an urgent need to remove John Ashley from his home and his life at once.

To his utter annoyance, John failed to follow. Instead, he'd taken a seat at the kitchen table. "Let's talk."

"We can do that on the road." Edgar stepped toward him menacingly, fists ready.

"No. Don't do that, Edgar." John waved him away. Brow furrowed, he had an idea. "Let's ask Laura to join us."

Where in God's name did she go? he wondered. She's holed up in their bedroom. What did that mean? It didn't look good.

"Out. Out of my house, now!" Edgar snarled and pointed to the door. "And take off that shirt before you go!"

"Sorry." John glanced down, embarrassed. "I only borrowed it so Laura could wash and iron mine."

"Not on your best day! Out! Take your dirty laundry! Now!" Edgar gestured as though scolding a dog he was about to kick.

John sighed, got to his feet, and slowly peeled off the shirt. How can I refuse to leave the man's house? he wondered. It's not right. But how can I leave without her?

"Okay!" Edgar puffed up, ready to fight. "I'll throw you out!" Despite his fury, he couldn't help but notice how muscular Ashley looked without his shirt.

"I'm not gonna fight you, Edgar. We have a lot in common."

"Get out of my house!"

"Not without Laura."

"What the hell?" Edgar's face contorted in disbelief.

"I'm ready." Laura sang out the words as she appeared like an answered prayer, in a blue traveling suit with a matching shirtwaist, the baby in her arms, and a valise at her feet. Her little girl, also dressed for travel, clung to her mother's skirt with both hands, one thumb in her mouth.

Weak with relief, John knew he'd never doubt her again.

"Why, John," she asked softly, "are you taking off your clothes?"

"Edgar wants his shirt."

"Damn right," Edgar said. "Where do you think you're going, Laura?"

"Away," she said calmly. "With John."

"No, you're not." He lumbered toward her.

"She is." John stepped between them.

"You're crazy if you think you can take my children anywhere."

"They need their mother," she said quietly. "Perhaps when they're older . . ."

"I'll never let you steal my kids! Never!"

Laura wilted. "I'm so sorry, Edgar."

"Don't be," John said. "It's my fault." He turned to Edgar. "I'm lower than a worm because I waited too long to—"

"No! It's my fault," she argued and squared her shoulders defiantly, "because I didn't wait for John. He's not responsible for this."

Edgar, sweating, his face beet red, lunged for the shotgun beside the door. His hands shook; he fumbled, nearly dropped the weapon, but then recovered and raised it grimly to his shoulder.

"Now, Edgar," his wife said gently, "stop that."

John rolled his eyes. "This isn't personal, Edgar. It's just that Laura and me,"—he gazed at her fondly—"we belong together. Always did."

She nodded.

"I'll blow you to kingdom come, you son of a bitch!" Edgar gingerly sidestepped the kitchen table and gritted his teeth, the shotgun barrel leveled at John's chest. His nostrils flared, his eyes narrowed.

"I don't care how well-liked you and your damn family are, Ashley. You're a dead man now. Nobody on earth'll blame me when I tell 'em how you sneaked into my home under false pretenses and took advantage of my wife."

"I never took advantage." John took umbrage. "Didn't touch her! Wouldn't do that under your roof, Edgar. I swear."

He saw Laura's mouth open, an eyebrow lift.

"Well, maybe a little touching," he conceded, "but that's all. In a nutshell, she is *not* your woman. Never was. Never could be. She's mine."

Laura nodded in agreement. "Don't you try to shoot him, Edgar. Now or ever. You're too young to die. I've seen John shoot hundreds of times. He never misses. Ever. And that shotgun you're holding? It's not loaded."

"I always keep it loaded." Edgar smirked like a card shark with the winning hand and slunk closer to his target.

"Not since this mornin'," Laura said, one hand on her hip. "Your rifle ain't loaded either. I threw the shells in the pond. Every last one." She proceeded calmly to the door. "We'll be going now. Please do not act up and frighten the children."

With a howl of rage, Edgar charged John, who caught the shotgun in both hands, wrestled it away, and sent him sprawling to the floor.

"You ain't getting away with this! Neither one a you!" Edgar scrabbled up onto his hands and knees and dove at John's ankles.

Laura hustled the children out onto the front porch so they wouldn't see.

"Laura!" Edgar screamed like a woman. "Don't go!"

Laura closed the door behind her, took a deep breath, and marveled at the brilliant and beautiful day. A great blue heron soared. She pointed it out to the children, whose big eyes followed its flight until they heard a crash in the kitchen. It sounded as though the table had been overturned. Scuffling sounds followed.

Laura reappeared in the doorway. The sun streamed in behind her, highlighting her hair, her posture, and her fiery eyes.

"Don't you hurt him, John!" she shouted, as the men grappled.

"Whose side are you on?" he demanded over his shoulder, as he pinned Edgar to the floor and held him there until he lay still, panting and sniffling.

"Calm down now and listen." John helped Edgar to his feet.

But Edgar would not quit. "You tomcatting, wife-stealing son of a bitch!" He swung wildly at John but missed.

Out of patience, John caught him square on the jaw with a roundhouse right. Edgar toppled like a tree, cracked his head on the metal stove with a loud clang, and crashed to the floor.

He stared up, glassy-eyed. John towered over him, holding the empty shotgun and rubbing his bruised knuckles.

"I need the wooden cradle and the diapers from the bedroom," Laura sang out from the porch. She peered around the door jamb.

"Didn't mean to hit 'im so hard, darlin'," John said apologetically.

"I love it when you call me that, John."

"Get used to it, sweetheart." He grinned, then found the items she wanted, hitched up the buggy, and loaded her things into it, along with the children.

Edgar clung to the front door for support, swaying as he watched.

"I need to borrow your horse and buggy," John told him. "You'll have them back by this evening."

"There's ham in the icebox," Laura called, "and a fresh loaf in the bread box."

Edgar stared in disbelief. "You leave now, Laura," he roared, "and you ain't never welcome back!"

She gave a quick nod, lips quivering, her eyelashes lowered, as John helped her into the buggy.

Edgar reacted with a savage cry. Shirt torn, bleeding from his nose, his busted lip, and the cut on the back of his head, he charged headlong down the front steps. Midway, he lost his footing, fell forward, and collided face-first with the ground. When he struggled to his knees, he appeared to have lost a tooth. Tears and blood mingled and his nose dripped as he blubbered, "No! Laura, please . . ."

"Stay down on your knees, Edgar," she told him. "Put your hands together in prayer and thank the good Lord I'm gone. You deserved a better wife."

"Don't go!"

She ran her hand through her hair, sighed, and turned away.

"Goddamnit! You'll burn in hellfire for this, Laura Upthegrove! You'll both burn!" He staggered after them and shook his fist.

She did not look back. Their little daughter did and began to shriek, "Daddy! Daddy! Daddy!" The baby began to howl, his tiny face red and puckered like his father's.

When they were finally out of sight, their mother joined in, first a whimper, then full-blown, shoulder-shaking sobs, punctuated by sporadic hiccups.

John listened in pained silence, his eyes on the road ahead. "It coulda gone better," he finally acknowledged, with a worried sidelong glance. "You sorry?"

She shook her head and wiped her eyes.

"Want to hear about Miami?" He took her hand.

She nodded, between hiccups.

"In Miami," he began, "they welcome the New Year with firecrackers and steamboat whistles. Last time I was down there, they had an organ grinder with a monkey, and a sightseeing boat that takes you up the Miami River to Alligator Joe's, where Joe, a crazy three-hundred-pound fella, wrassles the 'gators. Downtown there's two moving picture theaters, the Kinodrome and the Alcazar, right across the street from each other. For ten cents you see a picture show and vaudeville artists, along with a Tin Pan piano and a screechy Graphophone."

He winked as interest kindled in her eyes. "Of course, something else comes free with the show—a Turkish bath, 'cause the theater's so damn hot. They installed a buncha newfangled electric fans, but they don't stir much air. Last time I saw a show, the fire chief called the Kinodrome a fire hazard, threatened to shut it down. The theater manager cussed him out, said the chief was just ornery because no dogs are allowed and the fire chief refuses to go anyplace where his dog isn't welcome."

She smiled and crinkled her nose.

"The moving pictures get a little jerky and sometimes it's hard to read the captions, but they sure are entertainin'. Shows start at seven and nine o'clock. You can see both the same night, then go out for ice cream."

"Who did you take?" Her tears had stopped but not the occasional hiccup.

"Hate to say." John looked away, avoiding her eyes.

"Who?"

"Somebody special." He nodded slowly. "Name's Bobby. Took my little brother, Bobby, to Miami for his birthday."

She laughed aloud, followed by a tiny hiccup. "Don't tell me there's no girls down there."

"Sure, there are. Lots of 'em. A gal named Fanny, a real pistol, and a pretty little blonde, name of Bessie Burdine. Her daddy runs the trading post."

Laura stopped smiling.

"And that," he said quickly, "is where I met Carl Fisher, a millionaire from Indiana. Invented the headlights, or something, for Henry Ford's cars. Plans to build a city on that beach off Miami. Said it'll be a great place to raise a family. That we should settle down there." He gazed fondly at her and the children. "The man offered me a job, Laura. Said he needs all the help he can get."

"But I heard that beach is a swamp, nothing but mangroves." Laura's head rested on his shoulder, her hiccups gone.

"Don't you believe it, darlin'. Fella, name of Collins, plans to build a wooden bridge across the bay, all the way from Miami to the beach. The whole place is gonna grow like wildfire. It's where the future lies, darlin'. Our future." He kissed her hair. "The beauty of it all is that Henry Flagler, who's building the railroad, promised to keep a cap on it. Says he'll keep Miami a little fishing village, to provide services to his railroad, steamships, and hotels.

"Population's nearly seven thousand, and they predict it'll be ten thousand by 1910. Every minute I spent in Miami, I wished you were with me, darlin'. Miami is the city of the future, yours and mine."

"Is there a church?" she asked, her hand on his knee.

"Is there a church?" He laughed with such a joyous peal that she smiled. "Six of 'em! And every bell is different. People can tell 'em apart by the sound. There's two Methodist churches, one for Yankees and the Southern Methodist for the rest of us. Like Mr. Fisher said, it'll be a swell place for raising kids."

He smiled at the baby now asleep in her arms, then flashed his killer grin at Laura. "'Member when I was fourteen and you were twelve? I wanted to kiss you more than anything in the world, but you were scared it might cause a baby and you always ran away. But we did promise to raise kids someday. You wanted two, a boy and a girl."

"You still remember that?" she said dreamily.

"Damn straight, darlin'. But I never thought you'd go ahead and do it without me."

"Stop! Slow down, John! Stop! Right now!"

Startled, he pulled up the horse. "What's wrong, darlin'?"

She jumped down from the buggy, the baby in her arms, and walked swiftly down the rutted road ahead.

"Laura? What the hell are you doing?"

She ignored him.

"Come on, girl, where you going?"

She paused for a moment, her chin up. "Well, I can't go back to Edgar. You heard what he said. So I guess I'm going to my mother's."

"Why?"

Arlie, the little girl still in the buggy, yawned, sat up, smiled, and cut her eyes at him, so much like Laura that he had to stare. She quickly glanced away.

"God help the little boys you meet at school," he murmured. Arlie giggled.

"What did you say?" Laura demanded. She stood in the road in front of them.

"I asked you, 'Why?'"

"Because I refuse to spend the rest of my life listening to you discuss my mistakes. Hand that child down to me right now, John."

"Nope. If you leave me, I'm keeping her. I refuse to spend the rest of my life without hearing a female whine, cry, and hiccup." He winked at the little girl, who slid over and tucked her arm in his, then he turned to her mother.

"Come on, Laura. I didn't mean it, I swear. Won't ever mention it again, darlin'. Never. Now get back in here with me and your little girl before you turn your ankle. Your pretty skirt and nice shoes are getting all muddy."

She stopped to check her shoes and hemline. He was right.

He pulled the horse up beside her, made eye contact, then leaned across and reached out. She clasped his hand and he swung her up and back aboard.

"I already forgot whatever it was," he said. "The future is what counts, darlin'. And it's waiting for us in Miami. It's the perfect time to start out there, with the railroad, the steamship line, and the cross-Florida barge canal. Miami's got the only sewer system south of Saint Augustine. They already have sawmills, rock quarries, machine shops, and supply houses. Even three Chinese laundries! You won't ever have to wash my shirts, darlin', I promise." He crossed his heart with his index finger, then stretched his arms out wide as if to embrace the entire horizon. "It's gonna be big, Laura, and we will be too. We'll grow with it. Everybody will know our names. I know it. I can feel it in my bones. We can be happy there. Forever."

His smile faded slightly. "Though I may have to watch my back for a while. Did I thank you for unloading Edgar's weapons?"

"Anytime, darlin'," she said, his dreams of Miami and the future reflected in her eyes.

CHAPTER NINE

John insisted she close her eyes as he took a detour. "Okay, you can open 'em now," he finally said.

"I already know where we are." Laura smiled. "I hear it, and I can feel it in the air." She opened her eyes. "Oh, John, I was right. It's the river, where we . . ." Her eyes glistened and her voice trailed off.

He couldn't resist visiting the familiar place where they'd shared all their secrets and childhood memories.

"This reminds me," she said, softly, "a year or so after you left, the artist, Winslow Homer, came back. He'd aged a lot and looked frail. Sam wasn't with 'im. Said he grieved so when that little dog died that he never wanted another one.

"He was surprised that you'd gone. He said you'd be back. He was so sure; I should've known. I should've listened. I posed for him again down here by the river, but it wasn't the same without you. Nothing was. He said it took the two of us and the river to make magic."

"He was right," John said. "I still have his sketch of you. Built a wood frame for it. Think of you every time I look at it." He nuzzled her ear.

Her eyes closed again. They were sultry and heavy-lidded when she opened them. The glade shimmered in the afternoon sun and the water gleamed like green glass. He took a blanket from the buggy, his own buggy, which had been repaired.

He helped her down, backed her up against a young tree, and wrapped his arms around them both. "I had to be alone here with you again," he whispered, then kissed her.

It seemed the time had come to fulfill their youthful passions. Or maybe not.

"We can't," John said, as they reclined on the blanket. "The kids are awake."

"They're babies, John." Her skin felt scorched where he'd touched her cheek. "They won't remember."

"Hell, I'd remember their little faces. It's not right. What if they were scarred for life? I was when I finally figured out the reason for all my new baby brothers and sisters. It finally dawned on me that Mama and Pop were doing a whole lot more than sleeping together. Damn, no child needs to know for sure that their mother and father do it."

Laura's thick, dark lashes dropped. "You are absolutely right, John. We can't even strip naked," she said, her eyes anchored on his, "and take a swim to cool off, unless we go one at a time. The other has to stay to protect the children every minute. Why, they could tumble into the water and float downriver like baby Moses in the bullrushes. Even asleep, they're not safe. A rattler might slither out of that grass and strike. A cougar could carry 'em off. A bear would just devour 'em on the spot."

"Damn right." John touched her skin and winced as though it burned his fingers. "A big hawk could easy fly off with the little one. Or they might see us do things that would give 'em bad dreams."

"I'm glad you're so sensitive about their tender spirits," she whispered, her sweet mouth close to his. "I agree. We can wait. It'll just be five, six years or so." She sighed and tucked the tip of her tongue into his ear. "Then we can send 'em off to school and have a little bit of time alone together at last. Or maybe not. We might have to homeschool 'em ourselves."

She began to unbutton his shirt.

"You're right," he solemnly agreed. "We need to be strong, trust in Jesus, and control ourselves till they grow up and move out."

He unfastened his belt.

She stood up, stretched, gazed at the river and at her children, now asleep. She unfastened her skirt, let it fall to the ground, then sank back down into his arms.

Suddenly shoes, boots, and undergarments began to fly in all directions. "What if they wake up?" he said hoarsely.

"They'll get over it," she gasped. "This is something we started a long time ago. At last, it's our time. This place will always be ours."

They laughed. They shouted. She hiccuped. He moaned aloud and groaned in her ear. He explored, took a guided tour of her body as she whispered directions.

He held her tight.

"Are you as excited as you were back then, Johnny?"

"Do we have to talk about that now?"

"Yes."

Reluctantly, he quit what he was doing, caught his breath, and squinted as he tried to remember the question. "In a way, it was more exciting when we were kids," he finally said, "because it was forbidden. We knew we couldn't, shouldn't, and damn, it hurt like hell to stop. But in so many other ways it's better now." He ran his hand along the curve of her hip. "Back then, it was first love. We're grown now and it's still first love. I love you, Laura, and I sure hope I'm better at it than Edgar."

She laughed and rolled over to straddle him. "It's like we've never been apart, John. I swear, it's already hard to remember what Edgar looks like. I only see you."

He intended to linger there for only an hour or so because of the need to distance themselves from her husband, who by now had probably acquired fresh ammunition. But they couldn't bear to go. They lay in each other's arms, listened to the frogs croak, and saw thousands of birds flying in formation shadow the setting sun. Moist and damp like the air around them, the lovers were seduced by the familiar scent of the river. He listened to its voice, trying to make out the words as it rushed by. He slept briefly and was awed when he awoke and found the river girl in his arms. For a moment it was like a beautiful dream and he was amazed to find she was real and there with him.

Reluctantly, they began to dress but then simultaneously reversed the process and again began to feverishly remove each other's clothes. Later they watched the fireflies and yearned to stay the night. But it was time to head for home.

"You were right, Mama," John said solemnly, as Leugenia opened the door.

"Oh, Johnny." She looked up, hands clasped prayerfully beneath her chin. "Please say you found her."

He stood stock-still, without a reply for a long moment.

But he couldn't hide the answer in his eyes.

"You did! Oh Lordy, you did!"

He snaked his arm around the door behind him, caught Laura's hand, and twirled her around, as though presenting a rare and priceless work of art.

Leugenia welcomed her like a long-lost daughter. "You're all grown up! Look, how beautiful! Joe, come see who's here!" She hugged, shed tears, and prayed in thanks, scarcely raising an eyebrow at the two little children who came with her. Leugenia always had room in her heart for more little children. And all it took was one look at John, her golden child, whom everyone loved, to see his happiness. She was thrilled.

Lucy was not quite as taken when the family gathered for a celebratory supper two nights later. "I can't tell you how delighted I am to have been misinformed," she drawled to Laura. She did not appear delighted.

"Like Mr. Mark Twain said, 'Reports of my death have been greatly exaggerated.'" Laura laughed.

John heard her across the room, above the din, the music, and the laughter of others, and caught her eye. They glowed, lit from within, unable to keep their eyes or their hands off each other. Everyone felt the electricity between them.

"How did you meet Laura?" one of his little nephews asked, as John picked out "Black Is the Color of My True Love's Hair." He rarely used a guitar pick; John liked to feel the music and the strings on his fingertips and had the calluses to prove it.

"She was five," he said fondly. "I was seven. She wouldn't look at me. She always ran away. So I had to chase her. I've been chasing her ever since."

It made Lucy absolutely sick. "Well, bless your heart," she told Laura. She smiled sweetly at the children at play on the floor, happy and at home with the close-knit Ashley clan, which included children of all ages. "Looks like faster runners caught you a few times before John did."

Laura bit her lip and smiled. She and John had discussed Lucy at length before the two women were introduced, and Lucy certainly lived up to his description.

"Unfortunately, Lucy, we were the victims of falsehoods, rumors, and downright lies. As you may know," Laura said, "John was told I had died of yellow fever and I was informed that he'd married someone else." She laughed lightly, as though none of it mattered now. "Who on earth do you think," she asked, "could be so malicious?"

Lucy looked thoughtful and turned away.

John and Bobby began telling stories about Miami, where the lovebirds planned to settle. The city's current controversy raged over whether it should remain wet or go dry and prohibit the sale and consumption of alcoholic beverages. On their last visit they'd attended a big, week-long Miami tent revival. The next night an eerie procession had passed them on the street. Small children led the way, followed by a hundred young girls and women dressed in white and carrying flickering candles.

John and Bobby had joined the curious who followed it to the revival tent where Carrie Nation, the famous prohibitionist, was about to speak.

"Six hundred people were packed into that tent," John said.

They had watched from the back as the solemn women in white raised their right hands to recite the temperance pledge.

John repeated it from memory, hand over his heart, as his father, brothers, cousins, and nephews hooted and howled. "I promise not to buy, sell, drink, or serve liquor while I live. From tobacco I'll abstain, and never take God's name in vain."

"Then Carrie Nation stepped out," Bobby said.

"What's she like?" Laura asked eagerly.

"Somebody's grandma," John replied, "dressed in black, from her bonnet to her shoes. Except she carries a hatchet."

"Had a mean face," Bobby said. "Looks like Sheriff Baker in a dress."

The room erupted in laughter.

"What did she say?" Laura persisted.

"That she didn't choose her dirty work," John said. "Then she ranked herself right up there with the heroes of the Good Book. Said, 'The same God that put a staff in Moses' hand, a jawbone in Samson's hand, and a sling in David's hand put a hatchet in the hand of Carrie Nation! It's better to smash saloons than be smashed in hell!'

"She bust up any Miami saloons with that hatchet?" Joe asked.

John shook his head. "Said she quit smashing them up the way she did in Kansas. The hatchet's just a symbol now. In fact she was selling some as souvenirs. Said she's learned to go where the power is and is on to bigger things now. Kept yelling, 'On to Washington!'

"She wants national prohibition. Swears the whole country is going dry sooner or later. The crowd clapped and stomped."

The men all grew quiet, grimly pondering the prospect.

"Never happen!" Joe Ashley shook his full head of silvery hair for emphasis.

"Don't know, Pop. If women had the vote, Miami would be dry today," John said. "They put it on the ballot in the last election and the wets won by only forty-four votes." He paused for emphasis. "And Miami's chapter of the Women's Christian Temperance Union has more than two hundred members. They're on the warpath. Every church and one of the two newspapers stand with 'em. They've already shut down the saloons on Sunday, shortened operating hours, and hiked the cost of a liquor license from a few dollars to five hundred! And Dan Hardie, the new sheriff, promises strict enforcement of the law against selling liquor to the Indians."

His audience looked appalled.

"You should see how little girls walk to school in Miami." Bobby daintily demonstrated. "They zigzag back and forth across the street to avoid passing saloons. As though the devil and demon rum are gonna jump out at 'em."

"If Miami, the state of Florida, or the whole damn country goes dry, it's good news for us," Bill said. He lit up a cigar, despite Lucy's frown. "Those of us with our own stills will make a damn sight more money. People won't give up drinking."

"But operating a still would violate federal law," John said.

"Hell, the law ain't gonna crack down on people trying to feed their kids. Everybody around here has a still. And who drinks the most?" Bill asked.

"Lawmen and politicians," Joe said.

"Damn right, Pop," Bill replied. "Our best customers."

John nodded. "Sometimes a shot of whiskey is the only thing good for what ails you."

Even Leugenia had to agree on the medicinal value of alcohol along a wilderness frontier with few doctors and hospitals.

Joe shook his head sadly. "Don't see how prohibition could ever happen."

"Well, it's coming to a head and it's a fight to watch," John said. "Miami picture shows run short films now in support of prohibition. In one, a drunk beats his wife. In another, he pawns his baby's shoes and staggers to a saloon with the money."

The men smoked cigars and raised a drink while they still could, as John and Laura wandered outside to be alone. Silver light from the full moon spilled down through the shadowy treetops as he kissed her again and again. Just as he slid his hand under her dress, Blue, his father's favorite hunting hound, began to bay in a cornfield way down behind the barn.

"Sounds like he's cornered something," John said. "Could be the wildcat that killed all them chickens. I'll run down there to see. Go inside, I'll be right there."

"No," she said. "I'll wait here for you."

John, who'd worn a sidearm since he'd brought Laura and the children home, melted into the shadows like a ghost.

Laura hummed as she searched Leugenia's garden for the source of a uniquely fragrant aroma. She had ruled out night-blooming jasmine. This was more spicy than sweet. As she knelt to pluck a leaf from a small, staked plant, a man in black sprang from the shadows, caught her roughly by the hair, and clamped his hand over her mouth.

"Scream and I'll cut your throat, bitch."

She knew his voice.

She kicked his shins with her heels and fiercely elbowed his ribs. He grunted in pain. "I'll kill you right here!" he swore. He pressed a razor-sharp blade to her throat. When the knife nicked her skin she stopped resisting. Her heels dug into the soft earth as he dragged her around the side of the barn.

"I got her good," he said jubilantly to a man who waited in the shadows.

"Hello, Laura."

"Edgar! Why are you here?"

"To take back what's mine."

"Don't," she whispered. "Don't make John kill you."

He slapped her, hard, but she swallowed the cry that rose in her throat where the knife still hovered.

The man with the knife, Edgar's cousin Roland, jerked her head back to further expose her throat. All she could see were the treetops and a star-studded sky. Tears stung her eyes. The hound stopped baying in the distance and she heard other voices on the breeze. How many? she wondered. And do they have any idea how many Ashley men are in the house?

"Come to your senses yet, Laura?" Edgar asked.

When she didn't answer, he jammed the cold, hard barrel of a pistol to her forehead. She closed her eyes and silently repeated the Twenty-Third Psalm.

Another dark figure appeared and muttered something to Edgar.

His voice shocked Laura's eyes wide open. "Reverend Hasley?" she gasped.

"Give her to me." The preacher reached for her. "I have beseeched both Jesus Christ and your husband, Edgar, to forgive you. That was hard work, woman. So fall down on your knees, right here, and pray for forgiveness. Repent!" He caught her thick hair, wound it around his fist like a rope, and ripped the front of her dress as he slammed her to the ground.

The last time she'd seen him, he'd stood in the pulpit to preach God's love. He had baptized her baby son and her little daughter.

"Where's Dad and Sonny?" Edgar glanced over his shoulder.

He's brought his father, his brother, his cousin, and the preacher. Five in all, she thought, fighting the urge to scream.

"Here they come." Roland, still holding the knife, had drawn a pistol as well. "Let's grab the kids, decide what we do with her, take what we want, and get the hell out of here."

Two shadowy figures appeared, moving quickly. They were not alone. John kicked one in the seat of the pants to hurry him along. He had a pistol in each hand, another stuck in his belt.

"Sorry, son," Edgar's father said bleakly. "Ashley got the drop on us and took our guns."

"If you've hurt her, you all die, right now," John said, in a voice that frightened even Laura.

"Wasn't me that cut her," the preacher said. He let her go so abruptly that she stumbled forward onto her hands and knees.

Roland cursed. "It's Edgar's fault. Said he needed a posse to bring back his runaway wife."

"Shut up," Edgar said, a pistol in his hand. "Three of us are still armed. He's only one man. He can't kill us all before we shoot her. Don't anybody else give up a weapon."

"Hell," John said. "Which is where I'm about to send you. Now. You call this sorry group a posse? I didn't want anybody hurt over this. But now I'm provoked and might have to kill you. Did they hurt you, Laura?"

She hesitated. "No. There's just the five of 'em."

"Thank you, darlin'. You"—he gestured at the preacher with his gun—"help the lady up, then kneel, and ask her to forgive you."

The reverend helped Laura to her feet and dropped to his knees as she held the torn bodice of her dress together. "Sorry, ma'am."

"Not good enough." John's fingers tightened on the triggers of both guns. "Beg her. Now."

"Please, ma'am, please forgive me," the preacher babbled. "I knew not what I was doing."

"I'll think about it," she said coldly.

"Come stand behind me, Laura," John said.

"No," she said, without hesitation.

He looked startled.

"I won't stand behind you, John. I'll stand with you. Give me a gun."

He grinned. "Take the one from my belt, darlin.' Be careful, it's loaded. Don't squeeze that trigger unless you have to kill somebody."

"I can handle a gun," she protested.

"I know," he said. "You learned from the best."

She caught his belt with one hand, slid the weapon from his waistband with the other, then stood beside him, feet apart, hands steady, her weapon trained on Edgar's forehead.

No one moved.

Roland held the hunting knife in one hand; the other clutched his pistol, pointed at Laura. Beads of sweat stood out on his forehead.

The preacher froze, afraid to reach for his own gun.

They all stared at each other in the white-hot moonlight.

At that moment Bobby burst out onto the porch, ran down the front steps and into the yard. "John! Laura! Frankie wants you to play—" He took one look, skidded to a stop, then dashed back inside, taking the steps three at a time.

Seconds later, men stampeded out of the house. Some charged down the front steps, others vaulted porch railings—John's father, brothers, brothers-in-law, nephews, and cousins, all armed with rifles, shotguns, and pistols.

Inside, Lucy screamed, "Don't you go out there, Billy! Don't you dare get us involved!"

Bill was first out the door.

"Meet my posse," John calmly told the intruders. "The Ashley family, the fastest guns in Florida."

Roland shrank, dropped his gun, and threw down the hunting knife. He raised his hands and cursed bitterly at Edgar.

"Hold your fire, boys!" John shouted to his family. "We've got the upper hand."

He turned to Edgar and his companions. "If you want to see the sun rise tomorrow, leave now. But your weapons stay here and you have to swear you'll never come back."

Pastor Hasley, Edgar's father, his brother Sonny, and cousin Roland all agreed and ran for their lives, stumbling back through the woods.

"Edgar," his father shouted, from behind a tree. "Drop your gun and come on while you got the chance! She ain't worth it, son."

Edgar ignored him, as his father disappeared into the darkness. Alone, on a suicide mission, he stood his ground against more than two dozen armed men with weapons trained on him. He still aimed his pistol at John but couldn't steady his trembling hand.

"You coming, Laura?" His voice cracked. "It's your last chance."

"No," she said. "Of course not."

"Then give me my children."

"Not on your life!" John said, before she could even answer.

"You can't raise them alone, Edgar," she said softly.

"Yeah, I can. Ma and Pa came down. They'll stay to help."

"Drop that gun and get your sorry ass off my property. Now!" Joe Ashley advanced, his rifle in his hands.

"No," Edgar said.

The others moved forward as one, behind the patriarch. The sounds of metal on metal, guns cocked, rounds racked into chambers, resonated in the night.

Edgar ignored them and stared at Laura. "You can stay here and go straight to hell with John Ashley, but I won't leave without my children. They're my flesh and blood."

"Wait!" Laura stepped in front of Joe's rifle and turned to Edgar. "Then take them! Now! Take the children! Just promise you'll be good to them and always tell them their mother loves them."

"You ain't coming?"

"No!" she said impatiently. "Just take them and go. Will that satisfy you?"

Edgar nodded.

"Swear you won't be back?"

"Never, I swear."

"Don't do it, Laura." John sounded indignant. "You don't have to."

"I do. Yes, I do. Don't fight me, John."

She went back into the house where Leugenia helped her pack up the children's things, then brought them out. Edgar eagerly exchanged his gun for his baby son. Arlie, the little girl taken from her bed, was drowsy but reached out to Edgar.

"Daddy," she said, and rested her head on his shoulder.

"We're going home, baby," he told her.

"You're a good father, Edgar. Be kind. Don't speak ill of me to them, ever. Just say I love them."

He nodded. "Goodbye, Laura."

She and Leugenia kissed the small, sleepy faces for the last time. Then they were gone.

The adrenaline faded. The evening ended. The Ashley posse began to wander back into the house to gather up their own families and belongings.

John found Laura facedown on their bed. "My babies," she moaned.

"I'll go get 'em right now!" he said urgently. "I'll bring 'em back! They haven't gotten far."

"No!" she protested, as he reached the door. "Don't."

"Why? I can't stand to see you cry." He paced the room, restless and angry. "What can I do?" His voice rose. "For God's sake, Laura, what do you want me to do?"

"Nothing! Leave it be." Eyes flooded, she opened her arms.

"But why?" He held her tight, rocked her back and forth as though she were a child. "I'll be a good father. I promise," he said earnestly. "I swear, I'll work at it every day. You and me will raise 'em together. They won't even remember him."

"I know," she whispered. "But he'd never forget them. You saw how he was tonight. If I didn't give him the children, he'd keep coming back until one of you was dead. If you didn't kill him, he'd kill you. It nearly happened tonight." She gasped between sobs, her cheek pressed to his chest. "All those guns . . . It's a miracle that nobody died. I don't want to lose you, and I don't want the blood of their father on my hands, or yours. I can live without my children but not without you. This is how it has to be."

PART THREE

CHAPTER TEN

Chaos ruled in the lobby. The couple John had seen earlier was still there. She crouched behind the metal detector. The man, a cigarette clenched between his teeth, sat on the floor clutching his bleeding ankle.

"Medic! I need a medic over heah," he yelled, as a rescue van rolled up to the front door, siren screaming.

"Leon?" John sought out the homeless man, who now faced the wall, palms planted above his head.

Leon glanced over his shoulder. "That cop over there," he muttered under his breath, "told me not to move, talk, or look at anything."

"Don't worry about him." John steered him to a bench away from the confusion. "What happened?"

Leon appeared harmless, even inattentive, but wasn't. His talent was becoming invisible, disappearing into the background like a chameleon. After helping John identify the killer of several homeless men he'd become a valued confidential informant. Like most with his lifestyle, Leon admitted to a record of minor offenses: loitering, drunkenness, and trespassing. John had always empathized with those who chose a life free from utility bills, pesky neighbors, and permanent addresses. Some were drinkers, addicts, or mentally ill, a few were dangerous fugitives, but others were dreamers, seekers, and wanderers like the pioneers who braved heat, hardship, and danger to settle Florida. Some of their modern counterparts chose to live on the road, in the woods, beneath bridges, or in the treacherous wilderness of a big city. John sometimes envied them.

He also understood that there are no great detectives, only good timing, instinct, and great informants. And Leon's vision from the observation deck of life was an uncommonly clear one.

While he napped on the green grass at Bayfront Park, he said, a New York couple paused nearby to take photos. She put down her bag, shot a few pictures, then realized the bag was gone, along with their money, ID, and airline tickets.

They saw only one person nearby and shook him awake. Leon denied ever seeing the bag. The irate male tourist knocked him down and the female kicked him repeatedly. Several joggers and other homeless people intervened and Leon shuffled off to headquarters to make a complaint. As he described his attackers to the rookie at the front desk, they walked in to report the missing bag.

"That's them!" Leon pointed. "Don't let 'em get away!"

"That's him!" the tourists shouted. "Arrest him!"

Then two strangers walked in and identified themselves to the rookie as county deputies on business.

"I was here first!" Leon cried.

The noisy New Yorkers demanded that Leon be arrested.

"Did you see him take the bag?" the rookie asked.

"No," the man said, "but nobody else was there."

"Had to be him!" the woman insisted.

"Wasn't me! They attacked me for no reason!" Leon said.

The impatient deputies interrupted and said their business with Sergeant Ashley in Homicide took priority.

When the rookie spoke to John, his attitude changed. "Keep quiet!" he told Leon and the New Yorkers. "I've got a situation here."

The deputies reacted. "They got hinky," Leon said. "Said they had to go up to Homicide to conduct important business with you. Heard 'em say your name, Johnny. They wuz gunning for you."

The deputies walked toward the elevators. Only MPD personnel are issued elevator key cards. Yet the female, who'd identified herself as a county deputy, held one in her hand, ready to swipe, as they boarded. They ignored the rookie, who ordered them to halt.

He hit a button, deactivated the elevators, then reached for a switch to lock the lobby doors. Before he could hit it, the "deputies" drew their guns and told him to freeze. The female stayed near the elevators. Her partner advanced on the rookie and demanded he reactivate them. After a hopeful glance at the stairwell, the rookie saw no help in sight, and pulled his own weapon.

"Drop your guns!" he ordered.

The New Yorkers hit the floor and scrambled for cover. Leon watched from behind a potted palm.

The deputy fired two shots at the rookie, who blasted back. "Closed his eyes and pulled the trigger," Leon said, shaking his head.

They all missed.

The female deputy squeezed off two shots from the elevator. One hit the fallen officers' memorial plaque. The other ricocheted off the metal detector and slammed into the New York man's right ankle. The male deputy fired two more at the rookie and rushed the front desk. Hit, the young cop shot back twice as he fell to the floor. One slug shattered a glass display case of trophies from the Police Olympics. The other blew out a ceiling fixture. The fake deputy scooped up the fallen rookie's gun, jammed it into his belt and fled with his female accomplice.

"Who do you think they were, Leon?"

"Cops, Johnny," he said, without hesitation. "The way they fired, with the double tap, two quick shots. How they wore their badges and IDs in their belts. Their shooting stance. You only learn all that in one place, Johnny. The academy. It don't make 'em better shots, but it makes 'em look like cops."

"What the hell . . ." J. J. looked stunned, his radio to his ear as John returned to the Homicide Bureau. "Who's hit?"

"The rookie at the front desk." John focused on Laura, sitting in his desk chair, her left wrist cuffed, her face taut.

"The same kid who got shot last week?" J. J. asked.

"Right," John said. "Those 'county detectives' you were so happy to hear from tried to kill him."

"How bad?" J. J. demanded. "Is he gonna make it?"

"Yeah, but if it was me, I'd consider a new line of work."

"That kid's a magnet for bullets. The shooters split?"

"Yeah, your pals took off in a Crown Vic with county tags."

"Don't call 'em my pals." Agitated, J. J. paced the aisle.

"You couldn't wait to hand her over, could you?" John said bitterly. "No questions asked!"

"Who knew? Uniforms, the chief, a county car? Think they're the real thing?"

"Sure as hell looked like it." John gently removed the cuff from Laura's wrist, as she studied his face.

"They came for me," she said quietly.

"I hear you, girl," John said. "There's something you need to know. That return call from Cheryl came from a Montgomery County homicide detective, not her. Don't be upset, but he said—"

"Don't tell me," J. J. groaned.

John nodded curtly.

J. J. cursed. "What the hell is this?"

"Is Cheryl all right?" Laura's pleading eyes moved from John to J. J., then back. She looked pale.

"No. She isn't. I don't know all the details yet."

Laura gasped.

"What are the odds it ain't related to our cases?" J. J. said hopefully.

"Zero to none," John said.

The shooting team assembled along with their legal adviser. John handed over his gun, told them what happened, then briefed Captain Politano, who was en route to the station.

"They had a key card to our elevators," John said heatedly, "and IDed themselves as Miami-Dade County deputies."

The captain sighed. "Whatcha trying to say, Ashley?"

"If it looks like a duck . . ."

"We've had police impersonators for years."

John heard the shrug in his voice. Blue-light bandits were common—robbers, rapists, and police wannabes in uniforms, with badges, with blue flashers on their dashboards. One recently arrested impersonator was caught issuing traffic citations he printed himself. But nothing matched the 1980s when Marielito hoodlums and warring cocaine cowboys quickly discovered that police supply stores would sell equipment to anyone. They bought used patrol cars and motorcycles at auction, and on some hot, hectic nights in the bad old days, more fake cops than real ones patrolled Miami. Better armed and outfitted, they often looked more professional than the authentic rank and file. Civilians couldn't tell them apart and were advised to dial 911 to confirm when stopped by an officer. Many frightened motorists simply fled any flashing blue lights. But that was history; the problem hadn't been that serious for years.

"Even the worst," John said, "never walked into the station and shot at us. Two of the three girls with Eagle before he was murdered are dead. His killers just came for the third. It's only by the grace of God they didn't succeed—yet."

The captain sighed. "We should probably put her in protective custody."

"I can take her to the hotel," John said. The police and the state attorney's office housed endangered witnesses and victims at several nondescript hotels off the beaten path. Even that, he feared, might not be safe.

"We could turn her over to the state attorney's office," the captain said, "or to one of the female—"

"I'm the lead detective," John said. "She's my witness."

"How valuable is she? How much does she know?"

The hair tingled on the back of John's neck. Saying she was vital to the case might put her in more danger. But if he said she wasn't she'd be cut loose with no protection at all.

"Not sure. I'm still persuading her to talk," he lied. "I'm the only one she trusts. When she heard they'd come for her, she panicked and wanted a lawyer. She's from out of town, no rap sheet. I'm convinced she's no material witness for any joint investigation. I doubt one even exists. I should be responsible for her safety."

"She still want a lawyer?" the captain asked sharply.

"No, not after I said we'd protect her."

"What have they got in the Silver Spring case? Suspects?" Politano asked.

"All hell broke loose here before I could find out."

"Stay on it," he said. "Keep me posted. Take her to the hotel in Doral. I'll authorize the expense."

John chose another hotel. The one near Gulfstream racetrack at the north end of the county hadn't been used lately. The less anyone knew the better.

Jo Salazar, an assistant state attorney he'd consulted, spoke to a counterpart in the US attorney's office and Miami-Dade's legal adviser. "There doesn't appear to be any long-term investigation that involves your witness," she told John. She arranged for the wounded rookie and the witnesses to view more than three thousand photos of Miami-Dade deputies. Chances of an ID were slim. Witnesses grow weary and confused after seeing as few as fifty photos. John had little faith in the New Yorkers, who'd announced plans to hire their own lawyer. But maybe, just maybe, Leon might come up with something.

Laura spent the rest of the night at the upscale and historic Biltmore Hotel, too pricey for the city and too public to hide a witness. John left her in the protection of his brother Ed, the hotel's security chief, then whisked her out a side exit shortly before dawn.

Her new digs were secure, clean, and quiet. A new facade and structure fronted the street. Her room, in the original complex, hadn't been updated or renovated in decades. Burglar bars, installed after the riots, protected the room's few windows. Door hinges were secure, locks adequate but old. The room had twin beds, a big-screen TV, a small desk, and a tiny kitchenette with a mini fridge, small microwave, and a coffeemaker. Logistics were good. The old lobby, small and unmanned, was only a few steps from her door. Inside were tourist brochures, ice machines, and an armchair where he could pretend to read a newspaper while watching her room.

Warm rain spattered the car as they arrived. Steam rose like a thick fog off the parking lot pavement. They darted through the rain with their packages. He positioned her behind the door and checked the interior. "All clear," he said. The air was hot and sticky, but the cool and comfortable room welcomed them. She twisted the cap off a cold water bottle for him. Their fingers brushed and it felt like fire. Rain pounded outside but they were alone in a small space so quiet he could hear his heart beat. He reached for her. She kissed him back.

What was he doing? Sexually harassing a witness in his protection, he realized, let her go, and stepped back.

"Sorry. I didn't mean to take advantage . . ."

She looked tender, vulnerable, as though she hadn't heard him. "I knew you, John, when we met."

"That's how I—"

His cell phone rang and would not stop. Lucy. Is she psychic? he wondered. How could he talk to her now? What could he say?

"Nothing important," he told Laura, and let it go to message. Nothing was as important as they were now.

Lucy called again in thirty seconds, then in forty-five. Then again and again.

He finally answered in self-defense. "Yeah?"

"*Hola.* Remember? You. Me. Dinner with your folks tonight?"

"No." He closed his eyes. "I forgot."

"You need a secretary. How would you manage without me?"

"Can't make it."

"See. How lucky are you?"

"No, I meant tonight."

Laura flashed a secret smile as she unpacked the groceries he'd brought, and he forgot what he was saying.

"Can'tcha take a time-out from the case for a couple hours? Even an hour?" Lucy pleaded. "Your victims aren't going anywhere." She giggled. "I want to hang out in your mom's kitchen."

He frowned and tried not to look at Laura. Lucy had asked for copies of his mother's recipes, but she had none in writing, so Lucy had insisted on taking notes and photos in her kitchen.

"I can't be there," he said, "but you can go."

"Alone?" Her voice quivered.

When did this aggressive, kick-ass woman, who wielded a gun, Taser, billy club, and a flashlight heavy enough to smash a man's skull, become a shrinking violet? "They'd love to see you."

"No," she said, coldly. "Should have told me sooner, *mi amor.* But I know you're busy. How's your witness? Still alive?"

She wanted him to capitulate, sweet-talk, and tease. He wanted to avoid it all. He knew what he had to do, but not this way, not on the phone. "Have to go," he said, and hung up.

"Did I ruin your plans for the evening?" Laura asked softly.

"Don't worry about it, I'm not."

"John, are you married?" she asked wistfully.

"No."

"Ever?"

"Never."

She smiled.

"You?"

"No way." She shoved her hair behind her ear. "When I was a little girl, I used to sit down by the river and miss someone terribly, didn't know who, but it was somebody who was supposed to be there. Later I realized it had to be my soul mate out there in the world and that someday we'd meet and recognize each other instantly. Sounds silly, doesn't it?"

"No," he said. "Not now."

She nodded at his cell phone. "Was that the policewoman I saw you with at the station?"

He nodded. "Her name's Lucy. I made a mistake. We were engaged. Technically, still are. I haven't told her yet."

Laura frowned. "So, you two have a ring and a date?"

Usually he asked the tough questions. "A ring, no date."

"So you dodged the bullet."

"Yes," he said, "I did." It was as though they read each other's minds and communicated more with their eyes than with words.

"Treat her kindly," Laura murmured. "But tell her soon."

"I will."

The rain stopped. The parking lot puddles reflected a rainbow as he took his tool kit from the car to install the new Medeco double-cylinder dead bolt. He reinforced the door with metal stripping, lubricated the latches on the burglar bars, and showed Laura how to operate them from inside.

"I need a gun," she murmured. "Get me one, John?"

"People who want guns for protection have to be psychologically ready to use them."

"Think I wouldn't shoot a robber or rapist? Think again. I sleep with a gun and keep one in my car. When you hear noises in the night, or your car dies in a dark and lonely place, there is nothing like the comfort of cold steel in your hand. Never had to use one, but it's nice to know it's there."

"You won't need it," he said. "You have me."

She rolled her eyes. "What happens when I don't?"

"A police officer, Mona Stratton, takes over at midnight. I thought you'd be more comfortable with a woman."

Her eyes said he was wrong. "I can take care of myself," she said. "But what if you needed help?"

"Then we'd both be in trouble."

She shook her head and smiled. "Oh, no. That's when you want me next to you."

"I want you next to me, period."

"I'm serious." Her eyes flashed.

"Think I'm not?"

"You can rely on me, John. I don't panic, I surprise myself. The universe slows and the world comes into brilliant focus, as sharp and as clear as crystal, as though I've done it all before. I wish life could always be so clear. We're alike," she said, as though she always knew it was true.

He recognized it too. "The key is to have a plan," he said. "As a kid, I'd visualize the worst possible thing that could happen and what I'd do if it did. In the Marines, I'd wonder, What if I saw a sniper in that tree? How would I react? As a rookie cop, I'd wonder, What if the next driver I stop pulls a gun or goes for mine? What if those two men walking briskly out of the bank just robbed it? Keeps you on your toes."

"Visualization?" A shaft of sunlight from a window reflected in her eyes. "My gram believes in second sight. She says I have it."

He nodded. "Use everything you've got, all five senses—and the sixth. That's the one," he said, "that puts you in the right place at the right time. I once drove down an exit ramp as the dispatcher radioed the tag number of fleeing bank robbers. The car was right in front of me. I handled it. All the older cops said nothing like that had ever happened to them. Once you visualize what you'd do in any given scenario, your subconscious takes over. It's instinctive. You're ready."

"I know, I pulled a little girl out of the Caloosahatchee River once." She sipped her tea. "All us neighborhood kids swam like fish, but I'd wonder, *What if* one of them ever got in trouble, then decided what to do when it happened. I was eleven. At home. It was summertime and they were all down at the river, and suddenly I knew something was wrong. It felt too powerful to ignore. I wanted to run, but was afraid I'd look silly, so I walked fast, down toward the river until a little girl came racing up the path. I saw her face and ran in the direction she'd come from. They'd been diving for old bottles, and her seven-year-old sister hadn't surfaced. Her ankle was caught in a tangle of underwater weeds. She was unconscious."

"What happened?"

She shrugged and bit into a granola bar. "It went just as I visualized it. She's in high school now. Bright and beautiful, a cheerleader. I see her all the time when I'm home."

"You would have made a good first responder, lifeguard, firefighter, or cop."

She shuddered. "Never liked cops. As a little girl, I'd see sheriff's deputies on the street, stare at their guns, and just cry and cry, then have bad dreams. But I *always* loved to pose for pictures." She struck an exaggerated cover girl pose. "It's fun! As though I've done it forever. I'm so lucky. I fell into the profession. A *St. Pete Times* photographer came to shoot a photo essay on the river. Shot pictures of me wading, standing on the bank, in a rowboat. Two of them appeared in the Sunday newspaper, half a million circulation. An agent saw it and called me. I was sixteen. How cool is that? Some girls try for years to break into modeling, and I owe it all to that gorgeous, green river. I love it."

"If guns made you cry, why aren't you afraid of them now?"

"My granddaddy taught me to shoot his old muzzle-loader and I just took to it. I'm not afraid of a gun in my hands," she said. "Just afraid of other people with 'em."

J. J. called. "Got the witness situated yet?"

"Just about. I upgraded some of the security."

"Watch yourself, John," he said. "Don't forget number six on my top ten rules about sex. Never sleep with a woman who's got more problems than you do. By the way, the captain thinks Keith Baker is worth another look."

"What?" John paced the room. "We both know that poor guy is not the type and his alibi is rock solid. Last night's shooting at the station makes it obvious we're not gonna find the killer in Eagle's crank file."

"The cap still wants us to recheck his alibi. How did you get lucky enough to make it onto Eagle's enemies list?"

John sighed. "First time I saw him he was doing seventy miles over the speed limit on the boulevard in a black Ferrari with an expired tag. I was a rookie, on midnight patrol. Lit 'im up, but he ran. Finally pulled him over. Had two little blond girls crammed into the bucket seat next to 'im, no license or registration on him.

"He was big and arrogant, with lots of bling and a bad attitude. Had he stopped and been civil, I mighta just warned him. I never liked writing traffic tickets. But he gave me that 'Do you know who I am?' crap. I had no idea who he was, didn't care. His eyes were glassy, he slurred his words, refused a sobriety test, wouldn't sign the ticket, and became belligerent. I'd called backup, but we were busy and it took a while, so I took a better look at his passengers. Really young, in little shorts and halter tops. They were also under the influence and lied about their ages. One turned out to be a sixteen-year-old runaway, the other a fourteen-year-old missing for a week.

"He got really pissed. Tried to hand me a hundred-dollar bill, then threw it at me, so I added attempted bribery to contributing to their delinquency, DUI, and multiple traffic violations.

"My backup arrives, sees Eagle in cuffs, and says, 'You know who that guy is?'

"Didn't care. Inventoried his car before it was towed, found an unregistered gun, crack cocaine, marijuana, and ecstasy, and added those charges. He threatens me the whole time. 'I'll have your job. Do you know who I am? You won't get away with this.'

"As I'm booking him into the jail, my sergeant shows up and asks, 'Do you know who he is?' Next thing I know Eagle is unarrested, his ride released, and his contraband returned."

"Lucky him," J. J. said.

"He didn't think so. Wanted me fired. Threatened to sue. Needed to be sure I remembered who he was. Filed an Internal Affairs complaint. Raised hell with the chief, the mayor, and the city manager. With him, everything was personal. Every time I turned around, another cop would say, 'Ron Jon Eagle sends his regards.' If I'd seen him speed, drive drunk, or spit on the sidewalk, I'da done it again."

"With his clout and you a rookie, how come you didn't get fired?" J. J. asked.

"Luck and good press."

"I remember now!" J. J. said. "That girl at the bus depot. What was her name?"

"Helen," John said. "Her name was Helen."

CHAPTER ELEVEN

T ell me about her," Laura said later.

"Who?" John said.

"Helen."

"It's not pretty," John said.

She insisted.

Helen and her fiancé, college students from Great Britain, explored the US by bus that summer. Shortly after arriving in Miami, as she showered in the downtown bus terminal, she was attacked by three strangers who raped, stomped, and battered her into a near-fatal coma.

Earlier, John had seen the three young men swaggering down Flagler Street, sensed they were trouble, and followed his instincts. But as he watched them from a distance, he was hailed by an elderly couple. They'd lingered to chat too long after a concert, forgotten where they'd parked, and by the time they found their car, downtown was deserted. Then they ran out of gas, at 1:30 a.m. John called a tow truck and stayed with them until it arrived. By the time they were safely on their way, the suspicious trio had disappeared. The street was empty.

He couldn't shake a bad feeling about them. He circled every block, cruised the area. Nothing. The deserted bus terminal a few blocks away was the only place still open at that hour. He checked it on foot and found a young Englishman asleep on a bench near the front door. He told John that he and his fiancée, Helen, had been turned away from a nearby youth hostel until morning because their bus had arrived too late. She decided to use the ladies' shower and restroom at the back of the terminal while he stood guard at the front. They were unaware of an unlocked side entrance.

The young man asked John not to go back there because his fiancée was showering, but John did and drew his gun when he heard pounding that echoed like a pulse beat in his head. She lay unconscious on the tile floor, her hair wet, her pale skin glistening as the laughing trio took turns stomping her once-pretty face with their heavy boots.

He caught two, handcuffed them to a pipe, called for backup and rescue, then chased the third into the headlights of an arriving patrol car. He arrested all three but was sick that he hadn't stopped them sooner.

Helen's face was so swollen, her fiancé didn't recognize her. Paramedics, convinced she was circling the drain, gave her little chance to survive. But after three months, she awoke from her coma and eventually returned home, her mind a blank, unable to recall the attack, and barely able to speak.

In the meantime, she'd become a cause célèbre. Photos of her battered, bandaged face ran on front pages beside photos of the lovely, fresh-faced young girl she would never be again.

The rookie cop who saved her from certain death became Officer of the Month and received awards from half a dozen organizations, most related to the hospitality industry. John never believed for a moment that he deserved them because he could have, should have saved her sooner. The department, mired in the scandal of the moment, needed the positive press. John became their poster boy. He hated it. But then, at the peak of the publicity, he crossed paths with Ron Jon Eagle, and saving Helen saved his job.

"I still wish I really did save her," he said.

"You did." Laura sounded indignant. "Starting over, no matter how tough it is, beats being dead. Don't blame yourself for not arriving sooner. Blame the morons too stupid to put gas in their car, who hung around too late in the dark, people you had to save when you had more important business. They're the people who always expect others to take care of them."

She took out some yogurt and another granola bar. They gazed hungrily at each other. They wanted so much more. But food was safe; its pursuit would take them out of that small room dominated by beds. Since he was already expected, he invited her to his parents' for supper.

"Hm, low-fat yogurt or southern home cooking?" She pondered.

"Southern cuisine or condensed soup?" She shoved the yogurt back in the fridge and slammed the door. "I'll just be a minute."

She changed into blue jeans, a white blouse that hugged her body, and a leather belt with a western-style turquoise and silver buckle and brushed her hair. As she dressed, he pushed the bed nearest the door away from the wall.

Food, conversation, and company were always first-rate at Ashley family gatherings. John had four brothers and four sisters, along with spouses, nieces, nephews, cousins, and more. "The in-laws and the out-laws," as his father liked to call them.

John hoped to lift Laura's spirits and have the chance to brainstorm with his brothers, especially the cops—Robby, the youngest, a Miami-Dade deputy, and Frank, a North Miami detective.

After he was sure they weren't followed, they switched to his car, a silver Ford Expedition, then drove south to where he grew up. His parents lived in Morningside, a historic neighborhood a few short miles and a thousand light-years away from the endless traffic jams, neon glitz, and mirrored towers of downtown Miami and Miami Beach. Built by Miami pioneers in the 1920s, its wide, tree-lined streets skirted the bay east of Biscayne Boulevard.

Miami erases its history with bulldozers. But not here, he told Laura. With its wealth of restored art deco, Mediterranean revival, and mission-style homes, Morningside is the finest intact example of a suburb built during South Florida's early land boom. Open porches, built before air conditioning, catch the bay breezes. The stables, now garages, are behind the houses. The medians are wide landscaped islands in a sea of huge tropical shade trees.

"My family can be a noisy, nosy bunch," John warned her. "The first thing my mom will ask you is the date, time, and place of your birth."

"Is she a cop?"

"Nope. An astrology buff who wants to chart your horoscope. You don't have to tell her. Make up a date, any date."

"I never even read my horoscope in the newspaper," Laura said thoughtfully. "Given our current situation"—she melted him with a smile—"this might be a good time to start."

He laughed. "We tease her, but a couple of years ago she warned that

underground workers were in danger, because of Pluto, a planet connected to miners. Then whammo! Twenty-nine lost in a West Virginia
coal mine disaster. Then, on the same day something moved into Pisces,
ruled by Neptune, the BP oil rig blew, and we had the big Gulf spill.
Right after that," he said, "I was looking for a stockbroker who shot his
wife and kids to death. He'd dropped off the map. She did his chart, said
he was suicidal and most likely dead. Turned up in a bathtub at a Georgia motel. He'd shot himself."

"She's the perfect parent for a detective."

"Sure. But what do I do when I'm working a case and she calls to
warn me that Neptune is in retrograde?"

"You listen," she said, and patted his knee. "A boy's best friend is his
mother."

As he parked at the house, the front door flew open. His niece Lindsey, seven, and nephew Bobby, six, burst out, saw John coming up the
front walk, and dove at his knees.

They all discussed Lindsey's newly missing front tooth as they
stepped inside, where they were overwhelmed by mouthwatering aromas
from the kitchen, friendly conversation, lighthearted laughter, and a guitar being played in the Florida room.

John's mother bustled out of the kitchen after a bright burst of light
and nearly bumped into the couch. "Son! You've come after all and
brought someone!" She was tiny, her chestnut hair shot with gray, her
laugh lines untouched, her eyes sparkled as she spoke.

She greeted Laura warmly, still blinking as John introduced them.
"Something in your eye, Mama?"

"No, son." She sighed. "I'll be fine."

Laura inhaled, her eyes closed. "Mrs. Ashley! Your kitchen smells
like heaven, just like my gram's house! Is that corn bread?"

"Just out of the skillet, darlin'. When's your birthday, girl?"

Laura gave her the correct date, March 12, 1987.

"Pisces," cried his mother. "So is John! You are like-minded people.
Do you know your time of birth?"

"Mama always said it was four ten in the mornin', after 'a very long
night.' The midwife wrote it in my baby book as well, so it's most likely
accurate."

Laura cut her eyes at John as his mother pulled a pencil from her apron pocket and scribbled in a little notebook. "And where are you from, Laura?"

"Upstate, near Fort Myers, a little fork in the road along the Caloosahatchee River."

"A Florida girl! I knew it when I first laid eyes on you, darlin'! And that's where you first saw the light of day?"

"Yes, ma'am, at the home place where me and my gram still live."

His mother caught Laura's hands in her own. They couldn't have looked happier. He'd been right to bring her, John thought. Both seemed about to cry, but in a good way.

"Here comes the storm," warned Katie, his favorite sister. John frowned. From where Katie, the family beauty, sat, she couldn't see the sky.

"Uh-oh," chirped Anna Mae, his brother Frank's wife.

"Hear you're working on a big case, son."

"Where'd you hear that, Mama?"

She winked.

As he rested his right hand at the small of Laura's back, he heard a familiar voice.

"Fancy seeing you here, John. You are so full of"—Lucy restrained herself—"surprises." Her cheeks red, forehead moist, she had just stepped out of the kitchen. The camera she held explained the earlier flash of light and his mother's temporary blindness.

"Hello," Laura said, her hand still on his arm. She smiled sweetly at Lucy, who returned an icy stare.

John's sisters and sisters-in-law alerted like hungry wolves. His brother Robby stopped strumming his old guitar.

"Lucy was just saying how busy you are, how dedicated, how hard you're working." Katie struggled to keep a straight face.

"Mama always said they weren't a match," his sister Rose Ann said in a stage whisper.

"Mama scores again!" Robby thrummed his guitar in an ominous minor key.

"Do you want to leave?" John whispered.

"No way," Laura said. "I love it here, and I'm hungry."

His mother served southern-style pot roast surrounded by onions, carrots, and potatoes, with warm corn bread, pecan muffins, and sweet sun tea. For dessert, she ladled icing over fresh-baked Bundt cake, and served warm, extra-dark chocolate walnut brownies smothered in vanilla ice cream.

John wished Laura looked at him the way she did the food. Her sensual sighs and ecstatic moans after every mouthful set him afire as Lucy shot daggers across the table at them both.

"My gram fixes everything just the way you do," Laura told John's mother, "'cept she serves fried okra and tomatoes with it."

His mom smiled and returned moments later with a serving dish of fried okra and tomatoes. Serious eating created a conversational lull, until Lucy spoke to Laura. "Haven't seen you, honey, since they brought you up to Homicide."

A high-pitched meow came from the far end of the big dining room table. John glared at his brothers.

"That's right!" Laura licked her glistening lips, then patted them daintily with a napkin. "That's where I saw you!" As radiant as an angel, she pointed her finger at Lucy. "Aren't you Tracy, the one they all call Dick?"

Snickers.

"The name is Lucy. City of Miami Detective Tracy Luisita Dominguez," she said coldly. "John's fiancée." She waggled her left ring finger at Laura. The diamond glittered in the light from the dining room chandelier.

"How lovely." Laura admired it. "I once had an engagement ring with a similar setting."

"Did you marry him?" Katie asked.

"No." Laura shook her head and smiled. "That's what engagements are for, to decide if you're really a match. Sometimes, it's just not in the stars."

John's mother lit up.

Lucy's eyes widened.

"Rings aren't important," Laura said. "They're symbolic, and nice. But what counts is commitment and true love."

John's mother nodded, her eyes on his dad at the head of the table.

"So I gave it back, without a single regret. My heart," she placed her right hand over her breast as though the flag were passing, "said, 'Wait, find your soul mate.' I did wait and it's finally happened."

You could have heard a pin drop.

Lucy turned to John's mother as though she hadn't heard a thing. *"Mamacita,"* she asked, pen poised. "What's the secret to gravy this smooth? Look, no lumps. How do you do that?"

John's mother smiled shyly, then nodded at Laura, who spoke up. "The secret is to brown the flour with the butter, and add the milk very, very slowly." She drew out the last three words with her long, slim fingers.

"I didn't ask you," Lucy blurted. "I'm asking my future mother-in-law." She turned again to John's mother.

"Well, bless your heart, honey. It's just like Laura said. Brown the flour with the butter, then add the milk real slow."

Katie, the romantic, broke the silence. "Laura's right. Finding your soul mate is what matters. Did you see that story in *People*? Jewelry that the former king of England and the woman he loved gave to each other was auctioned for millions of dollars. The king could have had any woman except the one he wanted, an American divorcee. When he couldn't live without her, he gave up his throne, left his country, and spent the rest of his life in exile, with her."

"Musta been one hell of a woman," John's dad said.

"He musta been one hell of a man," Katie said, dreamily. "They called it the love story of the century."

Joe Ashley caressed his wife with his eyes. "They just didn't know about us."

The laughter and applause made her blush.

"Love is alive," Laura murmured, and gazed over the top of her glass at John.

"You're right," said his shy cousin Francie, who rarely spoke up. "It happened to one of our neighbors," she said. "She had two teenage boys. Her husband, Ralph, had a good advertising job. They were high school sweethearts, the perfect couple, an ideal family, until a quiet older man moved in down the street. He was a writer who'd been divorced a few times. Ralph came home one day and found Sandy stirring soup. She said she'd heard the new neighbor was sick, down with the flu, and all alone. She took the soup down to his house—and never came back."

"What do you mean, never?" Robby asked.

"Didn't even go home for her toothbrush," Francie said dramatically. "Ralph was beside himself. He finally divorced her and she married the writer who died one morning, twenty-two years later, asleep in his own bed, at home, while she, his much-younger wife, was out buying his favorite pastries for breakfast."

"Way to go," Frank said.

"You hear about people who fall in love at first sight and stay together forever, no matter what," John's sister-in-law Danielle piped up. "I knew two of 'em."

She pursed her lips and put down put her fork. "My mother's cousin, a journalist, went on an assignment to the Bahamas for the *Atlanta Constitution* and crossed paths with another reporter. They had lunch together and never slept apart again."

Katie hung on every word, eyes shining.

"But it wasn't all romance and smooth sailing," Danielle said. "Both were married and they had nine children between 'em."

Jaws dropped. Women gasped.

"That's right," she said primly. "He and his wife had four little ones; she and her husband had five under the age of twelve. The divorces were bitter. Both lost visitation, but they honeymooned for eighteen years, till she died of cancer. On her deathbed she told my mother that they knew they were soul mates the first time they looked into each other's eyes and were convinced they'd been lovers in a prior life."

"How romantic," Katie murmured.

"How cruel and selfish," blurted Ann Lee, Robby's outspoken young wife. "How could they, with all those little children?"

"It's soap opera"—Lucy stabbed her spoon into the heart of her ice cream-smothered brownie—"with no resemblance to real life." The chocolate on her chin weakened her argument as she glared.

"But we've all heard," Katie said earnestly, "about those rare moments when someone meets a stranger and knows instantly that nothing else matters, even if the timing is . . . inconvenient."

"Inconvenient?" someone asked. Others groaned.

Under the table, Lucy delivered a sharp kick to John's left shin. He stared sternly, to make it clear that was no way to behave in his parents' home. The hostile glare she returned made him glad she wasn't wearing her steel-toed shoes.

She left shortly after supper. "John?" she said, ignoring Laura, who sat beside him. "Would you walk me to my car?"

"Go," Laura whispered. "Be kind."

His father's old dog snored at Laura's feet, and his mother's tuxedo cat, usually invisible to strangers, purred in her lap. Robby had pulled up a chair and was demonstrating his finger work on a guitar fret, while next to her Katie chatted as though they'd been best friends forever.

"Sure." He followed Lucy out as eyes bored holes in their backs. Her red sports car was parked across the street, obscured by showy trees. She did not look at him as they crossed the median, but he heard her breathing, or hyperventilating.

"John!" Her voice startled him, like the sudden crack of a rifle. "How could you humiliate me in front of your whole family? Have you lost your mind? You, of all people, mixed up with some low-life witness. Flaunting a skank you don't even know in front of your family? Or"— she paused—"how long *have* you known her?"

"Sorry, Lucy. I never—"

"How long?"

"I met Laura the same day you did—"

"Don't you lie!" She cut him off. "I thought you were sensitive, en-lightened, a cut above." She spit out the words. "I never dated other cops until you. But you're just like all the others. Worse! You'd screw a snake! You don't love me. Never did. You lied! It was all about sex. Well?" she sneered, finally out of breath. "Do you have anything to say for your-self?"

"If you want to break the engagement and give back the ring," he said, "I understand."

"You just *try* to get it back," she said heatedly. "You lying, cheating . . ."

"All right," he said. "Keep it."

She walked away, then looked back, tears in her eyes. "John, you can't mean . . . Are we really over?"

"We are, Lucy. I'm sorry."

"You're sure?"

"I am."

"You pig!" Her cry cut through the quiet night. "How could I be so stupid? Was it *ever* real?"

"Of course," he lied.

"Don't try to tell me that!"

"Lucy." He tried to sound reasonable. "Let's rise above all this. It might be difficult for us to see each other on the job. If that's a problem, you might want to transfer out of the bureau."

"You son of a bitch! I'll still be wearing the badge long after you're history!"

She stomped across the street to her car, then hesitated. When he made no move to stop her, she wrenched the door open, slid behind the steering wheel, then peeled out.

He winced at the sound and the smell of burned rubber but felt relieved. It was over, at last.

As he walked back to the house, he heard something he'd never forget, something he'd heard before, but not like this. Robby was playing and singing a wistful, familiar folk song. But this time a sweet, sad, voice joined his. He listened from the porch as Robby and Laura harmonized.

Oh, Shenandoah, I love your daughter.

Somehow he knew he'd waited all his life to hear it.

For her I'd cross your roaming waters.

Robby and Frank had seen the news, heard the rumors, and promised to keep their eyes open and their ears to the ground.

Alone together at last, John and Laura switched back to his city car and he drove her north to her hotel.

The star-spackled sky seemed overwhelmingly bright, despite the city lights. Venus, spectacular on the high western horizon, outshone every other point of light in the night sky.

"Your brother Robby *is* a younger version of you," she said. "How flattering is it to have your brothers follow you into police work?"

He shrugged. "Look," he said. "There's Arch Creek, where there used to be a natural bridge. Everybody who arrived or left Miami by wagon or car used it. The bridge was a local landmark, a historic site, until one morning in the seventies, it was gone, scattered in a million pieces. They thought vandals blew it up. But apparently, it just collapsed without warning. Proof that nothing is forever."

"Some things," she murmured, "are forever, John."

He shook his head. "Recently, as preservationists began organizing to save it, a crew rolled in with sledgehammers and heavy equipment and demolished Saint Stephen's, a little church built by pioneers in 1912, in Coconut Grove. They worked fast, so nobody could stop them. In fifteen minutes they'd knocked the original cross off the roof. They smashed the bell tower next. How can people be so greedy, with no regard for the past? Whenever an old building goes we lose another piece of history."

She held his hand.

In an hour or so Officer Mona Stratton would report to cover the next shift. She'd been thrilled at the prospect of an easy night. He swung into the hotel parking lot. No one followed. No strange parked cars. Everything looked secure, with one exception. The parking lot was less brightly lit. One of the four security lamps was out. No broken glass. Probably just the bulb.

Laura moved closer. He wanted to kiss her, but didn't. He scanned their surroundings instead, opened the passenger side door, and walked her briskly to her room. The hotel key and the key to the new double dead bolt both operated smoothly. Nothing tampered with, all secure, exactly the way they left it.

Eager to be alone with her, he ached to throw caution to the winds and sweep her into his arms . . . but didn't. He opened the door. As they stepped inside, into the dark, his senses became instantly alert. Everything was wrong.

CHAPTER TWELVE

Time slowed. The air conditioner hummed as lustily as before. Yet the room was slightly warmer, the air moist. And John sensed, more than felt, a wraithlike summer breeze that carried faint traffic sounds and the calls of night birds. In the distance he heard a mockingbird burst into an eerily familiar full-throated, heartbreaking song in the night.

Somebody's in here, he thought. How? Who is it?

Laura sensed it too. "John? Something's wrong," she whispered.

He pushed her roughly to the floor between the wall and the bed and drew his gun. She gasped but did not resist or cry out. He saw the bathroom door now in brilliant relief. It stood an inch or two ajar. He'd firmly closed it before they left.

The door flew open and a shadowy figure opened fire as John dove to the floor.

The blast buzzed like a swarm of deadly insects over his head. He heard solid hits, pings, crashes, and whines. Dust rose from the carpet and drapes. The sound was deafening, the muzzle flash a blue flame a foot and a half long. What the hell is he packing? Shoulda worn a vest, John thought, as he returned fire one, two, three times at the shadow behind the flame. With each squeeze of the trigger, another question resonated. Who? How many? How did I let this happen?

Glass shattered. Wood splintered. The horrendous howl of a wounded animal, quickly followed by grunts, gasps, and desperate thuds as it scrambled and bounced between door frame and wall.

Is he hit? Diving for cover? Setting me up? Instinctively, John had returned fire in the dark. He knew the dangers of overconfidence.

He kicked shut the door they'd entered and threw the thumb latch to keep anyone else out. Instead of calling for backup at once, he trusted his instinct.

"Are you all right?" he whispered.

She hiccuped.

"Laura!"

"Yes, John. Are you?" To his huge relief, she scrambled to her knees, about to get to her feet, and hiccuped twice more.

"I'm fine. Stay down! Don't move!"

She dropped to the floor. No questions, hysterics, or drama. Only hiccups? Who is this woman? he wondered in awe.

He moved quietly toward the bathroom, light on his feet. Inside, something snorted like a wild creature, then gurgled. Blood-chilling sounds. The agonal breathing that followed would be difficult to fake. John paused until it stopped and the room went quiet. He stepped forward, gun in hand, flipped on the light switch, and blinked. A gloved man dressed entirely in black lay on his side, knees drawn up, his face concealed by a black hood, his gun still in his right hand.

John recognized the weapon, a Taurus Judge, a handgun that can fire both .45 caliber bullets and shotgun shells. The shotgun shells fired at them would leave no ballistic evidence, no match to the weapon.

He should have known; he had seen the weapon demonstrated for police officers. A shotgun shell fired from a Taurus Judge had pulverized its target, a frozen thirty-pound turkey. Tiny bits of flesh and bone had been scattered over a wide area. He kicked the gun out of the man's reach.

No need. The gunman, in a fetal position between the tub and the toilet, wasn't faking. He didn't move, but his blood did as it spread slowly across the pale green tiles and finally flooded the floor of the tiny room. Careful not to step in it, John felt for a pulse. Nothing. He reached for his cell phone to call it in, but something stopped him.

Laura, close behind him, hiccuped.

"I told you to stay down, darlin'," he said. "There may be somebody else outside."

"I checked," she said quietly. "No one's out there. Who is he?"

John knew better than to disturb a shooting scene, but he peeled the black hood away from the dead man's face.

One pale blue eye stared at the wall.

John grabbed his hair and lifted his head for a better look, then let it go and stepped back. "Holy shit!"

Laura gasped. "It's Manny, the one who drove away with Summer before she . . ."

"I need to get you out of here fast. Now! Get your things together! Wait, give me your cell." He took it from her and punched in a familiar number.

"I need you, bro," he said, when a voice answered. "There's nobody else I can trust. Everything's turned to shit. You know the place I told you about tonight?"

"Sure do."

"I need you to come get her out of here. Fast!"

"Got it. I'm on the way."

"No lights, no nothing. Slide in under the radar, soon."

"I'm a ghost."

John doused the lights, locked Laura inside, and walked quietly to the back of the building, flashlight in one hand, gun in the other. It was summer; surrounding rooms were empty and the commotion had apparently gone unheard. This older wing was solid and well built. Had someone called 911, he'd have heard sirens by now.

The window glass lay on the ground in the dark. The intruder had attached suction cups to it, used a diamond cutter, and lifted it out in a single piece. Then it was simple to reach in and open the latch to the burglar bars. John had underestimated the skill of his adversary. But the man had underestimated John and his desire to protect what was his. The man who tried to kill him was a city cop who'd advanced rapidly. He'd seen it all, learned from it, and clearly conspired with crooked county cops. How high, John wondered, does the conspiracy go?

He took photos with Laura's cell phone, returned to the room, and photographed the dead man from every angle. Then he doused the lights again and watched until a car rolled into the lot, headlights off. Robby had arrived faster than John expected. What a blessing a brother can be, he thought, and thanked God he was not an only child.

He flashed the room lights. Robby rapped moments later.

"What's up, bro?"

John showed him the bathroom.

"*Nice* shooting, bro." Robby frowned. "Where the hell did you fire from?"

"The floor."

His brother nodded, even more impressed.

"And what the hell was that dude firing?" Robby took in the damage, then crouched to take a closer look at the dead man's gun. "Is that a Judge? Yes, it is. Dumb son of a bitch fired it at my brother! Well, he knows better now."

John had hit him all three times, twice in the upper torso, once in the neck.

Robby's expression never changed. How cool is my little brother? John thought, impressed by the man he had taught to swim, swing a baseball bat, and shoot a gun.

"Anybody you know?"

"My captain," John said. "Armando 'Manny' Politano."

"Uh-oh." Robby gave a long, low whistle. "Damn. That complicates things. How'd he get in?" He jerked his head at the new hardware on the door.

"Cut the glass out of that back window, reached in, and unlatched the burglar bars."

"Slick," he said.

"The minute we walked in, we both knew somebody was in here."

Robby turned to Laura, who had set her suitcase near the door. "You okay?" he asked.

She nodded, as though they'd just crossed paths at the mall or at the supermarket. "Nice to see you again, Robby. Didn't expect it to be so soon."

Robby turned to his brother. "Your call, John. I'm up for whatever you wanna do."

"Just get her to a safe place. Then I'll call it in."

Robby blinked, his gray eyes puzzled. "That'll stir up a shit storm with you in the middle, John. Sure that's what you want?"

"No other option." John shrugged helplessly.

"We could come up with a few." Robby moved to the far side of the room and dropped his voice to a near whisper. "One is to take him outta here. Dump him somewhere, anywhere. Or plant him where he'll never be found. Let whoever sent him try to figure out what the hell happened to him."

He glanced at the bathroom, eyes speculative. "Shoulda rolled him up in that shower curtain right away, before he bled all over the damn place. We'll need lots of bleach, but the three of us can mop up this mess in no time."

"I hear you, Robby. But I can't involve her, or you. And that's not what I do. And you know that even if we did a bang-up job, the techs can always find forensics, or pretend to. I'm shocked at what they're teaching you over at the county, but thanks for sticking your neck out. I'm lucky you're my brother, but I'll go by the book and try to get to the bottom of it."

"You sure, John? Remember, a good friend will help you move. A very good friend, like your brother, will help you move a body."

"I'm sure." He checked his watch. "Hey, my replacement's due here in twenty minutes. Get Laura the hell out of here, to a safe place. Then I'll call it in."

"Okay." Robby turned to Laura. "We're gone."

"What about you, John? Come with us." Tears sprang to her eyes. "Let's both go with Robby."

"Can't. I want you long gone, miles from here before all hell breaks loose. Robby'll take good care of you. Keep down, don't let anybody see you in his car."

She nodded.

He kissed her, then asked Robby to buy her a prepaid cell phone.

"And a gun," she said. "Nothing smaller than a thirty-eight, short barrel."

"That can be arranged," Robby said, with a crooked smile.

This time John didn't object. Hell, she'd just seen that he couldn't protect her. Maybe nobody could. How could he, with any conscience, deny her the means to protect herself? Her grace under pressure spoke to him. They both came from Florida pioneer families who never asked for help or a handout.

"Protect her," he told his brother.

Robby nodded, picked up her suitcase, and took her arm. Her eyes, though haunted as she looked back at John, were fearless.

"We're ghosts," Robby said, and they were gone.

John wiped clean every surface she might have touched. If things went south, it might help to make her presence at the scene difficult to prove.

He waited twenty minutes, then used his cell phone to call his lieutenant and 911.

He had previously told only one person in the department their location. Just as he began to think she might have betrayed him, Officer Mona Stratton, a large woman, showed up late.

"Sorry, Sarge. Couldn't find you guys way back here." Breathless, she flashed a broad, gold-toothed grin.

She was in uniform. Perfect, he thought.

"Come on in," he said, "and join the party," as the sounds of sirens grew louder in the distance.

CHAPTER THIRTEEN

W onder what's shaking up in this neck of the woods?" Officer Stratton glanced over her shoulder as the incoming sirens built to a
crescendo, then converged. "Sounds like something big." She rolled her
eyes and chuckled in relief that it didn't concern her.

John nodded as she lumbered by him into the room. She set a tote
bag full of magazines, a paperback romance novel, and convenience store
snacks on the floor just inside and urgently glanced around. "Is that the
john?"

He frowned.

"I really got to pee." The big woman beelined for the bathroom.

"Don't go in there," John warned. "It's a mess."

She squinted at him over her shoulder but never slowed down. "Don't
worry," she sang out. "You should see mine."

"Wait!" John called.

She didn't. "Where's the witness?" Officer Stratton asked casually, as
she pushed open the bathroom door and stepped inside.

John sighed and counted down. Three, two, one. The shriek, more
high-pitched than he expected, preceded a roller coaster whoop, followed by a gag reflex and a series of terrified puppylike yelps.

Arms flailing, she nearly fell back into the room, eyes squeezed shut,
her feet pounding the floor like an Irish dancer.

"We had a problem," he said.

She paused, eyes growing wider as, for the first time, she took in the
damaged walls, furniture, and ceiling.

"What happenin' here?" she cried, as the earsplitting sirens stopped
outside and cops with guns burst into the room.

Three squad cars, Lt. Mac Myerson, and two marginal homicide detectives arrived simultaneously. Myerson walked directly to the bathroom. "Christ! It is him! How the hell did this happen?" he asked John and Officer Stratton.

"How'd he know where we were?" John countered. "I told no one, except Officer Stratton here." He looked at her and frowned.

Bug-eyed, she protested, denied, disavowed. "Had nothing to do with it. Not me! Don't ask me! I just walked in! Didn't see nothing. Didn't hear nothing. Don't know nothing!"

Only hours ago she'd been John's new best friend. Now she regretted ever hearing his name. This night was to be an easy shift babysitting a female witness, eating pizza, and watching TV, her feet up, the remote in her hand. Instead, it started bad and was growing worse.

"How we gonna tell his wife?" Lieutenant Myerson raked his fingers through his hair like a man who'd lost his best friend.

John believed he had a more important question. "Why did the captain try to kill me and my witness?"

"Where is she?" Myerson scanned the room.

John shrugged.

"What do you mean?" The red vein in the lieutenant's forehead bulged and throbbed. "You were protecting her!"

"Obviously, I couldn't. She didn't feel safe and split."

"You let her go?" he asked, alarmed. "Alone? When? Did she leave in a car?"

John shrugged again.

"Is she driving a vehicle?"

John paused to think. "Not to my knowledge."

"Did she call a taxi?"

"Not that I heard. But I was busy with your boss, who was trying to kill us. He didn't say a word. Let his trigger finger do the talking. I hit the deck, fired three rounds in self-defense. Had no idea who he was."

The lieutenant turned to Officer Stratton."Did you see her?"

"Who? Me? I didn't see nothing. Didn't hear nothing. Don't know nothing! I just walked in the door."

She refused to say more, demanded to talk to her union rep, plopped herself down on a shaky plastic chair outside the room, put her head between her knees, and inhaled noisy deep breaths.

Between frequent private phone calls, Lieutenant Myerson had uniforms rope off the area and check for surveillance cameras, then gave the room over to the homicide detectives. He and John moved to the small nearby lobby.

Myerson tucked his fat rear end into a chair behind the desk like a sinister clerk about to check John into a room. Where? John wondered. Hell? County jail? The state pen? Or a pine box?

"You know the drill, Ashley. Your badge and weapon."

John handed them over. "Three rounds fired," he said.

Myerson took the gun, his shaggy eyebrows raised, his expression mocking. "Ain't this the second time you've discharged a firearm in twenty-four hours? You must be almost out of hardware."

"I'll manage," John said. Myerson's attitude firmed his decision to talk no more that night.

The lieutenant asked for his cell phone as well.

"Nope. I don't think so." John shook his head. "A captain from our department tried to kill me tonight. Since I'm not sure why, I'm more comfortable hanging on to my phone. I may need it."

Lieutenant Myerson responded with an icy stare, then stepped away to use his phone. He returned more confident and less stressed.

"You look like hell, Ashley," he said. "You've had a long day, pal. Head home. Get some sleep and report to my office at eleven a.m. If it makes you more comfortable, bring a rep." He shrugged. "But I assume you have nothing to hide."

John hated to leave. What about the integrity of the scene, the collection and preservation of evidence? "Where's crime scene and the medical examiner? Shouldn't they be here by now?"

"On the way," the lieutenant said dismissively. "My office at eleven. And oh yeah, we need your city car." He instructed a young patrolman to drive John home.

Where the hell was the press? John hated to see his name in the newspaper, always had, but a masked police captain slain by one of his own sergeants under circumstances suspicious, to say the least, seemed newsworthy to him. This case would need the scrutiny of a topflight medical examiner, the press, the public, and the work of good crime scene investigators and photographers to ensure an honest and thorough investigation. Where was everybody?

The baby-faced young cop said little as they exited onto the Boulevard. John saw nothing reassuring on the horizon. No morgue wagon, no ME car, crime scene van, or media sound trucks.

"Where are the troops?" he asked. "Your radio traffic sounds light, seems to be a slow night. Crime scene, an ME, the shooting team, the brass, a PIO officer, and the news media: should be here by now."

The young cop shrugged. "The lieutenant's handling all that."

Myerson had stayed off police radio, used his cell phone exclusively. That could mean that neither the public, the press, nor other members of the department and support staff even knew there had been a shooting.

John got out of the patrol car in front of his building, swung the door shut, and watched the taillights until they were out of sight.

He felt weary but had things to do, places to go. His car was parked on level two of the garage. He took the stairwell instead of the elevator. As he approached the second level, he felt overwhelmed by a strong feeling that an intruder had been there on his turf. He could almost smell him. He scrutinized his car, searched it for anything missing—or added. Despite the aura of a hostile presence, everything appeared normal until he swept beneath the back bumper with his fingers and found something—a tiny tracking device. The same model that detectives in SIU, the department's Strategic Intelligence Unit, once planted on the personal car of a scandal-prone mayor.

When did they do this? he wondered. Had to be after he and Laura switched back to the city car. Why? How did they . . . ?

He duct-taped the device to a concrete pillar next to his parking spot, then drove to an all-night convenience store for several prepaid, untraceable cell phones. He knew he wouldn't be picked up on store surveillance tape. Just the other day, the manager had complained to him that his video system, damaged in a recent robbery-shooting, wouldn't be back up for at least ten days.

As he turned the familiar corner half a block from home, his eyes rose, as usual, to his balcony on the building's east side, his private little window on the world, with its patio chair, potted palm, and outdoor grill. He blinked, startled, as a flash of light bloomed in the dark behind the sliding glass door. He pulled over and killed his headlights to watch. There it was again. A flashlight beam. Somebody was in his apartment.

PART FOUR

CHAPTER FOURTEEN

H ey, look who's here, darlin'," John murmured.

Laura tore herself away from the bolt of shimmering blue silk the color of her eyes. The graceful, glistening fabric, perfect for a special dress she planned to make, spilled like water across the counter at Burdine's Trading Post.

It was their third brief visit to Miami.

"'Member when I told you about Mr. Carl Fisher?"

Laura followed his eyes and flashed her brilliant smile at the couple who entered. "Is that him?"

John nodded.

The tall, slender girl on Fisher's arm was full-faced, with a high forehead, dark hair, and bold, sparkling eyes. "Look at that elegant dress," Laura murmured. "His daughter's lovely."

"No!" John whispered hoarsely, as Fisher hailed them. "That's his wife."

Laura's eyes widened.

"Ashley, isn't it?" Fisher boomed.

"Yes, sir." John introduced Laura as his wife. That made life less complicated in Miami, where they planned to live. Husband and wife in every other way, they hoped to make it official soon. The day before, as they explored rustic, tree-shaded Coconut Grove, they stumbled upon a church construction site. The builder told them that Saint Stephen's would be completed and consecrated the following year. The design was clean and simple, the surroundings romantic. They decided it was where they would quietly marry when Laura was free and the church finished.

"We plan to take a boat out to see the beach before we leave," John told the Fishers.

Jane Fisher rolled her eyes dramatically and pushed her hair back off her brow, as though weary. "You poor thing," she told Laura. "You have my sympathy. Why Carl is so interested in that swampy sandbar, I'll never know. It's nasty." She shuddered delicately. "He took me there and I couldn't have been more disgruntled."

"Disgruntled?" Laura said.

The girl nodded, her eyes serious. "More than you can imagine. The boat ride made me seasick and millions of hungry mosquitoes swarmed all over me the moment we arrived. Right in the center there's a huge crocodile hole with all those ugly, awful creatures wallowing . . ."

Her eyes lit up. "Carl! Look!" She snatched the silk from in front of Laura. "Wouldn't this be perfect for my new ball gown? It's my color!"

"Laura liked it too, I believe she was thinking the same thing," John said.

By the time the clerk returned to say they had no more in stock, Miami's only bolt of blue silk was tucked possessively under Jane Fisher's arm.

Fisher mumbled something in his wife's ear. "Oh." She cocked her head in startled surprise. "Were you interested in it, too, dear?"

Laura smiled graciously. "You take it, Mrs. Fisher. It's special and will look absolutely beautiful on you."

Fisher urged John to contact him when he made his permanent move to Miami. John promised he would.

"Are you all right?" he asked Laura as they left.

"No." Slyly, she cut her eyes at him. "I am disgruntled." She mimicked Jane Fisher's little-girl voice. "More disgruntled than you could imagine. John, that girl can't be more than fifteen years old."

"You were even younger when I knew I wanted to marry you."

"But he's almost forty. The man is losing his hair."

"She was fifteen when they met," John said. "Must be sixteen by now. You really wanted that blue silk, didn't you?"

She nodded. "But that girl will go to more fancy parties than I will. And you may go to work for her husband." She shrugged. "I'm fine; she's welcome to it."

They stayed at the Price House, a small three-story hotel built by Henry Choice Price. A Georgia cotton planter before the Civil War,

Price became a firebrand blockade runner for the Confederacy, then morphed after the war into an upstate Florida citrus grower. He gave that up when a winter freeze wiped out his entire orange crop and moved his family south—to Miami.

The hotelman, an amateur military historian, loved to spin colorful tales and entertain his guests with jokes.

The hotel rate was two dollars a day. Hot breakfasts and lunches cost thirty-five cents each. Supper was fifty cents. Henry Flagler's Royal Palm Hotel had Miami's first and only swimming pool, but Price's guests had privileges.

John and Laura had never seen a swimming pool and were eager to try it out. She hated her woolen bathing dress which came with a matching hat adorned with a big bow in the front, and black stockings.

They'd both heard whispers about Jane Fisher's scandalous antics at the Royal Palm. She had peeled off her black woolen stockings and plunged bare-legged into the pool one hot, stifling afternoon. Men stared; women gasped and covered their children's eyes. No local women dared follow her lead, though Laura wished she could. The story gave her new respect for the millionaire's child bride.

"Don't even think about it, we plan to live here," John warned.

Laura understood but still fantasized. "The suits we wore to swim in the Caloosahatchee were so much more comfortable than this getup," she said demurely at the deep end of the pool, where John had just surfaced after a somersault off the diving board.

He slicked back his wet hair and spit out water. "But we didn't wear—"

"I *know.*" Embarrassed, she glanced furtively at the other bathers, mostly men.

"Sorry, darlin', that outfit can't hold a candle to what you wore, or didn't, in that river. You were so beautiful that day. But this bathing dress isn't bad. You look cute."

"Cute? It's hideous! It itches in places ladies can't scratch in public!" She splashed him fiercely.

He fended her off, caught her in his arms, and calmed her down with whispered promises that they'd soon swim sans suits again, this time in the gentle surf off Ocean Beach. "The sand is like silk and we can wade halfway to Cuba at low tide," he said.

While strolling back to their hotel, they passed the mortician's horse-drawn death wagon outside a small house nearby.

Mrs. Price, the hotelier's wife, stood outside with "Aunt Tilly." An angel of mercy Miamians turned to in times of crisis, Aunt Tilly had raised two orphans, delivered babies, tended to the sick, and laid out the dead.

"It's a sad day," Mrs. Price greeted them. The death wagon had come for Sandra Browne, a young mother of four.

"She was a little thing, excitable and high-strung," Aunt Tilly said. "Sheriff Hardie's in there now with the undertaker and her two little girls. They saw her die."

Laura shivered in the sun as she heard the story.

Cooley Browne had moved his family south from Philadelphia. His timid wife, Sandra, would hide in a closet during Miami's violent thunderstorms. Strangers, snakes, and scorpions terrified her. So did Indians. That day, as she and her girls baked bread, the door swung open and four Seminole Indian braves strolled into her kitchen.

She screamed, dropped her bread pan, and fell, in what appeared to be a dead faint. But her heart had stopped.

Indians came to Miami by canoe or horse and wagon. They bartered chickens for calico, had their horses shod, and thumbed through the Montgomery Ward catalog at the trading post. They didn't smile and rarely spoke but were not feared, despite their odd customs. For example, when they were hungry, they'd walk into the nearest home without bothering to knock, sit down at the table, and wait to be fed. They always were. Food was abundant in Miami. Everyone kept gardens. No one went hungry and the Indians' behavior was simply considered part of the local color.

"Here's the sheriff now," Mrs. Price said, as Dan Hardie emerged from the house. John and Bobby had seen the lawman on prior visits but never met him. Tall and lean, with clear gray eyes, Hardie had a strong jaw and a firm handshake.

"Sorry to hear the bad news," John said. "Do you think she was scared to death? I've heard that can happen."

"Maybe so," the sheriff said. "A sudden scare mighta killed her if she had a weak heart. I intend to talk to her doctor."

They watched the undertaker and his assistant carry Sandra Browne's covered body to the horse-drawn hearse on a stretcher.

Hardie said he'd interviewed her daughters, aged nine and eleven, and found no malice on the part of the Indians, who had since departed to dine elsewhere. "They made no threatening moves, had no weapons." The sheriff shook his head. "The little girls said they weren't scared until their mother screamed and collapsed."

"The poor children," Laura said softly. "How sad to grow up without a mother." She wiped her eyes. "Is there some way we can help?"

"Aunt Tilly has it under control," Hardie said. "She'll stay until the father arrives. He and his sons are on their way back from Knight's Key now. Mrs. Price will bring their supper."

Aunt Tilly returned to the girls, while John and Laura walked toward their hotel with Sheriff Hardie and Mrs. Price.

They turned the corner and moments later heard shouts; running footsteps pounded behind them. "Sheriff! Sheriff!" The mortician's pale young assistant sprinted around the corner and nearly collided with them.

"Hearse thief! Hearse thief!" he panted.

More angry shouts came from behind him.

"Horse thief?" Hardie frowned.

"No!" The young man gasped. "Hearse thief!" He bent over at the waist, hands on his knees, to catch his breath. "Robbers!" he croaked. "They stole the death wagon with Miz Browne inside!"

Two robbers had hit the hardware store. When employees began to shout, the driver of their getaway car panicked and sped away. The abandoned holdup men fled on foot with store employees in hot pursuit. The fleeing men spotted the unattended death wagon and scrambled aboard. One snatched the reins, cracked the whip, and off they raced, east toward the bay.

"They took that poor dead woman!" Aunt Tilly shouted, breathless as she rushed up to the sheriff. "What will I tell her husband and children?"

"We can stop 'em." John darted into the hotel for his Winchester, in a locked gun box in the lobby. He emerged in less than a minute and caught up to Hardie. The sheriff saw John's rifle and reacted.

"You are officially deputized!"

John liked the way that sounded and nodded. The mortician was far down the dusty street, chasing the death wagon on foot.

Hardie flagged down, then commandeered a passing Ford. He and John piled into the car, as the ousted driver begged Hardie not to wreck his new automobile.

John watched the sheriff shift gears, hit the gas pedal, and felt the Ford leap forward. He knew then he had to have a car of his own. Soon.

They raced after the death wagon. "They're headed for the natural bridge at Arch Creek," Hardie said, as they passed the huffing and puffing mortician, who gladly gave up the chase.

Arch Creek, over time, had created a natural stone bridge twenty feet wide. During the Seminole wars, it was used by the military. Everyone who arrived in Miami by wagon or automobile crossed the natural bridge.

"We can stop 'em now," John said, as the death wagon careened across the bridge ahead of them.

"How?" Hardie asked.

"I wouldn't shoot a horse, but I can bust the wagon's axle. That'll stop 'em. If they jump off and run, they can't get far."

"It's too long a shot." Hardie winced as the car bounced along the rutted, unpaved road. "Nobody could hit that axle from here."

"I can."

"Want me to stop so you can take aim?"

"Nope." John lifted his rifle, leaned out, stared down the barrel, held his breath and slowly squeezed the trigger. The rifle cracked with a puff of acrid smoke.

The death wagon continued racing ahead at breakneck speed.

"Told you . . . ," Hardie began, when the axle began to smoke, then snapped. The wagon veered sharply, jerked upright, tilted to the left, and tipped over. The two skinny robbers leaped off as Sandra Browne's shrouded corpse slid out the back.

"Damn," Hardie whispered. "Who taught you to shoot, son?"

"My dad," John said. "He's the best. My brothers are good too. So is Laura. I taught her."

The sheriff's eyes widened.

The robbers surrendered to an impromptu posse of Miamians who'd trailed the chase and swiftly surrounded them. The loot from the hardware store was recovered, as were the death wagon and the dead woman, a bit dusty, her shroud askew but no other harm done.

The robbers quickly identified the getaway driver who'd left them behind. In fact, they insisted, he was the ringleader who had organized the entire scheme. John was impressed by the number of local citizens who had joined the chase.

"That's the Miami way," Hardie said. "Folks here look out for each other, from Aunt Tilly to the businessmen and passersby on the street. Did you say you plan to settle here?"

John said he did and Hardie asked if he'd be available when needed for a posse. "They all volunteer," he said, "but none can shoot like you."

John agreed. "You know, my younger brother, Bobby," he said, "took a real interest in the Miami Rifles." The fifty-two young members of the military marching band and color guard performed in dedications, parades, and other events. Under the sheriff's command, they were affiliated with the National Guard. "We saw 'em at the opening of the new bank building," John said. "Bobby liked that marching music and those uniforms."

Hardie chuckled. "They all love those red jackets with the gold braid."

"He's a good boy, an excellent rifle shot."

"Have him look me up. Anytime," Hardie said, and shook John's hand. "We meet at the county jail and drill in front of the Twelfth Street firehouse, after dark, when it's cooler."

John and Laura cruised up the Miami River to the Musa Isle lookout tower aboard the tour boat *Sallie* the next day. A shop at the base sold postcards, guava jelly, and coconuts. At the top, they had a bird's-eye view of the "mysterious Everglades, endless watery flats where," a tour guide ominously intoned, "only Seminole Indians dare go."

John could barely contain his laughter. Laura looked amused.

At the suggestion of hotel owner Henry Price, they also took an excursion to Cape Florida's historic lighthouse, built in 1825. Rampaging Indians attacked in 1835, wounded the lighthouse keeper, and killed his assistant. The Indians torched the foot of the circular staircase in an attempt to smoke out the wounded man. Cornered in the lonely lighthouse tower, bleeding, outnumbered, choking on smoke, and certain he was about to die, the embattled lighthouse keeper made a brave last stand.

He flung a keg of gunpowder down the narrow stairs into the fire. He expected the blast to kill him but hoped to take out a few Indians with him. To his surprise, he survived. The force of the explosion was generated out, instead of up, and blew the fire out with it. The Indians fled screaming, several of them in flames.

The crew of a passing ship heard the explosion, and the lighthouse keeper was rescued.

John and Laura stood in the shadow of the lighthouse listening to the story. Laura looked so grave that John winked. "Ancient history," he said, with a reassuring smile. "Miami's civilized now." The tour guide grinned and agreed.

That night, when the other guests had all retired, John and Henry Price discussed the massacre that had started the Second Seminole War and triggered the lighthouse attack. Laura listened, curled up in a comfortable chair, as the men smoked cigars, talked, and drank.

An unexpected cold front had swept swiftly across South Florida that afternoon. After sunset, the temperature plummeted by thirty degrees. The winter night felt bitter. The only warmth and most of the light came from a roaring fire in the big stone fireplace. Its flickering flames threw eerie shadows across the walls and their solemn faces.

"I don't know why in hell they named this big county after Major Francis Langhorne Dade," Price grumbled. "His only claim to fame was getting hisself and his men slaughtered and scalped. Had Dade survived that fight, he woulda been court-martialed. Fool led his troops right into a massacre. It's embarrassin', as though this county is cursed. They coulda called it Biscayne, Miami, or Ocean County like some wanted, but no."

John and Laura had heard the story as schoolchildren, but Price knew details that never made the history books.

Dade, a Virginian, had served with Andrew "Old Hickory" Jackson in Pensacola in 1821, when Spain ceded Florida to the United States. Seminole Indians were scattered all across the peninsula then.

"Jackson forced the Seminoles onto a reservation up in central Florida," Price said. "His old buddy, Francis Dade, was an infantry commander in Key West by the time he was elected president. Jackson, a veteran Indian fighter, ignored the past promises and ordered all Florida's Indians to move to Arkansas. When they refused to go, Old Hickory set a deadline. On January 1, 1836, US soldiers were to round up all the Seminoles at bayonet point." Price lit a cigar, then continued.

"The Indians believed in their treaties and trusted Washington to relent. But Jackson refused to change his plans. So a young chief named Osceola took leadership and the Indians made plans of their own." Price's eyes grew sly in the shadows.

"General Wiley Thompson commanded a small garrison at Fort King up near Ocala. As the deadline neared, reinforcements were sent to back up Thompson and his handful of men.

"It was this happy time of year, the Christmas season." Price nodded solemnly. "Seventy-five years ago this month—an anniversary no one celebrates." He laughed without humor, puffed his cigar, and poured himself another drink.

"Major Dade never was supposed to lead those hundred soldiers on that march. But fate stepped in. Fate," he said quietly, "has a way of doing that." He sighed, then paused for a long moment. "The captain who was assigned to lead them dearly loved his young wife who had fallen gravely ill. The doctors said she was dying. So Major Dade volunteered to lead the march instead, so the captain could remain at her bedside."

"You have to give the major credit for that," John said.

"Don't be fooled, John," Price said sharply. He shook his head fiercely, the firelight reflected in his eyes. "Dade had other motives. He'd bragged that he could march a hundred men through the entire Indian nation without a scratch. This was his chance to prove it."

Price leaned back in his chair, sucked his cigar, and stared through the smoke. "They marched out of Fort Brooke on December twenty-third, 1835. One hundred and six miles across rivers, creeks, swamps, and pinewoods, straight through the heart of Indian country. Indians stalked 'em from the start, itching to attack. But Osceola, who'd planned the ambush, and Micanopy, another leader, had important business. Osceola had raced ahead on horseback to kill General Thompson at Fort King. Thompson had thrown him in irons that summer and Osceola was seeking revenge for what they'd done to his young wife, the daughter of a slave. The descendants of slaves were considered slaves too, back then, so white officers took her."

Laura gasped.

"Osceola planned to ambush Dade and his men but had to settle the score with General Thompson first. It was a matter of honor.

"Dade helped build the road between Fort Brooke and Fort King, so he knew the land, for God sake, and he knew the Indians." Price's voice rose indignantly. "He had advance and rear guards and flankers, all on the alert for Seminoles, but after he crossed the forks of the Withla-coochee River into open pine and palmetto country, Dade withdrew his scouts. His interpreter, a sharp-eyed mulatto slave, kept pointing out signs of Indians, but the major ignored 'im, argued that Indians never attacked in daylight in open country.

"Dade's column marched across open land at eight o'clock in the morning on December twenty-eighth. The weather had turned cold, just like today. Chilly rain kept falling, so Dade ordered his men to button their bulky overcoats over their muskets and ammo boxes to keep 'em dry." Price paused. "He did not send scouts out to sweep the sawgrass. Seminoles hid in the pines and palmettos and watched the troops march by like ducks in a shooting gallery.

"When Micanopy arrived, the soldiers had made it two-thirds of the way to the fort. He and two other leaders, Alligator and Jumper, assembled their warriors at Wahoo Swamp, five miles west of Major Dade, and decided to attack. The soldiers had finished their rum rations the night before and were hungover. Dade's romance with rum was well documented. He'd nearly been court-martialed before for being drunk and keeping sloppy records. He'd escaped it because he wasn't worth the trouble and had Washington connections."

"We never heard that," John said. "In school they called him a hero who fought bravely to the end."

"Don't believe everything they tell you in school." Price shrugged. "Dade's interpreter, that mulatto slave, warned him again and again, but the major turned a deaf ear. Said they were already in white man's territory. Didn't know that Indian country is wherever the Indians happen to be. He thought he made it. Major Dade left the column—only officers had horses—and pranced up to ride point. Shouted to his men as he passed. Promised 'em three days of rest and a belated Christmas celebration at Fort King.

"He was still shouting to them as Micanopy took aim, then shot him dead off his horse. The fusillade that followed killed or wounded half the command, cut down before they could wrestle their guns out from under their bulky, buttoned coats."

John sighed and shook his head.

"The surviving troops panicked as the Indians fell back to regroup. But"—Price's forefinger jabbed the air—"remember the captain's gravely ill wife? She'd made a miraculous recovery. Her husband had been riding all night to rejoin his men. He arrived during the attack, took command, and ordered the survivors to chop down pine trees and build a fortification."

"Instead of taking cover in the woods?" John said. "You're kidding me!"

"No, I'm not." Price's voice resonated in the frigid shadows of the room, as the fire crackled and sizzled. "They wanted to survive and worked as fast as they could. But the logs were only stacked knee-high when the Indians launched a second wave. They killed their last soldier by two p.m. One hundred three soldiers dead; five of them were West Point men. The captain died too. But his sickly wife lived another sixty-one years."

John reached for Laura's hand as she shivered in the cold.

"That mulatto guide, who'd warned Dade all along, survived along with four soldiers. The guide was welcomed into the Seminole nation on the spot. One of the four soldiers was caught and killed as the survivors fled back toward Tampa Bay. The last three made it to safety and said they'd been attacked by four hundred to a thousand Indians.

"The truth was," Price leaned forward, his voice a hoarse whisper, "the Indians had a total of one hundred and eighty warriors, three dead, five wounded. It was one of the Indians' most decisive victories over our soldiers. And it took place four years before the birth of George Armstrong Custer. Every schoolboy in America knows General Custer's name. But outside of Florida, nobody knows or cares about Major Dade, though the shot that killed him set off the Second Seminole War. Hope we never fight one like that again. Long, unpopular, and never won!" He slammed his glass down on the table.

"The Seminoles fought for seven bloody years." His voice rose. "The government finally sent forty thousand soldiers to fight fifteen hundred Indians! Cost us twenty million dollars and fifteen hundred dead soldiers, the most expensive, in lives and money, of all our Indian wars."

"Did Osceola ever make it to the fight?" John asked.

"No." Price grinned. "But he did what he set out to do. While Dade and his soldiers were being scalped, Osceola surprised General Thompson and a lieutenant as they walked outside Fort King to smoke cigars. He killed and scalped 'em both." Price pensively studied his own cigar. "That was three days after Christmas."

"Did Osceola ever find his wife?" Laura asked softly.

"No." Price shook his head. "He led his nation in battle for two years of the war. His guerrilla tactics baffled our troops; he was hailed as a military genius. When they couldn't kill or capture him, our leaders invited Chief Osceola to peace talks under a flag of truce. They guaranteed he wouldn't be arrested.

"They lied.

"Osceola arrived on horseback under a white flag, to seek peace for his people, was arrested and thrown into a dirty, wet dungeon, where he soon died mysteriously, at age thirty-four. His cause of death was variously described as malaria, pneumonia, or tonsillitis."

"Or a broken heart," Laura said solemnly.

Price smiled at her. "Chief Osceola was far from stupid," he said. "He refused to be treated by the white doctor the government sent. His instincts were right. That doctor displayed Osceola's head at traveling carnivals and used it to frighten his children when they misbehaved.

"The war ended in 1842, without a treaty, and most of the Seminoles relocated west of the Mississippi. Several hundred hid deep in the Everglades and survived. Their descendants now paddle canoes to the beach, string beads, and rassle alligators at tourist attractions during the season. Rest of the year they hunt, fish, and trap. But they haven't forgotten that white men lied and cheated their fathers. That Andrew Jackson forced them out so speculators could profit from their land.

"That is among many reasons why this beautiful county should not be named in honor of Major Dade, a dangerous, pompous misfit."

When Laura shivered in his arms that night, John thought it was the cold and tried to keep her warm, but she woke from a bad dream before dawn. "I'm afraid," she whispered.

"Of what?" he murmured sleepily. "I've known you all your life, girl. You were never afraid of anything. Wait, you were afraid to have sex when we were kids, but thank God, you got over it. But you never flinched from bullies, crack the whip, or leaving Edgar. When you stood with me against his so-called posse, I was so proud. What could scare a girl like you?"

"Bad dark days to come. I don't know and that's why I'm so afraid," she murmured. "The devil you know is better than the one you don't."

"I know what's wrong," John said confidently. He kissed her and folded his arms around her. "That poor woman who died of fright, the old lighthouse, and all those bloody war stories Price told in the dark. They'd spook anybody. But it's ancient history, darlin'."

He rubbed her back, kissed her shoulders, turned her over, and ran his tongue around her nipple. "Things like that don't happen now, not in our lifetime."

He gasped as she clutched his hair and roughly pulled his mouth to hers.

She seemed better in the morning, on the last day of their stay, so they went to the ocean beach off Miami.

"Oh, John." She looked radiant with anticipation. "Whatever else our house has or hasn't, we must have a verandah. Don't you agree?"

"Absolutely." He caught her hand as they strolled the shell-strewn shoreline of the island, a deserted mass of mangrove, palmetto, and tangled jungle rimmed by silky, sandy beach.

"A house is not a home without a verandah. I'll build ours big and wide so when we're old and creaky, we can sit out there in our rocking chairs, side by side."

Her nose crinkled and she laughed aloud at the image of them as doddering lovers. They had come by boat, and the entire ocean beach belonged to them that day. No other soul in sight for miles. Crashing waves glittered like diamonds in the sunlight, then foamed, swirled, and eddied at their feet.

"Here, I'll show you." He picked up a stick, sharpened it with his pocketknife, then outlined in wet sand the house he envisioned, as she knelt beside him.

"Here is your verandah." He sketched it in with broad strokes. "On chilly days I'll drag our chairs into this sunny spot where we can warm our bones, smell salt breeze, and watch the world go by."

"Promise?"

"Cross my heart." He traced a cross on his left chest.

"I will hold you to that," she said gravely. "And my memory is very long."

"It had better be." His eyes locked on hers, the color of the crashing sea and brittle blue sky that surrounded them. "Because I will never forget. I want you beside me, always."

"I will be," she said, as solemn as a vow. "Always."

After a long and tender moment, he continued to draw. "We'll plant shade trees here, here, and here, and I'll line up Australian pines like soldiers to keep the wind off our avocados and pineapples. We'll grow eggplant, onions, tomatoes, and cabbage too. Those we don't eat ourselves, we'll sell to hotel kitchens, then take the rest to the packing house to ship north."

Her lips curled into a smile. "Where will the flowers be?"

"Everywhere," he said. "In the garden, along the path, in the window boxes I'll build, and in your hair." He lifted her to her feet and swept her up into a long kiss as the ocean roared its approval and the seabirds swooped and squawked overhead.

"I love to hear the ocean and the seagulls," she said, eyes closed, arms tight around his waist.

They stood for a time, studied the drawing of their dream house, then strolled on down the beach, collected seashells, and paused to embrace. Backs turned, they never saw the wave that washed it all away in an instant, leaving only wet sand, smooth and pristine, as though nothing had ever been there.

CHAPTER FIFTEEN

About to head home from Miami, John stopped at Burdine's Trading Post. He asked Laura to wait, he'd just be a minute.

He wore a grin when he returned. She smiled, but asked no questions. Christmas was just around the corner.

The day was cool, the sun bright, with just enough wind to whisper secrets in the treetops, as if sweeping messages, knowledge, and memories up into the low-hanging clouds and on up into the universe.

A group of Indians stood beside their wagons near the natural bridge. John nodded and waved. They all stared. None returned the greeting. Laura rested her hand on John's knee as they passed, then looked back. The Indians still stared. She trembled, moved closer to John, and rested her head on his shoulder.

"Did you see how friendly Sheriff Hardie, Mr. and Mrs. Price, and the Fishers were?" he said, happily. "We won't be moving to a strange city, Laura. It'll be a homecoming. We're already welcome. Remember when I said, 'Everybody will know our names'?"

Their return to the Ashley homestead was like an early Christmas. They unloaded the supplies from Miami—new boots for Joe, household items, groceries, and dry goods for Leugenia—along with several mysterious packages John locked away until Christmas Eve. As the women prepared for the holiday, John left on a brief hunting/trapping trip with a secret detour to Miami to pick up the blue silk he'd ordered for Laura.

Why not? he thought. She deserved it as much as the rich man's teenaged bride.

John loved being in the wilderness, alert for predators, at one with nature, he reflected and mapped out his future beneath starry night skies. He stopped to make camp at dusk his third night out and heard faint, far-off voices carried on the wind that whistled through the pines. He quietly investigated and found Indian trappers camped nearby. Ordinarily, he'd remain alone, but he recognized DeSoto Tiger, along with several other Cow Creek Seminoles his brother Bill had befriended.

The Indians liked seeing Bill, who operated the family's moonshine still. So John ignored his initial instinct and stepped out of the shadows to greet them. The Indians welcomed his company. They'd trapped about eighty otters along the sloughs where the furry creatures fed on fish and smaller animals. Some of the males were as big as five feet long and more than thirty pounds, with pelts so thick and sleek that they'd bring as much as ten dollars each in Miami.

The trapping had gone well, but Tiger was impatient, eager to return home to Flora, his baby daughter born just before he left. Often, after accumulating a large number of pelts, the Indians would leave them for safekeeping with Captain Fowey, a trusted friend who operated a nearby dredging operation, so they could continue to trap. That night they agreed that Tiger would take their hides to the captain at dawn while they broke camp to return home for Christmas.

As morning mists rose from the water and a pink dawn streaked the sky, Tiger stacked the hides in his dugout canoe and shoved off. Moments later, John Ashley called out, his voice echoing across the water, and asked Tiger if he could go with him. Tiger agreed and poled back to shore, where Ashley, tall and husky, shouldered his Winchester and stepped into the canoe. Then they glided away across mirror-bright water and disappeared into the mist.

By high noon, a blazing sun reflected fire on the water and Tiger and Ashley had not returned. The puzzled Indians waited, then eventually returned home, expecting Tiger to follow or be there waiting when they arrived.

They never saw him alive again.

That night John Ashley arrived, unexpected, at the home of his brother Bill. Lucy invited him inside, but he left abruptly when she said Bill wasn't there.

John next surfaced in Miami. He sold a number of otter hides to Girtman Brothers for twelve hundred dollars, picked up his package at the trading post, and went home for Christmas, unaware that the world as he knew it was about to change forever.

CHAPTER SIXTEEN

A bloated, discolored body, the lips, eyes, and ears eaten away by marine life, was fished from the water twenty-five miles west of Fort Lauderdale, four days after Christmas.

The hardworking men on the dredging crew made the grisly discovery in the canal that would one day link Lake Okeechobee to the sea, part of a huge state project to claim hundreds of thousands of flooded acres as farmland.

The men had eagerly anticipated the New Year's Eve holiday, but what they saw on Tuesday, December 29, 1911, dampened their spirits. The dredge captain reported the find to Sheriff George B. Baker, who'd been appointed by the governor when Palm Beach County was created in 1909. The sheriff quickly identified the body as that of missing trapper DeSoto Tiger, a young husband, new father, and the son of a respected Cow Creek Seminole chief.

He'd been shot through the head.

Fellow trappers told Sheriff Baker that Tiger had vanished four days earlier and that they'd last seen him with John Ashley, a well-known marksman also known for his ability to wander in and out of the wilderness like a ghost.

Captain Fowey told the sheriff that Tiger and Ashley had never reached him, though he did see a canoe that morning. Off in the distance, among the marsh grasses, it was too far away to identify the occupant but Fowey was certain about one thing. It was a lone rider. The sheriff sent a posse to find John Ashley, now accused of murder.

The suspect didn't appear to be in hiding. On December 28, the night before the body was found, a Palm Beach deputy had cited John Ashley for reckless use of a firearm.

John had shared drinks that evening with strangers curious about his marksmanship, a popular topic of conversation in local saloons, pool halls, and barbershops. Men who hunted with him swore that Ashley was the finest marksman in Florida and probably the entire South. They'd seen him decapitate a small bird fifty feet away with a single shot from a handgun fired from a fast-moving wagon on a rutted dirt road. He could shoot the heads off rattlesnakes from a distance. And everyone talked about his flashy stunts with whiskey bottles, shooting out the bottoms without damaging the small openings through which the bullet passed. The skeptical strangers wanted proof that he was that good.

Bets were made. The bar emptied into the street to watch John try to shoot out the bottom of a bourbon bottle. He did. The stunned strangers bet he couldn't do it again.

So he did.

Twice.

The shouts, applause, and sporadic gunfire attracted a sheriff's deputy. Unimpressed by the show of marksmanship, the deputy charged John with illegally discharging a firearm inside city limits. He paid a twenty-five-dollar fine and left peacefully.

Two days later, Sheriff Baker informed the press and the shocked Ashley family that John was wanted for murder.

Then Baker heard a rumor: the fugitive was hiding out at a Hobe Sound encampment. The sheriff dispatched his two best men to make the arrest. Deputies Bob Hannon and James Barfield trudged down Dixie Highway carrying rifles as they searched the roadsides for a path through the palmettos to Ashley's campsite.

Suddenly their names were shouted out from behind them. They turned and stared down the barrels of handguns pointed at them by John Ashley and his younger brother Bobby.

"Drop 'em," John said.

The deputies put their guns on the ground.

"You boys looking for something?" John asked.

"Sheriff Baker sent us out to find you, John," Hannon said.

"You two couldn't find your way out of a rain barrel. You know as much about tracking as a dog knows about his father," John said. "If I hadn't called your names, you'd still be wandering on down the road.

Look at 'em, Bobby. No telling what kinds of varmints you run across in these here woods."

Bobby grinned.

"Now, John," Hannon said, his face sweaty. "We don't want no trouble. The sheriff just wants you to come in peacefully."

"Then why'd he have to go and tell my poor mother, who's all upset now, and the damn newspapers that I'm wanted for murder without even asking for my side of the story?" John's jaw clenched. "Nobody in my family ever had trouble with the law. We're good neighbors and law-abiding citizens. You both know that."

"John . . . ," Barfield said.

"Shut up," John said. "I'm provoked. Bobby, take their guns and badges and bring 'em to me. I'll cover you. Don't see why they give these boys guns anyhow. They ain't never shot nothing with 'em. Couldn't hit a barn if they tried. Either one makes a move, I'll shoot 'em both."

"Don't talk like that," Hannon pleaded. "You know we got nothing personal against you, John. We're just doing our jobs."

Bobby picked up their weapons, then asked for their badges. Reluctantly, they turned them over.

"These tenderfoots act more like little girls than deputies," John said. "Wonder how far they'd get with no boots? Let's see. Take 'em off, boys."

"No. John! There's rattlesnakes out here," Barfield complained.

"And it's all muddy back the way we came," Hannon said.

"Quit whining and take 'em off."

They muttered as they hopped about and removed their boots. Bobby gleefully retrieved them.

"This ain't gonna help your situation, John," Hannon said. "Sheriff Baker ain't gonna like this."

"Then give him a message from me," Ashley said angrily. "Tell Sheriff Baker that if he sends any more chicken-hearted men with rifles out here, they're gonna get hurt. Now git."

"You got to give us our boots back, John," Barfield whimpered. "There's all kindsa snakes and stuff out here. We'd never make it back without getting snake-bit and blistered. We never done nothing to you."

"Oh, all right." John sighed. "Give 'em their boots back, Bobby."

Bobby looked disappointed. "You sure?"

"Yeah. Let 'em have 'em," John said, disgusted.

"Our badges too?" Barfield asked.

"Hell, no. I'm keeping them." John studied their pleading, sweat-stained faces for a long moment. "Hell, all right. Okay, I'll get 'em back to you, I promise. Just make sure you deliver my message. Now git the hell outta here. Now!"

The red-faced lawmen trotted back up the road the way they came, with over-the-shoulder glances, as though they feared being shot in the back. They weren't. But they heard the Ashley brothers' laughter ring out behind them.

As promised, the deputies' guns and badges were delivered by messenger to Sheriff Baker, a day later, along with a matchbox. Baker slid the small box open. There was a bullet inside with the name BAKER scratched on it.

John and Bobby thought it was funny.

Baker didn't. The threat, his inept deputies, and being humiliated by John Ashley infuriated him.

"I'll get that son of a bitch," he swore to a newspaper reporter. "I'll see him hang."

Surprised that the sheriff couldn't take a good-natured joke, John insisted he was innocent and accused Baker of harassment.

CHAPTER SEVENTEEN

The stranger was clearly down on his luck. His teeth were yellowed and tobacco-stained, his complexion pockmarked, and the soles of his battered, oversized shoes flapped as he scuffed along the dusty road. He didn't appear much older than thirty.

At first he saw no one at the Ashley place.

Joe and the boys had left hours ago to chop wood for the railroad. John was away, building a fishing camp in the Everglades, and Laura had gone to pick wild blackberries for pie. The quiet house gave Leugenia the chance to tidy up the kitchen after breakfast, start a soup stock for supper, and tackle some laundry. She sang hymns to herself as she worked.

The man rapped at the back door as she was about to carry the washboard and wringer out to the wash pot. She'd heat the water over a fire, soak the laundry, scrub it on the washboard, then boil, rinse, blue, starch, and wring it out. Then she'd hang it on the clothesline strung between two trees. When the laundry was dry, she'd carry it inside, sprinkle each piece with water, heat the iron on the stove, and iron them all.

Her hair, mostly gray now, was caught up in a bun and she wore an apron.

"Howdy, ma'am." He held a battered fedora in both hands and stared at his shoes when she opened the door.

"I was hoping you could spare a body a bite to eat. I'm hungry. Ain't had nothing for days, and somebody I met on the road said that good-hearted people lived here."

The mother of boys nearly his age, Leugenia's heart went out to him. Wandering tramps were nothing new nowadays, she thought sadly, and wondered what the world was coming to.

"I can always put together a little somethin'. Come on in." She opened the door wide. "Been on the road long?"

He nodded glumly. "Too long. Came in on a boxcar yesterday, looking for work. Still picking the cinders outta my eyes."

He inhaled deeply. The room still smelled of biscuits and breakfast bacon. His eyes and mouth both watered.

"I'll fix you a plate," she said. "The pump's right out there if you want to wash up."

She threw a couple of fresh eggs on the griddle, fried up some bacon, reheated the grits, and warmed several biscuits.

He wolfed most of them down before she could even get the sweet butter to the table. She kept up a motherly, running conversation and suggested that her husband might be able to help him find work with the railroad or on a friend's farm.

Focused on the food, he answered in monosyllables.

He cleaned the egg yolk off his plate with the last of the biscuits, drank the coffee she poured, then looked up expectantly.

He'd eaten so fast, she assumed he was still hungry.

"I can fix a few more eggs if you like."

"Please, ma'am." He gazed at her with grateful eyes. "Haven't had home cooking like this for more than two years."

She fixed and served the eggs. It did her heart good to see how he dug into them.

His belly full, his eyes began to roam the room and the rest of the house. He still looked hungry. The only sounds were the birds outside and Leugenia's soft humming as she worked. "You said your husband might know 'bout a job for me. Is he here?"

"He and my boys won't be back till dark," she said. "They're chopping wood for the railroad today." She was at the sink, her back to him.

"So you're all alone here, ma'am." It was more statement than question. He picked up his empty cup and plate and carried them to the sink.

"You don't have to do that." She looked up at him kindly. He stood a full foot taller than she did. "I'll clean up the table."

"So nobody else is here," he repeated. Something in his voice had changed.

The tone triggered something inside her when she heard it. For the first time, she felt fear. "Some of my kin might come by at any time," she said. His eyes make her voice shake. She looked away and picked up a dish towel. "Can I fix you anythin' else?"

"There is something else I ain't had for a long time." He touched the bib of her apron, licked his lips, then yanked it off over her head. "You can fix that."

She shrank back, but he roughly pulled her to him.

"Stop that," she said. "I have a husband and nine children, sons your age." Her words sounded resolute as though she were in control, but the terror in her eyes gave her away.

"That don't bother me none," he said, his voice husky. "They ain't here now, and a woman's a woman." He held her in an iron grip, fumbling with the buttons on her dress.

"No," she cried.

"Then take it off!" His eyes changed, glinted like steel, as she began to weep.

Impatient, he threw her to the floor and lifted her skirt. She tried to roll away, but he caught her by the hair, tore it from the bun with one hand, and hit her hard in the face with the other.

"Lord, have mercy," she cried. "Help me, Jesus." Tears streamed down her cheeks. He unzipped his trousers and she started to scream.

That excited him more. He took a knife from the drainboard, cut away her dress, and bit her breasts and neck with his yellowed teeth.

The more hysterical she was, the more violent he became. When she fought, he reached up for the plate he'd eaten from and smashed it across her face.

Laura, three-quarters of a mile away, picking blackberries, stood up straight and cocked her head. What was that? A cry? Impossible from that distance, but some sudden inner voice demanded she go back to the house. It was as though she'd heard an ominous crash of thunder, though the day was breezy and beautiful beneath a blue, cloud-scudded sky.

She picked up the basket of berries and walked briskly toward home. Soon she broke into a trot then, filled with deadly certainty, she dropped the basket and ran.

How foolish, she thought, panting as she dashed across an open field filled with wildflowers. How would she explain to Leugenia why she'd returned so soon without the berries? She hoped her future mother-in-law would not think her stupid, silly, or superstitious.

No sign of Leugenia out by the wash pot where she'd planned to scrub the boys' work shirts and britches. Laura scrambled up the front steps, breathing hard, then pushed open the door, which stood ajar.

"Lu? Leugenia?" The hair on the back of her neck tingled and chills prickled her arms despite the heat of the day. The familiar kitchen, a place of warmth, good food, and fellowship, smelled of sex, blood, and fear.

Laura found her in the hallway just beyond the kitchen, seated on the floor, her back to the wall, trembling and barely conscious, stark naked except for one shoe and a torn stocking. Her clothing and corset cover had been cut into bloody shreds around her.

Laura quickly covered her with a soft quilt, then whimpering, in a fury, she ran for the pearl-handled revolver John had given her. It was gone, along with John's guitar, Joe's radio, a pair of his boots, and most of the food in the icebox. The attacker had also taken Leugenia's wedding band, which she had not taken off her finger for thirty-five years. Laura dropped to the floor in Bobby's room, dragged his hunting rifle from under the bed, loaded it, then checked every room, every closet, every cupboard. Then she checked the barn. She knew she would kill him if she could find him, whoever he was. But the man who had violated Leugenia was gone. Laura cursed herself for not flying home the second she sensed trouble.

She locked the doors and windows, washed Leugenia, half carried her to bed, treated her injuries as best she could, then made her some tea.

Bobby, fourteen, arrived home first. He'd been fishing and carried a bucket full of perch and trout.

Laura met him at the door, gun in hand.

He looked bewildered. "Is that my rifle, Laura?"

"Yes, Bobby. I had to borrow it. Go to your brother John now, as fast as you can. Tell him he must come home at once. Your mother's been hurt. Tell him she's alive but injured."

"Shouldn't I run for the doctor first?" Bobby stared wide-eyed at the broken plate and blood spatters on the kitchen floor.

"No," Leugenia wailed from her bed.

"Go, now!" Laura avoided the boy's questions and sent him on his way, then went back to sit with Leugenia.

"It was a tramp. He was hungry and I fixed him a plate," she said, weeping. Her face was cut and swollen, her body battered and bruised.

Laura fixed cold compresses for her face and gave her whiskey for the pain. She feared it would take hours for John to arrive, but she soon heard boots on the porch. Rifle in hand, gritting her teeth, she threw the door open, saw him, lowered the gun, and burst into tears. "How did you get here so fast?"

John had experienced a dark premonition, a sense of something wrong, about the same time she had, and headed home. He met Bobby on the road.

"Where is she?" he demanded.

"Inside." Laura gestured toward the bedroom but restrained him. "Before you see her, John. Don't ask questions. I can tell you all you need to know. She gave me the man's description. She's embarrassed, hurt, and humiliated, and she loves you too much to have to talk to you about it."

John caught his breath and closed his eyes as she whispered the details.

"I couldn't tell Bobby," she said, her hand over her heart. "That's for you or his father to do."

Bobby, upset, curious, and confused about what had happened, was dispatched on another mission, to fetch his father and brothers.

John and Laura sat on either side of his mother, each holding her hand as he spoke with her briefly. "He took my wedding ring, Johnny," she said, her lips puffy and swollen. "What am I gonna tell your father?"

"He'll understand," Laura said gently. "It'll be all right."

John left the room, unable to speak, his handsome face as hard as stone, his eyes dark and frightening.

His father and brothers arrived a short time later. Joe broke down and wept, then armed himself. The atmosphere became incendiary as the men shouted, cursed, paced, and punched the wall. "Save that energy," John said, "and help me decide what to do."

"Florida's penalty for the crime is death," Bill said grimly. "They'll hang him."

"If he's not gone on another boxcar before the sheriff decides to send somebody up here from the county seat," Laura said.

"Sheriff Baker and his boys would laugh," John said bitterly. "They're after me. You want those sons of bitches to question Mama about what he did to her?"

"They'd joke about it. They'd say that we can't protect our women."
Joe's eyes streamed, his fists clenched. The boys, who had never seen
their father cry, became more agitated.

"Then we'll handle it ourselves," John said.

All but Bill agreed. "You're already in trouble, John. If you take the
law into your own hands, I want nothing to do with it. Don't want to
know about it. I have a wife to take care of."

"That's fair," John said stoically. "I'll go. I'm already wanted for murder, so it don't matter. I'll find him."

Relieved, Bill headed for the door. "Lucy's waitin'," he told the others.
"I'll have her come by tomorrow to help care for Mama."

John and Laura exchanged a glance. Each knew what the other
thought. "No need," Laura said sweetly. "Why burden Lucy with this? It
might upset or frighten her. I'll take good care of your mother."

"But Lucy's family, you're not." Bill bristled at his wife's exclusion.

"Laura *is* family." John fixed his eyes firmly on his brother. "And she
is right. Not a soul outside this room should know about this. Mama
would be mortified if people knew. What happened to her today didn't
kill her, praise Jesus, but that would. We need to protect her."

They all knew that Lucy, an inveterate gossip, would relish repeating
the story and would most likely embellish the already shocking details.

"It's ugly," Laura murmured. "Why burden your wife? If John takes
care of it, it's not as though our neighbors need to know for their own
protection."

"You're right," Bill said. "Thank you, Laura."

The men all swore to keep Leugenia's secret.

At the door, Bill turned. "If you do this, John, be careful. Make sure
you kill the right man."

"I will." The words were a solemn vow.

First he had to fight his father, and his brothers Frank, Ed, and even
Bobby. All insisted on going with him. "You can't stop us, John!" Ed
shouted, his thin face pinched, eyes red. "I'm going after him, with or
without you." Armed with his own rifle and a revolver, he pushed past
John, toward the door. The others joined him.

"We're tougher than any posse!" Joe yelled. "Let's go get him!"

"Hold it!" John caught Ed by the shoulder, wheeled him around, and
confronted the others, his back to the door.

Ed flailed and took a swing at John, who shoved him against the wall as they scuffled.

"This is our fight!" Frank said. "Our mother. Don't expect us to sit by."

"That's right!" Joe yelled.

"Wait." John held out his hands, palms up. "I'm the only one here who's in trouble. None of you ever had a run-in with the law. You need to keep your reputations clean for the good of the family. Sure, we all shoot better than any posse Sheriff Baker could put together, but if we all ride out of here hell-bent on the trail of this son of a bitch, it'll draw attention. That's the last thing we want. The bastard is armed; he took Laura's revolver. If we all start acting crazy, some of us could get shot. That animal has already hurt us enough. And you know, I always hunt best alone."

He urged them to guard the homestead till morning. If he had no luck, he promised, he'd come back then and turn them loose. He won the argument.

He carried a shovel with him when he rode out that night. The tramp would probably head back to the railroad yard to hop another southbound boxcar. He had a head start but probably believed he had more time since the Ashley men were not expected home until dark.

The manhunt didn't take long. John's hunting dog loped along beside him. The tramp, slowed down by the load he carried, was headed for the railroad yard.

Not far from there, John's dog alerted him to a stash of clothing and other items in the brush off the side of the road. John's guitar, Joe's radio, and food from their pantry.

John waited quietly until the man returned from checking out the boxcars in the railroad yard. He wore Leugenia's gold wedding band on his pinky and carried Laura's gun in his pocket. Joe's boots on his feet were a dead giveaway. His long, dirty fingernails, yellowed teeth, and pockmarked face, all described by Leugenia, sealed his fate.

John took no joy in what he had to do, even when the tramp wept and whined that it was Leugenia's fault. After all, she had invited him into the house. John didn't regret killing him as much as he regretted the death of DeSoto Tiger. Why should his mother be victimized again and humiliated by the law? Why should the family name be dragged through the mud and the newspapers any more than it already was because of him? Why should she have to face her attacker in a courtroom full of strangers? The law mandated death by hanging as the penalty for his crime. In this case it was correct.

The tramp was lucky, John decided. How much easier it is to die instantly from a bullet in the brain than to be hanged, kicking and jerking, at the end of a rope.

John sent the bastard to hell but knew he had to live with what he'd done. He buried the man deep, in a place where he would never be found.

John arrived home, hollow-eyed and sick at heart, shortly before dawn.

He put his guitar, the radio, Joe's boots, Laura's gun, and the food on the porch. Laura was awake, waiting in the shadows.

"Is it over?" she whispered.

He nodded, then avoided her eyes.

"Thank God." She asked no questions. "We should be thankful," she said, instead.

He lifted his pained eyes to hers in search of solace. "What for?"

"Your mother's life. If he'd killed her, we never would have known who or why . . . And that I found her, not Bobby. I'm so thankful for that."

He smelled the familiar fragrance of her hair and fought the urge to weep in her arms like a heartbroken child.

The door flew open. "John? Is that you?" It was his father, the boys right behind him. No one had slept.

"I have a ring to return," John whispered.

Joe gave him a questioning look.

"He won't be back," John said. He dug in his pocket and handed his mother's wedding ring to his father.

Joe sniffed loudly, then hugged his neck. "Thank you, son, I'll take it to her."

CHAPTER EIGHTEEN

Sheriff's deputies hunting for a dangerous fugitive visited the Ashley place three times over the next seven days.

They displayed a wanted poster for Daniel W. Moody, who had escaped from a Georgia prison after serving only two years of a life sentence. Now sought for the recent assault and murder of a woman outside Atlanta, he was last seen hopping a southbound freight. Moody was believed to be in Palm Beach. Several local sightings had been confirmed.

Laura again suppressed her revulsion and calmly studied the poster during the lawmen's third visit. "Haven't seen him, and I'm sure I won't," she said truthfully. "We don't get many strangers way out here."

The deputies dismounted anyway, tied up their horses, and prowled the property as they'd done before, eyes darting, guns at the ready, more vigilant and wary than a routine visit warranted.

The tallest deputy, who had introduced himself as T. W. Stone, asked again to speak to the lady of the house. Laura replied that Leugenia had gone out once more, to pick berries in the woods.

"She'll be so sorry she missed you," Laura lied.

Leugenia was actually in the house, still recovering. No need for her to view her attacker's picture now.

Stone frowned and warned again that womenfolk should stay close to their men until the escapee was run to ground. Speaking of the Ashley men, T. W. wondered aloud if Laura might share some information on John's whereabouts.

Laura said she hadn't seen him lately. That was true. It had been at least ten minutes since he kissed her goodbye and climbed into the barn loft, where he now lay prone, his rifle barrel trained on Deputy T. W. Stone, his index finger on the trigger. How easy it would be to kill Stone, to put a bullet through his heart at that distance. But he did not.

John learned later that the posse also visited his brother Bill's place three or four times. Bill was always away, but T. W. Stone and Lucy spoke each time. John's neighbors said they'd only been visited once, some not at all. Baker's men were using the Georgia fugitive as a pretext, to snoop around the Ashley homesteads in search of John, who had no interest in shooting them, especially with his family in the cross fire. He finally retreated to his Everglades fishing camp, where Laura joined him two days later.

He unburdened his troubled mind as they lay together in bed. "This isn't what I planned," he said. "I want our life, the one in Miami. But it ain't possible with my picture hanging in the post office under the word *Wanted.*"

She sighed sympathetically and nuzzled his shoulder. Her black hair hung long and loose.

"I love Florida." He wrapped his arm around her waist. "We're a native son and daughter. Everything and everybody I love is here. But my family's embarrassed, and Mama's upset that I got Bobby involved. We meant no harm, didn't hurt anybody. Didn't know Sheriff Baker had no sense of humor. The man wants me dead, but I ain't ready to hang yet, not when I have you."

"What are you saying, John?" Propped up on one elbow, her right breast exposed, she searched his eyes for the answer.

"This all might blow over if I left for a while," he said. "Miami's memory is short. Some blame the Florida sun. Whatever it is, people here forget faster. Baker could lose his job or leave town. Then I could just ease back in and square things."

"You'd leave Florida?" Her eyes were wide.

He nodded.

"I'm going home," she said, and folded her arms around him.

His heart sank.

She smiled. "Ain't no home for me without you, John."

His eyes flashed fire. "You'd come with me, Laura?"

"Never told you a thing I didn't mean. Never will, John."

"It ain't right to ask you to run from the law with me."

"I sure as hell wouldn't let you run without me."

PART FIVE

CHAPTER NINETEEN

John had already been ambushed that night. Once was enough. What was this? He considered the possibilities.

Lucy still had a key. He scanned the neighborhood for her red Mustang. With all its extra chrome, flashy wheels, and the Cuban flag that dangled from her rearview mirror, her ride, like its driver, was hard to miss.

He didn't see it, but that didn't mean she wasn't there. However, if she was trashing his apartment, it was unlike her to do it in the dark. Stealth was not her style. She'd throw his things off the balcony with every light blazing.

The intruder was most likely from the department. Why? What they might find or steal was not as worrisome as what they might plant.

Or perhaps he or she was waiting for him there in the dark. While he pondered the thought, he called the medical examiner's office, identified himself, reported a fatal police-related shooting and asked for a medical examiner at the hotel scene. He did the same with the crime scene techs. No one had been notified, just as he'd suspected. He called Jeff Burnside, a reporter at Channel Six News, the NBC-TV affiliate. Burnside answered, awake and alert, said he'd call a cameraman and head up there.

Then he called Robby. "Hey," he said. "Did you take Laura to my apartment?"

"Hell no, John. You wanted her safe. Your apartment, or wherever you are, is probably the hottest spot in town right now."

"You can say that again, bro." He told Robby everything. "I'm relieved of duty, have to go in at eleven tomorrow."

"Be careful, John. Don't go without a lawyer."

"I've got a more pressing problem. Somebody's in my apartment with a flashlight."

"If they had a legit search warrant," Robby said, "the lights would be on while they tore the place up, and you'd see their vehicles downstairs."

"Don't see 'em, and I doubt they could get a search warrant this quick, even if they thought they had probable cause."

"You still armed, bro?"

"Yeah, though the way things are going, I probably need to invest in a few new weapons."

"I've got a couple, unregistered, serial numbers filed off, if you need 'em."

"Robby, Robby, we need to talk about what they're teaching you at the county. I'll pretend I didn't hear that."

"Whatcha gonna do?"

"What any citizen should. Call nine-one-one and report a burglary in progress."

He did but didn't stay to watch the fun. He distanced himself instead, drove to Bayfront Park, and roamed the dark on foot until he spotted Leon and three other homeless people sharing a pizza. John made eye contact, circled back toward the Boulevard, and waited at the bronze statute of pioneer Julia Tuttle, the mother of Miami. Recently dedicated, more than a hundred years late, the city had, at long last, honored the woman who persuaded Henry Flagler to extend his railroad to the small, swampy settlement by sending him fresh orange blossoms during a bitter northern winter freeze. The rest was history. It usually takes a long time for Miami politicians to do the right thing. Most often they never do it at all, John thought. He studied Julia Tuttle's strong, expressive face until Leon strolled up alone ten minutes later.

"Whatta ya know, pal?" John said. "See any familiar faces when you looked at the police ID photos?"

"Thought I saw 'em both, Johnny. But nobody wanted to hear it . . . Didn't take me seriously. Could be how I was dressed or that I don't have a permanent address or phone."

"What did you see?"

"The female shooter from the lobby, picture looked maybe six, seven years old. Had less mileage on 'er, less weight, different hairstyle. But it was her. Man who showed 'em to me said, 'Oh, can't be her. She's an Officer Friendly, assigned to a Kendall middle school.' Then I saw two who coulda been her partner. Saw one I was pretty sure was him, till I saw the other. They got to be brothers, twins, or first cousins. Must have the same last name, a common one, 'cuz there was only three, four pictures between 'em. Couldn't nearly tell 'em apart, 'cept one had a little different hairline in front. When I started flipping back and forth trying to see the difference between 'em, they like to close the book on it, copped the attitude that if I wasn't absolutely one hundred percent positive, it couldn't be neither one. Hada be one of the two, Johnny."

"Lots of families have uncles, brothers, fathers, and cousins in the same department," John said.

"Didn't have no names or badge numbers on the pictures, but they do have an ID number across the bottom," Leon said. "I got all three." He winked and focused his crooked smile on John.

"Where?" John took his notebook from his pocket.

Leon's grin grew larger. "Right here," he said, and tapped his temple three times with a gnarled right index finger. "Safest hiding place in the world."

"Shoot," John said hopefully.

Leon rattled off three six-digit numbers without hesitation.

"You're sure?" John asked, as he wrote them down.

Leon nodded.

"Their faces? On a scale of one to ten."

"Her? Nine and three-quarters."

"Him?"

"That it's one of the two? Nine point nine nine nine."

"Good. I've got something for you." He handed Leon one of the cell phones in a brown paper bag.

"I may call, might need you," John said, as Leon examined it. "Don't know who I can trust, except my brothers—and you. You've never steered me wrong. I could be in a real jackpot this time." He told him everything.

Leon listened, his grin fading into a grave expression. "What about her, Johnny?" he finally asked. "This Laura. You trust her?"

"With my life," he said. "I feel as though I've known her forever. I left Lucy, my fiancée, right after I met her."

"Your instincts are good," Leon said, "but beware the woman scorned, Johnny. Nothin's meaner. She can be dangerous."

Sounded good to John. If the intruder at his place was Lucy, he could live with that. She could cut up his clothes, slash his sofa, flood his bathroom. He wouldn't be happy, but it was better than the alternatives.

"It don't sound good, Johnny. But I won't letcha down."

"There's a charger in there," John said. "You've got five hundred minutes. You can use it for local and long distance. You might want to use it to reach out to family."

Leon's eyes were bright, the whites shot with red lightning bolts, but he didn't react.

"It needs an overnight charge. Can you do that?"

"Sure, Johnny. Little lady who works at Starbuck's 'ill help me out. Then I can probably plug it in once in a while over at the Salvation Army."

"Stay in touch." John scribbled his new cell number on a scrap of paper.

Leon read the number once, then shoved the paper in his pocket. "You can count on me, Johnny." Then he wandered off into the night.

John went home. Lights blazed in his apartment. Two empty patrol cars sat out front. The bubble machine atop one splashed eerie red and blue shadows across the building's facade.

He went to his apartment and feigned surprise at the manager and several patrolmen roaming about inside. He joined them. No sign of vandalism. Damn. It wasn't Lucy.

The manager, a rotund retiree named Miguel, wore pajama pants and a T-shirt. "Looks like a burglar got in, John," he said, sweaty and concerned, his brow furrowed. "A neighbor called the police, must be somebody on this floor. Sorry. I called the station, but you weren't there."

The two patrolmen looked friendly and engaged.

"Hey, Sarge," said a veteran named Melnick. "When they said it was your place, we got cars out here fast. Almost got 'im. Was inside when we pulled up. Saw his flashlight from the street. Came in, ready to boogie, but he was gone. Think he used your balcony to let himself down to the one below, forced the door, walked through an unoccupied apartment and down the stairs to the street, right past our cars. By the time Rivera starts chasing him, he's already around the corner. Couldn't find the son of a bitch. Musta had a car waiting."

"Description?" John said.

"Not much. Latin male, six feet, dark color T-shirt, jeans, sneakers. Nobody got a good look. Streetlight out there's busted, it's pretty dark, but a passerby got a quick glimpse as he ran by. Saw a gun in his belt, looked like a large caliber, chrome finish, and he was carrying a dark gym bag. Miguel here says there haven't been any other break-ins in the building lately. Wanna take a quick inventory? Check to see you're not missing any weapons? That's the important thing. Looks like your electronics, flat-screen TV, DVD are all here." His eyes roved John's living room.

John wished he'd confronted the SOB himself. Had he done that, the intruder would be dead or he'd be the one leaking into his own carpet, but at least he'd know who shot him. He didn't believe in coincidence. No random burglar stumbled into his apartment. He came to kill me, John thought. But if he had set up an ambush, in the dark, why would he use a flashlight? If he was looking for Laura, he didn't need it to see she wasn't here.

No, he thought, the intruder came to plant something. His gun cabinet was still double-locked. He opened it. Nothing missing, but something had been added. He closed the door, before the two cops caught a glimpse.

"Want us to send out a burglary detective?" Melnick asked helpfully.

"Sure," John said. "Have one call me tomorrow."

"If you find anything missing, make a list we can add to the report for insurance purposes," Melnick said.

They seemed disappointed that he didn't take his place apart as they watched. Maybe they wanted to be helpful. Maybe he was paranoid. Maybe not.

No sign of forced entry meant the intruder was a pro at picking locks—or had a set of keys. Too late tonight to change the locks.

The cops left, and he got rid of Miguel. Once he was alone, John drew the shades, then rechecked his gun safe. Where he had left two weapons, there were now three. A nine millimeter he had never seen before, recently fired, hadn't been cleaned. It had surely been used in a crime. The medical examiner had identified the weapon that killed Ron Jon Eagle as a nine millimeter.

He knocked back two shots of Jack Daniel's Black and began to think more clearly. He shot photos of the gun, close-ups of the serial number, then, careful not to touch it, put it in a FedEx box, addressed it to Robby, and drove out to drop it in a box at four a.m. The next pickup was at nine a.m.

At five a.m. he called Robby for Laura's new cell number. She answered instantly.

"I knew it was you, John." She sounded sultry. "It's about time."

"What are you wearing?"

She laughed with the easy freedom of a young girl, without a hint of fear after all that had happened. She was comfortable, she said, but sorely needed, missed, and wanted him. He didn't ask where she was.

They talked for more than an hour. By the time they said goodbye, he felt relaxed enough to catch a few hours' sleep.

He slept soundly for three-and-a-half hours, then awoke refreshed and ready. He showered, dressed, and headed for the station. He'd committed no crime, he told himself, had never jeopardized a case or betrayed the badge.

What's the worst they can do to me? he thought.

CHAPTER TWENTY

What's the worst they could do to me? he thought, again, on the way to the station.

He came up with a number of answers. None pretty.

Emma's was the first face he saw on the fifth floor. Small and prim, she had pale, lined skin, a tiny scarlet mouth, and big, sad eyes under half glasses. A civilian secretary, she'd been a fixture in Homicide for as long as he could remember.

"Good morning, John." She seemed to be fighting tears. A widow, she had a good heart and no surviving children. Her job was her life, her coworkers her family. He liked her, always had. Was she distressed about a personal problem? The job? Or could it be him?

"How's it going, Emma?"

She looked away quickly and blew her nose loudly. Uh-oh, he thought. She shifted folders on her desk and did not look up.

The blinds in the lieutenant's glass-enclosed office were drawn. He couldn't see everyone inside, but it looked crowded. He thought he glimpsed Jo Salazar, his favorite prosecutor. Her presence seemed positive. He'd consulted her on the Eagle case. He considered her a friend, smart and fair, a good woman.

Ten minutes early, he itched to go to his desk to check his mail and messages, as usual. But that might seem inappropriate. So he took a seat, like a visitor, watched the lieutenant's door, and waited to be summoned.

The door finally opened. Jo Salazar emerged alone, her face red.

"Hey." He got to his feet and smiled.

For the first time in all the years they had worked together, she didn't smile back. They were a kick-ass team. He had been to her home for pool parties and barbecues with her husband and kids. She understood cops. She'd worn the badge herself, back when female recruits had to be as tough as men to survive the academy, before standards were relaxed to the point that, in a city surrounded by water, cops no longer had to know how to swim. Cop by day, she'd studied law at night to fight crime in courtrooms instead of on the streets. They shared a mutual respect. So why did his good friend and colleague look at him now as though he were a dog that just bit her?

"Hello, Sergeant." Her voice sounded husky. She wore the suit she always wore when asking a jury to deliver a guilty verdict. The suit was dark. Her expression matched.

"What's with 'Sergeant'?" he asked. "What happened to John?"

Her warm brown eyes were distant. "I thought I knew you, John," she said softly. "I can't talk to you. I'm sorry. The best, and the only, advice I can give you is to hire a lawyer. A damn good defense attorney. Do it now."

She walked briskly away. Struck by the weight of her words and the gravity in her eyes, he felt his future fade with the departing click of her high heels.

How bad could this be? He had no idea.

"Wait a minute, Jo." He followed her. "Captain Politano ambushed and tried to kill me and our witness. I fired in self-defense. If you were told anything different, it's a lie."

She shook her head, did not look at him, and punched the elevator button. He would have boarded with her, but just then the lieutenant's office door swung open. Inside, John saw the Internal Affairs captain, the shooting team lieutenant, a court reporter, a major, an assistant chief, and the city attorney.

Lieutenant Myerson beckoned to him. John knew him well enough to recognize his smile as false. He had a liar's eyes, and despite looking as though he hadn't slept, he exuded a cocky confidence.

As John walked toward them a hangman's noose appeared in his mind's eye. What am I doing? he asked himself. My best friend in this dog fight just warned me to get a lawyer. Now. Robby had said the same thing. Time to listen up and lawyer up.

"Hey, guys." He tried to look self-assured. "I guess you all want to take my statement, right?"

Their hungry smiles made his decision. They looked like vampires at a blood bank. He checked his watch, frowned, and glanced over his shoulder, looking for a ghost. "My lawyer should be here by now," he lied, and watched their faces fall. "He must be waiting for me downstairs. I'll run down to check. Be right back."

He walked casually out of the office. As he passed Emma's desk, she spoke, without looking up. "Sergeant, I *have* to talk to you. Meet me in fifteen, at Macy's on Flagler, in the lingerie department."

Did he hear right? "Sure," he murmured. "See you there." Without slowing his pace, he went on to the elevator.

Macy's? Lingerie department? Am I crazy or is she?

He nearly passed on it. Lord knows he had other things to do, some of them urgent, but that tiny woman, treated by most detectives as though she were invisible, was no fool. They were friends. When she had no car, he'd volunteer to drive her home, especially when she was called in at night to transcribe statements needed in a hurry.

He had a head start and arrived first. Twice, saleswomen approached him as he perused bras, wired, padded, and apparently inflated, or molded from foam rubber. Racks and racks of bras, acres of them, resembled water wings; they could stand on their own. Women wearing them could be swept off ships in the mid-Atlantic and never sink. There were tiny panties to match, slinky nightgowns, and flowing robes. Like a drowning man, John saw his life flash before his eyes. His reputation was down the toilet, his career and pension circling the drain. He might soon be charged with a major crime. Yet there he stood, in Macy's lingerie department, fantasizing about how a lacy camisole with silk ribbons and a built-in bra would look on Laura.

He blinked, tried to clear his head, and decided to call Joel Hirschhorn. As he checked his wallet for the number, he saw Emma's solemn little face, dyed red hair, and big, sad eyes.

They walked to an empty corner near the elevator. "I'm so glad you're here." She sounded breathless.

"Why here?"

"Because"—she looked surprised—"we can't be seen together. And there's no bakery, coffee, donut, or bagel shop that won't have a police officer walk in at any moment."

Her eyes roved nervously, as though she feared SWAT marksmen with laser-sighted high-powered rifles were positioned behind every display. "But remember? You were hunting a fugitive once and told me that sometimes"—her voice dropped to a whisper—"the best place to hide is in plain sight." The corners of her small red mouth turned up. "I never forgot a thing you told me. I'd write them down at night, after I went home. Plain sight." She gestured at the racks of intimate items. "Yet no man in our department, and very few female officers, will ever walk in here."

"How can I help you, Emma?" He sounded weary.

"You can't!" she said fervently. "I'm here to help you. Thank God you didn't talk to them! The court reporter was late, so they called me in early." She paused to stare into his eyes. "They even took a statement from your girlfriend."

He blinked, mind reeling. "Who?"

"Lucy, Detective Dominguez," she said. "And your partner."

"They talked to J. J.?"

"And," she raised an eyebrow, "that young man from Ron Jon Eagle's law office, the one who came in and identified the body."

"Lonstein?" Why him? John wondered.

"Sergeant," Emma said, "you're my only real friend." She began to tear up.

"You have lots of friends, Emma."

"No. You were the only one from the department who came to my husband's funeral after I worked there for twenty-seven years. I'll never forget that. It's why I'm taking this risk." Again, her voice dropped to a whisper, her eyes darted both ways, like those of a child about to bolt across a forbidden intersection. "Lieutenant Myerson gave his statement too."

"And?" Made sense. He was among the first responders after he called in the shooting.

"The lieutenant said"—Emma spoke slowly and distinctly—"that he spoke to Captain Politano as they left the station last night. The captain was upset, he said, about you. Said his last words were 'Ashley's off the reservation, and I'm gonna find out what the hell he's up to.' He said you'd been told to lodge your witness at a certain hotel but didn't. He checked and found you'd taken her somewhere else instead.

"The lieutenant said he offered to go check it out himself, then urged the captain to give it to Internal Affairs, but the captain said he didn't want to write you up until he knew for sure what was going on. It was on his way home, he said, so he'd find out himself." She paused, out of breath, as he stared in disbelief. "John, they say the captain confronted you, you two argued, and you shot him."

"Did he mention the part where the captain broke into the witness's room through a window, waited in the dark, dressed like a goddamn ninja, in a black hood and gloves, and opened fire on us when we walked in?"

She shook her head solemnly. "A hood? None of that came up. Lieutenant Myerson said evidence shows that the captain tried to defend himself, got off some shots, but was killed. He got emotional. Said he saw the captain's body and knew 'It coulda been me lying there.'"

The news, the magnitude of the lies, staggered John, as he tried to explain. "The captain suggested I take Laura to the hotel in Doral."

She frowned. "You didn't trust him?"

"I didn't trust anybody. My job was to keep the witness safe. The fewer people who knew where she was, the better."

"I could lose my job for this," Emma whispered. "But I know you, John. I don't believe what they're saying. But you're in big trouble." Her words sounded accusatory.

"I am, Emma. But it's easily explained and straightened out. I swear, I did nothing wrong."

"But what about the Indian?" Her eyes misted. "Why did you shoot Ron Jon Eagle?"

"What? That's crazy. Eagle's my case, Emma! You know that. I'm trying to solve it along with the murder of Summer Smith, the dead girl in the Dumpster. Lucy knows. She'll confirm that we were together on the beach for more than an hour before Eagle's boat came flying ashore. There's no way I could have had anything to do with that." He heard his own words and wondered. Did he protest too much? Deny too vigorously? Did he sound like Officer Mona Stratton?

"Lucy gave a statement," Emma said. "I took it down verbatim. It broke her heart because you two are engaged, she said, but she had to tell the truth under oath. She couldn't give you an alibi, doesn't know where you were. Said she fell asleep on the beach and you might have been gone, had access to other boats, before Eagle came ashore."

"Lies," he said helplessly. "How can she say that?"

"Think this will break you two up?" Emma asked sadly.

"We're not engaged," he said. "We called it off."

"Well." Emma's eyelashes fluttered, her expression dubious. "She didn't mention that. She was wearing your ring. Couldn't miss it, kept twirling it on her finger during her statement."

He sighed. "Believe me, Emma. I called it off the other night. She didn't want to give the ring back, so I said keep it."

Emma fell silent for a moment. "There's something else." Her eyes watered.

What now? he wondered.

"The lieutenant and Captain Paulson from IA agreed that you should have taken yourself off Eagle's case, transferred it to another team, because of bad blood between you and the victim."

"Bad blood?" John rolled his eyes. "Sure, I busted him years ago. He deserved it; it was a righteous bust. How was I to know about all his connections? They immediately unarrested him, but Eagle had an ego. Stayed pissed off forever. I was pissed too, for about twenty minutes, then didn't give a damn. Literally. But the Indian wouldn't quit. Wanted to hang me." His last four words reverberated like an echo in his head. *Wanted to hang me. Wanted to hang me.* Was he losing it?

"I was a rookie, still on probation, but he couldn't hurt me, because I generated some good press for the department, which, as we both know, is rare."

"I remember," Emma said, "that lovely English girl . . ."

He nodded. "I didn't care about Eagle one way or the other, but I am the right man to work his case because I knew him, his lifestyle, and what he was capable of doing. Had he been a suspect, sure, somebody else should have handled it so he couldn't appeal a conviction on grounds that he was framed by a detective with a grudge. But Eagle was a victim, Emma. Why hand off the case?"

"They say you killed him as payback for an old feud."

"Payback?" He looked her straight in the eye. "That man wasn't even a blip on my radar. How many homicides did I work after that? I was too busy. He never crossed my mind."

"The young man from his office—"

"Lonstein?"

She nodded. "Said Eagle had an enemies list with you at the top. And your witness, that beautiful girl?"

"Laura?" His stomach flipped when he said her name.

She nodded. "J. J. and Lucy both swore that it obviously wasn't your first hello. You weren't strangers. You two knew each other before he caught her fleeing to the airport."

"I never laid eyes on Laura till the day Eagle was killed. She didn't 'flee.' She was going home." How and when had it all become so twisted?

Emma bit her lower lip. "I shouldn't tell you this. They're asking for a search warrant based on info from a CI who says you have the murder weapon, the gun used to kill Eagle."

He sighed. "Of course, I don't." Only because he had addressed it to his brother and dropped it in a FedEx box.

"You were walking into a minefield this morning," Emma said. "I was so relieved when you left."

"I won't forget this, Emma. I'm grateful. I'll never admit we talked."

"Please don't." She looked frightened. "I'd be arrested for interfering with an investigation, to say nothing of losing my job and pension. But I believe you, John. And I'm grateful to you. You've always been a good friend when I needed one."

They kept moving as they talked and were now back in the lingerie department. She must have seen him looking at the lacy camisole again. "Don't use a credit card, Sergeant."

He looked at that tiny, lonely, and wise little woman with new eyes.

"Remember," she warned, "what you always say about leaving paper trails."

She's right, he thought. He had to change his thinking, pay attention to his own words. What he knew about finding fugitives might help him survive as one, should it come down to that.

"The prosecutor, Salazar," Emma said. "She fought for you, but they finally convinced her that you're guilty. They even questioned whether Laura's alive or if you killed her too, because she knew too much."

"For Pete's sake, Emma. She's a witness I protected, but I do care for her. The first time we saw each other . . . It's why I called off the engagement. Laura came to Miami to work, met Eagle through another model, then he was killed. I met her that day. That's it."

"Lucy's story is so different." Emma face scrunched up as though wondering what to believe.

Leon was right. Beware the woman scorned.

"Keep your ears open," John said. "You kept me from making a huge mistake. Knowledge is power, and what I know now, thanks to you, puts everything in a new light."

"God bless, John. You know how to reach me."

He took the escalator, and she boarded the elevator to the first floor. They left through different exits, onto different streets. He walked beneath a blazing sun back to the parking lot where he'd left his car. He'd backed it into a space, so the tag wasn't visible from the street. Not enough.

A black-and-white was pulled up into the lot. The patrolman was looking at his license tag and speaking to the parking attendant.

John turned to walk the other way and saw a second patrol car coming east, in his direction.

He had to think fast. His survival instinct kicked in and he thought clearly. First he had to disappear off this street, then find Laura. He felt elation, almost relief, as though this was what he'd been waiting for all his life. Somehow he'd always known this day would come. Time to run. He felt as though he had done it before.

PART SIX

CHAPTER TWENTY-ONE

John and Laura left Palm Beach two nights later, giddy with anticipation about the adventure ahead. Their departure was bittersweet.
Leugenia wept. Joe's eyes grew shiny. Bobby begged to go with them, to
no avail.

"There comes a time when the wind shifts," John told Laura that
night they took to the road. "And this is it, girl. No regrets, no fear of
the future, we'll just live for the moment. Today is all we need."

The road led to New Orleans. They gave themselves new names.
John found work on a fishing boat and quickly advanced to captain.
They fell in love with music like none they'd ever heard before. He
played guitar, they sang, and they grew to love Cajun food and an entirely new and different lifestyle.

New Orleans wasn't home, but it was the next best thing— until
Mardi Gras.

They danced with abandon in the street, lost in the music, high on
the moon and the moment. Which was why, though they now answered
to other names, both responded to shouts out of the crowd: "John! John
Ashley! Hey, Laura!"

They wheeled around and saw familiar faces from their past. Henry
Choice Price, Georgia cotton planter, wartime blockade runner, Florida
orange grower, and Miami hotelier. Price bobbed, as big as life, a swimmer in a sea of revelry. He called again, waving enthusiastically. His
wife beamed and clung to his arm, mouthing a friendly greeting they
couldn't hear above the noise. She waved as well.

"Look," Laura said, eyes alight. "Look who's here!"

John took her elbow and steered her away, submerging them both in
the tidal wave of partyers.

"What are you doing?" She resisted for only an instant.

"Don't look," he said in her ear. "No. Don't look back. He knows. They've seen the posters, the newspapers. They'll remember any minute now. The man loves to talk. He won't stop. Neither will she. Back in Miami, they'll blab their brains out about where they saw us."

She only partially heard his words in the din around them but knew he was right. They rushed back to their room, careful they weren't followed, quickly packed up what little they had, and departed before dawn.

They headed to the north country, to Washington State, as far from Florida as one can go. He worked aboard a timber cruiser in a logging camp outside Seattle. Harriet and Langley—their new assumed names—lived as husband and wife. Far away, still free after nearly two years, they sent occasional postcards and letters home, signed with assumed names and no return address.

Neither acknowledged the magnetic pull of that wild and sultry peninsula where they were born. Aside from each other, all they loved dwelt there. Laura ached for news of her children. John missed the camaraderie of his close-knit family and the peace of mind he had always found in Florida's lusty subtropical wilderness.

One night, after weeks of chilly rain without a single patch of blue in gloomy skies, Laura finally said what they both felt. She stood at the wet, rain-streaked window and shivered, a light blanket around her shoulders. "I can't see the moon, not a single star," she said in a small, mournful voice. "Haven't seen 'em in weeks. It's like we're in a gray sea, lost in the world."

John nodded. "Nobody here or in N'Orleans tried to kill me, run me to ground, or throw me in jail. We're free as birds, thousands of miles from home, but oh God, Laura, I miss it."

She touched his hand, her eyes wet. "Me too."

"I don't call this living." He paced the small, narrow room. "It's just existing. I want our Miami lives, all the plans we made. I'm no murderer, Laura. I'd be acquitted if I went back to face the charge. They couldn't convict me for something I didn't do!" He turned to her, his face alight. "If there is any justice, I'd walk outta that courtroom a free man! Nobody could touch us then, not even Baker! We'd be free to live our lives. What a fool I was, Laura. I never should have let him run us out of Florida."

He quit pacing to face her. "If I went back, would you stand with me?"

She laughed, a glorious sound that made him proud. "Will the sun rise in the morning?"

He cut his eyes at the rain-streaked windows. "Don't think so, dar-lin', not in this neck of the woods."

They laughed together. "But"—she hugged him—"the sun *will* rise in Florida, every day, no doubt about it."

"I *need* blue sky," he said passionately. "Let's go find it, girl."

He dispatched a message for his father to deliver to Sheriff Baker: *John Ashley is ready to turn himself in and clear his name.* Joe hired a West Palm Beach lawyer to negotiate his son's safe surrender. John made only one request. Since he was coming in voluntarily, like a gentleman, he asked that he not be handcuffed like a common criminal. Sheriff Baker agreed.

Spirits high, John and Laura made the long journey east, then boarded a southbound train. Gravity pulled them home. He felt no fear and regretted running. "Had I stayed and gone to trial," he repeated more than once, "it would be over, and by now we'd be home, in Miami."

John never denied that he shot DeSoto Tiger but insisted it was self-defense. There were no eyewitnesses. The evidence was circumstan-tial. Sure, he sold the otter pelts in Miami. On an errand there anyway, he knew it was where they'd bring the best price. He intended to have his brother Bill, a friend of the Indians, deliver the proceeds to Tiger's widow, along with the bad news. No jury would convict him. He was sure of that.

Their first sight of Florida's flat, unearthly landscape with its miracle of light in a sky filled with bright birds and low-hanging clouds sent Laura into a paroxysm of hiccups and happy laughter. "We're going home! We're finally going home!" Radiantly happy, her skin luminous, she glowed, far more beautiful than he had ever seen her. He'd never loved her more.

"What are you thinking, John?" She held his arm tight.

"I wish," he whispered in her ear, "that we could draw curtains around these seats so I could jump you right here."

Her laughter made other passengers smile, convinced that the handsome young pair so much in love must be newlyweds on their honeymoon. "We'll be there soon," she whispered.

"But you know my family," he said plaintively. "We won't even have five minutes alone before I have to . . ."

They disembarked north of Palm Beach to quietly make their way south to the Ashley homestead. But Laura tugged at John's sleeve as he made travel arrangements.

"Isn't that a hotel over there?"

He nodded.

"I think," she said, "that we need to take a room."

He looked puzzled.

"I need to lie down for a while."

"Didn't know you were that tired, darlin'." He looked concerned.

"I'm not."

His entire demeanor changed. With springs in their steps and smiles on their faces, they turned to walk toward the hotel.

He swept her up and carried her across the threshold into their small, comfortable room. "Hello, little girl," he said in his sweet, soft drawl, as he kicked the door shut behind him. "Know how much I love you?" He set her down gently on the bed.

"Show me." She unfastened the waistband and kicked off her skirt, which slipped gracefully to the carpeted floor.

He loosened his tie. "What do you want, little girl?"

"Everything, Daddy," she answered in a breathless baby voice.

He unbuckled his belt and took a deep breath. "That's a tall order, but I'm up to the job." He glanced thoughtfully at the leather belt in his hands. "Have you been a bad little girl?"

"I'm about to be."

"Well, I may have to whup your backside with this belt to teach you a lesson."

"All right, Daddy, but if you do," she purred, "I'll be really, really bad—"

He smiled fondly.

"—and have to break that fancy glass lamp up the side of your head and smash that pretty wooden chair across your kneecaps, then set fire to the bed." She smiled sweetly.

He gingerly set the belt down on the dresser and backed away from it. "Only a passing thought, sweetheart."

"I thought so, darlin'." She opened her arms.

Strangers who heard their laughter down the hall smiled and looked wistful.

Later he kissed her throat. "In Miami we'll have beautiful daughters like you and a son I'll teach to shoot like me."

"I'm so happy," she whispered, her arms around his neck.

He smiled down into her eyes. "We're doing the right thing, girl. This can't be wrong."

They arrived home late the following day and enjoyed a thirty-six-hour family reunion. Then John kissed and hugged Laura and his mother and promised, "It'll all be over soon." He went, with his father and the lawyer, to the prearranged surrender site near the Ashley family home.

Alone and shirtless, hands in the air, John stepped into a clearing and approached the waiting deputies. They honored his request and used no handcuffs.

The sheriff's son, Deputy Robert C. Baker, was now the Palm Beach jailer. John was a model prisoner, helpful, agreeable, and eager to clear his name. Young Baker's priority was to please his father. The sheriff's thin-lipped son was a small, intense man. He favored well-pressed dark suits, ties, and stiff starched collars despite the steamy climate. His odd stare, beneath shaggy dark eyebrows, revealed the whites of his eyes beneath the pupils. Behind his back, his prisoners and his father's other deputies called him Crazy Eyes, a hated childhood nickname he could not shake.

John never expected to spend months in a small jail cell awaiting trial. Free to roam the outdoors for his entire life, he found confinement excruciating. Worse, young Baker had established his own set of rules. One was to make jailhouse visits available only to a prisoner's lawyer, blood relatives, and legal spouse. Laura was excluded.

"A rule's a rule," Baker said. "No exceptions."

Every day she stood in a doorway across the street so John could see her from the small, high window in his cell. His trial date could not come soon enough for him. When it did, at last, in June, he wore his good white suit and eagerly took the witness stand.

On the water, in the canoe, DeSoto Tiger wanted whiskey, John said. He refused, but Tiger demanded it. John testified that he carried only a small flask and knew it would never be enough. Tiger, he said, threatened him. Pointed a weapon at his head at close range, his finger on the trigger. John said he fired in self-defense, a single shot that knocked Tiger overboard.

John's extended family attended every day of the trial, as did scores of friends and neighbors. He was able to talk to Laura face-to-face during brief court recesses. The family felt optimistic; newspaper coverage was favorable. One reporter described John as "calm, well spoken, and well dressed."

Hopes soared as the case went to a twelve-man jury. If found not guilty, he'd walk free from the courtroom. A knock from the jurors signaled that they'd reached a decision. Excitement mounted. It was July third, 1914, the day before the county's big Fourth of July celebration.

Lawyers rushed to the courthouse. The defendant was marched in. Spectators crowded the room, the building, and spilled into the street outside, anticipating a victory party. Friends brought firecrackers to set off if John was acquitted.

But the decision the jury had reached was that they could not agree. Nine voted to acquit. Three to convict. None would budge.

The judge declared a mistrial.

He explained, to the shock and dismay of the bewildered defendant and his loved ones, that John would have to remain in jail until a new trial was scheduled. Perhaps then, the judge said, a new jury would agree on a verdict. Women wept. The men were furious. Instead of leaving together, John and Laura exchanged heartbroken looks as he was taken back to the jail.

John, now twenty-seven, counted the days, nights, and brief glimpses of Laura standing across the street for another four months. The new trial was set for November 1914.

The prosecution and defense attorneys began jury selection before

Circuit Judge H. P. Branning. Every potential juror questioned seemed to know John or his family. "I never met a more mannerly or nicer young man in my life," one swore. "He always has a smile, a helping hand, and a pleasant word," said another. And so it went.

Prosecutor John C. Gramling fumed and quickly used all twelve of his peremptory challenges to dismiss jurors who seemed biased in John's favor.

The defense attorney did not use a single challenge. He had no reason to do so. Unseasonably hot, the day dragged on. Fans fluttered in rows of spectators. By late afternoon, eleven men were chosen. Just one more juror and an alternate were still needed. But the hour was late and the judge impatient. When he said they would resume jury selection in the morning, spectators groaned, and the prosecutor rushed forward.

"There can be no fair trial here in Palm Beach!" he shouted, and demanded that John be tried in Miami instead.

His surprise request for a change of venue stunned the defendant, his family, and friends. Miami? Shocking. If the judge agreed, John would be moved to Dade County Jail, more than sixty miles south, to await yet another new trial date. His supporters insisted he be tried in Palm Beach where the crime took place, where everyone involved lived. A move to Miami would place a severe hardship on John's loved ones, who'd already exhausted all their resources on his defense.

Even more ominous, two defendants recently accused of murder in Miami had been quickly convicted and hanged. His family feared that John was being railroaded to the gallows. They protested and shouted objections until the judge ordered the courtroom cleared.

That bright fall day that had dawned full of promise and new beginnings had spiraled down along with the family's spirit and the weather. After a long, tiring day of confusing legal arguments, the sky had grown ominously dark. A strong wind began to howl. A violent thunderstorm burst overhead as the lawyers continued to argue.

Rain pounded the courthouse, nearly drowning out the judge, who agreed to consider the prosecutor's request overnight. The judge seemed to favor the move; he looked downright pleased. He saw a way out. The burden would be lifted from his shoulders if he could just lob this hot potato of a case over to a judge down in Miami. Let strangers to the south decide the fate of the favorite son of a large, well-known, and extremely popular Palm Beach family. It was a godsend for him and his future political aspirations.

The dark sky and wind-driven rain were seen by many as bad omens. John turned to seek Laura out before leaving the courtroom. They had had such high hopes. She tried to smile, then gasped. "Oh no," she murmured, then fell back into her seat as he was led away. Bystanders thought she'd felt faint, but it was something she had seen in his eyes.

CHAPTER TWENTY-TWO

Wind and rain buffeted them as Deputy Sheriff Bob Baker escorted John back to the jail. As usual, the defendant was not handcuffed. He had been a model prisoner from the start.

The storm grew wilder. Trees bent and limbs cracked overhead as they reached the jailer's residence adjacent to the lockup. Baker's drab-looking wife opened the door, squinted against the driving rain, and handed out a home-cooked meal Joe Ashley had left for his son.

Baker unlocked the gate in the ten-foot chicken wire fence that enclosed the jail yard. The two men stepped inside and Baker secured it behind them. He handed John the plate of food to hold while he switched on the bright light above the jailhouse door. The wind whistled fiercely as Baker, drenched, his feet soaked, unlocked the heavy door and pushed it open. As he did, Ashley dropped the plate, vaulted the fence, sprinted around the corner, and disappeared into the storm.

Stunned, Baker scrambled in pursuit. The fleeing prisoner was out of sight, but he heard running footsteps in the dark, drew his revolver, and emptied it in that direction.

Then he ran headlong to a nearby shed, dragged out his bicycle, and pedaled frantically through the torrential rain along the path he believed Ashley had taken.

All he found was Joe Ashley, the prisoner's father; Laura Upthegrove, his sweetheart; and Bethel Forsythe, a close family friend, chatting and waiting out the rain beneath the overhang of a nearby store. They said they didn't see anybody running.

"That's when I knew," Baker bitterly told the press, "that John Ashley's escape was a carefully orchestrated plan involving a number of people."

It had happened so fast that Baker never could explain to news reporters—or his father, the sheriff—how Ashley managed to scale a ten-foot fence during a fierce rain squall. "He just melted through it," Baker babbled to the press, the whites of his eyes reflecting in the flash-bulbs' glare. The reporters and others concluded that Baker had failed to follow his own strict procedures and, lulled into a false sense of security, neglected to lock the gate behind them.

"He was well liked, never gave us any trouble, and was a model prisoner—until he escaped," Baker complained. "We'll find him," he swore. "He can't get far."

Days later, pressed by reporters, Baker revealed that he had tracked John Ashley to Fresh Water Lake. There, he said, the wanted man broke into a shack, stole food and a shotgun, then vanished into the 'Glades.

CHAPTER TWENTY-THREE

Nearly a year after he surrendered to clear his name, John Ashley was hunkered down in his Everglades hideout again. Still wanted for murder, he now faced escape charges as well.

Laura arrived at dusk, days later. After so many months apart, unable to even touch each other, their reunion was bittersweet.

He heard her approach and stepped from the shadows, a gun in each hand. "Sure Baker's men didn't follow you?"

"I'm sure," she whispered. "I remember everything you taught me."

"Good." He checked behind her, then holstered one of the weapons and took her into his arms.

Reluctant to light a fire or even a lantern, they sat close together in the dark as night's blanket fell. But as he fumbled to unfasten her skirt, she didn't guide his fingers as usual. He sighed aloud. "What?"

"Did you rob the train in Fort Pierce three days ago?"

"Train?" He stopped what he was doing. "Huh, let me think about that. Why, hell no! I haven't left here since I arrived, except to do a little fishing yesterday before dawn."

"I knew you didn't!" She hugged him, then unfolded the newspapers she'd brought. "They say that you did, then shot a tourist for his money and luggage that night just south of the natural bridge."

"In Miami? What the . . . ? How could a man travel from Fort Pierce to Miami that fast? He'd need wings. Nobody can be in two places at once, at least I can't." He kissed her neck. "Wish I could, darlin', but I ain't been noplace but here."

It was too dark to even read the headlines, but Laura filled him in on the stories she'd read again and again. Since his escape John had been named and blamed whenever a gun was fired or a crime committed anywhere in Florida. Sheriff Baker called news conferences and painted lurid pictures for reporters. John Ashley lurked in the Everglades by day, plotting new crimes, Baker said, then emerged from the swamp after dark to commit them with his outlaw gang.

"Gang?" John said indignantly. "I ain't seen another soul, I swear, till you came. Where would I find a gang out here?"

A reporter from the Stuart newspaper had asked the same question, Laura said. Baker's reply? Easy, he said. John had recruited felons he met in jail while awaiting trial.

"That no-good, lying son of a bitch!" John said. "That man would rather climb a tree and tell a lie than stand on the ground and tell the truth."

"There's another story," she said sadly. "I wanted to tell you about it before you saw it yourself."

"How many more lies can they tell?" he said bitterly.

"I'm afraid this one is true. Mr. Carl Fisher—"

"Nothing's happened to him, has it?" His voice rang with concern.

"No, John. He's fine, in fact he's offered a five-hundred-dollar reward for your capture. Dead or alive."

She heard the breath leave his body, as though he'd taken a blow to the solar plexus.

"Think it's true?" he finally said.

"Yes, he was interviewed, had his picture taken, and I saw one of the posters."

"How could he?" he asked in disbelief. "The man knows me, asked me to work for him. I figured I still would after all this blew over."

Laura knew he'd never abandon their Miami dream. He still clung to the hope that someday it would come true.

"He said you were a public scourge, that you're bad for business, you hurt land sales and scare off investors. I brought some things," she added quickly, "to take with us."

"Where?"

"Anywhere they're not hunting for you, John."

"No!" he said angrily, his voice ragged. "I've had nothing to do out here but think. My first mistake was letting Baker run me outta Florida. The second was coming back. Lord, it felt so right at the time, but it didn't work out. I'm never gonna let the damn Bakers mess with my life again. Ever."

"We can make up new names, go to California, or Canada. Maybe a Caribbean island. What about Cuba?" Her words were wistful in the dark.

"Did you hear what I just said?" he asked irritably. "Last time we ran, we changed names so often that half the time I didn't know who the hell I was, who you were, or what name to answer to. They're not doing that to me again. I'm John Ashley." He jabbed his chest with his thumb and rose to his feet. "That's who I am and always will be. If Baker and his men mess with me again, I'll be their worst nightmare."

"I know you're angry," she said gently, "and hurt, but that's nonsense, John. You can't fight the law and win in the end. There's too many of them. You might win some battles, but not the war."

"Watch me," he muttered ominously.

Bobby also spent time with John at the fishing camp. Both he and Laura delivered news stories to John, reports of his "reign of terror," his "state-wide crime spree," brutal shootings, and ruthless robberies as his outlaw reputation loomed larger every day.

Finally, John had had enough. One night Bobby arrived at the fishing camp and found John had company, three tough-talking strangers he'd met at a ramshackle saloon at the fringe of the Everglades.

"This is Kid Lowe." John grinned. "Guess what he does?"

Bobby shrugged and offered his hand to the balding man, who painfully crushed his fingers in an iron grip.

"Banking!" the Kid boomed. "I'm into banking."

Everyone laughed as though it were funny.

"I'm wanted in Chicago," Lowe coyly confessed, "for making unauthorized withdrawals—of other people's money!" He smirked, laughed heartily at his own joke, and swaggered around the room.

With him were Clarence Middleton and Roy Matthews, also wanted men. The trio had fled south to hide out. Strangers to Florida's wild and unfamiliar turf, they'd seen the news accounts and heard talk about John Ashley's crime spree. They were thrilled to meet the high-profile fugitive.

"What were those guys doing here?" Bobby frowned, his fingers still numb, after the men departed. He had disliked Lowe, the balding bank robber, on sight.

"Listen," John said. "After all that time waiting in jail for trials, we're dead broke. Me, Laura, Mama, and Pop spent everything we had on my defense. I figured we'd win, I'd land a good job in Miami, make that money back and more. But we didn't win and now I'm a fugitive who can't land an honest job. Not when the newspapers write that I'm guilty as hell. Just like Baker and Carl Fisher, they don't even ask for my side. So the way I see it: they gave me the name, so I'll play the game. What choice do I have? Damned if I do and damned if I don't. They tell the world I run with outlaws, that I'm Florida's baddest man. So, what the hell? Why not make it true?"

"But why throw in with those guys?"

"Because they're pros, real outlaws." John leaned forward, eyes bright. "They know what they're doing. I can learn a whole lot from them."

Bobby looked thoughtful. "Does Laura know?"

"Not yet." John said.

She soon did, and was less fond than Bobby of John's new friends.

"All you have in common with them is that you're fugitives," she told John. "You're an innocent man. You were railroaded. They're bad men wanted for good reasons. You're not one of them."

"Nobody'd believe that if they read the newspapers," John said bitterly. "I can learn from them. I need to learn the ropes."

She argued against it. "If they were pros, good at what they did, then why are they fugitives? If they were that good, nobody would know their names."

He listened, but soon after, John and Kid Lowe set out to rob the Palm Beach Limited, a Florida East Coast Railway passenger train.

Unfortunately, Clarence Middleton, the team's third member, had indulged in opiates for days, a habit he'd brought from Chicago. Unable to sleep, he suffered severe tremors and paranoia and had been firing his pistol at rattlesnakes, rats, and others creatures that only he could see.

Kid Lowe insisted that Clarence participate anyway. "He'll be all right," Lowe said. "I've seen him a lot worse than this."

John disagreed, wrestled Clarence's gun away, and tied him to a chair.

Lowe insisted they needed a third man to act as lookout while they robbed the mail car. Bobby was thrilled when Lowe invited him.

John had serious reservations. But at least, he thought, he knew he could trust Bobby.

They set out with high hopes. The trio boldly boarded the train when it slowed at a crossing. John nodded and smiled politely at a female passenger. But when she saw his gun, she became hysterical, ignored his orders to stop, and ran shrieking through the train. Passengers panicked, and a fast-thinking porter rushed to bolt the doors between cars. The robbers, who'd forgotten their masks, were locked out and isolated. They escaped, red-faced and empty-handed, when the train stopped south of Stuart.

Furious, John blamed the confusion on lack of planning about who was to stand guard while the others looted the mail car. He'd assumed that Kid Lowe, the professional, would take the lead. Kid Lowe had assumed that John Ashley, the master criminal whose press he believed, would be in charge.

John began to realize that Lowe was not exactly the evil genius and master criminal he claimed to be.

"We need a plan!" John raged to Bobby and the Kid. "Nobody succeeds without one. We need to put it together, then stick to it. We've got to foresee all the things that can go wrong and plan what to do if they happen."

Once more, John's picture appeared on the front page of his hometown newspaper, under the headline "Daring Train Robbery." This time he'd actually committed the crime attributed to him and further embarrassed his loved ones.

Reporters hounded Sheriff Baker. Furious, he vowed to take immediate action but was frustrated. His deputies could find no trace of Ashley or his gang. Still beset by the press, Baker took action anyway. He had his deputies arrest John's father, Joe Ashley, a laborer who worked for him, and John's brother-in-law, Hanford Mobley.

Baker announced the arrests at a press conference, expecting positive publicity. But the men he'd arrested were respected citizens. None had ever been linked to crime. The press and the public were outraged. Irate editorials splashed across front pages, listing all the responsible jobs, achievements, and titles held by Mobley, a dynamic local businessman.

"His record is clear," the editor pointed out, "like the others'. Why on earth would Sheriff Baker arrest this fine man?"

Baker quickly released all three. Too late. The fickle press had switched sides. "Every bullet fired anywhere is blamed on John Ashley," one editor wrote. "He's only a man. No one should accuse him of DeSoto Tiger's murder until they can prove it in court," wrote another.

Humiliated by John Ashley again, the thin-skinned, publicity-conscious, politically ambitious sheriff lost sleep and began to grind his teeth.

John, too, lost sleep. He'd always been dead set against robbing banks, the local institutions where his family, friends, and neighbors deposited their hard-earned cash.

"It's not right," he told his new pals from Chicago.

But Kid Lowe could talk up a storm. "Where does the bank's money come from?" he demanded. "From up north. It's Yankee money! Ain't nothing wrong with robbing Yankees." That made sense to John.

On Tuesday, February 23, 1915, a teller looked up as a young man walked into the Bank of Stuart brandishing a high-powered rifle and shouted, "Hands up!"

The teller grinned, thought it was a joke, then saw the cashier, his hands already in the air. John Ashley suddenly appeared with a pistol in each hand and ordered the cashier to open the metal gate. The cashier complied and warned the teller, "Better put 'em up, Wallace! He means it."

"You bet!" The startled teller raised his hands, then asked, "What's next?"

John tossed him a gunnysack. "Put the money in there. That's next."

The teller stuffed all the money John could see, about $4,500 in greenbacks and silver, into the sack but never opened the cash drawer. John took the sack then demanded more. The teller used both hands to lift a hefty canvas bag that contained three thousand pennies. "It's only copper," he said.

"We'll take it anyway," John said. His knees nearly buckled when the teller dropped nineteen pounds of pennies into the sack he held.

John had never been inside a bank before, knew little about how they operated, and identified with the victims. "I'm sorry about this, Wallace. But we had some bad luck a few weeks ago," he told the teller, referring to the failed train robbery, "and we really need the money."

He insisted that the teller open his desk drawers, one by one, in search of more loot, but failed to notice the closed cash drawer that held more than $60,000. Then John marched Wallace into the vault, but the clever young teller convinced him it was empty.

When John asked him to open the safe-deposit boxes, Wallace said that only the customers had keys and the boxes contained just legal papers and other documents of no value to anyone else.

"Okay then, I guess that's it." As John thanked him and backed out of the vault, Kid Lowe burst in from the lobby.

"What the hell's taking so long?" Lowe demanded, then asked how much loot they had. When Wallace, the ever helpful teller, said it was about $4,500, Lowe demanded more and threatened to shoot him.

"Take it easy," John said, siding with the teller, who explained that the bank was small, that it kept little cash on hand, and they had already taken it all. Disgusted, Lowe roughly pushed the teller into the lobby, where Bobby still had the cashier and three customers at gunpoint, their hands in the air.

"Which one of you drives a car?" Lowe shouted. The cashier swore he didn't own an automobile and couldn't drive one if he did. The others said the same. Finally customer Frank Coventry, a businessman, admitted his car was outside.

"Good." Lowe jammed his pistol to the man's head. "You're gonna drive us out of town."

The bank customers and employees were marched outside at gunpoint and forced to face the wall. John warned them not to move. Kid Lowe forced Coventry into the car, then, furious and disappointed by the meager take, decided to prove he meant business. In a show of bravado, he began to fire his guns wildly. Bank victims and passersby either hit the ground or ran for cover. Bullets ricocheted off the building.

"Kid! What the hell you doing?" John shouted. He held the car door open. "Cut that out before you hurt somebody!"

Lowe, still firing, wheeled toward the sound of his voice and shot John Ashley in the face.

CHAPTER TWENTY-FOUR

The bullet slammed into John's right jaw on an upward trajectory and lodged in his left eye. Blood flew as he fell to his knees in the dusty street.

Lowe stumbled into the car. "Let's go! Let's go!" he screamed at the terrified driver.

"Don't you move!" Bobby leveled his rifle at the driver, told Lowe to shut up, dragged his barely conscious brother into the back seat, then climbed in with him. Coventry stomped the gas and they speeded away.

"You crazy son of a bitch!" Bobby screamed. "You shot my brother!" Frantically, he used Coventry's shirt to try to stop the bleeding. "You shot him! You shot John!"

"Didn't mean to," Lowe blustered. "It was an accident! He got in the way."

Bobby cursed at Lowe until he told Coventry to stop on an isolated road outside of town. They carried John from the car and let the abducted bank customer drive away. Once he was out of sight, Bobby and Kid Lowe bundled John, still bleeding profusely, into a Ford they had hidden in the woods.

John clung to consciousness, in severe pain and gravely wounded. His condition made it impossible to return to his Everglades hideout as planned. He needed immediate medical attention. John didn't know if he'd survive but knew he'd be caught. They hadn't worn masks, and at least five eyewitnesses could identify him. Barely able to speak, he insisted that Bobby and Kid Lowe leave him and run. "If I die," he told Bobby, "tell Laura I love her."

Bobby stopped at the first homestead they saw. He pounded on the door until a frightened woman opened it a crack. "We need help!" he pleaded. "My brother's been shot in a hunting accident!"

"Bring him in." She threw the door open and ran to clear her kitchen table. "Lift him up here."

They did. She turned pale at the sight of his shattered eye and the terrible wound, still gushing blood. His face, already swollen, continued to swell.

Bobby agonized. Lowe apologized, and the farm wife cleaned the wound. She tried to stem the bleeding as best she could, applied bandages, and said she'd pray for them.

"He has to see a doctor as soon as possible," she said. "You must get him to a surgeon. It's urgent."

They said they would, then left John in the woods twelve miles southwest of Stuart. Bobby finally found a telephone, called big brother Bill for help, and fled.

Bill had carefully avoided involvement in John's troubles but rose to the occasion. The Ashleys never let each other down. Joe and Leugenia had no telephone, but the Potters, neighbors two miles south, had a brand-new four-party line.

When she saw Roy Potter, age thirteen, gallop up on horseback, Laura knew something terrible had happened. She slipped out onto the porch and ran to meet him so that Leugenia would not hear.

"What's happened?"

The boy shrugged. "Bobby called on the telephone, wants to talk to you. He says it's important."

"Is he going to call you back?"

"No, ma'am. He's still hanging on the line, so nobody else can tie it up."

He lifted her up onto the horse, and they galloped back to his home.

The boy, his sisters, and their parents all stared. The big black telephone was a new, modern invention, and it was a major event when it rang, even if the call wasn't for them. Laura picked up the earpiece, turned her back to the family, and tried hard to focus.

"What's wrong, Bobby? Where are you?"

"John said he loves you, Laura."

"What's happened?" Her mouth suddenly felt dry.

"That's all I can say."

"Bobby." Her voice dropped into a register he had never heard before. "You tell me where he is, and what's happened, right now." She lowered her voice even more. "Is he hurt?"

"Yes, ma'am."

The blood drained from her face. "Is it bad?"

Bobby hesitated. "Yes, ma'am." His voice cracked.

"Don't you dare hang up this telephone. You tell me where he is. Right now, Bobby."

He told her.

"You left him alone?"

"He said we had to. Said to call Bill. He's going out there. He's trying to get a doctor now."

"Was it Sheriff Baker?" Laura asked quietly, her voice cold.

"No, ma'am. I have to go now." He hung up.

She turned. The Potters all leaned forward, hanging on every word.

She shook her head, shrugged, and smiled. "A little family matter. You know how these young 'uns are. Do you mind if I make a local call?"

Mrs. Potter signaled the go-ahead and Laura called Bill. The line was busy. Still smiling at the wide-eyed family, she fought tears and repeated the number to the operator for a second time, then a third. She whispered a silent prayer. This time it rang. Lucy answered.

"Can I speak to Bill?" Laura asked.

"Laura? Why would you call here? What do you want with my husband? Don't you try to drag him into John's problems. He ain't having no part in your—"

Bill asked who was calling. When Lucy hesitated, he took the phone from her.

Laura heard his voice and gasped with such relief that she thought her knees would buckle. "Thank God! I'm going with you."

"That may not be wise, Laura."

"Bobby told me where he is, Bill. And I will get there if I have to crawl."

"Where are you?"

She told him.

"All right. Good idea." He sounded artificially cheerful for Lucy's benefit. "See you soon, sis."

Sheriff Baker issued a statewide alert and assembled posses that fell apart. Young, able-bodied men eagerly volunteered but lost their enthusiasm for the chase when told who it was they were to capture. They suddenly remembered pressing engagements, pregnant wives, sick children, stalled cars, dead batteries, and bad tires. Some said they had no ammunition. Others had mislaid their weapons. Most were loyal to the popular, hardworking Ashley family, and none had the stomach for a gunfight with the best marksman they ever knew, despite word that he was wounded.

Two men, Naha and Tom Tiger, eagerly stepped up. The brothers of DeSoto Tiger, the man Ashley was accused of murdering, led the search, joined by Federal Indian agents, investigators from Florida's East Coast Railway, and the bank's company.

Laura could not wait another moment. She walked briskly down the unpaved road to meet Bill's car. It seemed like forever, but his Ford pulled up within the hour. With him was Dr. Paul Venable, a paunchy, red-bearded, middle-aged doctor from Stuart.

"Bobby said John's hurt," Laura said, as she climbed into the back seat and slammed the door. "Is it a gunshot wound?" Bill gave a curt nod and stomped the gas. Laura closed her eyes, prayed hard, and took deep breaths to keep from being sick.

The good doctor had grave misgivings.

"If anyone asks," Bill assured him again and again, "say I never mentioned the patient's name or the circumstances. All I told you was that a man was badly injured, and you did your duty as a physician. I promise, I'll swear to that. She will too."

"Yes, he's right. I will." Laura lifted her eyes to the jagged highway of blue sky between the tall trees bordering the road and wondered fearfully what they would find.

She spotted the turnoff Bobby had described before Bill saw it. He hit the brakes, backed up, and drove in behind the trees. She was running before Bill, with his box of supplies, and the doctor, with his medical bag, were out of the car. Branches caught her hair, scratched her face, and tore her skirt. She stumbled over tree roots and called out his name.

He lay beneath a tree on a makeshift bed of automobile seat cushions. The blood-drenched blanket that had covered him was now crumpled, tangled, and tossed aside by his thrashing. His blood was everywhere—on the ground, his clothes, his face, and the nearby bushes.

"John!" She dropped to her knees beside him to check for the source of all the bleeding.

"Is that you, Laura?" He reached out, groped for her hand as though in the dark. But it was broad daylight. His left eye protruded at least an inch and a half from the socket, wet and oozing like a broken egg.

"Yes, darlin', I'm here." She sounded calm and reassuring, even as dread and denial filled her heart.

"How'd you get here?" he gasped. "Come 'round to the other side so I can see you, darlin'."

She scrambled around him. Tears of relief overflowed when she saw his right eye focus on her. Bill and the doctor crashed through the undergrowth nearby. "Here, over here!" she cried.

"Bill and the doctor are here. You'll be all right now, sweet boy," she whispered. "What happened, darlin'?"

"I'm shot. It was a mistake. We robbed the Stuart bank."

She gasped.

"Sorry, darlin'."

"They drove you to it, John. You had to do something."

She fell back on her heels, tears streaking her face as the doctor took over. He instructed John to cover his wounded eye with his bloody, mud-caked hand.

"What do you see, son?"

"You, Doc. Your specs need a cleaning, and you've got brambles all over your jacket."

The doctor covered John's right eye. "What do you see now?"

"Nothing, sir. Just the dark, like the swamp at midnight with no moon."

"Are you in pain?"

John snorted, as if to laugh. "Hell, yeah!"

"I can give you morphine."

"That's the ticket, Doc. Thanks. Just make it quick."

After the injection, Venable stepped away to confer with Bill and Laura.

"He needs surgery." The doctor dropped his voice. "There's nothing I can do out here. We have to get him back to town, to a surgeon."

Bill objected. The doctor argued angrily. "He's half blind, a bullet's lodged in his eye. There is no exit wound! You have no choice."

"Okay." Bill's voice was tight. "I'll pull the car up closer so we can get him into the back seat."

"No!" John shouted.

They were all startled as he sat straight up. "Laura! Bill! Don't move! It's too late! They're here! We're surrounded! Don't you hear them?" He groped for his gun, but Laura had already slipped it into the doctor's bag. "Don't shoot, for God's sake! There's a woman here!" John shouted.

"He's delirious." The doctor frowned.

"No, he isn't," Bill said, and raised his hands.

Trees and shadows began to move around them. The stunned doctor stared. "Don't shoot! We're unarmed! I'm a doctor treating an injured man! Hold your fire!"

Naha and Tom Tiger and those with them emerged soundlessly from the woods, rifles raised.

Bill and Laura exchanged a despairing look. "How did they find us?" he muttered in disbelief.

"Lucy," she hissed.

"No! She wouldn't. Couldn't . . ." His voice trailed off.

CHAPTER TWENTY-FIVE

The bullet broke John's jaw and cost him his left eye. Surgeons removed it and planned to take out the bullet as well, but that meant more surgery and he refused.

"I'm gonna hang," he said bitterly. "Why bother?"

Taken to Miami in chains and under heavy guard, he again faced trial on murder charges. Having Dade County sheriff Dan Hardie see him that way added to John's pain and humiliation. He and Hardie had once shared a moment, a promise. The lawman had admired his skill, offered his friendship, had shaken his hand, and asked for his help when needed. John, once so proud to be of service, was now the man's prisoner.

"Don't apologize," Hardie said, as John was booked into the jail. "I never dreamed I'd see this day. I'm sure you didn't either. But remember, all men are innocent until proven guilty. Good luck in court."

John dreaded the shameful walk from the jail to the courthouse, wearing ankle, wrist, and belly chains, and a black patch over his empty eye socket, stared at by decent people he'd hoped would be his good friends and neighbors in what he thought would be the city of his future. Each step seared his soul.

Hardie guarded his high-risk prisoner well but treated him fairly. Unlike Baker, the Palm Beach sheriff, Hardie did not limit visitors to lawyers, spouses, and blood kin. Laura and other family members, especially his sisters, saw him regularly, in brief, monitored visits with no touching permitted.

Bill, Laura, and Dr. Venable, arrested with him, were released after witnesses confirmed that they had played no role in the bank robbery. Sheriff Baker had his long-sought prize, John Ashley.

How the posse found them so quickly remained a mystery. The sheriff said a tip from a confidential informant was so precise that the Tiger brothers were able to lead the posse directly to them.

John suffered another blow to his morale. The newspapers that had once supported him now embellished the story of his capture and retold in vivid prose the details of his escape and crimes. Traumatized victims and terrified witnesses were quoted at length: the woman who'd run screaming through the train, the clever bank teller, and Frank Coventry, the bank customer forced into the role of getaway driver. All told their harrowing personal stories of survival.

Editorial writers who had once criticized Sheriff Baker's heavy-handed tactics were now outraged at the hometown bad boy who preyed on neighbors and fellow citizens. One stinging diatribe concluded, "It's hoped that neither Sheriff Baker nor his deputies take any chances this time, and that John Ashley soon receives his just deserts."

John, who'd been so eager for his first trial, dreaded the public spectacle this time. Proceedings began on April 2, 1915. The defendant, in his white suit, black bow tie, and matching eye patch, listened intently, along with a packed courtroom, to the prosecution's first witness, the dredge captain who described finding Tiger's body with a gunshot wound through his head.

Unlike Palm Beach, the Miami trial took less than four days. On April 6, the jury swiftly returned a guilty verdict. The jurors recommended a sentence the same day and the judge agreed. Death by hanging.

Their fears realized, John's loved ones were inconsolable. He tried to comfort them. "We all get the death penalty," he said. "The only difference is that when you're sentenced to die, you have a date on the calendar instead of wondering when you wake up every morning if today's the day a bullet finds you."

His last hope was dashed ten days later when he was denied a new trial. He still insisted he was innocent and had acted in self-defense, but his grasp on life seemed tenuous at best. Public opinion turned against him and his family after the newspaper attacks. Even if his lawyers, who now worked without pay, won their appeal to the Florida Supreme Court, he would still face trial for robbery. And he suffered excruciating headaches caused by the bullet still lodged in his head. He languished in jail. His loss of weight and hope plunged those who loved him into despair.

Laura and his sisters, especially Daisy, the green-eyed family beauty, endured crude jokes, rude stares, and bold whistles from jailers each time they visited the condemned man. Yet they continued to deliver home-cooked meals all the way from Palm Beach, along with a tonic prescribed by Dr. Anna Darrow, of Okeechobee. Joe had traveled to central Florida to consult her. He hoped her tonic would stimulate John's appetite and help him heal. One afternoon, Daisy and Laura were so shaken by the jailers' cruel remarks and gestures that they inadvertently left their wicker food basket behind. They quickly returned for it and gasped. What they saw in the jail yard shocked them.

"Hey, you!" Daisy shouted. "What are you doing?"

"Stop! Please don't!" Laura cried, as Chief Jailer Wilbur Hendrickson poured out the bottle of tonic they'd brought and tossed it, along with John's meal, into a garbage bin.

Hendrickson ignored them.

"We saw what you did!" Laura said. "We'll see what the sheriff has to say about this!"

"What the hell you gals jawing about?" the cocky jailer replied. "What you want anyhow with that half-blind, thieving swamp rat?" He laughed and touched his crotch. "Want to try a real man on for a change?"

Daisy and Laura quarreled about what to do. Daisy feared that reporting the jailer's actions could make life behind bars more difficult for John. Laura insisted that Dan Hardie was fair and would not tolerate Hendrickson's behavior. But as Daisy pointed out, Hardie could not be at the jail twenty-four hours a day and John would surely suffer consequences. Laura reluctantly agreed. They said nothing to Hardie, but the family spiraled into a tailspin. Their favorite son, the man Laura loved, was doomed to die at age twenty-seven. If he didn't hang, he'd surely die of neglect and mistreatment behind bars.

Leugenia and her daughters wept and prayed. Laura, strong and dry-eyed by day, sobbed at night. Bobby, whose room was close to hers, heard her.

The youngest Ashley brooded. His father and brothers cursed Hendrickson, talked tough about a possible rescue attempt, but eventually concluded that the odds were stacked against a successful jailbreak.

Bobby began to secretly sneak whiskey to numb the pain of seeing his family suffer.

But that all changed on Thursday, June 1, 1915, a spectacular spring day. Bobby appeared cheerful at breakfast, was brimming with energy, and seemed to have regained his recently lost air of youthful expectation. Laura tousled his hair and told him how much he resembled John when he was younger.

Bobby smiled. It's as though she knows, he thought.

"Laura?" he asked, as she cleared the table. "What happened to that big blue sheet of wrapping paper?" A package of dry goods—muslin and cambric—ordered from the Sears, Roebuck catalog, had arrived days earlier wrapped in thick blue paper.

"It's folded in the pantry," she said.

"Can I have it?"

"Sure. Take it." She would regret later that she never thought to ask why he wanted it.

"Thank you, ma'am."

"Love you, Bobby," she said.

"It's Bob, ma'am." He flashed a conspiratorial grin.

Laura watched him go, bemused. Would he want to be called Robert after his next birthday? He'd always be Bobby to her. He so reminded her of John the year they swam with manatees in the Caloosahatchee River and lay naked on the bank. Sweet memories comforted her as she scraped and washed the plates. When her thoughts returned to the present, she wondered about young "Bob." What's he up to lately? They'd all been so worried about John that Bobby had been ignored, left on his own more than ever. She dried her hands on a dish towel and wondered, did he and that little Lummus girl spend time alone in some secret place? They definitely had eyes for each other.

Bobby's too shy, she thought, but she wished John was there to talk to him. John. Her eyes filled. What if he did hang? God forbid. How unfair, how insane! What would I do? She wondered. Where could I go? How could I live in a world without him?

She went to look for Bobby, but he was gone.

CHAPTER TWENTY-SIX

Bobby pedaled to the railroad yard. When no one was watching, he dragged his bicycle and a long package wrapped in blue paper into an empty boxcar on a southbound freight.

No one noticed until suppertime. Leugenia fixed Bobby a plate and listened for his quick steps on the porch; she became alarmed after dark. "This isn't like Bobby," she said.

"He's been gone since breakfast," Laura told her. "Did he go fishing?" But his fishing pole still hung in place in the barn.

Joe looked for him, had no luck, and came home scowling.

Bill and Lucy had come for supper. "That boy just craves attention," Lucy said. "When he finally straggles home, somebody should kick his butt!" She gave them a sugary smile. "You all have more than enough to worry about these days with all John's problems. How dare that spoiled young 'un show his ass like this."

"Bobby's never been a problem." Leugenia wrung her hands. "There are bears, rattlers, cougars, and Indians out there. What if he's been hurt? Or went swimming and drowned?"

"Bobby's smart," Laura assured her. "He's an excellent swimmer. He probably just lost track of time."

Bill promised to watch for him on the road, as he and Lucy left.

An hour later, Joe and Frank took their best tracking hound out to pick up his trail, while Ed rode to a married sister's house to see if Bobby might be there with his nieces and nephews.

The dark woods and dirt roads echoed with their calls. "Bobby! Bobby Ashley! Bobbeee!" No one answered. The hound treed a wildcat. His nephews swore they hadn't seen Bobby in days.

"Should we send for the sheriff?" Leugenia asked, at 3 a.m.

The men nixed the idea for the time being. None trusted the law after all that had happened. If deputies found him, he might be arrested for his role in the train and bank robberies. "Let's wait till morning. Maybe we can find him first," Frank said.

"Yeah, if he's not home by dawn," Ed agreed.

Laura suggested they ask the Lummus girl when she last saw Bobby.

"Who?" Joe frowned. He had no idea who she meant.

"That little blond-headed girl he always looks at in church," Laura said.

"With her sneaking looks back," Leugenia added.

"That's the one," Laura said. "What is her first name?"

"Rachel, I think," Leugenia said.

"Ben Lummus's girl?" Joe looked perplexed. "Thought all he had was little ones."

"Time flies," Leugenia said. "She's the oldest girl of five."

"Kids grow up too fast these days," Joe said wistfully.

At 4 a.m. they left a light in the front window and tried to catch a little sleep before dawn.

Bobby arrived in Miami at 4 a.m. He too waited for dawn. He counted the hours in the darkened railway depot, a block north of the jail. He and John had often visited Miami and he knew his way around. They'd worked there once for several days, had shingled a roof in Coconut Grove. The city had been exciting, a welcome adventure then. On this, his first solo trip, Miami was a strange and hostile place.

He thought of home. Do they miss me yet? he wondered. He hoped they wouldn't worry. It's time they treat me like a man, he thought. After today, they will.

Back in Palm Beach, Joe and Laura rode over to the Lummus place just after dawn. Ben, a hefty, middle-aged farmer, was outside at the pump, shirtless and washing his face.

"My youngest boy, Bobby, didn't come home last night," Joe said.

"I'll join if you're putting together a search party." Ben blinked in the bright sunlight as he dried his face with a cloth.

"Not yet," Laura said. "We hoped your girl, Rachel, might know where to find him."

"Rachel?" Ben's eyes narrowed. "How would she know?"

"They're friends, in school and church. I think he's sweet on her," Laura said. "Bobby's always dependable. We're so worried."

"*Rachel!*" her father bellowed, startling them both.

The slightly built teenager, with straight, almost white blond hair hanging down her back, padded barefoot onto the porch. She wore a loose yellow cotton dress with white trim. Her big gray eyes grew wider and she shyly hugged her arms when she saw visitors.

"You seen the Ashley boy?" her father asked.

She shook her head slightly, then lifted her eyes to watch a buzzard circling in the sky.

Laura feared it was an omen. "Rachel, dear, Bobby's been missing overnight and we're afraid something's happened to him. Can you help us?"

Rachel sneaked a glance at her, then looked away quickly, but not before Laura saw something in her eyes. Fear? Guilty knowledge?

"Mind your manners, Rachel," her father demanded. "Answer the lady."

"No, ma'am," Rachel said. "I'm sure he's fine. But I don't know where he's at." Her slender shoulders lifted in a halfhearted shrug.

"What did he say when you last saw him?"

"That I should call him Bob from now on." The girl turned and ran inside.

The café on the far side of the railroad tracks opened for breakfast at 7 a.m. Bob Ashley walked his bike across the tracks and ate a hearty meal of bacon, eggs, and grits. Afterward, still carrying his long blue package, he circled the two-story yellow brick jailhouse.

He had recently concluded that two things were true. One, John needed rescue. Two, the mission was his. He was, after all, the family's third-best marksman, after John and their father. On Tuesday night he had cleaned and loaded his weapons, all three of his guns: a six-shot revolver, a western-style pistol, and his Winchester repeating rifle.

John awoke with a violent start at 7:10 a.m. Lying on his bunk in his stifling jail cell, he struggled to make sense of his dark, disturbing dream. A buzzard circled, lights flickered in shadowed woods, familiar voices called, but he couldn't quite make out the words. Was it his name they called? His head ached. His left eye throbbed as though it were still there and festering. His tongue felt swollen, his throat parched.

He ignored his breakfast of cold coffee and coarse oatmeal and wished for cold water to drink and to wash his face. He lay on his bunk and tried mental telepathy. He and Bobby had seen it done at a stage show, back when Miami was still warm and welcoming. He tried to send Laura a message that he was thinking of her. He pictured what she'd be doing at that moment.

"Bobby's bike is gone," Laura said breathlessly. It was 7:20 a.m. "I didn't notice it missing last night."

"Where the hell would he . . . ?" Joe said.

Laura went to the boy's room and dropped to her knees to peer beneath his bed. It wasn't there. She scrambled to her feet, searched his closet, then the dresser drawers, panic rising. "Where is his rifle?" she cried out. "Where's Bobby's Winchester—and his pistol?"

"Oh, Lord," Leugenia said.

Frank and Ed searched the roadsides for his bike.

Laura was chilled to the core. No, she thought. He wouldn't. He couldn't.

At noon, Bobby pedaled past the Peacock Feed Store and the Miami Bank and Trust building. He smiled, imagining their faces at home when they heard the news. He'd obsessed, then schemed, dreamed, and plotted the jailbreak, ever mindful of what John had told him: "A man has to have a plan."

Bobby had thought out his plan. In order to break John out of jail, he decided, he had to break into the jail. He didn't tell anyone. They might try to stop him.

As Bobby watched from the depot, Sheriff Hardie visited the jail, then sauntered down the dusty street for lunch. It was 12:45 p.m. Time to make his move. Bobby inhaled a deep breath, aware that this could be the most important and pivotal moment of his life. He worried that he and John might have to go on the run after the escape but didn't dwell on it. John would know what to do, he was confident of that.

*   *   *

At 12:50 p.m., two stories up in his Dade County Jail cell, John ignored his lunch of watery pea soup with bread and butter. Instead, he paced his narrow cell, overwhelmed by a sense of dread, and tried to recall the details in his troubling dream.

"We got visitors," Joe Ashley said at 12:57 p.m. in Palm Beach. He peered at them through the front window and self-consciously rubbed the stubble on his chin.

Ben Lummus was outside with his wife, Rose, and their reluctant daughter, Rachel.

"Sorry, Joe," Ben said. "Girl never lied to me before. Come here, Rachel."

The girl climbed the steps like a condemned prisoner on the way to the gallows. She stood on the porch, a forlorn creature, red-eyed and cowed, the unhappy center of attention.

"'Pologize to Mr. Ashley and tell 'im what you told us," her father demanded. His wife watched, her lips a tight, thin line.

Leugenia stepped out onto the porch. She clutched a damp handkerchief between her hands, which were clasped, as though in prayer. "Don't stand out here in the hot sun, folks." Her voice shook slightly. "Come on in."

They stepped inside as Frank and Ed joined them in the kitchen. Laura, afraid her knees would give out, eased into a chair. The air felt thick with tension.

Bobby hopped off his bike at 12:59 p.m. and rapped on the door of the apartment behind the jail, the residence of Wilbur Hendrickson, the man with the jailhouse keys, the jailer who had tossed away John's food and tonic like garbage and insulted Laura and his sister Daisy.

He still carried his long blue package. He had a plan. He felt no fear.

A tall, dark-haired man, eyes piercing beneath fierce brows, swung the door open. His badge and posture made him look even taller. He loomed large in the doorway. He wore a puzzled frown, a long-sleeved shirt, and suspenders. He had seen this slender young man before, he thought, but couldn't quite place the face.

"Are you Hendrickson?"

"Yeah," the jailer said. "You have a delivery?"

"Yes." Bobby raised the package wrapped in blue paper and slipped his fingers inside.

"Who are you?" The jailer frowned.

"Bob Ashley. You know my brother, John, and my sister, Daisy." Bobby squeezed the trigger.

The rifle shot erupted like an explosion in the tiny room. Hendrickson staggered back a half step, then dropped to the floor, shot straight through the heart.

Not so tall now, are you? Bobby thought, and stepped inside, his ears ringing.

John sprang to his feet. That was a rifle shot! Other inmates—black, white, and Chinese—began to shout. He jumped up onto his bunk but could see nothing from the high, narrow window.

"Who's shooting?" he shouted down the cell block. "What's going on? Can anybody see anything?"

"Tell 'em!" Ben Lummus demanded.

Rachel fidgeted, pouted, then sniffed. Tears flooded her eyes. It was 1 p.m. in Palm Beach, sixty miles north of Miami.

"What is it, dear?" Laura said gently. "Can you tell us where Bobby is?"

The girl gulped and shot her father a fearful sidelong glance. The tears spilled over and skidded down her cheeks.

"Tell 'em!"

"Miami," Rachel bleated. "Bob said he was goin' to Miami to bring back his brother John."

"Oh, Lord!" Leugenia dropped to her knees.

"No," Laura whispered.

"We got to stop him!" Joe said.

Bobby crouched over the bleeding jailer and rifled the man's pockets for his keys. It was 1:01 p.m. It would take him only a few seconds to dash into the jail and find John. He hoped his brother heard the shot, knew he'd come, and was ready to run. Impatient, he rolled Hendrickson over. The man made an odd sound, like a sigh, as the air escaped his lungs. He was limp, a dead weight.

Bobby found the keys. As he fumbled, trying to yank them off the jailer's thick leather belt, a bloodcurdling scream rent the air around him and froze him in place.

A sturdy, brown-haired, plain-faced woman had burst into the room from the kitchen. He stared up at her shocked, his eyes wide, as she continued to scream. She had no part in his plan. Her skirts swished, and the skin on his arms erupted in goose bumps as she ran for the two rifles that stood in the corner. A small boy peeked from behind her as she snatched up one of the guns and swung it to aim at Bobby's head.

Still crouched over her motionless husband, Bobby stared at death down the barrel of the weapon less than two feet from his face and saw her squeeze the trigger. The gun clicked harmlessly. She screamed louder as she yanked the trigger again and again. The gun did not fire. The rifle was not loaded, to protect Wilbur Jr., age nine, the child behind her.

Bobby hesitated. So did she. They locked eyes for a moment. He saw the grief and horror, the rage and determination in her face. But he couldn't shoot a woman. How was he supposed to know that Hendrickson had a family?

Shrieking hysterically in panic and frustration, she flung the useless rifle at his head. He deflected it with his right arm as she continued to scream. The boy joined in with high-pitched, animal-like yelps of terror.

"Be quiet, ma'am! You too," Bobby sternly told the child, and got to his feet.

Neither listened. His plan had gone south in a heartbeat. People on the street heard the shot, heard her screams, and came running. Their shouts grew louder, closer.

"Over here!"

"It's the jailer's place!"

"That's Hendrickson's wife!"

He quit trying to rip the keys off Hendrickson's belt and ran.

* * *

The prisoners in the adjacent jail heard the commotion at 1:03 p.m.

"What the hell's going on?" John Ashley shouted.

Inmates shouted back that it must be Hendrickson's wife screaming, the woman who prepared their lousy meals.

"But what happened? Who got shot?"

More shouts and cries in the street below.

"He'll be fine," Rachel told the stunned adults at the Ashley homestead in Palm Beach, and tossed her blond hair. Joe Ashley took out his pocket watch. It was 1:05 p.m. The girl's lips curved into a smile. "Bob has a plan," she assured them.

Bobby burst out into the sun-drenched Miami street at six minutes after one. He did not have the jail keys or even a chance to hop onto his bike. The three big men who pounded after him shouted for others to join the pursuit. He sprinted through a shady garage, dodged from one street to another, to another, but couldn't lose them, and their numbers grew.

"There he goes!"

"Over there!"

"Get him, get him!"

"He shot Hendrickson!"

Jail inmates heard and picked up the chant. "He shot Hendrickson! Go, man, go! Run, run, run! He shot Hendrickson! He shot Hendrickson!"

Bobby stumbled across the railroad tracks, his heart pounding out of his chest, the growing mob in hot pursuit. They gained on him, were close on his heels. He stopped, turned, tore away the blue paper, exposed his rifle, then leveled it at them, his lip curled. The unarmed men saw the weapon, fell back, and took cover.

Panting, Bobby tried to think. His plan had failed, all because of that woman. Now he had to escape, rethink the situation, and concoct a new plan.

He darted into the street as a westbound bread truck rumbled toward him, stopped the startled driver, T. F. Duckett, at gunpoint, and leaped onto the running board.

"Keep going! Speed it up! Let's go! Let's go!" he shouted.

Duckett stared down the barrel of Bobby's rifle. "Drive it yourself, man!" he shouted, bailed out, and ran for cover.

Bobby had never driven a truck. Now he had to learn. Fast. He glanced back at his pursuers, blinked into the blinding midday sun, and saw two Miami police officers emerge like a mirage from the glare, running toward him. One, who held a revolver in his right hand, caught Bobby's shoulder with his left as young Ashley tried to slide into the driver's seat.

"You're under arrest!" he shouted.

"Like hell!" Bobby swung around, jumped down, grappled with the cop in the street, then stepped back and shot him pointblank in the jaw. The officer spun, as teeth, bone, and blood spattered Bobby's shirt. What will Mama say when she sees it? he worried, then took another angry step back and fired again. The officer, hit in the left chest near his heart, was thrown off his feet by the impact.

But the cop didn't quit. Bobby saw him jerk the trigger convulsively three times, three rapid shots, as though in slow motion as he fell. The first flew wild, over Bobby's head. The second slammed into his stomach with a pain that burned like fire. The third, fired from the ground as the cop's shoulders hit the street, caught Bobby under the jaw and blew an exit hole and a geyser of blood straight through the top of his head.

He fell back, jerking and gasping, into the bloody, dusty street.

The other cop commandeered the delivery truck to rush his wounded partner to the Miami hospital just north of Sixth Street.

Up in the jail, John Ashley heard a gun battle, screams, and shouting in the street below. Sick, his heart sinking, he knew somehow that it involved him and the dream he had that morning.

Breathless witnesses interrupted Sheriff Hardie's lunch with shouts that the jailer had been shot. At 1:10 p.m. Dan Hardie ran toward the scene, gun in hand, but on the way, he found a horribly wounded young man sprawled in the street, blood frothing from his mouth. Hardie commandeered a car and took him to the hospital. When he arrived he found his jailer, Wilbur Hendrickson, forty-four, dead, and wounded police officer John Rhinehart Riblet, thirty-one, struggling to breathe.

Thirty minutes later, Riblet, a US Army veteran from a small Ohio town, lost the struggle and died, the first City of Miami police officer ever killed in the line of duty.

Word that Riblet and Hendrickson were dead spread like wildfire. Men armed themselves. Angry Miamians gathered outside the hospital. The crowd grew. Some demanded that Bobby, drowning in his own blood and fighting to breathe, be lynched.

"Can you give him some morphine?" Sheriff Hardie asked the doctor.

The physician knew the dead lawmen and their families. The widows, Marian Hendrickson and Madge Riblet, had rushed to the hospital and were weeping inconsolably over their husbands' corpses. Each had a young son with her. Along with Wilbur Hendrickson Jr., there was Edward Riblet, age three. The doctor flat out refused to treat the killer in front of the dead men's loved ones.

"He's dying anyway," the doctor tersely told the sheriff. "There's nothing I can do for him."

The physician washed his hands of Bobby's case as the crowd outside grew still larger, shouting demands that the killer be turned over to them. When Hardie refused, they hurled rocks and smashed the hospital windows. Sheriff Hardie decided to move the young man to the jail rather than lose him to a lynch mob. He and two deputies rushed Bobby to the jail. Guns drawn, they held off the mob that followed shouting threats and curses. Hardie double-locked all doors, then secured the young cop-killer in a first-floor cell. The sheriff's clothes and those of his deputies were drenched in Bobby's blood.

"Can you hear me, son?" Hardie asked.

"Yeth thur," Bobby said, bubbling blood, his tongue split and his teeth shattered by the bullet. "Help me."

"Nothing more can be done for you, son, except prayer. You don't have much time. You're about to cross that river. If you want to save your soul, tell me the truth."

Bobby told Hardie his name and confessed all he'd done. Hardie asked if John knew about his plan. Bobby swore that he didn't, he had

told no one in his family. He confessed to his role in the robberies of the
Stuart bank and the Palm Beach Limited.

"Who was the other man with you?"

"Kid Lowe, wanted in Chicago," Bobby mumbled. "He shot John."

Hardie nodded, took notes, and asked more questions.

Bobby's injured brain began to swell. It had been more than two
hours since he'd been shot. The bright day faded as his world grew dark.
Now blind, he asked for his brother John, again and again.

Hardie believed Bobby but needed to be sure. He climbed the stairs
to John's second-floor cell. The waiting prisoner, fear on his face and in
his heart, saw him approach.

"John," Hardie said. "You have a younger brother, Bob?"

"I do." John held his breath, fearing what was to come.

"He the one you talked about, the boy interested in joining the
Miami Rifles?"

John nodded, a lump growing in his throat. "He likes the music and
the uniforms."

"He tried to bust you out of jail this afternoon," Hardie said, eyes
shiny. "Did you know about it?"

"No. I didn't, Sheriff, I swear. If I even thought . . . I woulda stopped
him. He's just a kid, Dan." His voice broke, then dropped to a whisper.
"Tell me he's all right."

Hardie shook his head. "I can't do that, John. He's dying."

"Where? Where's he at?"

"Downstairs, in a cell."

"Can you get him to the hospital, Dan?" John pleaded.

Hardie sighed. "I did. Nothing they could do for him. He's hit bad,
right through the head and the gut. He's not gonna make it. He killed
Hendrickson, the jailer, and a Miami police officer, name of J. R. Riblet.
Both their families are at the hospital now. The town's outta control. A
mob busted out the windows trying to take him. Had to bring him here,
or they would have lynched him."

John looked shocked. "Don't know how he coulda . . . He's a good boy.
I'm sorry, Dan. Can I see 'im before he goes? Please, can I see him?"

Hardie nodded and unlocked the cell door. "He's asking for you,
John. Sorry, I have to do this," he said, and handcuffed John's wrists.

Halfway down the narrow stairs they met a breathless deputy on the way up. "Sheriff," he said, fear in his eyes, "the crowd's growing! There's more than a thousand people out in the street now." He glanced at John. "And the prisoner who killed Hendrickson and the officer—his eyes look glazed and he's got a death rattle in his throat."

Hardie rushed John into his brother's cell moments later.

Too late. Bobby was dead.

CHAPTER TWENTY-SEVEN

Wild rumors that Joe Ashley and other heavily armed gang members were on their way to Miami to avenge Bobby's death spread with lightning speed. The Ashley patriarch was actually in Palm Beach. But panicky Miamians armed themselves. The mob outside the jail grew, demanding that Bobby be turned over to them.

Sheriff Dan Hardie defused the immediate threat of violence by bringing Bobby out on a stretcher. His deputies carried the body up and down the streets to show the would-be lynch mob that the cop killer they wanted was beyond any earthly punishment.

Young members of the Miami Rifles covered Hardie, who strode grimly behind the stretcher with a shotgun, determined not to lose young Ashley's body to the mob. It worked. The target of their wrath looked so young and pale in death, his wounds so grievous, that even hard-core agitators lost their stomach for the idea of hanging him from the nearest lamppost, dead or alive.

But Hardie's worries were far from over. A scrawled note nailed to a tree at the edge of town, further fueled public fears.

> We were in Miami when one of our gang, young Bob Ashley, was brutally shot to death by your officers. All of Miami is about to pay for what you've done. And if John Ashley is not given a fair trial and turned loose, we will be back to shoot up your whole Goddamn town again, no matter what. We'll be there. Soon.
> Signed, Kid Lowe and other members of the Ashley gang

Rumors that the gang was poised to invade Miami and free John from jail spread through a long and sleepless night.

Sheriff Hardie warned the Ashleys not to send family members for Bobby's body. "I can't guarantee their safety," he told Joe. An out-of-town relative, Edward Rogers, an in-law, risked his own life to take Bobby home. Hardie's deputies escorted him safely out of Miami. On his own after that, Rogers managed to accomplish his mission and deliver his sad cargo to Palm Beach.

He was lucky. Trigger-happy Miamians were heavily armed, angry, and in most cases, drunk enough to shoot anyone named Ashley on sight. Many wanted John lynched after rumors spread that he'd paid for his defense with the loot from the Stuart bank robbery—despite Bobby's dying declaration that he and Kid Lowe had split the take after John was wounded.

Hardie was well aware that a mob broke into the county jail, then located in Juno, twenty years earlier. Determined to lynch a man accused of killing a sheriff's deputy and two residents, they murdered a jailer who tried to protect the prisoner, whom they hanged and left swinging from a signpost at a major intersection.

He'd be damned if he'd let that happen on his watch. Despite bitter protests, Hardie closed the saloons until further notice. Lynch mobs were bad, drunken lynch mobs far worse.

Frightened families packed up and fled the city. Those who stayed stripped the shelves at the trading post and hardware store of all their guns, ammunition, and emergency supplies. Businesses shuttered. Banks closed. The Miami Rifles patrolled and every man and boy was armed and jittery.

A group of leading citizens urged the mayor to ask the governor to send in the National Guard to protect the public and keep the peace. The mayor conferred with Sheriff Hardie, then refused. "The situation is under control and being well handled by our own authorities," he said, labeling as "groundless" the rumors of lynch mobs or gang members coming for John Ashley. Hardie himself wired the governor, said Miami was in good hands, and urged him to ignore "sensational stories from unreliable sources."

It was a gamble. Hardie and the mayor didn't want the world to think they had lost control. Pride was a factor, but the rest was strategy. Hardie believed their refusal to request outside help would assure residents that mob violence would not rule and the Ashley gang would not raid the city. But he also issued sawed-off shotguns to a dozen extra men assigned to guard the jail.

Sporadic shootings erupted throughout the county. Jumpy citizens with itchy trigger fingers blasted away, as they mistook family members, farm animals, wild animals, and their neighbors for members of the Ashley gang.

The newspapers called for calm. "There probably is no Ashley gang," opined the writer of one front-page editorial: "If a few members of that misguided body are left, they have fled. The remaining family members are peaceful, quiet citizens who should not be punished by this constant suspicion of all who bear that name."

"Life is short and full of trouble . . . ," the pastor read from the Book of Job at Bobby's funeral, "like a flower that quickly grows, then dies away . . . like a shadow, here for a short time, then gone."

He did not speak of how Bobby's short life had ended.

Young Rachel Lummus and her parents were among the mourners as Bobby went to his rest close to home, on the Ashley property. The family feared a grave elsewhere might be robbed or desecrated.

John, under tight security in jail, was denied permission to attend the funeral.

Services for Officer John R. Riblet were held in Fort Pierce, where his wife, the daughter of Florida pioneers, was born. The pastor praised the officer's bravery in risking and losing his own life trying to take Bobby Ashley alive, instead of shooting him down from a distance.

Hundreds attended the funeral for jailer Wilbur W. Hendrickson at Miami's Southern Methodist Church. Pallbearers carried his casket from the courthouse to the city cemetery as a band played a dirge. Only a month before his death Hendrickson had warned city officials about poor security at the jail. He had told a reporter for the *Miami Metropolis* that the jail was "dangerous and a disgrace to the county."

Several days after the story was published, Hendrickson physically overpowered a violent prisoner to thwart an escape.

The jailer may have had a premonition foreseeing his own death. He'd pleaded for help, better security, more manpower or a different job, but fate intervened. The day he was shot dead, the inmates of his small, overcrowded jail included four accused murderers and three men, including John Ashley, already sentenced to hang.

Like Riblet, Hendrickson was born in Ohio. The son of a Great Lakes steamboat captain, he piloted steamboats in Florida until the railroad arrived, then became a master printer at a newspaper. He quit to wear a badge. A former West Palm Beach marshal, and a deputy sheriff in Miami for six and a half years before he became jailer, he had recently set his sights on and campaigned for the job of Miami police chief. The primary election was held the day before Bobby Ashley pedaled up to the jail with his long blue package. Hendrickson lost. Crestfallen, he told friends he planned to move upstate to grow vegetables on a twenty-acre tract his father-in-law owned.

On that election day before he died, the county commission had agreed, based largely on Hendrickson's pleas, to levy a special tax to build a bigger, better, safer jail. But he wouldn't live to see it.

His widow, Marian, recalled later that her husband had warned her that one of the two rifles kept near the front door wasn't loaded, but in her panic she'd seized the wrong one. Had she only picked up the other, she easily could have killed Bobby Ashley. She had seen the young man with the blue parcel circle the jail earlier, she said, thought it was suspicious, and planned to tell her husband about it when he came home for lunch. But he'd walked in laughing in his big, booming way about something funny he'd seen and began to tell her about it. As they laughed and chatted over lunch, the slender youth on the bicycle slipped her mind until she saw him again, in her living room rifling her dying husband's pockets.

Officer Riblet's widow, Madge, had always feared guns and swore on her husband's grave that she would never allow their young son, now fatherless at age three, to use, touch, or own a firearm.

Her husband, a popular member of the eighteen-man Miami Police Department, was known to be especially protective of young mothers with baby carriages. He'd stop all traffic at busy intersections so they could safely push their precious cargo across the dusty streets.

The Stuart bank's insurance company wrote the widow, described her husband as a hero who paid the ultimate price "to capture and fatally wound one of the bank robbers," and enclosed a one-hundred-dollar reward. City officials pledged to continue to pay her dead husband's twenty-five-dollar-a-month salary.

The triple shooting touched everyone, including John Ashley. Bobby's violent and ugly death rekindled a flame that barely flickered in his condemned older brother. John's malaise and hopelessness vanished like smoke. He suddenly burned to the core with a fiery determination to survive. If he did not, Bobby's sacrifice would be in vain. John had to live free again, for himself, for Bobby, Laura, and his family. He'd live for Bobby, make Laura happy, and repay his parents for the misery he'd brought them.

He immediately planned his escape. No guns, no outside help. His only tool: a metal spoon. He broke through his cell's cement floor and used the spoon to dig for more than a month. Each day he'd excavate as much dirt as one can with a spoon, hide the dirt under his bunk, flush it away with water later, or allow it to sift slowly through a tiny hole in his pocket as he strode the corridors during his daily hour of exercise.

While John walked one day, a conscientious jailer searched his cell, discovered the dig, and alerted Sheriff Hardie, who advised the jailer to keep quiet and do nothing—for the time being. Hardie wanted to know if anyone else was involved and, if so, to what degree. He and the jailer watched and waited as John dug for weeks. The project, Hardie thought, would keep the prisoner occupied, too busy to plot other schemes or escapes.

John's excitement mounted as he inched closer to freedom. Less than two tantalizing feet from fresh air, sunshine, and a sky full of billowing cumulus clouds, he was dragged from his cell and locked into a more secure cage. He refused to talk and concealed his fury, certain he'd been betrayed by fellow prisoner Floriah R. Johnson, a condemned murderer in an adjacent cell. The next time the men passed in the corridor, Ashley lunged, threw Johnson to the floor, and tried to strangle him. Two jailers—Clyde, a husky former farmer from Georgia, and a portly, red-faced, sweaty man named Sutter—rushed to rescue Johnson as he struggled for breath.

"Don't you choke him!" Sutter bellowed, panting as he tore John's shirt and waistband in an attempt to drag him off the man. "You can't kill him, John! We got to hang him!"

"Didn't do it! Didn't do it! Wasn't me!" the man cried. Johnson had used the same defense at his trial. Nobody believed it then; John didn't believe it now.

Clyde, the farm boy, wrestled John into a headlock. "Don't do it, John," he panted into his ear. "We'll do it for you." John could have hurt him but didn't. His appeal to the Florida Supreme Court was still pending. The jailers were decent men doing their jobs, and someday he might need their good will.

John remained the best-behaved, most closely guarded prisoner in Dade County Jail until August 1916, when the high court reversed the judge who had denied him a new trial. He'd just won a new chance at life.

Fear, unrest, and paranoia still roiled in Miami. The politicians didn't want another controversial, high-profile murder trial for John Ashley. The defense attorneys seized the moment to negotiate a deal. The prosecution would drop the murder charge. There'd be no new trial or future prosecution in the case of DeSoto Tiger. In exchange, Ashley would plead guilty to the Palm Beach bank robbery. He had never denied robbing the bank, had no problem pleading guilty, and was sentenced to seventeen and a half years' hard labor in the state penitentiary.

Prison officials waited at the gate to welcome John to Raiford in November 1916. Two, in fact, were so delighted to meet and greet their notorious inmate, they posed happily for photos with him. The wardens wore dark, somber suits and traditional ties. One carried a Bible. Ashley wore his black patch, a white tropical suit, a jaunty bow tie, and a bemused expression as he stared directly into the camera. The three could have been at a garden party. The only hint that the occasion had more gravity was the stone wall looming behind them.

During his stay, prison doctors fitted John with a glass, blue-gray artificial eye. As charismatic as ever and, as always, a model prisoner, John was assigned to a chain gang that worked out of a road camp in Milligan. Happy to be outside prison walls in the great outdoors, he even enjoyed the hard work and strenuous exercise, but not enough to stay.

John and fellow bank robber Tom Maddox escaped on a breezy spring night in 1918. They left behind the ankle chains they were required to wear at all times. An assistant warden had helpfully unlocked the twenty-pound chains after John pointed out the possibility of shackle sores that could cause gangrene.

Bloodhounds and a posse failed to pick up a trail. Lawmen were baffled until witnesses in a nearby town reported seeing two men who fit the escaped prisoners' descriptions speeding south in a flashy Maxwell motorcar driven by a striking young woman with black hair. Officials later recalled that Ashley's dark-haired sweetheart, Laura Upthegrove, had recently visited him at the road camp.

Eventually they called off the search.

Ashley was gone.

CHAPTER TWENTY-EIGHT

The young woman in white stumbled as she ran, her blond hair pale in the moonlight. She carried a satchel and paused from time to time to catch her breath and regain her bearings. The endless woods looked so different, so forbidding at night. The only light was the quarter moon, and the path, when she could see it, lay in shadow. But, on a mission, she felt no fear.

She slowed and stared uncertainly at faint lights up ahead. Was she lost? If she was on the right path, there should be nothing but dark woods between her and her destination. Why, she wondered with a sigh, must this always happen at night? And what *is* that up ahead? She had thought she was alone in the wilderness. Focused on the mysterious, moving lights, she never saw the man in the mask until he stepped directly out in front of her, brandishing a rifle. The barrel glinted in the night. She'd seen up close what such guns could do.

"Halt!" he ordered, his voice raspy. "Don't move."

A bandana concealed the lower half of his face. All she saw were his eyes and the rough hands grasping the weapon. She gasped as he took a long stride toward her. What had she stumbled into?

He had heard her approach, glad that the arriving intruder was not stealthy, but on edge that anyone at all was out there in the dark.

Now, for the first time, she saw the rope stretched across the narrow, rutted, unpaved road ahead.

"Turn around now and don't come back here," he said gruffly. "Don't say nothing to anybody."

"I won't say a word, but I'm not turning around either." Still panting, she firmly stepped forward. "I'm Mrs. Nils Jorgensen, from White City. Ingrid. I'm a nurse. Stand aside, sir, and let me pass."

"Turn around, ma'am, or I'll shoot you."

She did not flinch but stood her ground. "My neighbor who lives up yonder made an urgent request that I hurry to help his wife, who's in childbirth labor. He's gone to Fort Pierce by horse and wagon to fetch the doctor. It's at least a two-hour ride. The woman is alone and needs me. Now."

"No. You can't . . ."

Ingrid Jorgensen, her eyes adjusted to the low light, now saw men unloading cases of liquor up ahead. Later, when she had time to think about it, she realized what they were doing. But all she thought of at the time was the young mother and baby who needed her. Chin up, she shook her finger at the man. "I'm on my way to help a mother birth her baby, and you won't stop me."

"Watch me . . ." The rifleman's words trailed off as another man, well built and a head taller, emerged from the darkness without a sound.

"Who is she?" he asked the gunman.

The rifleman shrugged. "She just come up outta nowhere. I told her to go home or get shot."

"Lower your gun, Sam," the tall man said, with a sigh. "We don't point guns at women."

"Sir"—Ingrid Jorgensen turned to the newcomer and introduced herself—"I am a nurse."

He nodded. "John Ashley, ma'am."

"Thank God. I thought it was you, Mr. Ashley. But it's so dark . . ." She ducked under the rope and rushed to him.

"I need your help," she said, still breathing hard, her hand over her pounding heart. "It's Seth Miller's wife. Their first little one. It's been a hard . . ."

John's attitude changed. "We'll get you up there as fast as we can, ma'am. Here, let me carry that for you." He took her satchel and scowled at the rifleman.

"Please don't delay her husband and the doctor when they come!" she said, over her shoulder.

"He won't," John said. "I promise you that, ma'am." He turned to the rifleman. "When he comes with the doctor, take them right to Miller's door."

The nurse was breathless as she kept up with John's long stride. "Do you need any help?" he asked. "My wife, Laura, is here somewhere. She's at her best in a crisis." He searched the darkness and the golden pools of lantern light, as men labored to tote heavy cases of moonshine from the still and load it into mule-drawn wagons. "Laura," he called. "Laura!"

The workers parted and she appeared from their midst carrying a lantern, a .38 caliber revolver strapped to her waist. Her blue eyes widened when she saw the woman, her fine blond hair wild and free in the night breeze. John explained. Laura nodded. "I have clean towels in the wagon," she told the nurse. "I'll get them."

"Take some whiskey too," John called after her. "If the patient doesn't need it, I'm sure Seth Miller and the good doctor will before this night is over."

"I knew you'd help." Ingrid Jorgensen gratefully clasped his hand. "I've heard about all the good things you do. God bless you."

After escaping the chain gang, John kept his promise: to love Laura, make her happy, live for Bobby, and try to repay his parents for all they'd lost.

Still not married, John and Laura could not have cleaved more to one another. She participated wholeheartedly in whatever John did, legal or illegal. Newspapers had dubbed her "Queen of the Everglades," their base of operation, and true or not, she was widely believed to be a powerful influence on John, his gang members, and their entire enterprise.

Both clung to the dream of exchanging vows at Saint Stephen's Church in Coconut Grove. Initially, they'd hoped to be the first couple married there, but the simple mission-style chapel with its arched door and bell tower had opened on schedule without them in 1912, when John was a fugitive, wanted for murder. The little church was still their dream. Its early members were the Mathesons, the McFarlands, and the Munroes, all pioneer Miami families, rock-solid citizens John had hoped would be their friends and neighbors.

Honest work was not available for chain gang fugitives pictured on wanted posters, so John operated the Ashley family's three moonshine stills in Palm Beach County. The business prospered and grew under his management.

Palm Beach sheriff George Baker suffered from health problems and had lost a leg but never stopped his pursuit of John Ashley. A few volunteers had initially stepped forward. The reward had grown. Those eager to claim it assumed that a legendary marksman who'd lost an eye was no longer to be feared. But his would-be captors found, to their dismay, that he was as good a marksman as ever. John, they concluded, had probably always closed his left eye when he aimed. His skill, and his growing popularity, made it difficult to recruit men to hunt him. He possessed all the qualities that pioneers admired. Brave and kind, he excelled as a marksman, hunter, trapper, and fisherman, remained loyal to only one woman, had a contagious sense of humor, and never hesitated to thumb his nose at authority.

As their business prospered, the Ashley family shared with others, as always. Everyone in Palm Beach County had stories about John Ashley and his gang. Sick, poor, unfortunate people found money tucked beneath rocks left on their porches. Elderly widows and young mothers with hungry children found food and supplies on their doorsteps. When the Ashleys stocked up on necessities, they always ordered extra for those in need.

John also took great pains to protect the legitimate businessmen with whom he dealt. He rented mules and wagons to haul heavy loads of whiskey to paved roads where it could be transferred into waiting cars. Each time he rented them Ashley paid the full purchase price and had the owner fill out an undated bill of sale to show the authorities if the gang was ever caught using the wagons and animals in an illegal operation. When they were safely returned, the owner would reimburse the gang for the full amount, less the rent.

Prosperity beyond their wildest dreams was just around the corner. Prohibition, in 1920, forever changed the future of John Ashley and those he loved. With liquor sales banned nationwide, the demand soared.

John expanded the business. He and his brothers Frank and Ed, experienced boaters like so many others in South Florida, took to the sea. The British sold the most popular brands of liquor, and there was a huge demand to fill. The Ashley Gang smuggled liquor from Bahamian warehouses into the Jupiter Inlet and Stuart. They ran liquor to Florida from West End in the Bahamas. No US government ever had or would have enough federal agents or police to protect the entire Florida coast, with all its inlets, islands, coves, and deserted beaches.

The Ashleys were not alone. Many prominent families engaged in bootlegging and rum-running, which burgeoned into a lucrative business for all. Entire populations of frontier Florida towns were either engaged in transporting and selling contraband liquor or were customers of those who were. Liquor for medicinal purposes was a household staple in nearly all Florida homes. And most of the population saw Prohibition as another example of federal regulation that their parents or grandparents had rejected when they seceded from the Union. Men reaped fortunes. Competition flourished. Lawmen and politicians happily pocketed payoffs to look the other way.

In for a dime, in for a dollar. Break one federal law and it's easier to ignore others. The Ashleys embraced the premise that it was no crime to rob trains and banks. They were simply reclaiming Confederate wealth stolen by damn Yankees.

So when the weather grew too rough to go to sea, the gang raided banks from Stuart to Fort Meade, Avon Park, and Boynton Beach. His neighbors respected John's code of ethics. The well-planned robbery of a major South Florida bank was aborted at the last minute when John learned that a childhood playmate was the bank's president. It wouldn't be right, he said, to do that to a boyhood pal. So they didn't.

Laura enjoyed her role. At a time when women were slowly achieving a few basic rights, she participated fully in John's business. She drove getaway cars faster than any man. She flounced into banks, posed as a customer, and cased them for robberies. She smiled, waved, and drove carloads of bootleg whiskey past Prohibition agents who waved back.

Even John's nephew Hanford Mobley, son of the businessman of the same name, joined the gang in his early teens. Popular and athletic, full of fun and pranks, he reminded everyone of the uncle he idolized. Hanford often drove his family's Model T Ford to school and was often seen with eight or nine school pals piled into the car cruising on their lunch break.

Inevitably, Prohibition's huge profits attracted money-hungry mobsters from New York and Chicago. They showed up in South Florida, sweating in woolen suits, slogging through swamps in shiny shoes, attempting to muscle in and take over the action. But they didn't know the coastline, the currents, the Gulf Stream, or the swampy countryside. Even more important, they didn't know the depth of pioneer Floridians' dislike for intruders, particularly Yankees. The final shot of the Civil War, an ancient echo, had been fired fifty-five years earlier, but the war still raged on in the hearts and minds of South Floridians.

Sheriff Baker was still obsessed. When a tip came that John was out hunting alone, on foot, he sent his seven best deputies to lie in wait and shoot him. They tried, several times, but missed. They demanded he surrender. He laughed, climbed a tree, and pinned them down with rifle fire from somewhere inside the dense foliage. He shouted that he had them covered and they froze. He called out their names to prove he could see them all, and swore to kill the first one to move. Then he quietly climbed down and left.

The deputies lay facedown on the ground in the scorching midday sun, afraid to move a muscle. Hours later a local homesteader rode by on horseback. When he stopped to ask what the hell they were doing, they frantically warned him to dismount and hit the dirt. John Ashley, they said, was high above them with a rifle and had them all pinned down.

"He'll kill you!" one cried. "Get down, for God's sake, man!"

"No, he won't. I have no quarrel with John." The man squinted up into the trees but saw no one. "He's a good neighbor; he'd give anybody the shirt off his back." Then he rode on. Nearly an hour later, the man spotted John Ashley up ahead on foot and caught up with him. "John," he asked, "do you know deputies are still hugging the ground back there, sure you'll shoot 'em if they move?" They shared a good laugh and sips from John's silver flask, a gift from Laura.

Baker would not have been as upset if the homesteader hadn't repeated the story until it reached the ears of a reporter, who interviewed him and put it in the newspaper.

Embarrassed again, unable to recruit a posse, Sheriff Baker sent out a hit man to kill John Ashley.

One afternoon, camped near one of the stills, Shine, John's favorite dog and constant companion, began to bark furiously. He caught a young black man, his rifle aimed, about to kill the animal.

"Don't you shoot that dog!" he shouted, and lifted his own rifle. "If you do, I'll kill you!" John took the man's gun away and examined it. "Where'd you get this weapon?" he asked.

"Sheriff Baker give it to me," the would-be killer whined. "It's from the National Guard armory. I got to give it back. Sheriff Baker," he said, "sent me here to kill you." John became so angry that the terrified man fell to his knees, began to cry and beg for his life.

Baker, the man said, offered to drop charges against him if he'd kill John; if he didn't he'd go to a chain gang for life.

John felt sorry for him. "Here." The man flinched as John gave him a bullet. "Tell Baker this one's for him. If he wants me dead, tell him to come out here like a man and do it himself." He told the would-be hit man to run, but instead he continued to quake, cry, and beg for his life. John sighed, took out his billfold, handed the man five dollars, and told him to leave. Before he did, the man asked John to give back the rifle.

"Nope," John said. "Tell Baker I'm not giving it back until he comes out here and asks me himself." John thought it was funny.

Baker was livid.

John and Laura were at his parents' for dinner when the second-biggest story of the year broke. Frank and his little red-headed wife drove up in their yellow Ford with the news. "Wait till you hear this, Johnny! Sheriff George Baker is dead," he announced. "Natural causes—a heart attack."

"I can't believe he's gone!" John said. "You sure, Frankie?"

"Funeral's set for Thursday."

"I don't wish nobody ill," Leugenia said, "and I'll pray for his family. But nobody will miss that man. Ain't no lawmen like him with the Lord."

"You know what this means?" John whispered to Laura, beside him. "Our lives are changed!"

"You sure it's for the better?" She looked troubled.

"Are you kidding?" Frankie was exuberant. "What new sheriff could be worse than Baker?"

"Damn straight." Joe Ashley, the family patriarch, lifted his glass, smiled his crooked grin, and reached for Leugenia's hand. "Happy days are here again!"

* * *

"Marry me," John said when they were alone that night.

"It's time," she agreed.

They arranged to slip into Miami and quietly exchange vows at Saint Stephen's Church in June 1921. A piece of their Miami dream would finally come true. The long feud with Baker was over. They believed life was about to become simpler, better, and more forgiving.

They could not have been more wrong.

CHAPTER TWENTY-NINE

The bad news hit hard.

Palm Beach had a new sheriff. His name was Baker. The governor had appointed Bob Baker, the late sheriff's son, to fill out his father's term. The new sheriff was the former jailer from whom Ashley escaped on that stormy Palm Beach night. He'd been humiliated, belittled by the press and other lawmen—including his father. No one ever let him forget it.

Baker lacked his father's physical stature and his reputation as a lawman. But he had ambition, a long memory, and a hunger for revenge that kept him awake at night. John Ashley had taunted, tormented, and ridiculed his father. He swore the man's health had suffered and his life had been shortened by the frustration and lack of respect he'd endured at Ashley's hands. Payback time had come. He vowed to make it happen.

Leugenia burst into tears at the news. The Ashley men were grim. Baker was a pipsqueak and a coward, but his single-minded obsession could only bring them grief, and they had no shortage of that in their lives.

John found his share on a three-day business trip. As he unloaded cases of contraband liquor at a Wauchula garage, northwest of Lake Okeechobee, he was confronted by Hardee County Sheriff John Poucher. The delivery had been so damn routine that John had left his pistol in the car. The rural sheriff had no idea who he was, so John peacefully surrendered, gave a false name, and hoped he'd be able to post bond quickly or escape from the local jail before anyone had a clue to his real identity. His face was famous in South Florida but not way up in Hardee County. He remained calm, casual, and low-key. So far, so good. But as he was booked into the jail, another inmate began to shout.

"Lordy! It's John Ashley, the outlaw!" he cried. "That's him! Right there!" He pointed, as all heads turned. "The sheriff done brought in John Ashley! John? How'd you ever let 'em catch you up here, man?"

John sighed and replied with an icy stare. Too late.

The sheriff choked on his cigar, broke into a cold sweat, locked John into a solitary, high-security cell, and assigned several men with shotguns to guard him.

John was immediately returned to Raiford Penitentiary to finish his seventeen-year term.

Laura agonized. She should have gone with him. He never let his guard down when she was beside him. She would have had the pearl-handled revolver he'd given her. She would have had his back, could have distracted the sheriff or gotten the drop on him. Could have, would have, should have.

Their scheduled wedding date came and went.

Laura conducted business on the mainland while Ed and Frank continued to run liquor in from the Bahamas, operating as best they could without John's personal touch, insight, and business acumen.

And John, during a long, dark night in his North Florida prison cell, experienced a clear and lifelike nightmare so unsettling that he awoke flailing, in a cold sweat, tears on his face. That morning he sent urgent word for his father to come at once.

He'd had the same sort of ominous and disturbing dream in his Miami jail cell the morning of that fatal day when Bobby came to town. He'd experienced a similar, waking vision the day the tramp found Leugenia home alone. But this new dream was far less vague. Details this time were as sharp as knife thrusts, an entire scenario he could not prevent from unfolding around him in horrific three-dimensional color.

He neither ate nor slept. How could he? He prayed and paced for days until a jailer said he had a visitor.

"Pop!" He slid into a seat behind the wire-mesh screen that separated him and his father. Their skin looked sickly gray behind it and the harsh lighting cast unkind shadows on their faces.

"What is it, son?" The family patriarch, low-key and taciturn as usual, looked pinched, his shoulders hunched as if in defeat. The trip had been long and hard, north from Palm Beach to just south of the Georgia border.

"I'm worried about Ed and Frank, Pop. You know how I dream sometimes?"

Joe nodded slowly.

"I had a dream so real it scared the hell out of me. Warn the boys. Give 'em a message as quick as you can."

"Tell me the dream, son."

John sighed. "Ed and Frank were on a run to the Bahamas aboard the *Sea Spray*. They loaded 'er up with good whiskey and started home in rough seas, but they were hijacked, robbed by some of the competition, those three bastards who work out of Vero Beach: Donny Ridgeway, Jack Allen, and Will Holliwell. Same ones tried to cross us once before. I never trusted them. Didn't like—"

"The dream?" Joe persisted. "What happened?"

John took a deep breath. "They shot Ed and Frankie, hijacked their liquor, then scuttled the *Sea Spray* with them aboard."

Joe gave a slight nod.

"Talk to 'em, Pop. Tell 'em to watch out for those guys, avoid 'em, don't turn their backs on 'em. Never. And if they ever make any false moves, tell the boys to use their guns. I mean it. They're dangerous."

Joe sat quietly, eyes downcast.

"Will you do that for me, Pop? Right away?"

Joe paused. "No, son. I can't."

John's eyes widened. "Why?"

"Ed and Frankie took the *Sea Spray* to the Bahamas last week, with thirteen thousand dollars for a load. Your brothers didn't come back, son. Young Hanford and Joe Tracey took the other boat over to look for 'em. They were told that Ed and Frankie loaded up but bad weather delayed 'em overnight. When the weather didn't let up the next day, they pushed off for the mainland anyhow. The crew who helped 'em load said conditions were hazardous and the boat was overloaded."

"God help us," John whispered. "But if they're gone"—his voice rose—"it wasn't weather! It was those bastards!"

"Hanford's a smart boy, like you," Joe said. "He asked what other crews were there when our boys were. He came back with a list. The names you mentioned are on it, son."

Neither Ed nor Frank Ashley was ever seen again. No trace of their boat, money, or liquor was ever found.

Laura believed that John's arrest in Wachula and his return to prison may have saved his life. Had he been free, he might have been lost at sea with Ed and Frank.

John was sure that if he hadn't been arrested, he would have been with his brothers, and might have saved them.

While he served time at Raiford, gang members operated the business. Clarence Middleton and Roy Matthews spent most of their time hijacking other bootleggers' whiskey when it was being moved by boat or car.

Hanford Mobley, more creative, came up with another idea. He visited Laura at the Ashley home one afternoon. She always had been fond of John's favorite nephew but was startled when Hanford asked if he could try on, then borrow, one of her long skirts and frilly blouses. He'd only wear them once, he promised, and asked her to keep it between them. Joe and Leugenia needn't know. More than ever, Laura wished John was there for a man-to-man talk with a younger family member.

She helped Hanford select a long black skirt, a white blouse with lace-trimmed sleeves, and a fussy hat with a smoky veil that draped across his face. They fit Hanford, a slender lad, perfectly.

The next morning, in nearby Gomez, Mobley, in his girly getup, frantically flagged down a passing motorist. When a driver braked to assist what appeared to be a damsel in distress, Matthews and Middleton burst out of the bushes, hijacked his car, and tied him to a tree.

Soon after, John Taylor, the cashier who still worked at the Stuart bank, found himself, in a moment of déjà vu, being robbed by the Ashley Gang. Again. This time it wasn't young Bobby who walked in and held everyone at rifle point. Instead, it was a fashionably dressed creature in a black skirt, white blouse, and veiled hat. The attire was definitely feminine, but the gait, hairy arms, and voice were not. Hanford Mobley's accomplices, their noses pressed up against the plate glass window out front, burst in on cue and robbed the bank.

The robbers fled in the stolen car, but Sheriff Bob Baker was soon hot on their trail. He immediately alerted sheriffs all over the state. Fast action and better means of communication worked. Mobley and Middleton were arrested halfway up the west side of the state, at Plant City, in Hillsborough County.

Hanford and Clarence stonewalled, refused to name the third robber or even speak to Sheriff Baker, who shouted, punched, kicked the wall, and vowed to bury them in prison for life. Frustrated, Baker modified his tactics. He questioned Clarence alone. Still somewhat drug-addled, Middleton immediately confessed to all he knew and more, then begged the sheriff to keep it secret because Mobley would surely kill him if he knew. He not only implicated Matthews, he helpfully told the sheriff precisely where his friend had gone to hide out in Georgia. He even drew a map. Matthews was found and arrested.

Mobley made several unsuccessful attempts to escape from the Palm Beach County Jail, so Baker booked all three prisoners into the more secure Broward County Jail, a fortified, escape-proof facility in Fort Lauderdale.

Hanford Mobley became a model prisoner. Like his uncle John, he was helpful, friendly, and nonthreatening to the newly appointed jailer, W. W. Hicks, right up to the moment he and Matthews escaped. Middleton refused to go with them at the last minute. He claimed he was scared he'd be shot in the back as they fled. What he actually feared was that his friends knew he'd confessed and would kill him. He felt safer in jail.

Hanford, weary of revenge-crazed sheriffs named Baker, fled the state and traveled as far west as a man could go. He gave up crime and drove a taxicab in San Francisco. He marveled at the cable cars, the people, the tall buildings. Soon restless, he went back east and signed on to go to sea again, big-time. A crew member aboard a transatlantic ocean liner, he made several trips to Germany. But as much as he enjoyed new places and strange sights, they all paled compared to Florida. Her sons and daughters are hooked for life, he realized. You can leave Florida but it will never leave you. He began to write home for news.

For his part in the bank robbery, Middleton was sentenced to fifteen years in the state pen at Raiford, where he was happily reunited with

John Ashley and Joe Tracey, Laura's half brother, and made the acquaintance of their new pal, Ray "Shorty" Lynn.

Ray, from an old Florida family like the Ashleys and the Upthe-
groves, had married young. An outdoorsman, he loved to hunt, trap, and
fish. One morning, in a patriotic fervor after a long night of drinking, he
enlisted in the army. He quickly regretted it. The free-spirited country
boy who'd grown up roaming frontier Florida at will found military
rules, regulations, and regimentation unbearable. He went AWOL, much
to the alarm of his young, pregnant wife, in need of a nest and a husband
who could provide for her.

She refused to join Ray in hiding in the Everglades. That was
no place for a pregnant woman, or any woman, she told him. His
explanation—that he hoped to meet John Ashley and join his gang—
appalled her even more. He did not meet Ashley. His wife divorced him.
Then he was arrested. Prison life, he feared, might be worse than the
army, until there, behind bars, he met John Ashley! He felt his luck had
changed, that this was meant to be. Eager to be part of an enterprise he
could relate to, with like-minded companions, he was thrilled to join the
Ashley Gang.

John, the model prisoner, was sent to a road gang. Again. Soon after,
a former customer of John's in Okeechobee was fixing his supper one
evening when a pebble struck his kitchen window. Then another, and
another. He snatched up his shotgun, charged out onto his porch, and
there, crouched behind the front steps, was John Ashley.

"Hey! Come on in, John." He waved him inside.

"You alone?"

"Yup, my wife and kids went down to Fort Pierce to do a little shopping and visit her mother. Damn good to see you again, John. Heard
they sent you off to Raiford for a long stretch."

"They did," John said as he climbed the steps.

"How'd you get out?"

"Broke out." John grinned, as his host handed him a drink.

"How'd you do that?"

John winked. "Bribed a guard." He downed the drink and scowled.
"Where'd you get this rotgut, Ernie? You make it yourself? I can get
you some really good, smooth whiskey."

"Good deal, John. I'm in the market."

After a good meal and a long chat, John said goodbye and disappeared, alone, into the night, headed south.

His reunion with Laura and his parents was just the beginning. Soon after, Joe Tracey was released from Raiford. Then Ray Lynn and Clarence Middleton escaped from a road camp in Marianna, up in the far northwest section of the state. All three found themselves free close to the Georgia and Alabama borders, but all three beelined back to South Florida, the Everglades, and John Ashley.

And when Hanford Mobley heard from relatives that John and the boys were back in business. He quit his job to race south and join them.

The newly regenerated gang expanded operations into a number of counties. They stole so many cars to haul moonshine and bootleg whiskey that Sheriff J. R. Merritt up in Saint Lucie County recovered thirty-five stolen automobiles in less than a month, courtesy of the Ashley Gang, who left them parked when they no longer needed them.

Business boomed, and John decided to give Laura a diamond ring. In fact, he thought, all the gang's women deserved diamonds. The gang members all ordered rings sent COD from a fine New York jeweler. Notified that their packages had arrived and could be picked up, the gang picked them up. They broke into the express office that night and took only the packages addressed to them. Yankee insurance companies could cover the loss.

Shortly after the gang reunion, the three hijackers in John's death dream about Ed and Frank also vanished at sea. Like Ed and Frank, no one ever saw them or their boat again.

Laura wore a new sparkler on her finger and drove a seven-passenger Lincoln with wooden wheels, an open car with a green body, a black hood, and an aluminum radiator.

The gang robbed stores and banks and hijacked boat- and carloads of liquor. Their escapades made the newspapers regularly, along with the more mundane news about ice cream socials and tea dances and the obituaries of local luminaries gone to their reward.

The gang hijacked so many shipments of illegal whiskey being smuggled in from the Bahamas that they nearly put out of business the big-city bootleggers whose importation and distribution of foreign liquor had undermined local moonshiners. Ashley and his men proved so effective that rum-running on the Florida coast virtually ceased while they were active.

The gossip in barbershops, pool halls, and bars revolved around the gang's latest crimes and sightings. Support leaned in their favor. Newspaper editorial writers railed against the lawlessness, and one Florida politician said John Ashley was the greatest threat to the state since the Seminole Wars. But most people rooted for the local bad boys. Why not? They made the Yankees pay, poked fun at the law, and kept the whiskey flowing despite the overbearing and paternalistic federal government.

John Ashley had become a folk hero to poor Florida crackers, a symbol of resistance to Yankees, big banks, and the law. He and his gang enjoyed warm public support and were treated with respect when they appeared unexpectedly in one town or another to play pool, have their hair cut, their cars serviced, and dine on good restaurant meals.

Sheriff Bob Baker doggedly stalked them. One night he received an inside tip that John and the gang were expected at the Ashley homestead for supper. He and several heavily armed deputies hid their cars in brush off the main road at dusk, walked a distance, approached the house on foot, and settled in to sit surveillance in the woods that surrounded the place.

The winding, unpaved road that led up to the house from the main drag was half a mile long. While they watched, waited, and swatted mosquitoes, Leugenia Ashley, the family matriarch, appeared several times. She swept the front porch, carried a burlap sack out to the barn, then went to the well, but never looked up, or around, or noticed a thing. The tiny gray-haired woman had aged, they noticed, as had her husband, after losing three sons in the prime of their lives. She doddered about, focused on household chores.

"She doesn't suspect a thing," Sheriff Baker chortled to his most trusted deputy, T. W. Stone. It was just a matter of time now. They had their guns at the ready.

They'd been swarmed by mosquitoes and worried about snakes and fire ants for hours when a telltale splash of headlights suddenly reflected off the towering pines and oak trees. A car swung onto the shadowy road to the house.

"This is it," Baker muttered. "We got 'em. Here they come!" Eyes glued to the road, they paid scant attention to Leugenia, who had stepped back out onto the porch. They didn't even notice her until she raised her arm high above her head, and fired a pistol into the air three times. Then she doddered back into the house, closed the door, and never looked back.

The deputies hit the ground at the sound of shots. Down the road, brakes screeched, a powerful engine roared in reverse, and tires squealed as the car bounced back onto the paved road and peeled out. The stunned deputies ran for their own cars hidden in the brush a half mile away. But by the time they reached them, the fleeing car was long gone.

Bob Baker had underestimated Leugenia. She was no harmless old woman, no sad and grief-stricken matriarch of a doomed and dwindling clan. A true Ashley, she had sensed their presence, seen the deputies squatting in the bushes from the start, and had protected her own. Sheriff Baker now hated her with as much passion as he hated John and the others.

Baker received a bullet, delivered the next day. In the accompanying note John wrote that he had another one just like it, with Baker's name on it. Baker, apoplectic, sent back a note in which he swore that he'd soon wear Ashley's glass eye on his watch fob. He released it to the press as well, to be sure Ashley got the message. A local paper even played it on the front page.

On a bright November day in 1923, Joe Tracey hired a taxicab and had the driver take him out to a remote area, where the rest of the gang emerged from the woods to join them. They shared their picnic lunch with the driver: fresh boiled shrimp, slices of just-picked tomatoes, homemade potato salad, and lemonade. They passed around a flask, practiced target shooting in the woods, then tied the cabdriver to a tree. The man begged John not to take his taxi. He said he needed it to earn a living.

"So do we," John said. He explained that they planned to use it in a bank robbery and told him exactly where to find it later.

"If we're lucky," he said, "it won't be damaged. No bullet holes. And this is for you." John counted out a stack of bills for use of the cab. "And this"—he placed a rifle bullet on top—"is for Sheriff Baker. Give it to him and tell him that John Ashley is still waiting for him in the 'Glades."

An hour later, the gang robbed a bank in Pompano of five thousand dollars cash and eighteen thousand dollars in negotiable bearer bonds. As they fled, John tossed the cashier a rifle bullet. "A souvenir," he said, "of my career."

The cashier later told reporters that John "seemed a little wistful," as though robbery had not been his first career choice. The press speculated that maybe he had wearied of it after taking nearly one million dollars from at least forty banks between 1915 and 1924.

The cabdriver eventually struggled free, hitched a ride to town, and found his cab, undamaged, with no bullet holes, exactly where Ashley had promised.

Sheriff Baker took Ashley's message personally and waited to make his move. In February, another inside tip informed him that Ashley and his family were camped overnight at one of their stills. Baker moved quickly. He borrowed high-powered automatic rifles from the National Guard armory, and without warning, at dawn on January 10, 1924, Baker's brother, Fred, led a dozen deputies who opened fire on the Ashley camp.

John's dog, Shine, detected the intruders first. He left his master's side and ran out barking furiously to raise the alarm. Hit by rifle and shotgun fire, he was the first to die.

Shine's barking and the shots that killed him woke John and Laura, sleeping under a tarp stretched across a dry ditch nearby. Joe Ashley and other gang members were asleep in a tent near the still when the shooting started.

John held off the deputies with a handgun as he pulled up his pants. "Run!" he told Laura, and sent her to the tent for shelter with the others. "Stay with Pop," he said, and picked up his rifle. "I'll be there in a minute. Tell him it's Baker's men, looks like about a dozen. Go! Now!" He used both guns to fire a barrage at their attackers as she ran to the tent.

She stumbled inside as Joe, his rifle beside him, sat up and began to pull on his boots. "Get down!" he told her, as the gunfire continued. The others scrambled for their clothes and weapons.

"John said there's a dozen deputies! They killed Shine!" Laura said breathlessly, her eyes wet. She looked for John, then turned back to Joe as a large piece of his skull flew through the air and landed near her feet.

She saw his brains and blood splattered across the pillow, and began to scream. Then she was hit by a spray of shotgun fire.

John heard her cries and sprinted to the tent, firing back toward the deputies, who dove for cover. Inside the tent he saw her struggling to her feet, her clothes bloodstained, her arm and both legs bleeding, and rushed to help her.

"No! No! No!" she screamed. "It's Joe. Pop! Your father!"

He turned in time to see his father stop moving, and his eyes roll back in his head.

John paused, then walked out of the tent in full view, and took careful aim, as the deputies scattered. He killed Deputy Fred Baker with a single shot.

"I killed the son of a bitch," he told Laura as he ducked back into the tent. "I killed Baker's brother."

The others had slashed an opening in the back of the tent and were fleeing into the swamp. "Let's go." He took her arm.

"I can't. I can't." The wounds from the buckshot in her legs, thighs, and arm bled profusely and made it too painful to walk.

"I'll carry you." He moved to sweep her up into his arms.

"No! You go, I'll be all right. You shot Baker's brother! Run! Now!"

"I won't leave you."

"You have to. I need a doctor. I'd slow you down. You can't carry me all over the swamp while they're chasing us. You'll be caught and it will be my fault, all for no reason. Baker won't do a damn thing to me. You're the one he wants. And"—she turned to look at Joe, sprawled on his back, with one boot on, his rifle across his thighs, half his head gone, his blood spilling into the hungry earth, then averted her eyes—"I need to be with your mother now, John. You can't, but I can." She looked deep into his eyes. "This is how it has to be, John. You know it. So go now."

He did.

Her arrest was worse than she'd anticipated. Manhandled by deputies, she was held for more than twelve hours before a doctor was called to treat her painful injuries.

But worse than that, Fred Baker, a more popular man than his father or brother, had a host of caring relatives, friends, and neighbors. Furious at what Sheriff Baker described as his brother's brutal murder, a large crowd rushed to the shooting scene. They attacked the moonshine still with sledgehammers, got drunk, torched the camp, then piled into cars and wagons and raced off to attack first the Ashley and then the Mobley homesteads. Both were burned to the ground. Leugenia, rescued by her daughter Daisy and son Bill, lost both her husband and her home in a few short hours.

The newspapers condemned the mob violence toward innocent family members, and their homes were rebuilt with the help of neighbors and volunteers. But Joe's sudden, violent death struck the hearts of both the family and the gang. Their luck had begun to run out.

CHAPTER THIRTY

The gang paid top dollar for a load of whiskey on a Bahamian run and discovered too late that the bottles contained water, not whiskey. John called in every available gang member for a retaliatory raid on the liquor warehouses in the village of West End on Bahama Island. They planned their ambitious strike for a brief window in time, after the bootleggers had all paid cash for a week's supply but before the money was sent to the bank.

Heavily armed, adrenaline-charged, and ready to go to sea, the gang learned, again, that Sheriff Baker had advance knowledge of their plans and a posse was waiting in ambush at their departure point. Impatient to go, they had to outwit Baker's men as time ticked away. In a major change of plans, they departed instead through Hobe Sound and used the Jupiter Narrows for access to the sea. They sailed undetected, but the detour cost them dearly in time. Then bad weather delayed them more. Luck was not on their side.

They were late, and the regular express boat had arrived early at West End. It had departed ahead of schedule shortly before the gang arrived, taking with it $250,000 in cash for deposit in a Nassau bank. The gang's take was a paltry $8,000. But their efforts could not have drawn more attention.

For the first time in more than a hundred years, American pirates had attacked a British Crown colony. The United Kingdom struck back with a vengeance. The Brits declared Ashley an international pirate and sent warships to capture him and his gang or blast them out of the water.

John laughed, thumbed his nose at the British, called them "a pack of thieves," and retaliated. He robbed their bank in West End and outran their warships.

*   *   *

The Everglades hideout soon rang with heated debate. Hanford Mobley tried to persuade his uncle John and the others to flee Florida for new lives elsewhere. Hanford had enjoyed honest employment, weekly paychecks, and life free from trouble with the law. The world outside Florida, he said, was so big, so promising, so booming, they had no need to resort to crime. Men like them, he said, young and willing to work, could easily succeed without guns, while their current path would lead them to prison, at best.

John listened. He hated to let go of his Miami dreams but admitted that though he and Laura had sorely missed Florida when they were on the run, they now fondly recalled the simple pleasures of that time together. There was no way for them to enjoy simple pleasures in South Florida. Not while Bob Baker was sheriff.

The feud between Sheriff Baker and John Ashley had become bitter and obsessive. John's talent for escape, his ability to elude capture, his taunts at the law, and his popularity among the native crackers had ignited a fire in the bellies of law enforcement officers now determined to get Ashley, no matter what it took or how they did it.

Missing the big score in West End was a sign, an omen, John thought. He agreed, it was time to go.

CHAPTER THIRTY-ONE

Y ou promised not to leave me again, John." Laura's voice rose. "You swore!"

"I'm *not* leaving you!"

She backed away, her eyes red and swollen. "Then what do you call it?"

"I'm just going on ahead, darlin'."

She shuddered and hugged her arms. "Don't ever say that!"

"You know what I mean, darlin'. We'll find the right place, then I'll send for you and Mama. It's safer."

"Safer? Tell me, how? I'm a better shot than all three of the boys you're taking along. And they don't love you like I do," she said passionately. "We're safer together. But you're right about one thing, John. If we stay, we'll die before our time like Bobby, Ed, Frank, and poor Joe. But if we go, it should be the way we did it before. Together."

He brooded, eyes dark, then shook his head. "Too risky. I want to grow old with you, Laura. That's all I want in this life."

Her eyes flared in defiance. "What makes you think I want to grow old, with you or anyone? I never said I did! My grandma says growing old is hell. I want you, love you, need to be with you for whatever time we have."

His eyes softened. "It's too risky to travel together. You know that." He spoke slowly, persuasively, as though to a stubborn child. "My face is on every other tree, pole, and fence, under 'Wanted, Dead or Alive.' And since that damn picture of us hit the newspapers, every two-bit bounty hunter in Florida is locked, loaded, and hunting us."

"And tell me who," she asked, her voice brittle, "gave that photo to the newspapers?"

Leugenia had taken the full-length snapshot of John and Laura with a new Kodak camera Bill bought her. In it, Laura wore a holstered revolver around her waist. The photo had disappeared from the family scrapbook Leugenia carefully kept.

"We been through that a dozen times." John sighed bitterly. "We have our suspicions, but no way in hell to prove 'em."

Laura dropped to her knees beside the bedstead, her voice muffled as she buried her face in the handmade quilt. "How can you leave me? You swore you never would. I left my husband, my children, my home . . ."

"Why in hell did you ever marry that sorry-ass son of a bitch when I said I'd be back?"

"Be back?" She wheeled to face him. "When? After how many years with no word? You swore you'd never bring that up again! Promises mean nothing to you."

"Goddamnit, Laura. I meant every word I ever said to you since you were five. And I never woulda mentioned Edgar again, 'cept you just brought him up!" He paced the room angrily. "I thought I knew you, girl. But the way you've been carrying on, a man can't win. How can I even . . ."

So engrossed were they that neither heard Lucy arrive. Leugenia, who'd been shucking sweet corn, welcomed her into the warm and fragrant kitchen.

"How are you, Mama?" Lucy sweetly kissed her cheek.

Leugenia, mourning her husband and three sons, wore black from head to toe. Lucy's flouncy dress was sunshine yellow and white, colors of hope and innocence.

Agitated voices came from the room John and Laura shared. Lucy cocked her head. "My word." Her eyes widened, her hand flew to her lips, and she hitched her shoulders in a gesture of genteel surprise. "Can I believe my ears, Mama? Have the lovebirds fallen out?"

Leugenia nodded, eyes welling with tears.

Lucy's face lit up as John shouted, "Quit it now, Laura! Quit arguing. This is how it's gonna be, and that's it."

"No!" Laura cried. "I know I'll never see you again!"

"It ain't like it sounds," Leugenia murmured softly in the quiet kitchen. "They love each other dearly. Always will."

"Well, if your son Billy ever used that tone of voice to me . . ." Lucy's eyes rolled, pale lashes aflutter. "I should go, I s'pose, though I hate leavin' you alone here in the middle of a family fight. Think there'll be bloodshed?" She seemed to brighten at the thought.

"Oh, no, dear. Of course not." Leugenia looked back, startled, as she tended a sizzling skillet on the burner. "And don't feel you have to go, Lucy. You're family, always welcome in this house."

Lucy smiled as she edged into the hallway to better hear the rapid-fire exchange of words. "Whatcha fixing now, Lu?" Her pert nose twitched, like that of an animal testing the breeze. "It's way past suppertime."

Leugenia hesitated for only a moment. "Johnny's leaving," she whispered. "No one's s'posed to know."

"Leaving Laura?" Lucy's eyebrows and bosom rose simultaneously.

"Oh, no," Leugenia said earnestly. "He'd never do that. But since that picture of 'em got in the newspapers, Sheriff Baker has everybody huntin' the two of 'em together. So he and the boys are gonna leave, find a place to start over and go straight. Johnny says it's the only way to stop the killin'." She twisted her worn gold wedding band and looked wistful. "He's sending for Laura and me when they're settled."

Lucy dropped into a chair, fanning herself dramatically, as though shocked. "I had no idea," she breathed. "Lu? You'd leave Florida?" Her feral eyes darted about the room as though inventorying the furniture. "Does Billy know?"

"I'm not sure." Leugenia looked confused. "I think so."

"When are they going?" Lucy asked, all wide-eyed and innocent.

"Bright and early tomorrow. I'm fixing 'em a basket of eats to carry with 'em, fried chicken, ham, baked beans, and biscuits."

"They driving? Taking the big Ford?" Her eyes grew as stealthy as a big cat stalking prey.

Leugenia didn't see Lucy's expression as she checked the biscuits in the oven. "Drivin' up to Fort Pierce," she said, "then north through Sebastian tomorrow night. Johnny wants to stop to see his sister Daisy and her family upstate. Then they're on to Georgia and wherever the road and the good Lord leads 'em."

* * *

"What about Miami?" Laura's question echoed from their room. "Our plans?"

John paused. "Miami'll still happen for us, darlin', I promise."

"How?" She shook her head in disbelief.

"Darlin', you know everybody in Miami came from somewhere else. Only Indians and a few babies were born there."

In the kitchen, Lucy strained to hear John's words.

"Miami has a short memory," he said. "When there's trouble, it's big, but it blows over fast. Baker'll lose his badge one way or the other. How can that man not go down in disgrace? Next thing you know, we'll be forgotten. Nobody will even remember us. We'll be together there one day, Laura. I promise. I just can't stand you hating me right now."

"You know I could never hate you."

He reached for her. This time she kissed him back, again and again until they moved as one to the four-poster bed.

"At least they ain't fightin'," Lucy said smartly, as she gathered her things.

"Don't go so soon, dear. I'll fix us some tea."

"Sorry, Mama. Just remembered an errand I forgot to run, and Bill's already waitin' on me at home."

As she reached the front door, they heard a muffled cry. A door slammed. John stomped down the hall and burst shirtless into the kitchen, hair uncombed, his face dark.

"Son?" Leugenia said gently. "Can I get you something?"

He shook his head, stared hard at Lucy, then brushed by them both to carry a bulky canvas bag to the barn.

Laura's sobs sounded from the bedroom.

Lucy bid her mother-in-law a hasty goodbye. As she passed the barn where John stood peering under the hood of the car, she turned her face away to hide her triumphant smile.

Neither spoke.

He straightened up after a moment, wiped his hands on a rag, and watched thoughtfully as she rushed away. She never looked back.

"Mama?" John asked a short time later. "How long was Lucy here?"

"Just a few minutes, son. Billy's waiting on her at home."

CHAPTER THIRTY-TWO

Deputy T. W. Stone sat in his car at the four corners where they often met. When he saw her car approach, he drove to a lonely spot in the piney woods where he pulled off the road into the shadow of the trees.

She followed. "Hello, T. W." She glowed, almost giddy, as he opened her car door.

"What's got into you, blondie? You look like the cat that ate the canary."

"Oh, it's lots more excitin' than that, handsome, so much more." Her pouty lips parted in a huge smile. "I'm about to give you something you won't forget."

He turned to take the blanket from his car.

"Oh, I can't stay for all that, sweetie. Next time. I just stopped by to drop off some news and then go home to my husband. You'll earn yourself a big bonus for this," she said coyly. "Listen." She drew him close, then whispered her news in his ear, his right arm around her waist.

His body language morphed from sexual to serious business. "You're sure?"

She nodded, eyes alight, still smiling.

"What are they driving?" He let her go and fingered his thick brown mustache as he processed what she'd said.

"The Ford touring car."

"How many?" He took a pencil and small notebook from his pocket.

"All four of 'em, honey—John, Hanford, Ray Lynn, and Clarence Middleton."

"Armed?"

"That's like asking do I 'spect the sun'll rise in the mornin'. A course. What'd you 'spect?" She giggled as he took a deep, excited breath.

"Knew that would get your attention, sweet boy. Don't say I never did you any favors, T. W."

"I'll never let on who told me," he swore.

"Tch," she sighed aloud, as though annoyed. "But honey, after you nail 'em, everybody'll be asking how Sheriff Baker got wind of it. And when they do, I want you to tell the whole world, 'specially the newspapers."

"But—"

"Here's what you're gonna say, sunshine." On tiptoe, she whispered again.

His head jerked back in disbelief. "You're a helluva woman!" He laughed heartily. "You're brilliant. You sure you want me to say that?"

"Knocks two birds outta the sky with a single stone, don't it?" she snickered conspiratorially.

"You are a piece of work, gal. Hope you never set your gun sights on me."

"Now, why in the world would I ever do that, T. W.? Promise that's what you'll tell 'em?"

"Sure." He shrugged and grinned. "It's beautiful, Lucy. Perfect. Like you."

She licked her lips, then kissed his mouth hard. Their embrace was brief. Each was now preoccupied with urgent business elsewhere.

"How can you be sure?" Sheriff Baker whined from behind the oversized desk that dominated his small office. He loved that imposing piece of furniture, unaware of how much smaller he looked when he sat behind it. "Smells like a setup. Ashley's gunning for me, you know. He's snake smart and rabbit fast. He'd sell his soul to get me in an ambush."

"Woman's never lied to me yet," T. W. said. He leaned forward in his chair. "I'd swear on the Bible that everything she's told me is the whole truth and nothing but. You said yourself a dozen times how valuable it's been for us to have a confidential informant inside the family."

The sheriff scowled and got to his feet. He wore his brown three-piece suit, a slick silk tie, and his ever-present gold pocket watch. He loudly jingled small change in his pockets as he rocked nervously. "Lucy probably lies down for John Ashley too." He pointed his index finger at T. W. "Whatcha think about that?"

"Never saw or heard a hint that he's ever showed interest in any woman but Laura. But even if he did, he'd never do his brother like that. Got to admit, if nothing else, the Ashleys stick together. And 'sides, Lucy ain't his type."

"She's sure your type, ain't she?" Baker said irritably, and loudly jingled his coins.

The sound and Baker's attitude set T. W.'s teeth on edge, but he refused to show it.

"She sure is," he answered, "so long as my wife don't find out. When I pinned on that badge and took the oath, I didn't know all the sacrifices involved."

"You mean extra benefits, don'tcha?" Baker leered.

T. W. grinned and stroked his mustache. "The woman likes me well enough. She'd never lie to my face. If you coulda heard 'er, Sheriff, you'd believe 'er. Couldn't wait to spill the news."

Baker paused at his desk, shoulders hunched. He shook his head, his thin lips pursed. "Ashley knows I'm running for election. He'd never leave without trying to kill me first."

"Not so sure 'bout that," T. W. said mildly. "Despite all his bullets, bad jokes, and threats, you and me both know he coulda kilt us all a dozen times or more. But he didn't. The man finds no joy in killin'. He's more a good old boy who wisecracks to get your goat, then has a good laugh when he does."

"Tell that to my brother's widow and the kin of that dead Indian," Baker snapped.

"But Ashley didn't shoot your brother Fred till after you kilt his daddy," T. W. said reasonably, "and they dropped the charge that he kilt the Indian a long time ago."

"Doesn't mean he didn't do it!" Baker shouted. "Judges and juries can be plain stupid or on the take! You know how that goes!" He tried to light a cigar, but his hands shook too much to keep the match alive. The flame trembled and died.

Convinced his information was solid, T. W. didn't quarrel with Baker, who was obviously afraid of Ashley. Instead, he said, "Sure, this whole deal could be an ambush, one that *we* set up." He leaned closer and lowered his voice. "Only route north from Sebastian by car is acrost that bridge at the inlet. After dark it's like the bottom of a well out there, with plenty of cover for us to set up and wait. It's our last chance. Once they're outta Florida, they're like the wind. Could be anywhere. But you know John Ashley, we all do. This here's his turf. Sooner or later, he'll be back, like a homin' pigeon. But we'll have no clue when or where he'll turn up like a bad penny. You really want to spend the resta your life feelin' your blood run cold, your heart beating faster, every time you hear a quiet footstep behind you?"

Baker chewed his lower lip and jingled his change. The sound seemed to comfort him. "Trouble is nobody hears Ashley's footstep till it's too late. The man's a goddamn ghost! What I hate the most," Baker said, his face reddening, "is every time we lock up somea his gang, the ones we didn't get never stop till they bust 'em out. They've escaped from jails in Miami, Fort Lauderdale, and Palm Beach, from chain gangs, from Raiford Penitentiary, and every convict camp in this godforsaken state." His eyes narrowed. "If we could just git 'em all in at the same time, we could shoot 'em, hang 'em, or lock 'em behind bars till they're too old to stand, much less lift a pistol. That stinking swamp rat's a public menace and will be till the day we put him in the ground. You know the rule my daddy lived by: 'Your enemy is your enemy until he is dead.'"

He paused to relish the words.

"Well, we can make that happen sooner rather than later," T. W. said. "Maybe tomorrow night."

Suddenly galvanized, Baker strode across the room and snatched his hat off the hook by the door. "Let's go, T. W."

"Where to?"

"Sebastian Bridge is in Saint Lucie County, Sheriff Merritt's jurisdiction. J. R. Merritt is a tough old bird, an old-school son of a bitch. If we play 'im right, we can get him to handle it for us. I'm headed to the telegraph office. You round up Clyde Padgett and Dan Nelson. Send 'em over to the National Guard armory to borrow some big guns, tell 'em we need the best they got, and lots of ammo. While they pick up the hardware, you spread word around town that I'm gone, left to visit kin upstate."

Baker swore the telegraph operator to secrecy, then wired Merritt that he had urgent, immediate information to divulge. The two talked for an hour by telephone.

"Thought John Ashley and his gang were your problem," Merritt drawled. "He don't bother us much up here." The slow-talking lawman seemed to lack any interest in taking action.

Baker insisted his source was impeccable, and one hundred percent accurate. He'd send help, of course, his best deputies, men who knew Ashley and his companions on sight.

"The lawman who ends John Ashley's reign of terror'll win more than a feather in his cap," Baker said. "He'll be a household word. Newspaper coverage alone will be enough to launch him right into the governor's mansion, if that's what he wants. It's all in your hands now, Merritt. I'd do it myself, but he'll be on your turf, and I ain't the kind to intrude on another man's jurisdiction. You wouldn't appreciate that, neither would I. Ashley's a menace; he and his gang have to be stopped. Permanently." Baker paused. "We don't need no more games, no more trials, appeals, or prison breaks. You know what I mean, Merritt. This needs doing. It'd be a favor to me, to the governor, and the public. They demand it. We all need it, bad."

"I understand," Merritt said slowly.

CHAPTER THIRTY-THREE

Clyde Padgett, Dan Nelson, and T. W. Stone returned to the sheriff's office at midnight, heavily armed and ready to drive north to cut Ashley off before he could leave the state.

"We got the firepower," T. W. informed Sheriff Baker outside his office.

"Good work." Baker leaned into the open driver's side door. "Sheriff Merritt's waiting on you," he said heartily. "Good luck." He closed the door and stepped back.

The three deputies waited.

"You ain't coming?" T. W. finally asked.

"It's me Ashley's after. It'd just complicate things if I went up there," he whined. The whites beneath his eyes glinted in the dark as he took another step back.

"Do what Merritt says. He's the man in charge, not me. It's his jurisdiction. But don't you boys forget John Ashley's glass eye. You bring it to me. That's my trophy. I made that outlaw a promise, and I owe it to myself and the people of this county to keep it. I said I'd wear his eye on my watch fob someday. That day is here." His voice rose. "And don't you come back here without it!" He stuck out his chin, took out his pocket watch, and checked the time in the yellow light of a streetlamp. "You best get moving now, while ya still have a good head start."

"Son of a bitch," T. W. blurted, after they drove off. "That little man is sending us to do his dirty work."

"Ya see his crazy eyes?" Clyde said.

"He's scared shitless of John Ashley," Dan Nelson said. "He's a goddamn coward."

"Always has been," T. W. said. "Sure don't take after his daddy. That old man must be turning in his grave."

John and Laura fought, made love, then fought again throughout the night. He finally dozed fitfully as Laura lay beside him and stared into the dark. She never closed her eyes.

Hanford and the others arrived before dawn. In the privacy of their room, Laura begged John once more to take her with him.

He refused.

"Then we'll never see each other again."

"Don't talk foolish. You can't shut me off so easy." He flashed his killer grin. "We'll be together again before you know it, darlin'."

Unconvinced, she refused see him off, to kiss him goodbye in front of the others, to appear with swollen eyes, her face haggard from lack of sleep. Nothing she could do or say would stop him, and if she went out there, she knew she'd make a scene.

"Will you come out to wish me and the boys good luck?" he asked.

She did not answer and refused to look at him, just sat and stared at the wall.

Hating to leave her like that, he paused hopefully at the door. But she had no change of heart, her profile etched in stone.

"I promise to send for you and Ma as quick as I can," he finally said, with a sigh, then closed the door behind him.

When she heard the front door slam, she sprang to the window and watched Leugenia carry her food-laden picnic hamper to the car. Bill had come to say goodbye as well.

"Where's Laura?" Hanford asked, as John started the car.

"Inside," John said tersely. His passengers exchanged glances. "She's upset," John acknowledged.

"Woman always wants her way," Ray Lynn said, as the car moved down the lane to the main road. "They're all like that."

Laura gasped as they drove away. How could she let him go without saying goodbye? Heart in her throat, she burst barefoot from the room in the silk kimono he'd bought her in Miami. She rushed by Leugenia and Bill, who planned to stay for breakfast. They called her name but she did not look back as she darted through the vegetable garden, cut through an adjacent field of sweet corn, and heard the car again.

Morning mists rose toward a pink dawn as she scrambled up the stony embankment of an open drainage ditch just as John's car passed on the other side. Breathless, she waved her handkerchief over her head, just as the blazing sun pierced the cloud-strewn horizon.

"Hey," Hanford cried. "There's Laura!"

John saw the morning sunlight and a brisk breeze play in her hair, tapped the brake, slowed down, hit the horn three times, and waved back.

I love you, she mouthed, and blew kisses. She felt the warmth of his grin even at that distance and continued to wave until the car was out of sight and sound. Then she walked numbly back to the house.

"Did ya see him?" Leugenia asked.

She nodded. Leugenia reached out to comfort her as Bill scooped up a stash of breakfast biscuits to take with him and left.

"John has always been our most intelligent and loving child, our golden boy," Leugenia said, after Bill left. "We need to trust in his judgment—and in God Almighty."

"I'm scared I'll never see him again," Laura whispered.

"Let's get on our knees right now and pray to God you're wrong," Leugenia said.

Unable to rest, despite her exhaustion, Laura drove off that afternoon. She ran a few errands, then took a long, solitary walk, grateful for the cool, quiet air.

"If she was mine, I'da brung her," Ray said after they passed Laura.

Middleton agreed. "Ain't nothing like the comfort a good woman can bring on a long, cold night."

"You done with her, Uncle John?" Hanford asked.

"Hell, no." John glared at all three. "She's my woman. I'm protecting her, keeping her safe, and when we're together again, I'll treat her like a queen. Give her everything she wants and more. I broke promises in the past, but I'll make it up to her. I can," he added. "Never had a problem making an honest living. Now let's quit jawing about my personal life."

Hanford mentioned that Sheriff Baker was traveling north as well, to visit kin in Tallahassee.

John frowned. "When'd you hear that?"

"Pa came home late last night, said he heard it at the barbershop and at the trading post. So it must be true. Hope we don't cross his path."

"Unlikely. But I wish to hell we would." John smacked his palm against the steering wheel. "I'd love to sit down face-to-face, man-to-man, pour us a drink and try to piece together, for my own peace of mind, how this whole mess got started. I believe Baker and his father always knew I didn't murder that Indian, but if he thinks I did, I'd make him understand that it ain't true!"

"Then you'd shoot him?" Middleton sounded eager.

"Hell, no!" John sounded exasperated. "You ever listen to anything I say? *No more killing.* How many times do I have to tell you that?"

"He'd never talk to you," Middleton said. "You'd need to shoot him in the foot, take his gun, and tie 'im to a tree afore he'd ever listen."

"So be it," John said grimly.

"Who cares what he thinks?" Hanford said. "He's just a little man who hates us. Let's leave him be."

John sighed. "That's what we're doing."

CHAPTER THIRTY-FOUR

The deputies made excellent time on the first leg of their mission. But then, without warning, the leaves on the trees began to shudder. Branches swayed violently in wind so wild that leaves, foliage, and other debris pelted the windshield.

"Confound it! What new hell is this?" T. W. grumbled.

Dan Nelson, next to him, squinted through the windshield into the darkness.

A flash of forked lightning and an earsplitting crash of thunder startled Clyde Padgett awake in the back seat. "The hell's happening?"

"Storm come up," T. W. drawled.

"Jesus, sounded like cannon fire. Thought we drove onto a battle-field."

The wind whistled, screamed, and howled. Treetops roiled wildly. "Hell, it's like onea them nasty summer storms we never get this timea year," Nelson said.

"Pull over till it passes," Padgett said.

"No damn way," T. W. said. "My job is to get us there. We don't keep moving, we'll wind up caught in a flash flood or stuck in the mud." He slowed down, as rain began to pound the car as though with a vengeance.

"The wrath of God," Padgett whispered, his face pale in the dark. "Never liked this whole damn deal from the start. Has a bad feeling, a rotten smell. If Baker's so damn hot to git Ashley, why ain't he here with us?"

"And if we do get him," Nelson said, "Baker'll steal the glory for his-self somehow. Don't like that little sumbitch, never did. How the hell did he get to be sheriff?"

"Inherited the badge from his daddy," T. W. said. "Everybody knows that. When the old man died in office, his buddy, the governor, appointed Baker's little rat-faced son to finish his term. But now he's facing election, next week. That should be interesting."

"Don't everybody know he's a crazy-eyed coward who still sucks his thumb and wets the bed?" Padgett said.

Nelson hooted, his laugh lost in a crash of thunder and a blinding explosion of light that turned night into day.

T. W. hit the brake. The others cursed and cringed.

"What the hell?" Nelson blinked, temporarily blinded.

"Back up! Back up! Hit the gas!" Padgett shouted.

T. W. responded without question. The car hurtled in reverse as an immense live oak toppled toward them, its leaves on fire. The huge tree narrowly missed the car's passenger compartment and slammed onto the roadway directly in front of them. The uppermost branches grazed the hood and cracked the windshield.

"Was we hit by lightning?" T. W. asked.

"Damn close! Hit the tree instead." Padgett's voice dropped again. "His terrible swift sword. I knew it from the start. Ashley don't need to kill us, God's on his side. This storm'll do it for 'im."

He and Dan, both white-faced and shaken, wanted to turn back. T. W. argued against it. "What we gonna say? A thunderstorm scared us off? We'd be a laughingstock. Baker'd never buy it. The deal he made is that we back up Merritt and his men. If we don't show and Merritt lets him down, Baker'll have our hides and our badges in a heartbeat. If Ashley gets away, we'll get blamed and never live it down."

"Being laughed at and outta work is better than pushing up daisies," Padgett said. "I got me a wife and kids to think about. I ain't going no further. You don't turn back, I can get out right here."

"Listen to me," T. W. persisted. "Okay, it's nasty out here. But if you're hunting for the devil, you got to go to hell. And we have the biggest gun, the element of surprise. That's the weapon that wins wars. Ashley and his boys never expect to see us up there. We've got the advantage."

He tried to find a way around the downed tree, inching the car in reverse. The heavy, still-smoking branches dug deep scratches in the dented hood as he backed out from beneath them. It was impossible, the road impassable. When the storm finally began to let up, they got out and tried to move the tree off the road, using a crowbar, tools from the trunk, broken branches, leverage, and muscle. Cursing, sweating, dirty, and wet, they argued the entire time. After two hours, they finally managed to roll most of the massive tree off the roadway.

Personal pride and professional duty demanded that they complete their assignment, T. W. explained as they hauled singed branches out of the car's path. "We nail Ashley and we have our pick of jobs. Might even snag somea that reward money."

"Dead men don't need jobs or money. What if he kills us first?" Padgett said.

"He won't," T. W. said confidently. "Like I said, we got the upper hand. Sheriff J. R. Merritt's a helluva man, knows his stuff, and he don't play games. We partner up with him and his deputies, then surprise Ashley and his gang. The odds are with us. It'd be a different story if Baker was here running the show."

"Yeah," Nelson said. "First time he heard a twig snap, he'd drop his gun, scream like a girl, and pee his pants."

"What the hell's that smell?" Padgett wiped his face on his shirt and grimaced.

"Shit!" T. W. said. "Goddamn it to hell! There's dead skunk under these burnt branches."

J. R. Merritt shook his head and spit tobacco juice after Baker's "best men" rolled into town late, dirty, and disheveled in a scratched and dented car with a busted windshield. "Figured the storm musta slowed you down some. So Bob Baker hisself isn't joining us?"

"The sheriff wanted to be here," T. W. lied, "but had important business back in Palm Beach. Said to follow your orders."

Merritt nodded, then frowned. "Good God! What's that smell? You boys pick up a family of polecats on the road?"

John Ashley, his nephew Hanford, Ray Lynn, and Clarence Middleton refueled the touring car that afternoon in Fort Pierce, then strolled down to the local barbershop for shaves and haircuts.

Afterward, they proceeded to the local pool hall. Money changed hands as John and Hanford took two out of three from Ray Lynn and Clarence Middleton.

Then they crossed Main Street for a restaurant supper. A young red-haired woman in a white dress smiled real friendly and waved to John as they passed the window of the real estate office where she sat behind a desk. He grinned and waved back.

"You know her?" Ray Lynn's jaw dropped and he lagged behind for a better look. "I hear redheads have hot tempers. But I'd take my chances with that one. Introduce me, John."

Ashley shook his head. "Never seen 'er before."

"That's life for famous outlaws," Middleton said. "Ladies love bad boys."

"Shut your mouth," John said quietly. "And don't use that word again."

"What word?"

"*Outlaw*," John said softly. "We're done with that. And this ain't the time or place to meet a woman, Ray. We have to hit the road at dark. We want out of Florida, fast." He inhaled a deep breath and studied the horizon. "And we'll have to drive through bad weather."

Ray Lynn and Clarence Middleton squinted at the bright blue sky and exchanged skeptical glances. "Nah," Middleton said. "Perfect traveling weather."

Ray agreed. "Not a cloud in the sky."

"Let's go eat," John said.

They dined on thick rare steaks, apple pie, and coffee, then left Fort Pierce during a brilliant sunset. But an hour later, leaves and tree limbs began to stir, then churn above them. The wind built. Thunder rumbled like distant cannons and advanced like an army. Lightning pirouetted across the night sky, touching down closer and closer.

The wind howled like a thousand banshees as nickel-sized hail pounded the car like machine-gun fire. Torrential rain followed, punctuated by lightning and thunder crashes.

Forced to stop in zero visibility, they discussed turning back. "No point!" Ashley shouted to be heard above the storm. "It's movin' south. No way to outrun it. Let's keep heading north and ride it out."

Only Ray Lynn, deep in fantasy about the redhead back in Fort Pierce, disagreed. The storm fury swept south and the turbulent skies slowly calmed as they continued north. Starry shafts emerged from between inky black clouds, revealing a frail quarter moon, their solitary beacon in the semitropical darkness.

A wild creature hurtled across the road directly in front of them, big luminous eyes aglow for a heartbeat in the headlights. John stomped the brakes and the animal vanished into shadow.

"What the hell was that?" Hanford leaned forward.

"Panther, I think, " John said.

"Where?" Clarence Middleton asked from the back seat, his gravel voice groggy. "Maybe a gator?"

"Way too fast." Ray's cigarette tip reflected red in the rearview mirror. "Coulda been a bear."

"Faster than a bear, unless he was desperate to catch something," Hanford said.

"Or desperate to escape something," Ray Lynn said, his voice low as he stared into the darkness.

"Nothing out here that'll scare a bear," John said. "Only men with guns. Whatever it was, it's lucky, and so are we, that we didn't hit it. Maybe it's a good omen," he added hopefully.

"Hope so," Ray muttered. "I'm so tired of running and sick of staying. Be nice if things work out for us this time."

"It's a big country," John said. "We'll find us a place. Maybe California. We could try gold mining, maybe strike it rich." He looked back. "Do me a favor, Ray. Crank down that window to clear out the cigarette smoke."

Ray obliged. The rush of cool air that followed the storm was refreshing, but the shroud of darkness and dense wilderness made them feel small, lost, and alone on the vast Florida peninsula.

"Look at that," Hanford said. "The storm musta brought down that big live oak. Somebody already hauled it halfway off the road. Look at them drag marks."

"Nice to know there's somebody else alive out here," Clarence said. "I'm not sorry to say adios to Florida. This here's a dark and lonely place. No lights, no cars, no people. Darker than a mine shaft. It's like we're traveling alone on the road to hell."

"Close the window," John said. "Somebody hit a skunk out here."

"One thing I won't miss is Florida's critters," Ray said. "Or that swamp fulla skeeters, snakes, and gators."

"I liked crossing the Atlantic, being out at sea under the stars," Hanford said, "but didn't think much of the people over there. I missed Florida."

"Me and Laura felt the same way when we were on the run," John said. "Missed home, kinfolk, good friends. 'Member how tight we all were? But those I missed most are gone now, because of me." His voice tightened. "No better man than my pop ever walked this earth. Baker's men shot him dead in his bed before he could pull his boots on. Three brothers gone, Laura hurt, homesteads burned. And they damn near hung me. That's over now. Once we find a place to settle, I'll live a good life like the ones we had before all the trouble. I'm looking forward to that."

CHAPTER THIRTY-FIVE

Sheriff Merritt, four of his deputies, and Baker's men moved fast, formed a plan, then drove to the bridge across the Sebastian Inlet, the deputies in two cars.

Merritt, in his own car, brought a heavy chain and stopped at a farmer's house to borrow a lantern. They hid the cars, Merritt's off the road on the north side, the deputies' in the woods on the south side of the span.

"What if Ashley turned back because of the storm?" a deputy asked, as they stretched the chain across the narrow bridge.

"If Ashley's half the man they say, no storm could keep him off a road he intended to take," Merritt said. He hooked the lantern to the center of the chain, stepped back, and smiled. The lantern glowed like an ominous red eye in the dark.

"Check your weapons, boys, split up, move fast, and take cover on both sides of the road," Merritt said. "Hold your fire till you can't miss. Don't be shooting acrost the road and hitting each other. No smoking, no talking, no drinking. Remember who we're dealing with. Look sharp, stay alert, and stay alive."

"Laura's madder than a wet hen that you wouldn't bring her with us," Hanford said. "Think she'll wait for you?"

"I know she will," John said. "The girl's more sad than mad. She knows bounty hunters are looking for us together."

He wiped the inside of the windshield with his sleeve and squinted into the dark. "Look!" He grinned. "That's the Sebastian Bridge up ahead. We'll make good time now."

PART SEVEN

CHAPTER THIRTY-SIX

John ducked into a Flagler Street shop that sold electronic gadgets, souvenirs, sunglasses, and swimsuits to tourists. He bought an over-sized T-shirt, shades, and a baseball cap, put them on, and was back on the street in minutes.

He left a message on Robby's cell. "You're one helluva weatherman. Ran into that storm you predicted. Shoulda listened. Rough seas today. Thinking about a little getaway and want to pick up my girl. Call me."

He started to leave a message at the house but decided not to involve Robby's wife. It suddenly occurred to him that he didn't really know the girl. Something about her pale eyelashes and bold stare turned him off, along with her hooting laugh. It reminded him of something unpleasant he couldn't quite remember. Was he becoming paranoid? He'd always liked his siblings' spouses.

John doubled back to Macy's, took the escalator back to the second floor, then the footbridge over the street to reach the parking garage. He rode the elevator down, left by the north exit, and ducked into the historic Seybold Building, constructed in the early 1920s and now known for floor after floor of fine jewelers. He drank a cortadito at a Cuban café in the lobby. Still wearing his shades and baseball cap, he cold-shouldered the surveillance cameras. There were dozens in the building, all monitored by security in the lobby.

Leon answered his phone immediately.

"Hey," John said. "I'm downtown and need to leave under the radar without wheels. Somebody made my car in the parking lot where I left it."

"Take the Metromover right by FedEx and get off at the Omni sta-tion. Meetcha there."

John glanced at the monitors as he walked by security. Two police officers were approaching the entrance he'd used. He punched the button at the elevator bank. The ornate doors opened immediately. He hit six but got off on seven, took a stairwell down to four, opened a window, stepped onto the fire escape, and descended at top speed. As he jumped the last four feet to the pavement, a middle-aged security officer appeared.

"Whatcha doing, buddy? What's the story?"

"Good news. The fire escapes meet code. A-plus for this inspection." He scribbled in a notebook from his back pocket. "City Building Department." He flashed his ID, with his photo and the city seal visible. His thumb covered the word "police."

The security man glanced at it and nodded.

John hadn't taken the Metromover in years. He watched the action below from a bird's-eye view as the cars skimmed over the city, disembarked at the Omni, headed for the street, and spotted Leon, nearly invisible among throngs of commuters.

"You're damn good, Johnny," Leon said. "Most people wouldn't have seen me. Your clothes ain't bad, but you walk like you're military. Makes you stand out. Use the homeless shuffle."

"Shuffle?"

Leon nodded. "Hunch your shoulders, keep lookin' at the ground, and insteada picking your feet up, shuffle. That's it, you got it. Let's go. How are ya for cash?" he asked, as they shuffled.

"Strapped, just ten, fifteen dollars on me till I see my brother. I'm headed there now."

Leon nodded.

A Yellow Cab sat at the curb just off the busy thoroughfare. The husky, bearded, middle-aged driver did not lift his eyes until Leon tapped on the window.

"This here's a friend," Leon told him. "Take 'im where he needs to go. Nothing on the log or radio. You don't know him. Never saw him." The cabbie gave a quick nod. Leon handed him a bill. "See me if the tab is higher."

What is that? John thought. A fifty? It was a fifty-dollar bill.

"Leon," he muttered, as he slid into the back seat. "That was a fifty."

Leon lifted his eyes, and for a moment, John saw a flash of something he had never seen there before, a clear, formidable, and single-minded vision.

"Tell you about it sometime, on a need-to-know basis. I'll go by the diner, see what I can pick up. Cops go there to shoot the breeze and cadge a free lunch. You know how cops gossip." He winked, the look gone, a harmless, homeless, unnoticed man shuffling down a busy street full of hurried, harried commuters with places to go, people to see.

Did I imagine that look? John wondered. He asked the driver, a large man with a well-trimmed jet-black beard and mustache, to drop him at an address a mile or so from the Miami-Dade Police substation where Robby worked.

The hack license, driver ID photo, and cab number required by law to be on display at all times were nowhere to be seen. The driver sat as solid as a rock behind the wheel and was just as communicative. Unlike most Miami cabbies, he appeared to understand English but replied with only grunts or monosyllables. When John asked the driver how long he'd known Leon, he hunched his huge shoulders and made a noncommittal sound.

John's prepaid cell rang during the trip. "Sorry," Robby said. "Had the phone off. I'm en route back to the station. What's your location?"

"On my way up to your neck of the woods. How's my girl?"

"Snug as a bug, hanging out with Katie, her new BFF. Ma called. Had visitors. Tell you when I see you."

"I'll call when I'm close. I'm five to ten away."

A mile from the substation, John got out and reached for his wallet. The driver held up his beefy hand like a traffic cop and shook his head. Then, surprisingly, he spoke several complete sentences.

"Good luck, pal. If it doesn't come your way and you need a ride, gimme a call. Watch your back." He handed John a crumpled business card from a long-defunct Miami auto dealership, a phone number scribbled on the back. "Ask for Tyree," he said.

John nodded as the cab eased into traffic. He called Robby as he walked through a tiny strip mall, then took a seat in a laundromat with several other customers waiting for their wash. Minutes later Robby's unmarked rolled slowly past the door.

John got up, sauntered around the corner of the building back to the Dumpsters, and got into Robby's car.

His brother, working undercover, wore jeans and a black T-shirt with white lettering: I AM THE PERSON YOUR MOTHER WARNED YOU ABOUT.

John frowned.

"Yeah, ma hates it too." Robby grinned engagingly.

"She had visitors?"

"Yeah. 'Bout an hour ago, a pair of hangdog detectives with a uniform right behind 'em. Scared the hell out of her. Thought one of us got shot or something. You know how cops' wives and mothers are—always afraid they'll answer a knock at the door and see other cops there to break bad news. What the hell's wrong with those guys? Don't they have mothers?"

"Probably not. Most crawled out from under rocks. What did they want?"

"You, man. Were looking for you. Must be nice to be so wanted."

"What'd she tell 'em?"

"To check the station, that you were probably working, like always. They asked when she last heard from you. Said she wasn't sure. They told her to tell you it would be in your best interests to come down to the station. She asked what for. They said it was serious, then asked for her permission to come in and look around! Can you believe those guys?"

"What'd she say?"

"No way, said she was busy in the kitchen, closed the door on 'em, and called me. Our mother's small, not stupid."

John filled him in about the meeting and what he'd learned.

"Holy crap!" Robby said. "What'd I tell you, bro? Virtue is its own punishment. This whole damn thing sounds FUBAR—Fucked Up Beyond All Recognition. What the hell is going on?"

Robby's police radio crackled to life and broadcast a routine countywide BOLO, a Be On the LookOut. But this one was different. The subject being sought was Miami Police sergeant John Ashley. They stared at the radio, as the dispatcher's cool, ethereal voice gave John's physical description and date of birth and requested that he be detained for questioning in a homicide. "Be advised," she warned, "Ashley is armed."

"Did I hear that right?" Robby said, stunned.

"You heard it too?" John sounded weary. "I hoped I was hallucinating."

"We should be so lucky," Robby said.

John felt unexpected comfort at Robby's use of the word *we*. You're never alone, he thought, when you have family.

"I never thought I'd hear a BOLO like that in a million years." Robby's voice rose. "You're the Boy Scout, John! The cleanest, most dedicated cop in this county! If they can do this shit to you, nobody's safe. Nobody! You need a lawyer, bro. Fast. If they put that out on the air, an arrest warrant isn't far behind."

"Where's Laura? I need to see her."

"She's hot, John, but believe me, your time is better spent with your lawyer."

"I don't want to talk about that now. Where is she, Robby?"

He sighed. "She's been bugging me too, wants you, asks where you are. She's with Katie, bro. Think I wouldn't take good care of her? They're having the time of their lives at the Sea Spray."

The name resonated oddly in John's memory. He blinked. Where had he heard it before? Was it a fast boat?

"It's a new, high-rise oceanfront condo," Robby said, as he made a U-turn toward the causeway to the beach. "Finished right as the real estate market crashed. Timing is everything. Speculators who signed contracts and made deposits on expensive units walked away, took the hit. It's less than twenty percent occupied. Way less now because it's off-season. Snowbirds and foreign investors who use them as second homes are gone for the summer. Listen to this, it's got a fully equipped gym, spa, Olympic-size, infinity-edge pool, and cabanas, with nobody using 'em, except for our little Katie and your little Laura. Let me tell ya, they've been busy on the beach, in the pool, the gym, and the spa."

John lifted an eyebrow. "What's Katie's connection there?"

"Remember her patient, the girl in the plane crash?"

Katie, a registered nurse, had befriended a former patient, a wealthy young Frenchwoman who suffered serious back injuries in a light plane crash that killed her fiancé in the Florida Keys. Slowly recovering after several surgeries, Robby said, she bought an apartment at the Sea Spray to be near her doctors, hospital, and therapists. Now in Europe for the summer, she'd left Katie to house-sit, enjoy the amenities, water her plants, and care for her little dog.

"Isn't it dangerous for them to be alone in a big, dark complex at night with no neighbors?" John frowned.

"Not to worry. You know Katie—and Laura," Robby said. "They're armed to the hilt. And building security isn't bad, though at some point it's bound to get hairy with so few owners paying maintenance fees. Luckily, most of the buyers who did close have the bucks to protect their investment and keep the place up until the market revives. Katie says the management company plans to launch a leasing and rental program, that could save the day."

Robby called ahead but didn't mention he had company. Katie said they were at the beach, on their way to the pool.

"They're not neglected," he told John. "I check on them. Called 'em a couple times last night. Laura's never alone. Katie's taking comp time the hospital owes her; you know how much she works. They're not paying OT because of budget cuts, just giving the staff comp time."

The lonely monolith was white, tropical, open, and airy. Flaming red and purple bougainvillea draped from latticework, balconies, and gigantic flower boxes bordering the parking garage. The Sea Spray looked like the tropical dreams in glossy real estate brochures sent only to multimillionaires.

They parked, saw no one, and walked through the building. No one at the front desk. The massive marble lobby echoed like an empty museum. The beach was breathtaking, the water a brilliant blue, bluer than the sky. The heavy white lounge chairs all stood empty, as though waiting for the party to begin. But there was no party, nothing to celebrate. Investors had lost their shirts.

But the locale and spectacular structure would endure until things changed. John and Robby walked out onto a huge, elevated pool deck and saw them approaching, two tanned and beautiful girls in bikinis. They'd left their bright sarong-like wraps on beach chairs. They put them on, then spotted Robby. John stood in shadow just inside the slatted door of a cabana.

The cabanas were as lavish as the rest of the building, but the interiors were unfinished. There were hookups for wet bars, HDTVs, stereo systems, mini refrigerators, and microwaves. The basic amenities—half baths with showers, daybeds, couches, card tables, and chairs—had all been installed.

The girls ran up the already weathered wooden steps from the beach to greet Robby on the pool deck. Laughing, their hair loose in the sea breeze, their sun-kissed skin glistening with coconut oil, they looked happy and lighthearted, without a care in the world.

"That," Robby said softly, over his shoulder, "is how all young girls should always look. Too bad life gets in the way. Remember this moment, John. We don't have many."

He's right, John thought, surprised by Robby's sudden introspection, so unlike the wild and fearless boy he'd helped raise. This break would be good for both girls, he thought. It gave Katie a brief respite from the sterile, often grim atmosphere of intensive care, and Laura would feel safe from the threat of sudden violence.

The girls hugged Robby; all three laughed and talked at once. John heard his name. "Is he all right? Have you seen him?" Laura asked wistfully. "He hasn't called." The sound of her voice made all that had happened that day seem unimportant by comparison.

Robbie walked them back toward the cabana, an arm around each of them. As they passed the cabana, John reached out and swept Laura inside. Katie gasped. "It's okay," Robby whispered in her ear. She relaxed and began to laugh.

"She's really crazy about John," she told her brother. "I hope I feel that way about a man someday."

"You will," he said

"I don't know," she said thoughtfully, her green eyes pensive. "What they have is rare. Most people are never that lucky."

She stopped, her arm around her brother. They looked back at the cabana. The door was closed and they heard Laura's laugh, a clear and joyous sound.

"Shall we wait for them?" Katie asked.

"No," Robby said. "They've waited so long. And there's so little time."

"Let's go upstairs," she said. "I'll fix you some lunch."

CHAPTER THIRTY-SEVEN

She lay in his arms, the door half open so they could feel the ocean breeze on their skin, see clouds, ships, and blue water, and hear seabirds and the surf.

Eventually he explained the trouble he faced. She sat yoga-style between his open legs, her eyes never leaving his face.

"No matter what other people think," she said, when he finished, "we both know you're innocent. We'll work through this together. But most important, don't ever leave me again, John. Katie, well, she's the sister I always wanted. It's as if we've known each other forever. And Robby is so cool. We're simpatico. I already love him like a brother. But you and me"—she tossed her lush, long black hair back over her naked sun-kissed shoulder—"we have to stay together no matter what. I've never felt more sure about anything in my entire life."

Despite his relief, he warned her about the dangers, how unfair this might be to her, her career, and her family. What about her family?

"Doesn't matter; nothing else does." She shrugged. She'd spoken to her gram, actually her great-grandmother, as she did every day. "She's fine," Laura said. "About a hundred years old, she lives alone when I'm away, drives her powder-blue 1985 Oldsmobile Calais with almost thirty-five thousand miles on it to church on Sunday, then has lunch with friends. It's the high point of her week. She's lost friends, family, and neighbors over the years, survived two husbands, and sorely misses those who've gone ahead. But she lives in the family homestead where she grew up. She's lived a wonderful life, and still does."

Laura smiled. "Do you know she never wore shoes till she went to school in a one-room schoolhouse on her granddaddy's property, with all her cousins and friends? Her granddaddy hired the first teacher. She's living history. You'll love her," she said, her voice tender as she reached for him.

When the cell phone Robby insisted she keep with her rang, they scrambled, looking for it among their tangled clothes on the floor. It was Katie, inviting them up for supper.

Both were ravenous. John hadn't eaten all day. Robby had gone, but was just a phone call away should they need him.

Katie had baked sweet potatoes and grilled salmon steaks with lime, spinach, tomatoes, and mushrooms. The beautiful apartment was cool and fragrant with the aromas of good cooking. After the empty halls and vacant, unoccupied space, it gleamed, a jeweled oasis in a barren desert. The sunset from the wraparound terrace was beyond spectacular.

The day that began badly had become so memorable for John and Laura that even the nightly TV news could not diminish their bliss. But it came close. They were still at the dinner table, as Katie poured the last of the wine, when Robby called.

"Check Channel Seven," he said, tersely. "I'm recording it."

All four local news outlets led with the same story. Miami's police chief had grimly announced at a press conference that a first-degree murder warrant had been issued for one of their own. Homicide Sergeant John Ashley was being sought in the murder of his supervisor, Capt. Armando Politano, shot to death at an Aventura motel. The chief, a strip of black mourning tape across his badge, released few details and evaded reporters' questions. All he'd say was that the investigation was ongoing, with more charges expected.

The press conference had been delayed until after the captain's swiftly arranged funeral. Police officers from all over the state and even Georgia had come to pay their respects, to honor Politano as a fallen hero, which irked John. Had the captain survived his last act, he could have, should have, lost his job, his certification, his freedom forever, and perhaps even his life. How wrong for a badge-wearing criminal to share space on the same plaque as Officer John R. Riblet and all the other real heroes killed on the job.

Aerial news footage caught hundreds of patrol cars, lights flashing, mounted patrolmen, motorcycles, even a SWAT team van. The creeping procession stalled traffic for miles. News reports covered the final sign-off on police radio, taps, the twenty-one-gun salute, and the mournful wail of bagpipes. All for a masked man who broke into Laura's room to ambush and murder them both.

The white-gloved honor guard presented the folded flag to the widow, her children at her side. The TV news report then returned to highlights of the press conference in which John was described as yet another cop gone bad, a cautionary tale, proof again of how tough a cop's job is, both physically and to the psyche. The chief, who hadn't uttered more than a dozen words to him in years, now pleaded like an old friend: "For God's sake, John, surrender like a man, before anyone else is killed or hurt. Come in, for your own safety."

The chief went on, "We believe he's still in the area, and may be accompanied by this woman." He identified her as Laura Groves, her professional name, and displayed for the camera what appeared to be a mug shot.

"I look like a criminal!" Laura gasped. "What terrible lighting! Where did they find such a bad picture?"

"Probably off your driver's license or concealed weapons permit," John said.

"We're not sure," the chief was saying, "if this woman is an accomplice or another victim. She is a known associate of attorney Ron Jon Eagle, whose murder Ashley was investigating."

"'Known associate'?" Katie said. "That sounds like mob talk!"

"Where and when was Sergeant Ashley last seen?" asked TV Six reporter Jeff Burnside, the first news person called upon.

The chief frowned, conferred with a detective behind him, looked unhappy with the answer, then cleared his throat. "This morning, at police headquarters," the chief mumbled, then looked hopefully at other reporters for simpler questions.

But Burnside didn't quit. "So John Ashley voluntarily came to police headquarters this morning but wasn't detained, and now you want tips from the public to find him?" Burnside looked confused, though the light in his eyes was not at all confused.

"The situation changed rapidly," the chief said. He glanced sharply at the detective and quickly ended the conference.

"How dare they say such things about us?" Indignant tears glittered in Laura's eyes. "I thought people are presumed innocent until proven guilty in a court of law. And why would they use a terrible photo that looks like a mug shot when so many better pictures are available?"

"It's deliberate," Katie said accusingly. "They're showing their asses. Look how they're treating John. He's a hero, the best they have. He's won more awards, plaques, medals and citations for bravery than the whole department put together. They're jealous. He's their top marksman, the best in the state and probably the country. He learned to shoot from our dad like we all did. But John's the best. He's won the gold medal for marksmanship in the Police Olympics every year except one, when his automatic jammed. Which is why I like a good revolver," she added.

"Me too," Laura said. "And they don't jam or spit out hot shells that can fall into your blouse or bra."

"Damn straight." Katie swished her long, flowered skirt angrily as she paced the room in her strappy gold sandals.

Their conversation sounded surreal to John, still staring at the TV, the remote in his hand. He switched back to Channel Six. Jeff Burnside's report was the most fair and balanced, he decided. He replayed it:

"Hero cop John Ashley, accused of fatally shooting his captain in a bizarre motel room confrontation, was the only member of his department to seek press coverage of the incident in which he is charged. Miami's police chief said today that Ashley reported to headquarters this morning and was allowed to leave. Yet hours later, the chief called a press conference and appealed to the public for help in finding him."

Burnside gazed into the camera, his clear eyes sincere. "Sergeant Ashley has a sterling record of service to this city and his department, which has had an unfortunate history of cover-ups and corruption. Viewers may remember the young English tourist Sergeant Ashley rescued from brutal attackers in a downtown bus terminal, saving her life, only one of many high profile cases for which he earned recognition. Some colleagues say that he deserves the opportunity to tell his side before being accused of the ultimate crime. In our system of justice, a man is presumed innocent until proven guilty."

"See?" Laura cried. "Isn't that what I just said?"

"I love that man," Katie said.

"Me too," Laura said.

"He's an honest reporter," John said. "That's rare in this town."

Laura plucked a glossy folder from her suitcase and removed copies of her modeling composite. "I'm sending photos to the press and the police chief, asking them to correct the impression that I have ever been arrested or in any trouble whatsoever. I want the chief to publicly retract his comment that I was *a known associate of Ron Jon Eagle*," she said, mocking his solemn delivery.

Both women turned to John for his reaction. He laughed aloud. His career had crumbled, he was a wanted man, but he was with Laura and more content than he ever had been. He had just shared the most exciting and satisfying sex in his life, then enjoyed great food and good wine with two people he loved. How could he even dignify the insane allegations against him by taking them seriously? That they had been made at all seemed ludicrous.

"Sure, darlin'," he told Laura. "If that's what you want to do, it makes perfect sense to me. Maybe it is time for us to fight back."

"You wouldn't turn yourself in? Would you?" Katie asked.

He shook his head. "I can't. I'd be denied bond, couldn't be with Laura, or try to clear my name. Nobody else seems interested in what really happened, so it's up to me."

"Us," Laura said firmly.

He called Robby again. "Is that package I sent you in a safe place?"

"Sure is. Want me to get rid of it?"

"No," John said. "I need to know it's safe, secure, and doesn't fall into the wrong hands."

"I hear you. What now?" Robby asked.

"We need to send some mail that won't be postmarked from this zip code."

"Gotcha. I'll pick it up early in the a.m., take it to Homestead or up to Broward. I'll bring stamps. Don't want face time with some postal clerk who has a photographic memory."

While Laura wrote her demand letters, John downloaded photos from her cell phone onto Katie's laptop, then printed several sets on the printer in the study. The photos revealed Capt. Armando Politano, minutes after his death, still clad in his black garb, gloves, and hooded mask. Others focused on the window glass Politano had removed in order to ambush them in Laura's motel room: the screen, the diamond cutter, and the suction cups he used. The time stamps showed the photos were taken shortly before John called in the shooting.

He called Joel Hirschhorn's office and left a message asking the lawyer to represent him. And if so, asked him to subpoena the phone records of his calls to the lieutenant and to 911 that night. He also asked Hirschhorn to arrange a lie test for him with a respected polygrapher used by both the FBI and police. Results were not admissible in court but they could influence both investigators and prosecutors.

He typed a chronological account of what happened that night into Katie's laptop. Unwilling to involve his family, he simply said that he and the witness had dinner in Miami and noted the time that they switched back to the city car to return to the motel. He described the events as they happened, then had Laura read it to be sure he hadn't missed anything. He printed copies for the FBI bureau chief in Miami; the medical examiner that autopsied Politano's body; Hirschhorn, the lawyer; and Jeff Burnside at Channel Six.

In her letters, Laura angrily protested the photo and accused police of smearing her character and damaging her reputation. "I am not a victim or an accomplice," she wrote. She detailed how and when she first saw John Ashley and cited witnesses, including the photographer and the makeup artist.

"You are the one," she wrote the police chief, "who announced that Sergeant Ashley and I were linked. We are now, by circumstance. We never met prior to that day. Why," she concluded hotly, "is no one investigating what really happened? Who killed Ron Jon Eagle? And my two coworkers? Why did Police Captain Politano assign Sergeant Ashley to protect me, then try to kill us both? Isn't anyone investigating the real story?"

Robby joined them for Katie's breakfast of sausage, eggs, grits, and gravy. He brought bagels and the morning paper. The story had made the front page, along with photos of John and Laura.

"Don't look," John told her.

She did. "Oh, no! It's that picture again!"

"Warned you not to look."

"The bad news is they put it in the newspaper," Robby said. "The good news is, nobody will recognize you. Doesn't look like you at all; it looks like your evil, ugly duckling twin."

"Thank you, very much," she said testily, and swatted him with the sports section.

"It's not so bad," John said. "It's sort of cute."

"Cute! It's hideous!" She took another photo from her portfolio, a prim and proper close-up in which she wore a crisp, tailored blouse with a Peter Pan collar and pearls, all-American girl with a million-dollar smile.

She slipped it into an eight-by-ten manila envelope along with a copy of her letter and addressed it to the reporter who'd written the story.

Robby said he'd given the family a heads-up, assured them that John had done nothing wrong and warned them not to believe anything in the press. He planned to take a prepaid cell phone to their parents so John could call them himself.

"It's heavy." Robby looked pained. "I'm getting calls from people I hardly know. But they know or have worked with you and are blown away by the news. I tell 'em all that you're the best cop I know and have never done a goddamn thing to tarnish the badge or your rep." He looked hollow-eyed and tired. "You okay, John?"

"Never felt better, Robby."

Robby stared. "Then you obviously haven't grasped the gravity of your situation, bro."

"Don't forget to mail the envelopes," John said.

"Neither rain, nor snow, nor gloom of night will deter me from my appointed rounds." Robby grinned and took off.

John's cell rang a short time later. "Are you all right, John?" Emma sounded breathless.

"Using the phone I gave you?"

"Yes."

"Good. Where are you?" He heard traffic sounds in the background.

"On a bench in that little park across from the State Building. Didn't want to call from the office or the car, just in case . . ."

"Good thinking. What's up?"

"It's a madhouse," she whispered. "They're searching for you everywhere. The tip line hasn't stopped ringing since the news broke. One caller even insisted he saw you posing as a homeless man near the Metromover station at the Omni," she chuckled.

John raised both eyebrows.

"Dozen of calls from people who say they saw you at the airport, checking luggage, at the ticket counter, or passing through security. One swore you were working as a screener, in a TSA uniform, forcing elderly passengers to take off their shoes. Lots of tips from Little Havana. You were seen drinking Cuban coffee at Versailles. One man said that when he called you by name, you put your finger to your lips to shush him, then left in a hurry. And a couple insisted they saw you playing piano at a nightclub on South Beach last night."

"Always wanted to break into show biz," he said.

"John!" She sounded shocked. "You saw the news, right?" She sounded on the verge of tears.

"Sure."

"Then how can you joke? They're watching your apartment and your parents' place. I think they're trying to get a warrant for a wiretap. I don't know where you are and I don't want to know. But the best leads they've had either put you behind the wheel of a sports car headed south on US One toward the Keys or watching a movie at the Regal Theater on South Beach."

"Which movie?"

"John! Stop that! They're taking it seriously. The caller insisted he knows you, was convinced it was you with a girl who looked like Laura, the witness."

"Did they follow it up?"

"You bet. Sent a team right out. Beach police and fire assisted, activated the fire alarm, evacuated all eighteen theaters, and checked every patron. Several people on the escalator fell in the panic and confusion, and three had seizures brought on by the flashing laser lights and high-pitched sirens. The theater complex is in a building that covers the entire block. It also houses high-end shops, a beauty salon, ice cream parlor, pizzeria, bar and grill, and a jeweler. There's just one central fire alarm system for them all, so everybody had to be evacuated. Lots of arrests. People refused to leave, some fought police and firemen who ordered them out. With no fire or smoke, some people just flat out refused to leave with bleach on their hair, half a haircut, or a meal, hot pizza, or drinks in front of them. Some bikers took on the Beach cops, half a dozen tourists joined in, and—"

"I get the picture," John said. "It wasn't pretty."

"Right. You escaped in the confusion, the detectives said."

"A close call," he said. "But it was a lousy flick anyway."

She sighed in exasperation.

"Sorry," he said. "I'm in a situation where if you don't laugh—"

"You cry," she finished, her tone sympathetic. "But be careful, this is nothing to be cavalier about. You have stacks and stacks of messages. People who had beefs with Captain Politano called to wish you well. Most didn't leave names. Others cheered you on. Here, I wrote down one I thought you'd like."

He heard her fumble in her purse, paper being unfolded.

"Here it is. 'Run, Johnny, run! Safe journey! God bless, and stay safe, man.' I thought that was nice. A flood of calls are also coming into Homicide from people whose cases you handled. They're supportive, shocked, and upset. They say they need you, want you on the job; some say without you, there'll be no justice in their cases."

John turned away from Laura and Katie for a moment. Frightened witnesses and victims needed his support and encouragement, to help them find the courage they'd need to testify in court.

"There's another message; actually it's the reason I called. It might be important, John."

"Go," he said.

"It's from that assistant, Lowenstein or Lonstein, Eagle's office manager—"

"Right, Gil Lonstein."

"That's him. Says he has new, urgent information. Really important, related to the case. He sounded excited."

"Did he talk to anybody else in the office?"

"Not that I know of. He said it was for your ears only. When I offered to transfer him to another detective, he hung up. He's called twice since. I told him that, under the circumstances, the Homicide Bureau was the last place he could expect to find you. He'd seen the news but didn't know how else to reach you and hoped that maybe, somehow, you'd get the message. Here's his number."

John jotted it down. "What do you think, Emma? You're a good judge of character. What's he got?"

"I don't know the man," she said proudly, "but he's convinced it's a life-and-death situation."

"So, on a scale of one to ten, with ten life-changing and earth-shattering?"

"I'd give it a nine-plus," she said. "Consider the source, John. The man ran a high-profile lawyer's entire office operation. He must have some credibility, don't you think?"

"You're right. Thanks. Be careful, and stay in touch. I need you."

He called the number. Lonstein answered. "John Ashley here, Gil."

"Thank God, you got my message! I've been looking all over town for you, tried everywhere. How do you find a man the whole damn police department is looking for and can't find? If they really do want you. Come on now, Sarge." He sounded coy. "You're in no real trouble, are you? They fed that story to the press to put you undercover with the bad guys. That's it, isn't it?"

"What message?" John said, to protect Emma. "I got no message. Just thought I'd touch base, see if you had any new ideas. Since nobody else is investigating, it's up to me."

"Don't tell me! You needed my help and called on your own. I knew it! We're on the same wavelength, Sarge."

"Call me John." He rolled his eyes.

"John, I have news for you. Really, really big news."

"I'm listening."

"Listen."

John rolled his eyes again.

"I finally got around to opening the wall safe in Ron Jon's office. I'd nearly forgotten about it, hidden behind a Carol Garvin painting of the Key West lighthouse. I open it and right on top is a manila envelope with my name on it, underlined in black ink. That was Eagle. That's his style. Inside is a little red envelope with a key and a hand-printed note. Here, let me read it: 'Gil, enclosed is the key to our safe-deposit box at the Wachovia branch on the Boulevard at Fifty-first Street. You may have forgotten that you're my cosigner. Get over there ASAP. Open it. Now. RJE.'

"Hadn't thought about it for years," Gil said. "We opened the box my first year on the job, had our fingerprints entered into the electronic ID system. I was given an entry code but no key. Never gave it another thought. Now I have the key."

"What do you think is in there?" John looked longingly across the room at Laura, who was speaking loudly on the phone to her great-grandmother, who seemed to be hard of hearing. "I miss you too, Gram," he heard her say. "You'll love him as much as I do."

"I don't *think* anything," Lonstein replied. "I *know*. I've seen it!"

"And?" John asked.

"A gold mine!" Lonstein sounded breathless. "I went to the branch. You have no idea what I went through. Despite the key, my fingerprints, and my signature on file, I was personally unknown to anyone at the branch. They have an overweight woman obsessed by minutiae in charge. Her joy in life must be to jerk people around."

"What did you find, Gil?"

"A big, fat, overstuffed manila envelope."

"And?" John's eyes lingered on the tilt of Laura's chin, the sleek curve of her hip. His attention drifted.

"It said, 'Eyes Only. To be opened only by Gil Lonstein.' "

"So you opened it?"

"Damn right, on the spot."

"What's it about, Gil?" John asked, as he focused on her legs.

"You. It's about you, Sarge."

CHAPTER THIRTY-EIGHT

W hat did you say, Gil?"
        "Listen to me, John! This is big! Really big!" Lonstein's boyish voice shook with excitement. "A stack of receipts and spreadsheets, and another note from Ron Jon. I swear, it's eerie, like a message from the dead. It *is* a message from the dead!"

"What's it say?" John reached for a pen.

"I copied it verbatim, John. Listen."

> *Gil,*
> *If you're reading this, I'm dead and you're the only one I trust to do the right thing, to bring down my killers. You know how I am, Gil: I always want the last word.*
> *People I associate with are becoming increasingly paranoid and most likely plan to whack me. I'm doing everything I can to avoid that possibility, but some things are inevitable. So, just in case, I enclose an affidavit. You know my signature. Notarize it, date it two weeks before my death, then do me one last favor. Take the entire package to Miami homicide detective John Ashley, the only honest cop in town.*
> *He'll do the right thing. Trust no one but him. Tell him I'm glad I couldn't have him fired. Ironic, isn't it, how the game of life plays out?*
> *R. J. Eagle*

Suddenly on his feet, John paced, phone to his ear, his voice charged. Katie stared. Laura closed her eyes and prayed for good news.

"Did you read the affidavit, Gil?"

"Skimmed it, John. It's heavy. Names names, identifies conspirators, people you know from the city and county police departments. Your late captain, Politano, is one of them."

"Holy crap!" John said. "You have the papers with you?"

"Hell, no, they're too dangerous to have around. They're incendiary. I shoved 'em back in the safe-deposit box until I found you. Didn't know how long that would take."

"We need to get copies to the right people," John said. "I'm in Miami. How soon can we meet?"

Laura quietly left the room.

"I'm in Broward," Lonstein said, "but I can be down there in half an hour."

"Good. I'll meet you. You said the bank's at Fifty-one and the Boulevard?" John said.

"Right."

"Does anybody else know, Gil?" John's question was almost an afterthought. The pause that followed made his heart sink.

"I mentioned it to my partner. He said not to get involved, said to shred everything, then we'd get out of town for a few weeks, take a cruise. But I'm a loyal man, John. My boss was difficult but good to me. He saw my value and that's priceless. How could I ignore his last request?"

"Anybody else?"

Another guilty pause. "Well, when I found the first note at the office, I told one of the paralegals. I mean, it *was* mind-boggling. A note from the dead. But after I went to the bank and saw the documents, I wouldn't tell her anything. She asked, but I told her it was confidential."

John sighed. "Don't talk to anybody else about it."

"I won't," Lonstein said. "You can count on that." Then he recalled something more. "When I was leaving messages all over for you, I got a call back from your Lieutenant Myerson. Asked what it was about, if he could help. Sounded like a good guy."

"Don't talk to these people, Gil. They're dangerous."

"Maybe I can draw him out, pump him for a little intel that might help you. I'm willing to do that."

"No, I'm serious. I'm warning you, Gil."

"You surprise me, John." He sounded cocky. "You don't need a badge to have a feel for what goes on in the human mind. It's instinct. Pure instinct. You have it, or you don't. I have a hunch that if I—"

"Gil, thanks for the offer, but don't."

"John?" Katie tapped him persistently on the shoulder. "John."

He frowned at the interruption, then saw her face. "What is it?"

"Just heard your name on TV, a news bulletin."

"Hold on, Gil."

"Wait, John!" he cried. "Your picture just flashed on TV. Breaking news. Wow! They said you just robbed an armored car driver at Dade-land Mall, shot him, and fled south on US One. Are you in a high-speed police pursuit? Police and TV choppers overhead, following your car?"

"What the hell?" John said. "What station you watching?"

"It's on all of them," Katie whispered, her eyes huge.

"Where are you, John?" Gil demanded.

"Nowhere near Dadeland, Gil. I guarantee no choppers are following me." He closed his eyes in dismay as the unmistakable thud of chopper blades filled the room. "That's the TV, Gil. Somebody just turned up the volume."

Katie and Laura, who had changed into a denim shirt, blue jeans, and cuff-high boots, stared at the screen.

"Talk to no one, Gil. I'll meet you in the bank parking lot in forty-five minutes. What are you driving?"

"A 2011 silver-blue BMW."

"Good for you, Gil. I'll find you," John said.

He joined Laura and Katie in front of the TV. A female newscaster, sweaty and windblown at the scene, breathlessly reported that a lone, bold bandit had shot a Brink's employee as he wheeled a hand truck loaded with money bags from a mall department store to his armored car. The gunman escaped with two bags containing a large amount of cash.

Two witnesses described his getaway car as a late-model dark-blue Dodge Charger with a Florida tag.

"The armored car driver caught only a brief glimpse of the robber who *killed* his partner. That's right." The reporter nodded solemnly. "The victim has been pronounced dead at the scene, despite the efforts of passersby and paramedics who tried to save him. His killer is described as about six feet two or three inches tall, with sandy brown/blond hair, blue-gray eyes, and a light complexion. The robber fled south through midmorning traffic with police in pursuit. Our eye in the sky chopper is in the air and will provide continuing coverage of the chase in a few moments.

"The fleeing gunman remains unidentified, but an unnamed police source has confirmed that the killer fits the description of rogue Miami cop John Ashley, a fugitive charged in the murder of his own captain and a person of interest in other cases. Police say Ashley had been seen in the Dadeland area earlier. Several calls to the Miami police tip line reported sightings. Ashley is believed to be desperate for cash to flee the country."

"What?" John, Laura, and Katie echoed. They stared at one another.

"You are a busy man, John Ashley." Laura batted her eyelashes seductively.

"You certainly get around, bro." Katie shook her head. "That must be how you solved all those cases, by being in two places at once."

"This is crazy!" he said. "Dadeland's at the other end of the county. And the tip line's had reported sightings all over the tri-county area. I don't believe this."

A male reporter at the Dadeland scene urgently reported new information. "We have just received reports of two robbery shootings in the Dadeland area last night. The gunman fits the description of John Ashley, who police say may be on a crime spree after killing his supervisor."

John fumed. "They're blaming me for every crime that happens anywhere." He pulled out his notebook, then punched a number into his cell phone. "Hey," he said, "I need you to patch me in to Jeff Burnside. I know. It's important. This is John Ashley. Yes, that John Ashley. I need to talk to Jeff, now."

He picked up the remote and switched the big flat-screen, high-definition TV to Channel Six. Burnside was visible in a wide shot of chaos at the mall, in the background, talking to a security guard. They watched as the reporter answered his cell phone.

"Jeff! Yeah. This is John. John Ashley. No joke. It's me. Remember, we last talked the night of the motel shooting in Aventura? Listen, Jeff, let me assure you, swear to you, I'm nowhere near Dadeland. I'm not driving a Dodge Charger and have no police or news chopper on my tail. Don't buy it! They're piling it on to make me sound like somebody I'm not and never could be."

"I wondered, John," Burnside said. "So, you're saying that next they'll say you shot JFK and masterminded nine eleven? It may be safer to turn yourself in."

"No way, Jeff. I'd like to avoid dying mysteriously in jail or doing time for crimes I didn't commit. Who's investigating what really happened the night Politano was killed, who murdered Ron Jon Eagle, Summer Smith, and Cheryl Ann Sutter? I may be able to prove what happened, but not from behind bars. I just need more time."

"Hold on a sec, John."

On the TV they saw Burnside speak briefly to someone behind him. "I just heard on a police radio, John, that they have a positive ID on you as the killer of this Brink's guard, that you abandoned your stolen Charger and fled on foot."

"Do I sound out of breath? Do you hear rotors stirring up a storm over my head?"

"No, but that doesn't mean—"

"Look, we were having bagels when . . . Wait a minute." He beckoned Laura and Katie and handed them the phone. "Say hello to my friend Jeff at Channel Six."

"Hi, Jeff," Katie sang out. "Love you, watch every night."

"Me too," Laura said. "You're the best. When all this is straightened out, we want autographed eight-by-ten glossies, suitable for framing. And I swear"—she giggled—"the only person in pursuit of John Ashley at the moment is me."

"Is he still there?" Burnside asked.

"Sure." She handed John the phone.

"Good," Burnside said, "because police radios just broadcast that you jumped from the stolen Dodge Charger after crashing it into a tree and are swimming across a drainage canal."

"You hear any splashing, Jeff?"

"No, I don't, John."

"I just hope they catch the son of a bitch," he said, "so everybody will know it wasn't me." John checked his watch. "Gotta go, Jeff. I'll be in touch."

"Wait, John, I want to set up an on-air interview—"

"Have to call you back." He hung up. "I need to go to a meeting," he told Laura and Katie.

"I'll go with you, John." Laura picked up her handbag.

He'd hoped she wouldn't say it but was glad she did. "No, I have to meet a guy. I believe him but don't know if I can trust him. It might be dangerous."

"More reason for me to be there, to watch your back. Two guns are better than one." She trembled as though caught in a cold wind from the past. Her eyes locked on his. "You promised you'd never leave me again."

"You're right." He frowned. He knew he'd made that promise, but when? "They're not sure if you're a victim or an accomplice," he said. "If things go wrong, I'd rather have you treated like a victim."

"Not on your life," she said.

He saw the unflinching determination in her eyes. "Okay," he said. "Let's go."

CHAPTER THIRTY-NINE

The spiky heels of Laura's boots echoed eerily off the concrete as the wind swept through the open sides of the parking garage. The empty structure reminded John of a lonely, unused mausoleum silently awaiting the dead.

"Here's our ride." He took the keys from the top of the right front wheel of a used Toyota Robby had left for them on the second floor of the parking garage at the Sea Spray. Except for the grayish green Camry, the entire level was unoccupied, as were the others above. "I like American-made, myself." He opened the passenger side door for her.

"So do I. Why would someone buy a car this color?" Laura wondered aloud.

The interior was dull beige, a pine-tree-shaped air freshener hung from the rearview mirror, and there was a child seat in the back.

"You see them all the time in traffic. There must be more people than we think who are like us, who need to blend in and stay under the radar." He turned on the radio to catch the news. Both were startled by an earsplitting blast of raunchy hip-hop.

"That can't be what Robby listens to," Laura said, in mock disbelief. "It must be the prior owner's favorite station."

John listened. Live voices punctuated the raunch with shout-outs, gang slang, obscene challenges, and threats. "Nope, it's Robby." John grinned. "Definitely Robby."

"Coulda fooled me. Thought he was into folk, Bob Dylan, and old-time country-western."

"He is. But Robby looks young and works undercover in the Gang Unit from time to time. What we're hearing is a street gang's pirate radio station." They rolled out of the gloomy garage into blinding summer sunlight. "The boy's just doing his homework. Listens for intel, keeps tabs on the gangbangers." Miami gangs, he said, rent small homes, erect 130-foot antennas, plug in their electronics, and launch their own pirate radio stations. These pirates had forced a classical music FM station off the air and hijacked its signal to broadcast their raucous music and live on-air insults, slurs, and challenges to rival gang-bangers.

John turned it off so they could talk.

"I told Gram all about you." She cut her eyes at him in a way so familiar, he was sure he'd seen it all his life. "I asked her not to talk or answer questions from anyone, locals or strangers," Laura said. "She promised she'd do her usual act."

"Which is?"

"Gram doesn't like strangers, so when they show up, she looks bewildered, cups her ear with her hand, and replies to everything with 'Say, what?' It's easy to pull off at her age."

Leon called as they crossed the big, blue bay to Biscayne Boulevard. "Figured you might be too busy to answer, Johnny. Hear you shot a guard, knocked off an armored car, crashed a stolen vehicle during a chase, then dove into a canal, and swam away."

"Haven't been near that end of town, I swear."

"Didn't think so," Leon said. "They're tightening the screws, racheting up the pressure."

He'd been to the diner directly across from the historic Miami cemetery where Julia Tuttle and other city pioneers were buried. "Your situation's split the police department right down the middle, Johnny. Everybody's taking sides. Most of the rank and file swear you were set up by the crooks who run the show."

"Nice to hear," John said. "But I can't count on help from the troops. When a cop gets in trouble, the rest run like thieves. Every man for himself. No cop wants a beef with his bosses. They can ruin you. Kill you. Look at me.

"But we may be onto something. I'm on my way to meet a man. Now."

"Good luck, Johnny." Leon chuckled. "Hope yours is better than theirs. Heard about the mini riot at that movie theater across the bay. They turned South Beach upside down and shook it out looking for you.

Anybody who remotely fit your description, which means any white man between fifteen and sixty, had his balls to the wall being frisked. Hope you were miles away sipping a cold one. Got something for you, Johnny, from a friend a mine in your neighborhood, the nighta your so-called burglary."

"Tell me."

"There *was* a burglar who *is* a thief. But it didn't go down like they said. Thief's name is Harry. Last name sounds like Ryder or Ridder. His claim to fame is some press five, six years ago, that got him the moniker of the Matchstick Burglar. Moron didn't own a flashlight. Worked at night and left a trail of burnt-out matches as he prowled houses looking for valuables he could carry. Didn't own a car either. One night he's burglarizing a house in Wynwood, dropping matches behind him as he searches for jewelry and cash, and winds up in the laundry room. Didn't know the lady of the house was soaking sweaters in some kind of flammable cleaning solution in a basin on the floor."

"Don't tell me . . . ," John said.

"Yup, drops a match, the fumes ignite, go *whooosh*, and he runs screaming down the street, lit up the night with a three-alarm fire in the seat of his pants. Police find him at Jackson's burn unit. Couldn't sit down for a year. Had skin grafts, the whole nine yards. Cost the taxpayers a bundle. You know how fire victims like Phantom of the Opera, Freddy Krueger, or that guy Jason in the mask have charred, scarred, shriveled faces? That's what his ass looks like. At least that's what I'm told, ain't seen it myself. Did time for burglary and arson, was paroled early. Got busted for burglary again a couple, three weeks ago. But oddly enough, they didn't revoke his parole. He was released. First place he goes is yours. Not his usual MO. Usually hits houses and small businesses. Didn't leave no burnt matches either. Did he?"

"Nope," John said. "Not a one."

"*Humph*," Leon said. "Another friend in your hood says Harry just strolled around the corner that night, all nonchalant. Then the two cops who said they chased 'im come tearing around the corner all breathless and putting on a show. Soon as they're outta sight of your place, they slow to a walk, high-five, laugh, and chew the fat for a while. Then they go back and say he outran 'em."

"The Matchstick Burglar," John said. "With that street name, Harry shouldn't be hard to find."

"Right," Leon said, "could be reluctant to cooperate, unless he hears a major investigation is coming together and he'll be protected."

"Hopefully, that'll happen," John said.

"Watch yourself, Johnny. They're making it more dangerous for you. Once they convince the world you're a deranged outlaw on a violent crime spree, it's open season—on you."

"Got it," John said. "Let me know if you get a handle on where Harry bunks. I'd sure as hell like to talk to the man myself."

"Sure thing. Watch your back."

"Somebody's doing that," he said, as he and Laura exchanged a sweet glance. "Things are looking up, man. Stay in touch. I need all the help I can get."

The sun glinted off cars in the bank parking lot. John spotted the silver-blue BMW at the back with Lonstein still behind the wheel. John drove by at a crawl, gave him a nod, and made eye contact or tried to. Lonstein wore huge, mirrored aviator shades. John saw a departing SUV free up a space closer to the entrance.

As he swung the Camry into the spot, Laura gasped.

"Oh my God. He's James Bond!"

"For Pete's sake," John said.

Lonstein walked toward them. Along with the shades, he wore black Nikes, fingerless black leather driving gloves, and a black turtleneck under a dark jacket, despite the heat. A metal-sided attaché case appeared to be chained to his left wrist. With every stealthy catlike step, every swing of his shoulders, he swiveled his head, scanned the landscape, and peered over his shoulder. He gave the wary appearance of a man guilty of something and certain that he's being followed.

A noisy white minivan rolled by packed with children and driven by a harried woman in search of a parking space, Lonstein stopped, stared, then riveted his eyes on the license plate, moving his lips as though committing it to memory.

"What happened to his preppy look?" John asked.

Lonstein focused on an elderly couple, the man hobbling slowly on a walker, the woman using a cane. He lowered his chin to study them so intently that, alarmed, they picked up their pace.

"Nine-one-one will probably be flooded with calls before he even walks into the bank," Laura said.

"I should have mentioned," John said, "that he fantasizes about being a detective. Said he missed his calling."

"He's role-playing," Laura said. "More actor than investigator."

"And not doing very well at it, unless he plans to play Inspector Clouseau in a Pink Panther flick," John said.

Lonstein approached, his back rigid, eyes straight ahead. Abreast of their car, he slowly surveyed his surroundings, then muttered, "Hey," out the side of his mouth.

"Hey." John sighed. "You have the key?"

Gil nodded, then made eye contact with Laura over the top of his shades. "A familiar face," he said suavely. "Glad to see you looking so well."

"I'm spectacularly well," she replied, and cut her eyes at John.

"My name is Lonstein," he said. "Gil Lonstein."

"Laura," she said.

"Yes. The lovely model." He cocked his head at John. "You coming?"

"You don't need me," John said. "Sign in as you did before, use your access code, hand over the key, then bring out the package, all the paperwork."

"Should I ask the clerk to make us copies?"

"No. We can do that in a less public place."

"It'll leave the box empty. Shall I ask them to close it?"

"No." John was becoming impatient. Lonstein, in his getup, stood out like a sore thumb to every passerby on the street, every passing car on busy Biscayne Boulevard, and all the foot traffic in and out of the bank. "Let's just get the package Eagle wanted you to give me. You can close it later. And Gil, do me a favor, lose the shades before you go inside. The gloves too. Relax. Act normal."

Lonstein looked startled.

"We don't need negative attention," John explained. "Bank robberies are up, employees are alert. Sunglasses, hats, packages, anything out of the ordinary spooks 'em and can create problems."

"All right," Lonstein said curtly. He plucked off the aviator glasses, stuck them in his pocket, peeled off one glove, then struggled with the other because of the attaché case chained to his wrist.

People stared. "Okay. Okay. Just leave that one on," John said.

"I'm going in," Lonstein muttered dramatically without moving his lips.

"Good. Good luck, Gil."

"If I'm not out in fifteen minutes, make a run for it. Godspeed, go for broke."

"You'll come out. It's all routine," John assured him.

Lonstein squared his jaw and, without looking back, trotted up the five steps to the double glass doors. He opened one and turned to give a thumbs-up with his gloved hand, which caused the attached metal briefcase to bounce painfully off his groin. He limped inside as the door swung shut.

John stared. "Did you see what I saw?"

"At the door," Laura whispered, her face pained, "when the wind caught his jacket, I saw a bulge."

"Me too."

"Oh, no," she murmured.

"He never mentioned that he had a gun, a permit to carry, or knew how to shoot," John said.

"Even if he did," she said, "it's illegal to carry a firearm into a bank, bar, school, or public building."

"He's crazy," John whispered.

"Probably considered it a vital accessory to his *Mission Impossible* ensemble," Laura said. "Let's go." She touched his arm and glanced around the parking lot. "Let's get out of here, now."

"If Eagle's papers are what he described, we can't risk losing them. It may be the evidence we need. Our future rides on this. Sorry. I shouldn't have brought you, darlin'." He turned the key and the engine kicked in. "I'll drive you about twenty blocks north, drop you at a bus stop, and be back here before Gil comes out. If I don't pick you up in twenty-five minutes, hop the next bus north toward Robby's jurisdiction. Stay on until the end of the line, then call him or Katie. You were never here. Got that?"

"No," Laura said, "I am here, I always will be. Cut the engine, now. I will not get out of this car."

"Listen to me—"

"Look," she said.

Lonstein exited the bank, stopping to hold the glass door open for a small, elderly woman. She gazed up gratefully, and he returned a benevolent smile, tough guy with a heart.

He swaggered toward them, still smiling.

Behind him a bank security guard, in his early sixties, wearing a blue-gray uniform, stuck his head out the same door.

"Uh-oh," John and Laura said in unison.

The door swung all the way open. The guard raised his arm and shouted at Lonstein. "Sir, sir!"

Lonstein heard him, looked back, walked faster, then ran the last few yards to the car.

"You have it?" John said.

"In here." Lonstein gasped. He fumbled with the key to his attaché case as the guard walked briskly toward them.

"You locked it?" John said, exasperated.

"Damn straight." Lonstein panted. "This stuff is dynamite. I need to go with you. I want a copy."

His hand shaking, he finally managed to turn the key. The case flew open and the file spilled into the parking lot. Lonstein froze and stared down wide-eyed at what he had done.

John and Laura bailed out opposite sides of the car to retrieve the papers. Most were clipped together in a large manila envelope. Only two loose sheets fluttered away among the parked cars. Laura chased and caught both, as John snatched up the overstuffed envelope.

Lonstein looked up at the approaching guard, yanked a gun from beneath his jacket, and pointed it, his outstretched arm shaking, at the man.

"Halt!" he cried.

The gray-haired guard froze. He had never even thought to draw his own weapon. In his hand he held the aviator sunglasses Lonstein had inadvertently left in the safe-deposit box cubicle. "Sir!" he said, eyes wide.

Startled, Lonstein opened fire.

When he did, the weapon seemed to take on a life of its own. He could not stop squeezing the trigger. Passersby screamed, hit the ground, or ran, as bullets ricocheted off the walls of the building. The security guard dropped and rolled.

"No, no, stop!" Laura screamed from the far side of the car.

"Put the gun down!" John shouted. "Stop it before you kill somebody!"

Still firing, Lonstein wheeled toward the sound of John's voice and shot him in the face.

CHAPTER FORTY

The bullet slammed into John's right jaw on an upward trajectory and lodged behind his left eye. Blood flew as he fell to his knees in the parking lot.

Lonstein, his smoking gun now empty, looked wild-eyed.

"You shot him!" Laura screamed. "You shot him!"

"Didn't mean to, it was an accident!" Lonstein stared down at John, gasping and choking, on all fours. Blood covered his shirt. The envelope, now blood-spattered, lay beside him.

"Hand me those papers!" Lonstein waved his empty gun at Laura. "And give me that envelope!"

"No! Go to hell! Get out of here or I'll kill you myself."

He ignored her and rushed toward John and the envelope. Laura snatched her own gun from its holster at the small of her back, hidden by her denim shirt. "I *will* shoot you!" she said, her voice husky with rage and fear. She never wavered, her hands steady.

Lonstein stared, his face red, then turned to run. He took several steps, then dashed back to pluck his aviator glasses off the blacktop where the guard had dropped them, then fled to his car.

Laura snatched up the envelope, then half dragged, half carried John, bleeding and barely conscious, to the car. Grunting, she wrestled him into the passenger seat and fastened his seat belt. With no more shooting, passersby zoomed in like sharks. They pointed, stared, babbled on their cell phones. As Laura slid into the driver's seat, she heard voices in the crowd: "It's them! The ones on TV! In the newspaper!"

"It's the cop who killed the guard at Dadeland!"

"Somebody shot him!"

"It's John Ashley and Laura!"

She inched the car in reverse as bystanders closed in around it like a mob. The security guard, back on his feet, appeared dazed but unhurt. She tried to move the car forward, but people blocked the way, leering, pushing their faces up against the windows, staring at John and at her. She leaned on the horn, prepared to drive through them whether they parted or not, but suddenly, Lonstein's silver-blue BMW hurtled forward, burning rubber, from the rear of the lot. He never slowed down. Bystanders scattered, ran for their lives. Laura seized the moment, floored it right behind him, and raced out of the lot in Lonstein's wake.

"You'll be all right, darlin'," she repeated, again and again. Her voice trembled, as she willed it to be true. "You're all right, John. Speak to me. Dear God, oh please, please, let him be all right."

He groaned. "I can't believe the son of a bitch shot me," he muttered. "Did we get Eagle's papers?"

"Yes, darlin'. We have 'em and we're goin' to the hospital."

"No! No hospital!" he said vehemently, then gasped in pain.

"You've been shot. You need help."

"No! Chained to a bed? Held without bond? Behind bars?"

"Alive!" she cried fiercely. "Alive!" She choked back sobs, turned off the Boulevard onto a shady side street, and pulled to the curb. No one in sight. Sirens sounded in the distance. She didn't have much time.

She pressed her handkerchief to the wound under John's chin and called Robby. "Please pick up, oh, please pick up," she whispered, tears streaming. He didn't. She inhaled a deep breath and steeled herself. It was up to her. Her small hanky was instantly blood-soaked and dripping. She wiped her nose and her eyes on her sleeve, tried to sound calm, and left Robby a message. "Emergency in progress. Please, call ASAP."

She slipped off her denim shirt and pulled the sleeveless T-shirt under it over her head.

"Where are we?" he mumbled. He coughed and spit up blood.

"Just stopped for a sec, darlin'." Wearing only a lacy bra from the waist up, she fashioned the T-shirt into a crude compress.

"I'll drive," he mumbled. "Need to get you out of here." He fumbled, trying to unfasten his seat belt.

"And risk wrecking this wonderful car? Robby'd be furious, darlin'. I'll drive. Want to hear some pirate radio?"

"I'd rather have whiskey for the pain," he whispered.

"We'll get you some soon, darlin'." A patrol car zoomed by like a heat-seeking missile on the Boulevard, so swift, so close that it brought tears of fear to her eyes.

"Laura?" he moaned. "Damn. I can't see you—"

She fought back a cry.

"—or nothing out of my left eye. Nothing. My right eye's okay. Lemme see you."

"Here I am." She gently shifted him and pressed his hand to the soft compress on the wound to slow the bleeding.

"Can see you now," he muttered. "Love you too, girl, but this ain't the time to take off your clothes." He tried to laugh but grimaced in pain instead.

She kissed his cheek, his neck, his shoulder. His blood stained her bra, her hands, her chin. She couldn't bear to see his pain. She shrugged into her denim shirt, buttoned it, then caught her breath as another siren howled nearby. A police car raced south on the Boulevard, half a block away, speeding to the shooting scene at the bank. A chill swept across her shoulders and down her spine. Thank God that cop didn't turn onto this street, she thought. But one will. Soon. They'll fan out. A police chopper will appear overhead. I have to get him out of here.

She called Katie, who answered. "Thank God you're there." Laura fought tears. "John's alive, but he's been shot."

Katie gasped. "Where are you, girl?"

"In the car. Not far from the bank. I tried to stop the bleeding." She sniffed and wiped her nose. "I have to get him out of this neighborhood. The police are everywhere, they'll be all over us in minutes. He needs to go to the hospital but refuses."

"Good sign." Katie choked back a sob. "So he's conscious?"

"In and out."

"How bad is it?"

Laura turned away from John and dropped her voice to a whisper. "I'm scared. He's in pain, hit on the right side of his face, under his chin. There is no exit wound." She fought hysteria. "The bullet is in his head! And he can't see anything out of his left eye."

"He needs surgery," Katie said coolly. "Has to go to the hospital. Did you get the evidence?"

"Yes."

"Okay, hospitals must, by law, report all bullet wounds to the police. If you take him to the ER at Jackson, there will be delays. He will be arrested before he's evaluated. It could take forever. He needs to go to Bascom Palmer Eye Institute. If there is any chance to save the vision in that eye, they can do it. They have an emergency room. They're the best. Patients come to them from all over the world. If we can just get him there safely, he'll have the best shot."

"They'll arrest him, Katie."

"I know, darlin'. If it was simple, maybe I could handle it, or we could take him to some Little Havana clinic where they bend the rules. But it's not simple. At Bascom he'll be evaluated and in surgery before the police arrive."

Laura heard an odd rhythmic thudding as Katie spoke. "I hate to see him arrested," Laura whispered mournfully.

"So do I. But he'll be alive," Katie panted.

Laura now recognized the thuds. Katie was running. "And they'll arrest me too."

"No, they won't," Katie said breathlessly. "I'm getting in muh car now. I'm on the way. Stay calm, girl. I'll take him into the hospital. I know someone there. I've worked with 'im. I'll call ahead, tell 'im I came home and found my brother injured, his vision damaged."

Laura heard the car door slam.

"The key," Katie said, gunning her car out of the parking garage, "is to git him there before the police stop you. If not, he'll go to Jackson, then sit in chains for hours without pain meds or treatment. You have to do this, girl."

"But Katie, won't you be in trouble too?"

"Why? He's a family member. Haven't seen my brother for a while, came home, found him injured, took him to the hospital. For all I know, he had a hunting accident or was robbed. That's my story and I'll stick to it, unless I thinka somethin' better. Does Robby know?"

"I left a message."

"Good. Here's how you get to Bascom Palmer."

She gave clear, succinct directions. "Don't panic, girl. Focus on your cargo and driving carefully. Don't get distracted tryin' to reach Robby. I'll find him. You just get John there safely. That's your mission. I'll meet you there."

"We're on the way," Laura whispered. "If you hear anything on the news, call to tell me what they're saying and where they're lookin' for us."

She hung up and eased the car away from the curb.

"Who you talking to?" John mumbled,

"We're goin' to meet Katie. You'll be all right, darlin'."

"You don't know your way around Miami," he protested.

"No better time to learn, sweetheart." She sounded calmer than she felt. The most direct route to Bascom Palmer took them back past the bank shooting scene. She used the avenue behind the bank instead of the Boulevard in front.

"Don't let FHP or the cops stop us," he mumbled, rocking in pain.

"Then I need you to help me, tell me what to do," she said, hoping to keep him conscious and talking.

The bank's parking lot was being cordoned off with yellow crime scene tape, amid a sea of flashing blue lights. Laura slowed down like other motorists and stared curiously. It would seem odd if she didn't.

"Don't speed, don't get noticed," John said, eyes closed, words slurred. "Stay in the middle of the pack, darlin'. Hunters go after stragglers that stray from the herd. Stay within five, ten miles an hour of the cars around you. Cops look for drivers traveling faster than those around 'em. Use the signals, don't be aggressive, and never . . ." His voice trailed off. He'd passed out but was still breathing.

Minutes later, he opened his eyes and picked up where he had left off. "This is a perfect car. It's why Robby picked it. Flashy, tricked-out cars attract cops, not nondescript, ol' family cars like this one. Robby's good."

"Yes, he is, darlin'." She found the entrance ramp for State Road 836 and merged into the heavy westbound traffic stream. Her heart stopped as a highway patrolman swung into her lane behind the two cars following her.

She watched him in her rearview mirror. He's going to pull me over. Her mind raced. What should I do?

The Twelfth Avenue exit was coming up fast. She saw the name, Bascom Palmer Eye Institute, on the building. So near, yet so far. The trooper made his move, gunned his engine, roared past the two cars between them, and cut into traffic directly in front of her.

"John," she began. "I think we . . ."

His head lolled forward. "Wha, darlin'?"

The trooper stomped his gas pedal, hit his siren and blue flashers, then accelerated across three lanes of traffic, headed due west, and disappeared in a sea of brakelights.

Her knees weak, Laura breathed a sigh of relief. "Nothing. We're almost there."

Her cell phone rang. "Ah see you. I'm coming off Eight Thirty-Six right behind you," Katie said, her voice tense. "I'm 'bout six cars back. Pull up just before the entrance. I'll come up behind you and we'll switch cars. I'll drive John up to the door in the Camry. You take his gun, his phone, his wallet, those evidence papers, and all your belongings with you and drive my car back to the Sea Spray. See you there. Hold on a sec."

She came back on the line moments later. "Slight changea plans. Robby's right behind me. Musta drove like a bat outta hell. He's parkin' in the lot across the street. When I get John out of the Camry, Robby'll drive it back to the Sea Spray. When I leave the hospital, I'll drive Robby's car home."

Laura hated to leave. John made it easier.

"Katie's here," she said softly. "You may need surgery and this is the best place. They'll give you something for pain now."

He frowned, dazed. "They're gonna arrest me, Laura. Get out of here, now, before . . ." He gingerly explored his sightless eye with his fingers, as if to determine whether it was still there. "Lonstein," he murmured, bewildered. "What the hell did Lonstein . . . Why? Don't let go of that envelope, darlin'. Now go! I have always loved you, girl."

"I have always loved you more, John. We'll be together soon, I promise." She heard running footsteps come up behind her. It was Katie.

"You did it, girl! Now go, go, go," she urged. She hugged Laura and pressed into her hand the keys to her Chrysler convertible. "Sure you've got everything? Go! He'll be in good hands now. I'll call you, quick as I can."

Laura went, after a last look over her shoulder.

Katie turned to her brother, slumped in the passenger seat. "John," she demanded, "what the hell happened?"

He looked up and blinked, still pressing the blood-soaked, makeshift compress to the gaping hole in his chin. "Cut myself shaving."

"Told you to toss that damn straight razor a long time ago."

"What are you doing here?"

"Who else would be here? What happened?" she demanded again.

He paused. "Don't want you involved."

Robby appeared from nowhere, out of breath, fire in his eyes, his face pale. "Who shot you? Who did this, John?"

"Lonstein. Showed up dressed like Tom Cruise in *Mission Impossible*, saw a bank security guard, panicked, pulled a gun, and started shooting. When I yelled at him to stop, he shot me. Don't think he meant to, he's just stupid."

Robby sighed and tightened his lips. "They're saying on the air that you, Laura, and an unidentified white male tried to rob the bank and were thwarted by a security guard."

"Goddamnit," John mumbled. "None of that's true."

"I know," Robby said grimly. "This piling on has got to stop."

"Get out of here, bro," John murmured. "Go. Don't want my shit to rub off on you."

"I'll be back," Robby said. "When you see me, look surprised."

Katie had disappeared into the emergency room and emerged moments later with a wheelchair. Robby helped John from the car into the chair. As Katie rolled him into the ER, she glanced back and made eye contact with Robby. He nodded, slid into the Camry, and drove off. Moments later, he pulled into an abandoned gas station, changed the license tag on the Camry, then used peroxide, cold water, and a sponge to clean up the blood as best he could. Alone, he lost his cool when he saw how much John had lost. "My brother," he repeated again and again, his voice cracking as he scrubbed. He tossed the baby seat, air freshener, sponge, and peroxide into a Dumpster, then drove north.

Inside the ER, Dr. Sander Dubovy, an associate professor of ophthalmology and pathology, greeted Katie. "They said you'd arrived."

"Sandy," she said breathlessly, "it's my brother."

"Let's have a look at him."

As she hoped, John was taken for an immediate scan, then straight to surgery.

"He has a bullet lodged in the orbit of his left eye," the surgeon told her. "Luckily the globe was undamaged, but blood or bone fragments compressed the optic nerve and caused his loss of vision. If we can remove the bullet, the bone fragments, and drain the blood inside the orbit, the pressure should be relieved and he stands a good chance of re-gaining most or all of the vision in that eye. He's lucky you got him here fast. Otherwise it might have been irreversible."

Laura prayed, paced, wept, and raged back at the Sea Spray. Katie called when John went to surgery and again to say police had arrived and he was under arrest but would remain briefly at Bascom Palmer for postop care.

"Here's the *Reader's Digest* version," Katie told her. "The eyeball sits inside a bony structure called the orbit. Blood filled the orbit, cre-ated pressure on the optic nerve, and caused his loss of sight. Surgeons drained the blood, removed the bullet, and relieved the pressure. They expect the nerve damage to be temporary. They'll know for sure in the next day or so. It could have been permanent if he hadn't arrived here as fast as he did. Or if the bullet had been bigger; it was a twenty-two long."

"The gun looked like a Walther P twenty-two automatic," Laura said. "Looked like the fool had never fired it, or any other firearm, in his life."

"Beginner's luck," Katie drawled.

"I'd like to wring his scrawny neck," Laura said.

"Join the club." Katie's voice dropped to a whisper. "The cops all knew John had been shot, so many witnesses saw it. But nobody knew the bullet had damaged his eye. Cops were at every ER in Miami-Dade and South Broward but never thought of the Eye Institute."

"Thanks to you," Laura said.

"You were the ambulance driver, I only helped you navigate. We pulled it off," Katie said, with relief, and promised to call back, which is why Laura dove for the phone the next time it rang. She answered to dead silence, heard someone breathing, and said hello again.

"Hi, this is Gil. Is John there?"

"No, he isn't," Laura said tersely. "You shot him, you moron, re-member?"

"No need to cop an attitude," Lonstein said peevishly. "It wasn't de-liberate."

"Do you even realize what you've done?" She could hardly restrain her anger. "If you had killed him, he'd be dead, deliberate or not." Her voice rose. "What were you thinking?"

"He isn't dead," Lonstein asked cautiously. "Is he?"

"No. No thanks to you. He's in surgery. The doctors don't know yet if he'll ever see out of his left eye again. And he's been arrested on murder charges, thanks to you."

"Bummer," Lonstein said. "Didn't know I hit him in the eye."

Laura shuddered, gritting her teeth. "What do you want?"

"All the Eagle documents, and a copy of the official murder case file, if possible."

"May I ask why?" she said. "Eagle requested that you deliver those documents to John, to help convict his killers. If you wanted copies, why didn't you make them yourself when you first found them? Why now?"

Lonstein paused for a long moment. "You see, I had no idea how valuable they could be."

"Gil, if you even think about trying to blackmail any of the criminals or corrupt cops involved, you're dumber than I thought. It's dangerous. Don't do it."

"Oh, Laura," he said pettishly, "give me credit for a little common sense. I wouldn't dream of that."

"So, what is it?" she asked, curiosity piqued.

"Those things are gold," he said intensely. "Don't get any ideas now, I've got first dibs and a leg up already. A friend of mine with TV and publishing connections has *Forty-Eight Hours, Twenty/Twenty, Prime-time*, and maybe"—he sucked in a deep breath—"even *Sixty Minutes* excited about the story."

"The story?" Laura resisted the urge to kick the phone like a foot-ball. Is he crazy, is the whole world crazy?

"Can't you see it?" he said. "High-profile murder case, sex, money, powerboat racing, a spectacular crash, dozens injured, beautiful models knocked off, bodies found in burning Dumpsters, a handsome homicide sergeant framed for murder, the victim's young office manager who investigates on her own and uncovers the clues that break the case. Eagle's notes to me from beyond the grave are dynamite! Once it's on TV, a book and/or a movie contract is sure to follow. It's a gold mine!"

"I'm out of work, woman. This could launch my new career. Show biz! A franchise based on sexy high-profile murder cases. Could be the best thing that ever happened to me! Admittedly," he conceded, "it's at the expense of others, but shit happens. Not my fault. It takes a smart and savvy guy to salvage something good out of it, to spin shit into gold."

Laura slumped, exhausted, into a chair, listening in open-mouthed disbelief.

"Play your cards right, Laura, and you might play yourself in the movie. The big screen," he said reverently. "If I'm executive producer, I might put in a good word for you. I mean, you are a goddamn model, pretty enough to play yourself. All you need is a crash course in drama training."

"I have enough drama in my life already, thank you. And those models who were 'knocked off,' as you put it, were friends."

"What'd I just say, Laura? Drop the attitude. Golden opportunities don't come often. When lightning strikes, you have to seize the moment. It may never come again."

"Is that why you shot John?"

"I told you, that was an accident. Faced with a high-hazard mission, I armed myself. All Americans have that right. Bought the gun but didn't have time enough to completely acquaint myself with its operation before I needed it. Now, where and when can I pick up copies of my papers?" he asked persistently.

"I swear, if you so much as cross my path, I will slap the snot out of you, you inept, impossibly stupid, wannabe warrior! What you really are is a pitiful, small-time wuss who probably still sucks his thumb and wets the bed!"

"No movie role for you," he sang out maliciously. "You just blew your chance! Those personal notes from Eagle belong to me! Nobody else! The attorney I consulted confirmed it!" Lonstein shouted angrily, as she hung up.

She wondered, with a sinking feeling, how many people he'd talked to, and shook her head.

"He's nuts," said Robby, who called a short time later. "He has a lot more important things to think about. Doesn't it strike you as odd that the Miami police haven't talked to him yet? That's ominous. He did business, signed papers in that bank. Surveillance cameras caught him inside and outside. Witnesses and the cameras saw him, his car and tag. They know who he is, where he lives, and what he looks like. Strange, isn't it, that all these hours later, no cop has pulled him over or knocked on his door? I wouldn't want to stand next to the man in a public place right now," Robby said.

CHAPTER FORTY-ONE

Katie feared she'd be followed when she left the hospital, so she went to her North Miami townhouse instead of the Sea Spray. The police had grilled her for more than an hour.

She switched on all the lights, sorted her mail, paid a few bills, then showered, dressed, and turned out the lights, as though she'd gone to bed. Thirty minutes later Robby arrived at the back door and drove her to the Sea Spray.

"Thank God we came through for John today." Robby looked and sounded bone weary.

"Of course." Katie nudged his arm. "Ashleys always stick together, no matter what."

"Damn straight." He smiled for the first time that day.

"Have you eaten, Rob?"

He thought for a moment. "Not since breakfast on the run."

"You need more meat on your bones, boy. Come on up, I'll throw some burgers in the broiler. Betcha Laura's awake and hasn't eaten either."

She was right.

Laura had never even tried to sleep. After Lonstein's call, she copied the Eagle papers on the copy machine/printer in the apartment's small office. As she stapled six copies, she muttered, "And not a single one for you, Mr. Lonstein. Sorrrry."

She ran to open the door when she heard Katie's key in the lock.

"They're giving him high doses of steroids to reduce inflammation around the optic nerve," Katie said. "First thing he asked when he woke up was if you were safe. I said, 'What? Who? I thought you were still seeing that fat-ass cop, you know, the big-mouthed Latina.' Shoulda seen his face. Then I winked. They had a cop, a really creepy big guy, parked in a chair on John's blind side.

"His eye is bandaged shut. The doctors will know more in the mornin'. But I tell you, girl, I'm optimistic. So's the surgeon."

That was good news. The bad news was that John was handcuffed to his bed, with a tug-of-war under way between Miami homicide lieutenant Mac Myerson, who demanded that John be moved to the county prison ward at once, and doctors who preferred that he have a few days of postop care at the institute.

The patient's brother, sister, and sweetheart dined on medium-rare cheeseburgers with homemade slaw at 2:30 a.m. Only Françoise, the absent owner's little shih tzu, ate with gusto. She ravenously finished her own and some of theirs.

When Robby was ready to leave, Katie picked up the dog's leash. "She needs a walk. I'll go downstairs with you."

"I'll come too." Laura slipped on her shoes.

"No way," Robby said emphatically. "It's too late, too dark, too deserted. Nobody else knows that you're here, as far as we know. But we can't count on that."

"But Françoise has to go out," Katie protested, "to pee, poop, get some fresh air and exercise."

"Walk her out on the terrace in the dark. No lights," he said. "Clean up after her. Do what you have to. Before you turn on any lights after dark, close the drapes tight. When the rest of the building's dark any light in here stands out like a beacon, a neon sign. We have to take extra precautions because it's tough to tell the good guys from the bad. Don't count on anything or anybody. It's just us. I brought you another car. The Camry's gone," he told Laura. "It's in the same space as the Camry but two levels up. The keys are on the right front tire."

He hated to go. "I should stay," he said. "But Ann Lee worries when I'm out all night. She's either scared I've been shot on the job or that I'm with another woman. She'd rather I get shot." He flashed his boyish grin. "Early tomorrow, I'm having breakfast at Morningside with Mom and Pop. The rest of the kids will be there so I can fill them in without repeating myself and talking too much over the phone. All I said tonight was that John'll be all right."

"Kiss 'em all for me," Katie said. "Tell 'em I love 'em and I'll be at the hospital first thing in the morning."

Robby hugged them both and left.

They walked Françoise up and down the big wraparound terrace in the dark. Katie carried a plastic bag and paper towels.

"You always take Robby's advice?" Laura asked.

"Most of the time. He's my brother; he's got my back. They all do. The one I *always* listen to is John. He's the best, the brightest, always does the right thing. He's solid gold, the real deal. We all, even our parents, look up to John. But now, with him indisposed, I turn to Robby. I'd be stupid not to. I can't help but think of him as a kid, 'cuz he is the youngest and I remember him learning to walk, but he's a real man—a little wilder, but smart, quick, and resourceful like John."

"Runs in the family," Laura said. "You were so cool, spitting out split-second decisions when we needed them. You brought us through it."

"I'm so glad you're gonna be an Ashley too," Katie said. "Welcome to the family."

They gazed down at quiet Collins Avenue from the darkened terrace. A convertible cruised by, top down, its stereo blasting Phil Collins's "In the Air Tonight." A man was driving. The blond hair of the woman close beside him whipped like a banner in the wind.

"Honeymooners, I bet," Katie said, wistfully. "It must feel good to be that free together in this mellow night, with the sea breeze and the music washing over you . . ."

They went to bed, still restless after the adrenaline-charged events of the day. Each dozed fitfully in separate rooms, until Françoise, the fluffy little black and white shih tzu, began to bark frantically in the dark. She jumped off Katie's bed and ran out, growled viciously, and hurled herself at the front door.

Katie and Laura nearly collided moments later, dazed, hair tousled, in their nightgowns in the dark outside their rooms. Each held a loaded revolver pointed at the floor.

"Think someone's out there?" Laura whispered.

"For sure," Katie whispered back. "She never acts that way for no reason."

"Maybe it's a neighbor coming home late."

Katie shook her head. "No other neighbors on this floor."

Laura inhaled deeply. "The owner?" she breathed hopefully. "Maybe she's back from Europe."

"She called from Switzerland this morning, having a wonderful time, asked me to send some of her things."

"Crap," Laura whispered.

As Katie edged along the wall toward the door, the knob slowly turned. The dog erupted in a frenzy of wild barking.

"Get out of here!" Katie shouted fiercely. "My husband's got a gun! The police are on the way!"

The little dog growled, her body stiff. She dove at the doorsill and, still growling, began to dig furiously as though trying to burrow beneath it to reach her prey.

"Good dog," Laura murmured.

Françoise turned and stared at them, her shiny button eyes mournful in the night, then raised her head and emitted a shiver-inducing, eerily high-pitched, brokenhearted howl.

"She never did that before either," Katie said, trembling.

"Oh my God!" Laura gasped. "She may sense something."

"If she does, it's not good luck coming our way." Katie's big, luminous eyes looked haunted in the filtered moonlight from the terrace.

"Shall we call Bobby?"

Katie shook her head. "Did you see how he looked tonight? He's overtired, stressed out, juggling a demanding job, the rest of the family, his own wife, who's a handful, and what's happened to the big brother he's always idolized. He's also taking care of us. Don't want to add to his burden with anything but an emergency we can't handle ourselves."

Laura wearily agreed. "Will this night ever end?"

Katie smiled sweetly. "Don't worry. In Miami, the sun will always rise in the morning."

Both swore they were not superstitious, but the dog's behavior so unnerved them that Katie called the hospital to allay their fears.

"John," the charge nurse said, "is resting comfortably."

"I hate to sound silly," Laura said after the call, "but it made me think of all those old wives' tales about dogs howling when somebody's about to die."

They dragged a heavy sofa, braced it against the door, double-locked the windows and sliding glass doors, then camped out in Katie's bedroom for what little was left of the night.

Laura's cell phone rang shortly after they finally fell asleep. She fumbled for it in the dark, unsure where she was for an instant. She found the cold steel of her revolver beside her, then the phone, and tried to keep from waking Katie.

Too late.

"Who can it be at this hour?" Katie mumbled, and sat up.

"Don't know," Laura said, her heart clutched with fear. A phone call in the wee hours is almost never good news. The scare at the door and the howling dog seemed omens of disaster to come.

Katie switched on a bedside lamp as Laura answered.

"Wait," she told the caller, her face shocked. "What are you talking about? Do you know what time it is? . . . Who? . . . Which ones? . . . What was that? . . . No! Oh my God! No! Don't do that!"

CHAPTER FORTY-TWO

L aura? You've gotta help me!" He sounded frantic, out of breath.

The shameless poseur, the reckless wannabe who shot John, the man who'd rudely dismissed her as unqualified to play herself in his demented and grandiose movie plans, needed her help. And it was four thirty in the morning. She rolled her eyes at Katie, crinkled her nose, and silently mouthed the name *Gil Lonstein.*

"Wait!" she said, suddenly. "What are you talking about? Do you know what time it is?"

"They're here!" he cried.

"Who?"

"The cops!"

"Which ones?" Her voice changed from exasperated to wary.

"Looks like Miami and the county!" he panted.

She heard a shattering boom, as though a car had hit a house. "Oh, no!" he said.

"What was that?"

"They're breaking in! They yelled for me to throw out my gun, then surrender. If I didn't, they'd shoot! I don't have the gun. It's in the car. So I slammed the door and ran out through the kitchen to the garage to get it. I'm scared! They're gonna kill me, Laura! Laura? I'm getting in the car now."

She heard the car door slam.

"Okay. I've got the gun. I'm gonna open the garage door and drive to the Miami Lakes Police Department for protection!"

"No! Oh my God! No! Don't do that! No," she screamed again as he started the engine. She heard the rumble of a heavy garage door opening. "Wait!"

"Stop him! Get him! Get him! Get him!" men shouted. A barrage of gunfire. Crashes, breaking glass, the slam of bullets into metal never seemed to end. She heard at least thirty shots.

A high-pitched scream at the start was followed by a moan, several seconds of labored breathing. Then silence.

"Throw out your weapon! Throw out the gun!"

"Jesus! We got 'im! We got 'im. Let's get him outta there! Artie, come on! Get him out. Get him out. Now!"

"Son of a bitch! Get that phone!" Fumbling noises as someone picked it up.

"Hey! Who is this!" a man hoarsely demanded in Laura's ear.

She held her breath, frozen, listened to his heavy breathing for a moment, then hung up. She stared at Katie.

"I think they killed Gil Lonstein," she whispered.

Hands shaking, she called Jeff Burnside.

"Jeff, Jeff," she said as he answered. "This is Laura. Please listen."

"I'm here," he said. She heard him moving about, as though he'd rolled out of bed and was dressing. "Where are you?"

She ignored the question.

"Gil Lonstein," she said breathlessly. "He's the man who shot John at the bank yesterday."

"Right. I know who he is. They issued a warrant for him, or were about to, last night. He worked for Eagle."

"That's him. He just called in a panic. Said the police were trying to kill him. I heard at least thirty shots. I think he's dead."

"Where?"

"Lonstein said he went into his garage. Has to be at his home. He lives in the north end. Said he was going to try to drive to the Miami Lakes Police Department for protection. I may be able to find the address. Hold on."

"Okay, let me call a cameraman on another line. Don't hang up."

"I won't." She dashed barefoot to the small office next to the kitchen, still clutching her cell phone.

Katie, seconds ahead of her, was already booting up the computer on which John had been documenting the case, including lists of witnesses, suspects, and contacts, for Joel, his lawyer. She smoothly vacated the desk chair as Laura slid into it, then ran for John's notebook and coffee, as Laura scanned files.

She returned to peer over Laura's shoulder. "Hit edit," she suggested, "then find and replace, and type in Lonstein's name."

"There! There it is! I've got it!" Laura said moments later. She repeated Lonstein's Miami Lakes address to Jeff Burnside.

"We're on the way," Burnside said.

She told him, as he got into his car, about the files and letters Eagle had left. "That's why we were at the bank," she explained. "Lonstein found them in a safe-deposit box he shared with Eagle. I'll try to send you a set today. Lonstein talked to too many people about what he knew. That's why he was killed. He sounded so scared. Said they ordered him to throw out his gun or they'd shoot. He ran to the car to get it. By then they were breaking into the house. He knew they'd kill him, so he tried to drive to a safe place for protection."

"Call me later," Burnside said.

"What should I do now?" she asked.

"Write down everything you heard during his call. Try to recreate the entire conversation, all the background noises, names, and what was said while it's still fresh." He paused. "Laura, there's an arrest warrant for you too. If you're in a safe place, stay put. Try not to be alone, and be careful."

"A warrant? On what charge?"

"Attempted bank robbery, aggravated battery, obstructing justice, gun charges, and criminal conspiracy."

Laura teared up as Katie prepared to leave for the hospital. "I hate to see you go without me. I'd give anything to see John and tell him I love him."

"I'll tell him as much as I can, with that cop in the room. Hope it's not the same creepy one as yesterday." Katie shuddered, then hugged Laura. She took two copies of the Eagle documents with her in manila envelopes, one addressed to Jeff Burnside, and the original to John's attorney, Joel Hirschhorn.

Françoise, the shih tzu, trotted to the door behind her. The women exchanged a startled glance as the same thought occurred to both. "Françoise was right," Laura said.

"She didn't even know Lonstein," Katie said thoughtfully.

"Yes, but she sensed something. Dogs are so intuitive. We'll walk you to your car." Laura buckled the little dog's red leash to her collar. They locked the apartment and walked down the empty hall to the elevator, talking quietly.

Katie gasped. "Look!"

Cigarette butts, two of them, had been dropped, then ground into the plush carpet in a small alcove across from the elevator. Both were Marlboros, smoked down to the filter.

Someone had waited and watched their apartment on the otherwise empty floor.

"The prowler at our door last night must have left them," Katie said. "If they'd been here when Robby and I came home, we would have seen them." They stared at each other. Katie sensed what Laura was thinking and shook her head. "Wasn't him. Robby doesn't smoke, never has."

She gripped Laura's arm tightly. "Wish I didn't have to go, but I want to be there when the doctors check John's vision. Don't take Françoise out; walk her on the terrace. Try not to be seen from the street." Katie checked her watch. "Time to fill in Robby. He's on his way to Morningside to brief the family."

The elevator door yawned open and they hugged. "Be back, quick as I can. Pray for good news. Wear your gun and cell phone at all times. By the way, there's a pistol-grip shotgun under my bed. It's loaded. Get it out and keep it with you."

The doors closed and she was gone.

Laura and the dog trotted back inside and returned minutes later. She plucked the cigarette butts from the carpet with tweezers, dropped them into a Ziploc bag, and sealed it. As she rose to her feet, she saw that the elevator, at lobby level where Katie left it, had begun to ascend with a new passenger or passengers. Two, three, four, it kept rising. As it approached their floor, Laura and the little dog ran back to the apartment and barricaded the door.

CHAPTER FORTY-THREE

Figured it was Lonstein," Robby said, as Laura poured his coffee. "Heard that a task force of city and county cops killed a male subject wanted in the bank robbery attempt and shooting. Said he was armed, resisted, and forced them to fire in self-defense when he tried to hit them with his car."

"Don't believe that," Laura said. "He tried to run to a safe place because he knew they'd kill him, and they did."

"Remember what he said to you yesterday? 'Shit happens.' He was right," Robby said.

"But dead wrong about himself," she said. "He thought he'd found a new career, a promising future. Instead he had no future at all."

"What they did was cold, premeditated," Robby said. "And the best time to do that is four a.m., which it was. No pedestrians, joggers, or nosy neighbors, no mailman, no lawn man mowing the grass. No witnesses."

"Why on earth would he call me for help?" Laura asked, as they sat in the cheery kitchen. "Last time we talked, I promised to smack the snot out of him."

"He thought you'd know what to do," Robby said. "Or it was an accident."

She nodded. "Scared, in a panic, he may have accidentally hit redial. His last call before that may have been the one to me. I threatened him, called him a small-time wuss."

Robby grinned. She gave him a reproachful look.

"Hey, I won't miss his sorry ass. He shot my brother. He's lucky I didn't see him first."

She looked serious. "Are your folks okay?"

His parents were on the way to see John in the hospital, he said. "Mom was up early fixing chicken, dumplings, and the works. The girls are going this afternoon, Ed and Frank later. Won't be much chance once he's transferred to JMH. That's a locked-down prison ward. It won't be easy."

"Is there a way I can call him?" she said.

He shook his head. "His calls are monitored."

He had her write the time, the date, and where the cigarette butts were found on the Ziploc bag and said she and Katie should have called him immediately when the intruder was still outside. "There is a remote chance," he said hopefully, "that the prowler last night was one of those creeps who strip foreclosed houses and vacant condos. They steal a/c units, generators, appliances, everything but the kitchen sink, and sometimes that too. Or a pervert who saw you and Katie on the beach, quite a sight in your bikinis."

"I wish it was a two-bit thief or perv," Laura said. "Them we could handle, but not a bunch of trigger-happy cops who want us dead."

"Dial nine-one-one as a last resort if they show up. You'll get the cops in this jurisdiction. Ask if they have officers at your door. When they say no, tell them you're alone, scared, and that armed men who claim to be police officers are breaking into your home. They'll give it top priority."

He took a copy of Eagle's documents with him. "Now," he said, "I need to find you an alternate exit."

He studied the wraparound terrace, took measurements, left, and returned in thirty minutes with a nine-foot length of scaffolding nearly two feet wide and weighted at both ends.

"You're not afraid of heights are you, Laura?"

"I'm not phobic." She hesitated. "But I'm not one of the Flying Wallendas either."

He took the scaffolding to the far end of the terrace, around the corner of the building, and left it lying against the wall where it couldn't be seen. "If the time ever comes when you or you and Katie have to leave in a hurry, just slide this under the rail and push it across to the next terrace, which is five feet away. The ends are weighted, the bottom railings will hold them both down. You'll have two feet overlap at each end. Just step over the railing and walk across to the next terrace if it's not windy; if it is, crawl across, holding on to the scaffold. Then drag it over to the other side and leave it against the wall. I stopped by the super's office on my way out. Nobody there, so I borrowed the keys to that next apartment and made copies.

"And here." He opened a package from Home Depot and unfurled a sturdy rope ladder. "They make these so people in upstairs bedrooms can escape house fires. You fasten the ropes to the railing like this, make sure it's tight, then climb down to the terrace below. That apartment's also unoccupied. I copied the keys. That set is green, the ones for next door are red."

He gave them to her on a single key chain attached to a sturdy leather cord she could wear around her neck.

"Once you're out of the apartment, there are two elevators across from the stairwell on the south side of the building. Push the buttons for all the lower floors including the lobby, then take the stairs to the penthouse level. On your right you'll see a covered bridge to the parking garage. You know where the car is. It's an older-model gray Volvo. The key's in the usual place. They'll be watching the exit, so you leave through the entrance on the other side. There's a yellow button on the mechanism that operates the gate. Get outta the car, hit that button, and it will open. Drive south. Or simply walk out of the garage onto the beach, like a tourist taking a stroll south along the surf. Then call me or Katie if she's not with you."

She nodded. "Hope I don't need it. But thanks, either way. If I go, I'll have to bring Françoise, can't leave her behind."

"If she slows you down, don't," he said. "Now I'm headed to the hospital to see John."

"Tell him his friend, Leon, called and is concerned. He's been helping John with information."

"Leon's on our side." Robby nodded. "John trusts him. We need to stay in touch with him."

"I have his number now." Laura copied it for him.

"Nice to have another sister." He smiled, kissed her cheek. "Lock the doors," he warned, and left.

CHAPTER FORTY-FOUR

Miami police officer Frank Miguel had never enjoyed his job more. He liked seeing John Ashley, with all his goddamn medals and awards, helpless and handcuffed to a bed.

The real fun was to frisk the prisoner's family, especially the good-looking ones. Even Ashley's mother wasn't bad for her age. He liked to paw through their personal possessions as they watched and to grope their bodies, especially his sister, the one who was there the most, the tall, long-haired, big-eyed Katie. She was uppity, a registered nurse, thought she was hot shit. He'd take her down a peg or two.

Miguel was notorious, held the departmental record for the most citizen complaints in his personnel file. He had more Internal Affairs investigations into allegations of brutality, excessive force, sexual assault, and harassment than anyone else. He took pride in that. Nothing anybody could do to him. He had the right rabbis. Maj. Rod Martinez, Lt. Mac Myerson, and Capt. Armando Politano, from whom he personally took orders, until Ashley, that son of a bitch, killed him.

"What are you doing?" Katie gasped, as he ran his rough hands across her breasts, rubbed his thumbs across her nipples, and slid his thick fingers down over her hips.

"You'd be surprised how many a you broads smuggle weapons, drugs, or some other shit in their bras. Or inside, down under." He leered suggestively at her crotch. He grasped her long, lush hair in both hands, squeezed the silky strands, then rubbed the back of her neck and fondled her ear.

He saw her expression. "You don't like that?" He shrugged. "Then stay outta here. Every visitor to this room is frisked or, at my discretion, strip-searched. It's the price of admission." He stripped her naked with his eyes. "Just doing my job." He let her go, then whispered, "But I know you like it."

She shivered and glared at him in distaste.

In response, he snatched up her handbag, which she had placed on a chair before lifting her arms to be frisked. He yanked the zipper open, upended the purse, and shook out the contents over the room's second, unoccupied bed. He pawed through her wallet, hairbrush, lipstick, and other personal items. Under any other circumstance, she'd immediately report him to both hospital and police officials, but he was the one assigned to guard John and clearly the type of man who'd take it out on the prisoner if she did.

Despite the curtain drawn around that side of his bed, John heard part of what was said and tried to protest but couldn't reach the curtain because of his handcuffs.

The surgeon and another doctor who examined John's bullet wound and checked his vision were pleased, but not as elated as John, Katie, and their parents. He had vision in his left eye! It was blurred, but before there was none and now he could distinguish one person from another. He could see! And doctors were confident that his visual acuity would improve daily until he'd regained most or all of his eyesight.

Officer Miguel frisked Ashley's parents, leaving the mother, who'd arrived smiling and eager to see her son, in shocked tears. He even opened the meal she'd brought her son, crudely sniffed it as if it were garbage, then probed it with unwashed fingers.

Joe Ashley was furious, but his wife and Katie calmed him down for John's protection. It was Officer Miguel's job, except that the way he did it and the pleasure he took in it bordered on the perverse.

Then Robby arrived. He saw Miguel and raised his hands to be frisked.

Miguel stared at Robby's police ID. "Where's your weapon?"

"Off duty, didn't bring it." Robby grinned. "Thought I'd make your job easier."

"Don't do me no favors, punk."

"What did you call me?" Robby said softly.

"You heard me. Turn around, spread your legs."

Robby paused, then did so. Miguel patted him down and began

groping his thighs. "Man, you touch my junk and you're toast," Robby warned.

"Take it easy, Rob," John called from behind the curtain.

"We've got good news, bro!" Katie said, trying to defuse the moment.

"Robby, come listen to this," said his mother.

Miguel sneered at them.

Robby gave him a cold, contemplative stare, then joined his family around John's bed.

"What a surprise," John said. "Good to see you, Robby."

Miguel made a derisive guttural sound.

The visit ended when a nurse arrived to take John's vital signs. "The girls will be here later," his mother told him.

Miguel licked his lips and smiled in anticipation.

While the others waited at the elevator, Katie dashed back to John's room for the notebook in which she had jotted the doctors' findings and instructions. The nurse was gone, the curtains were drawn around John's bed, and Officer Frank Miguel was emptying John's homemade meal of chicken and dumplings into a plastic trash receptacle.

"What are you doing?" Katie demanded. "That belongs to John! You have no right to do that!"

"I decide what's right here, bitch. I'm in charge."

She burst into tears.

Robby appeared in the doorway. "Katie?" he said.

She blinked and said nothing.

"Do they know which jail my brother will be transferred to after Ward D?" Robby asked Miguel.

"Yeah." Miguel grinned. His dark eyes glittered. "We're gonna keep 'im in the hole, the holding cell at the station, for the first few days so every cop who comes in can spit on him, then he's going to the pysch ward at the jail."

Robby took a step forward.

Miguel puffed up, held his ground, daring him to take a swing. "Ain't you embarrassed?" he said in Robby's face. He snorted and curled his lip in the patient's direction. "If that was my brother, I'da disowned the piece a shit by now."

John's cuffs rattled behind the curtain. "Rob? Katie? Don't let . . . Rob, he's trying to goad you into getting arrested. It's what he wants."

"Damn right." Miguel rubbed his knuckles, his smile malevolent. "Hear there's more like you, Katie. Can't wait till the *girls* get here. I'm getting hard just thinking about it."

Robby swung and connected with his jaw. Miguel, heavier and slightly taller, with broader shoulders, fell straight back. He knocked a pitcher of water and a basin off a metal cart, which clattered loudly to the floor.

A nurse rushed in, looked around, and said, "Don't make me call security."

Miguel sat on the floor, dazed.

As Katie and Robby started to leave the room, Miguel shouted after them, "You're under arrest!"

Robby turned. "And you're in a world of trouble," he said quietly. "Listen for my footsteps behind you when you least expect it."

He and Katie turned to the nurse, a middle-aged supervisor who had heard complaints from young nurses since Miguel got the assignment.

She looked Robby in the eye. "I didn't see a thing."

"Call security," Miguel told her, as he struggled to his knees.

"I don't work for you, sir," she said, and left the room with the others.

CHAPTER FORTY-FIVE

When Joel Hirschhorn arrived at Bascom Palmer to meet with his client, he insisted that Frank Miguel, John's police guard, leave the room.

"Is that who I think it is?" the harried lawyer said. "The man's notorious. What's it like to have an eight-hundred-pound gorilla in your room? And what the hell happened to the gorilla's jaw?"

"Long story," John said, "but my brother Robby probably won't be visiting here again any time soon."

"Doesn't matter." The lawyer said. "You won't be here." He brought bad news. Hirschhorn had come straight from an emergency hearing. He fought John's imminent transfer to the county hospital's prison ward, but lost. The judge ruled for the prosecution after a Jackson Hospital physician testified that John was ambulatory, could soon be moved to the jail, and until then, would receive adequate care at Jackson.

John's initial court appearance would be later in the week. No chance he'd be granted bond. In fact, it was rumored that more charges would be filed against him.

"What about Eagle's affidavit, his own admissions in those notes to Lonstein?" John asked.

"The problem we have," Hirschhorn said, "is the death of the only person who could testify that the documents actually came from Eagle. With Lonstein gone, it's difficult to prove. I've lined up a handwriting expert to authenticate Eagle's signature and the notes. But those spreadsheets, bank records, and receipts will be a ton of work for forensic accountants. Each allegation, every conspirator has to be individually investigated.

"The copies you sent that TV reporter make for interesting reading, but his bosses and their lawyers won't allow any of it on the air until two or three independent sources verify the allegations as true. You may have more luck with a newspaper reporter who has more time and resources. But it would take a whole newsroom of investigative reporters, a good lawyer, and a forensic accountant weeks to go over all that paperwork."

"What about the FBI?"

"Terrorism's their top priority, so they're less likely to investigate local corruption, but if you know somebody there who might take an interest, it could help."

John sighed in frustration. "I took pictures right after Politano died, the whole shooting scene before they cleaned it up and changed everything. And I'm sure that the murder weapon that killed Eagle is the gun that burglar planted in my apartment. We can subpoena him and the witness, the homeless guy who saw him that night."

"My investigator's already looking for Harry, the burglar," Hirschhorn said. "His parole officer can't find him either. I'm hoping he's still alive. And where do we send the subpoena for the homeless witness? Possession of the murder weapon is not a plus for us unless we can prove how you came to have it. I'm all over this case, John. It won't be easy, but I guarantee you, I'll give it my best." He grinned. "Have briefcase, will travel."

"What can I do to help?" John asked his lawyer.

"Pray for a reasonable, seasoned prosecutor," he answered.

But it was too late for prayer.

Jeff Burnside called Laura. "I wanted you to know before you see it on the air."

"What is it?" she asked, dread in her voice.

"The state attorney is holding a news conference this afternoon to announce that they will seek the death penalty in John's case."

"No," she whispered. "What about a story based on the documents Eagle left?"

"They're sensitive and hard to authenticate," Burnside said. "They could decimate the leadership of two of the biggest departments in South Florida, the biggest police scandal in years. But we need at least three reliable sources willing to be quoted before we can use any of it. I'm working on it, but it takes time and investigation. Miami's a hot news town and we're already short-staffed. How's John?"

"Healing, physically. But Jeff, that good man is . . ." She took a ragged breath. "He's accused of crimes he didn't commit. The system wants him dead. He's handcuffed to a bed, guarded by an obscene, intrusive goon who leaves John's sisters, his mother, and even the men he frisks feeling sexually violated. Otherwise, things are swell."

"I'm sorry. Keep the faith."

"I'm sorry to dump on you, Jeff. I'm glad you called. It is easier to hear bad news personally than to see it on TV."

John's phone rang again so quickly, she thought Burnside had called back. She answered to silence, said hello several times, then hung up. Few people had the number. Was one of them in trouble? Did the police have their phone?

Her mind raced as it rang again.

"Hello? Please say something," she said.

"Hello?" The woman's voice sounded small and uncertain.

"Who are you looking for?"

"Can you get a message to John?" she whispered.

"I can try." Laura instantly realized who it was. "You must be his friend. Someone he worked with."

"Please don't say my name on the phone."

"I won't, I promise. What message do you want me to give him?"

"Tell him to be careful, to watch his back." The woman's voice grew stronger. "He's in danger. He's not safe."

"He's in the hospital," Laura said.

"I know. But they're moving him tomorrow. They say he'll never see the inside of a courtroom."

"Oh, God," Laura murmured. "Thank you. Please call if you hear anything else."

Her hands shook as she called Robby on her cell. As he answered, John's rang again.

"Emma called!" she told him. "Hold on for a sec. John's phone is ringing."

"Hey, Laura," the caller said.

"Leon!" she said.

"You sound busy. But this is urgent. Is there a way I can reach Johnny's brother? The one who works for the county?"

"Yes. What is it, Leon?"

"Johnny ain't coming outta this alive. He's gonna die in custody. Another inmate suicide, or they'll say he was knifed by a prisoner he put away. They're running a pool on how many hours he'll survive in the system."

"A pool?"

"They make bets, put money in the pot. The bettor who comes closest to predicting John's official time of death wins it all. Don't want to scare you, sweet girl, but we have to do something. Fast."

"I'll have Robby call you right back."

"Yes, ma'am. Sooner, the better. He's being moved tomorrow."

She repeated the conversation to Robby. "Can this really be happening?" she whispered.

"I figured it would," he said solemnly. "Don't cry, Laura. I'll handle it."

CHAPTER FORTY-SIX

The brief glimpse of towering white clouds and Miami's wide blue sky took John's breath away as Officer Frank Miguel shoved him roughly into the Corrections Department van. Could I live without seeing that sky or Laura for the rest of my life? he wondered.

Is she safe? Does she know where I am? Where is she? He tried to focus on sending her a message. Was it over? Was his life slipping away?

Officer Frank Miguel rode shotgun as a corrections officer drove. John was being transported to Ward D at JMH, a half mile away, but their circuitous route would take them far afield.

Nothing in Miami is ever simple, sensible, or easy.

John had to be booked into the jail in the civic complex, less than a mile away, first. The cash-strapped county had recently suspended prisoner intake at all but that single location. Police from all over the two-thousand-square-mile county were now required to drive further and wait longer to process their prisoners. On busy nights, the streets outside the jail were jammed bumper to bumper with idling police cars.

A few municipalities, small departments unable to spare on-duty cops to spend hours in line for their prisoners to be fingerprinted, photographed, and screened, instituted catch-and-release programs. Suspects they arrested were asked to sign a promise to show up in court and then released.

Earlier in the week, Miami-Dade's prisoner processing had become even more problematical when a major roof leak in the booking section shut down the antiquated electrical system at the main jail. As a result a shuttered facility in another part of the county was temporarily re-opened.

That's where John Ashley would be processed and booked into the system, along with two other prisoners in the back of the van with him. The two were talkative. One had fought cops who tried to eject him from a Miami Heat game for repeatedly harassing a referee. The other had shotgunned his big-screen HDTV and held off a SWAT team for twelve hours after the Mets beat the Marlins three in a row. Both bitched and moaned about lousy plays, bad calls, and their painful hangovers, until one asked John his story.

"I'm innocent," he said, "but they're asking for the death penalty."

The booking process seemed to take forever. Forbidden to bring firearms into the jail, the cops had to lock their guns in their cars, parked blocks away in a high-crime neighborhood.

The perp walk from the van to the processing center, paraded past so many fellow police officers and their prisoners, was humiliating. John was not only handcuffed but hobbled by ankle chains that threw him off balance whenever Miguel shoved him or jerked his cuffs. Miami was his home, the city where he'd made a difference and was recognized for his work. The people he cared about lived there. How quickly his life, his reputation had changed.

A few cops snapped cell phone photos. "Good luck, Sarge. We're with you," said a young cop he'd trained. Officer Frank Miguel glared, then stared at the officer's name tag, intimidating others who said nothing, though a few nodded to John.

One prisoner spat in his direction.

Miguel loved it. What a pity, he thought, that no one had alerted the press. There should be cameras, he thought. He hated reporters but decided to tip them off himself next time.

"How's it going, John?" A silver-haired jailer he'd known for years took his fingerprints.

"Could be worse." John tried to smile. "I don't know how, but I'm sure it could."

"Hang in," the man said, eyes watery.

By the time all three were processed and back in the van, Miguel was hungry, so he and the driver stopped for Cuban sandwiches. When they were finally back on the road, rush hour had begun.

Traffic on the Dolphin Expressway was bumper-to-bumper, with westbound drivers blinded by the blazing late-afternoon sun. They were headed for the Twelfth Avenue exit, which feeds traffic into the Civic Center, which includes the jail, the Justice Building, and the sprawling

Jackson Memorial Hospital complex, which has more than twenty buildings and parking garages. The prison ward, now called the Rehabilitation Center, was in building eighteen. Elevated Metrorail commuter tracks ran parallel along NW Twelfth Avenue with its Civic Center station part of the complex.

A blue, nondescript older model Ford sat in the far right breakdown lane, a black-haired woman behind the wheel, cell phone to her ear. Anyone who saw the way she scrutinized approaching traffic in the rearview mirror might think she was watching for a tow truck. But she wasn't.

A car also sat in the same lane at the approach to the Seventh Avenue exit, a small red-haired woman behind the wheel, cell phone to her ear. "I think I see it! It's passing now. That's it! The license number is correct. Good luck."

She started her car, drove down the Seventh Avenue exit, and returned to work.

The woman in the Ford up ahead passed the word along.

A helmeted motorcyclist in dark jeans approached the Twelfth Avenue exit, slowed down, exchanged a long, meaningful look with the dark-haired woman in the Ford, then proceeded down the exit.

She checked her rearview mirror. Now she too saw what they all waited for.

The afternoon sun blazed its brightest. Even motorists wearing shades pulled down their overhead visors. Reflections and the painful glare off hoods and windshields made them blink and squint.

An older man in work boots, a bright orange hard hat, a Department of Transportation jumpsuit, mirrored shades, and an international orange safety vest walked up the grassy side of the exit. He stopped at a traffic barricade on the grass, picked something up from behind it, carried it back toward the exit, and gazed to the east, where he too saw what they all waited for.

He grinned and waited for a moment's break in traffic. "This one's for you, Johnny," he said, and flung what looked like a pair of long sticks across the twenty-foot-wide exit ramp. They hit the pavement as traffic began to stream down off the expressway. He walked away briskly before anyone even realized what he had done.

CHAPTER FORTY-SEVEN

The first three cars drove over the spike strips used by police and the military to flatten the tires of fleeing vehicles. A pugnacious criminal defense attorney drove the first, a Cadillac Escalade. A Haitian family of six was packed into the second, a rusting Honda Civic. Two tattooed Cuban brothers and three of their cousins, gang members en route to post bond for another brother, were in the third, a black 2011 Camaro, with red flames on the hood, oversized tires, and expensive hubcap spinners.

The spikes flattened every tire. The drivers braked and blocked the bottom of the exit ramp, as all the occupants piled out to assess damage. The driver of a white Hyundai suddenly saw men, women, and children milling about in the roadway in front of him and stood on his brakes. A bipolar senior citizen off his medication was driving his handicapped twenty-four-year-old daughter with Down syndrome to pick up her mother, a juror in a carjacking case. The driver behind him, a lost and bewildered New Jersey tourist in a rented Nissan Sentra with his wife, two children, and the sun in his eyes, plowed into the back of the Hyundai and forced it into the Camaro.

The next vehicle, halfway down the ramp, was the county Corrections Department van. The driver squinted through the glare, saw trouble ahead, and braked too late to back up. Traffic piled up behind him.

Frank Miguel unleashed a torrent of curses. The driver jumped out to urge motorists to move their damaged cars off the ramp. No one was hurt but the scene was chaotic. The eighteen men, women, and children who had emerged from all five cars began to look like a mob.

The gang members swore and shouted in Spanglish, nearly drowned out by the earsplitting hip-hop blasting from their stereo, tuned to pirate gang radio. The lawyer shouted, cursed, and, late for a contempt hearing, pointed repeatedly at his Rolex, which drew the gang members' attention to the timepiece, clearly a mistake. The milling Haitians berated the gang members in Creole. The gang members retaliated and menaced the Haitians. The bipolar senior went for the gun in his glove compartment, and his handicapped daughter wandered away to pick wildflowers on the grassy slope.

At that moment the long-legged motorcyclist left his bike and walked, with a loose-hipped stride, back up the ramp. The corrections officer, who had given up trying to reason with the other drivers, returned to his van. He opened the door to climb back behind the wheel as the cyclist walked by. The cyclist, who had never even looked at the officer, suddenly turned and, hidden from view by the van's open door, jabbed the barrel of his gun into the small of the corrections officer's back. He snatched the officer's weapon from its holster and shoved it into his own belt.

"I don't want to hurt you or anybody," he said in the man's ear, "but I will, if I have to. It's up to you. Give me the keys to the back, the handcuffs, and the leg irons. All three. Now!" He pushed the gun harder, as the man hesitated.

Officer Frank Miguel had watched the escalating scene on the ramp with disgust at first, then with growing annoyance. He turned to complain to the driver, saw what was happening, and reached for the gun in his shoulder holster. Too late.

Robby had learned to shoot from the best. Three rapid shots hit Miguel in the forehead, the throat, and the left chest. "Told you to look over your shoulder," Robby said quietly, as he took the dying man's gun.

The ashen corrections officer immediately surrendered his keys. "Don't shoot," he whimpered.

"I won't," Robby said. "We're on the same side. Don't do anything stupid."

"Not me. I won't," the man swore.

John and the other prisoners in the windowless van heard shots but had no idea what was happening. The other two were more startled than John when the back door opened.

"Hey, John." Robby grinned. "Come on! Let's go!" He unlocked his brother's cuffs, then the ankle chain with steady hands, and gave him the correction officer's revolver. "You guys want out?" he asked the other prisoners, who sat wide-eyed, their mouths open.

"Why not?" said one, caught up in the moment.

"What the hell! Sure," said the man who had killed his HDTV.

Robby tossed them the keys. "You're on your own," he said.

He and John jumped out the back. So did the others, moments later.

"She's at the top of the ramp in a rusty blue Ford," Robby said. "She knows what to do. Go!"

John rubbed his wrists, eager to run. "You coming with us?"

"I've got my bike; I'll head out Twelfth. That'll add to the confusion. Go, now! Meet you back at the place, bro. By the way, I killed Miguel." Robby shrugged, stuck his gun back in his belt, and tossed Miguel's weapon into tall weeds off the side of the ramp.

"No! Shit, Robby. I'm sorry."

"I'm not. Go!"

John sprinted up the ramp, now jammed with cars. Impatient motorists scuffled, swore, and leaned on their horns.

Laura saw him, gasped in relief, and started the car. He wrenched open the door, slid into the passenger seat, and drew her close. Their kiss was electrifying.

He knew this had happened before.

He knew Laura felt that way as well when she smiled, cut her eyes at him and said, "We have to stop meeting like this, John."

"I can't believe you're here!" he said.

"We have to go. Now!" she said, and swung the Ford out into the westward stream of rush hour traffic.

They didn't hear, as they raced into the setting sun, the gunfire that rang out behind them, back down on the ramp.

CHAPTER FORTY-EIGHT

Robby watched John sprint to where Laura waited. His eyes followed them safely into traffic and out of sight. He smiled as he turned to mount his cycle a few yards away but was confronted by the corrections officer, now bolder and brandishing a .308 Remington 700 rifle.

"Where'd you get that?" Robby asked.

"Mounted under the dash," the officer said, with a wicked grin. Cold sweat beaded his brow.

Robby frowned. How did he miss that? They had organized the mission so quickly that he'd had little time to plan.

"I have no beef with you," Robby said.

"Think I'd let you take my prisoners, kill a cop, and walk away?"

Robby hesitated. He couldn't shoot a man wearing a badge and just doing his job. The officer was young, wore a wedding ring. Killing Miguel was different.

Sirens sounded in the distance. He had to get away. They stood less than ten feet apart. I can take him, he thought.

The corrections officer must have read his mind.

The high-velocity shot from his rifle took off the top of Robby's head.

Leon had boarded Metrorail at the Civic Center station and sat in an already crowded, air-conditioned, elevated car. The route afforded a view of the chaos below at the Twelfth Avenue exit ramp.

"Look at that mess!" said the large black woman sitting next to him. "Aren't you glad you're not down there trying to drive an automobile through that?"

"Yes, ma'am," he said, heart sinking.

Emergency vehicles had begun to arrive.

Laura's Ford was gone, hopefully to safety with John. A lone tattooed gangbanger stood next to his Camaro. A black family was seated on the grass, being questioned by a uniformed officer. Paramedics were treating a bloodied man next to his Escalade. A deputy in a brown corrections uniform was bent over at the waist, one arm leaning on his van. He appeared to be vomiting. Leon didn't see Robby's motorcycle, but he could not take his eyes off the centerpiece of the violent tableau, the cycle's rider lying on his back in a growing red sea of blood.

Nobody was treating his injuries. Leon watched a policeman take a yellow plastic sheet from his car and walk toward the body.

"Oh, no," Leon murmured. What the hell went wrong? Other commuters craned their necks and commented.

"Oh, my," the woman beside him said. "Somebody dead down there. Lord, have mercy. Looks like a big accident. That van musta hit 'im."

"Looks that way," Leon said, eyes shiny, as the train speeded up and the scenery changed.

The lawyer was mugged by two of the gang members, who took the Rolex, his wallet, and the gun he kept in his Escalade. The bipolar senior panicked after his disabled daughter wandered away. He fired two shots into the air, hoping to attract police who would find her. Instead it attracted the tattooed young men from the Camaro. They took his gun, watch, and wallet. One had seen Robby pitch Miguel's gun into the weeds. It took only a few moments to find. Now they had three new weapons.

They trotted across the westbound lanes of the Dolphin Expressway, which were now at a standstill, and used the guns to carjack an eastbound motorist who had slowed down to gape. Now one of the two Cuban brothers and two of his cousins were driving east toward Miami Beach in the victim's new Lexus. The sweaty motorist, forced from his car at gunpoint, was spotted by police as he dodged cars in the eastbound lanes. They tased him, threw him to the ground, handcuffed him, read him his rights, and radioed that they had successfully apprehended a suspect in the shootings as he tried to escape on foot.

The other cousin from the Camaro had taken Robby's motorcycle and headed south on NW Twelfth Avenue. When he stopped in Little Havana to examine his new bike, he found a bonus in the saddlebags— a loaded pistol, handcuffs, and a police badge.

The lone Cuban gang member who'd stayed with his Camaro, as any good citizen should, told police he didn't know those other guys, the ones who'd mugged the lawyer and the senior citizen. Brow furrowed, eyes sincere, he swore he'd never seen them before, didn't know where they came from or which way they went. Asked what they looked like, he paused, then gave precise, detailed descriptions of four hated rival gang members, down to their missing fingers, gold teeth, telling tattoos, and distinctive attire. Eager police recognized them at once and broadcast their names and descriptions on the air, with a warning to fellow officers that they were armed, dangerous, and linked to the Twelfth Avenue cop killing.

The Haitian family tried earnestly to tell the increasingly frustrated Spanish-speaking officer what he wanted to know, but they could not understand his heavily accented English and he failed to comprehend a word of their native patois.

A police K-9 dog led his handler to a DOT jumpsuit and vest discarded in a thorny tangle of bougainvillea planted along both sides of the expressway by jail prisoners during a state beautification project. The work boots and hard hat were already gone, now worn by a homeless man who had stumbled upon them.

Hundreds of people had seen the man who wore them first, the man who threw the spike strips, yet investigators could find no one who clearly remembered what he looked like. No one could say with certainty whether he was black or white. Witness estimates of his height ranged from five feet, three inches tall to six feet, four inches, his weight between 120 and 210 pounds. His hair was first described as silver, but others said he was dark, swarthy, and wore dreadlocks. Several insisted he was bald.

John and Laura spent little time driving into the sunset. She took the next exit, at Twenty-Seventh Avenue, and drove into a Days Inn parking lot. John had changed his clothes in the car, adding a baseball cap and big sunglasses Laura brought. They strolled around to the front of the building as a Yellow Cab pulled up. Leon's friend Tyree, behind the wheel, scarcely looked at them as they got in.

He took them to I-95, then east across the bay.

Katie, waiting at the apartment, was jubilant.

"Where's Robby?" John asked.

"I don't know." She shook her head. "He said he'd be here before you." The TV blared. All local affiliates had interrupted regular programming for live reports from the scene of John Ashley's daring and bloody escape.

Reporters barraged police with questions. What exactly happened here? They needed to know. Now. They were on deadline for their six o'clock news broadcasts. Police still had no clue about exactly what happened or who was involved. All they knew for sure was that a veteran cop had been shot dead, along with a still-unidentified man, and John Ashley was gone.

John stared at aerial shots of the exit ramp on TV and felt as though they were discussing someone else, a total stranger. "Look," he said at one point, "that must be Frank Miguel in the passenger side of the van. Robby said he killed him."

"Then who's that out on the pavement under the sheet?" Katie said.

Laura gasped. "You don't think . . ."

"The reporter said two men were killed." Katie's eyes filled with tears.

"No," John said. "Robby's too smart, too sharp to stumble. His cycle is gone. It's not in any of those shots. That means he got away, took Twelfth Avenue."

"Then why isn't he here?" Katie said. "If Robby was all right, he'd call."

John's cell phone rang. "What did I tell you?" he said, relieved. "Robby?"

"No," Leon said, "it's me."

"Leon," John said. "We're good, but Robby isn't here yet."

"Johnny," he said, gravely, "he's not coming. He didn't make it."

CHAPTER FORTY-NINE

Katie rushed to be with her parents.

John called ahead to prepare them.

They already knew.

"Robby's wife called," his mother gasped between sobs. "She screamed so much I couldn't understand a word she said. A man finally took the phone from her, said he was a homicide detective, taking her to identify Robby—at the morgue. Said my son, my baby is dead." Her voice shattered. "Shot down in the street. Oh, Johnny," she said, "what on earth happened?"

"He did it to rescue me, Mama. They planned to kill me in custody before I ever saw a courtroom. It's my fault, but I swear, Mama, I didn't know he was gonna do it until he opened the back door of that van with a gun in his hand."

Laura stood behind him, arms around his waist, her cheek pressed against his back as though she'd never let go.

"The kids are all here now," his mother said, "except you, Katie—and Robby." She choked back a sob. "Does your sister know, son?"

"She's on the way to you. Left a few minutes ago. We want to be there too. But we can't."

"I understand. Your dad and I love you, son. We all do. Please be careful. Don't let 'em hurt you too."

"I nearly forgot." Laura handed John a locked leather briefcase. "Robby brought it this morning. Said to keep it in a safe place and give it to you or your lawyer if things went bad. Here's the key. He said it has to go to the right person, somebody at the FBI or Justice Department."

Did Robby, always so savvy and confident, feel a sense of foreboding? John wondered. Did some dark premonition trigger his need to put things in order?

Inside were the photos John shot at the motel after Politano was killed, a fully charged police radio with an earpiece, and a loaded gun.

The neatly organized papers included Robby's copy of Eagle's documents, labeled and filed, along with bullet points for John's defense attorney. Robby had included his own taut, typed narrative that included the abuse by Officer Frank Miguel and his history of brutality complaints. The last items in the file cited the time-of-death pool at Miami police headquarters and medical examiners' reports on half a dozen suspicious deaths in Miami police custody over the past two years. He had also put together intelligence and background on half a dozen high-ranking members of the Miami Police Department and a number of the Miami-Dade County police personnel with whom they associated, along with allegations of wrongdoing against them.

"He put so much work into this, did a thorough and complete job," John said. "We can't let it be in vain."

"You're right," Laura said. "We have to get through this, not only for us but for Robby and your folks."

Katie called from her car minutes later.

"Mom knows you're on the way," John said.

"I couldn't go in, John. I was there!" she cried. "The house is surrounded by police cars, flashing lights, and paddy wagons. Before I could jump outta the car to see what happened, a neighbor ran up and said I shouldn't or I'd be arrested too. So I drove on by."

"Arrested?"

"Yes," she said emotionally. "They arrested everybody, paraded Mama and Daddy, our brothers and sisters, their husbands and wives, out in handcuffs in front of the whole neighborhood. And they snatched the kids. They're sending 'em to Child Protective Services. Eddie Woodruff, across the street, heard the mothers' screaming. He went over to tell the police he and his wife would take the kids till relatives pick 'em up. The cops said no, and when Eddie saw how the officers, in SWAT gear, flak jackets, and ski masks, were tearing up the house and carrying things out, he objected. So they arrested him too."

"What things are they taking?"

"Daddy's guns, cell phones, computers, tax files, insurance policies, bills, family pictures. Every piece of paper in the house. What can we do, John? Our whole family is going to jail and not a one deserves it. Not one of us has ever been arrested before! The kids must be so scared. If I'd showed up a few minutes sooner, I'd be in handcuffs with 'em."

"Where are the kids now?" John asked bitterly.

"Crying and screaming in the back of three or four police cars. They put Daddy and all the men in one paddy wagon and Mama and the girls in the other."

"On what charges?"

"The neighbors say they heard it was harboring a fugitive, aiding and abetting, I don't know."

"Come back here," John said. "Stay calm, be careful, and don't let anyone follow you. I'll call Hirschhorn. We've got to get the kids back, can't let 'em go to foster care."

He asked Laura to tip off Jeff Burnside, while he called the lawyer.

"Do you know?" Jeff asked when he heard Laura's voice.

"Yes," she said. "Now something else terrible has happened."

Burnside, already covering the manhunt for John, went to Morningside, found a video a neighbor had shot of three generations of the Ashley family in handcuffs. He interviewed witnesses, shot footage of the hysterical children pounding on the police car windows, and spoke briefly to family members locked in the vans until police stopped him. He had enough for the 11 o'clock news.

"What?" Hirschhorn said. "They can't do that! But that's what they do, John. Damn! Your family will beat the rap but not the ride. I'm sorry. Where are they now?"

"Still outside the house in paddy wagons, the kids in the back seats of police cars, while cops trash my parents' home and carry out personal property."

"The good news is we have a helluva civil rights case against them." Hirschhorn sighed. "I hoped you'd call me, John. You can't keep running; this only gets worse."

"It has. The second dead man out there today, the one whose name hasn't been released? He's my kid brother, Robby."

"No! The one who works for the county, right? Testified in a couple of my clients' cases. Smart as a whip. The one who punched out the eight-hundred-pound gorilla."

"That's the one," John said.

"That makes tonight even more of a nightmare for your family. The charges against them are bondable, but given the hour . . ." He sighed. "By the time they're transported, processed, and jerked around, they'll still be in holding cells well after midnight. A bondsman can have them out first thing in the morning. Did they take the entire family?"

"Everybody. Except me and my sister, Katie. She's a registered nurse."

"Perfect! She's responsible, with good family ties, she's a nurse, their aunt. I'll get someone who can file a petition for the children's release to Katie at an emergency hearing in Family Court. She's perfect."

"She is," John said solemnly. "I'm lucky she's my sister."

"The charges against your family seem highly suspect. The state attorney's intake office reviews arrests made without warrants. The woman who reviews them is smart, a seasoned prosecutor. She'll decide whether they should be dropped."

TV reported that the manhunt for accused cop killer John Ashley was the biggest and most intense in modern Miami. Every police department in the county canceled vacation time and days off until Ashley was killed or captured.

"We can't stay here," he whispered to Laura, as they sought solace in each other's arms. "We need to leave town for a while. They won't stop till they find us, and if we stay, they will. What they did to my family was designed to increase the pressure. Sooner or later, somebody who knows that Katie is house-sitting will tell them about this place. They may know already."

When Laura told him about the prowler at the door shortly before Lonstein was killed and the cigarette butts in the hall, John became even more convinced they had to leave. "The sooner the better," he said. "There's nothing to keep us here. I can't even go to my brother's funeral."

"The car Robby left us is still in the parking garage," she said urgently. "Let's take it and go now."

He paced, fighting mixed emotions. "It's not right to ask you to run with me. When they find us, they'll try to do what they did to Lonstein. I don't want you there when that happens."

"Then we'll have to make sure it doesn't," she said sensibly, "because I *will* be with you."

"It'll be tough to get out of town," he warned. "We can't show our faces anywhere."

They dressed in jeans and dark shirts, packed up a few things, some clothes, supplies from the pantry.

"I know the perfect place," he said. "My family's used an old fishing camp out in the Everglades for generations. A relative built it way back. Did a pretty good job. It's primitive. But nobody will find us there.

"I've been thinking," he said, "about an FBI agent I used to know. We were good friends. He got promoted, transferred four, five years ago. Haven't heard from him for a while. Don't know if he's still based in Washington. If I can find him, he'd listen."

Laura made three trips to the car with Robby's briefcase, some clothes and other things, while John wiped down every surface, eliminating any trace that they'd been there.

On the last trip, she returned quietly. She found him removing the hard drive from the computer. She stood in the doorway of the little office. "John," she said softly. "They're here."

He sprang to his feet. "Where?"

"I heard men's voices, echoes in the parking garage, and the sound of police radios. They're in the building, sweetheart."

CHAPTER FIFTY

S he cut the lights as he snatched up his cell and called Katie. "Where are you?" he asked urgently.

"Almost there," she said.

"Don't come! They're here."

"Oh, my God, John! Please, don't let them kill you!"

"I'll try not to. Go to Joel Hirschhorn's office in Coral Gables, on Biltmore Way, the building with the big stone lions out front. Hang with him until the family's free. Love you, sis."

He stepped to a window with a street view and, from behind the shade, saw a number of unmarked cars and clusters of armed men and women. He recognized a dark, armored van parked across the street as one used by SWAT. He turned to Laura. "Time to go, darlin'."

She ran to pick up Françoise, but John shook his head. "We can't," he said. "Not now." She nodded, tears in her eyes.

They moved quietly to the front door. He gently turned the knob, opened the door slightly, and listened. Too late. They heard boots on the stairs and pings from the elevator. He closed and double-locked the door.

They slipped out onto the wraparound terrace, locked the glass door behind them, and edged along the wall. John had attached the police radio to his belt and wore the earpiece. Laura had the leather lanyard with the keys around her neck and had tucked it into her T-shirt. She carried several thick bath towels to muffle the sounds. Working swiftly, they wrapped the towels around each end of the scaffolding and secured them with belts. John carefully slid the scaffolding under the bottom rail and pushed it straight across empty space and beneath the bottom rail on the next terrace.

"Robby said we should have two feet at each end."

"Got it," he whispered. "Don't look down. Keep your eyes on your destination. I'm right behind you."

Françoise began to bark inside the apartment. "Good little dog," she whispered. "Hope they don't hurt her."

She slipped off her shoes, soft little ballet slippers, and put one in each pocket. He helped her over the top railing, held her arm steady, and said, "Go."

She walked across quickly, barefoot and graceful, ignoring gusts of wind that lifted her hair and made him catch his breath, then grasped the far railing and vaulted over it onto the terrace.

He wanted to applaud. What a woman, he thought. He'd been afraid she would panic. He should have known better.

He swung a long leg over the rail, then the other, and ignored his own advice. He looked down. A mistake. No one was in the street below, which was good. But the height and the strong wind made him uncertain. He looked down again.

"No," she whispered hoarsely from the other side. "Look at me, John." She held out her arms. "Come to me."

He did, and held her moments later. Together they gently pulled the scaffolding to the far side.

"Wait till I tell everybody that big, bad John Ashley is ascared of heights."

"I am not," he whispered. "I looked down to see if anybody saw us and it threw me off a little."

Far behind them, Françoise's barks grew frantic.

They moved quickly to the far end of the terrace and let themselves into the vacant apartment. Empty, it smelled of fresh paint. Paint cans stood in the living room, along with a ladder, a shirt, spattered overalls, and a painter's cap.

Laura rolled up the clothes and put on the cap. "We might need these later."

They listened at the door. All the action seemed to be around the corner, back down the hall.

"Let's go," he said. "Before they bring in K-9s." He took her hand and they fled swiftly, quietly down the carpeted hallway toward the stairwell at the far end of the building. They saw and heard no one until, just a few yards from the door, they heard voices.

They literally skidded to a stop as two cops in flak jackets opened the door and stepped out of the stairwell. John pulled Laura back and around a corner. Flattened against the wall, they tried not to breathe.

"If they come this way," John whispered, "I'll try to take them. No guns." He and Laura were armed, but shots would rain hellfire down upon them in a fight they couldn't win.

The cops came closer.

"Nobody living here. It's spooky as a morgue," one said.

"Like a goddamn graveyard," agreed the other.

New sounds and voices came from behind John and Laura. What they said wasn't clear, but the voices grew louder.

Trapped, they were caught in a vise, with no way out.

"Is this the right floor?" asked one of the cops who'd come out of the stairwell. "Are we headed in the right direction?"

"Wait a minute," said the other. "We're s'posed to head 'round to the east, the beach side. That's back the other way."

"Goddamnit, let's go. Betcha ten it's another false alarm."

Their grumbling receded as they walked in the opposite direction. John and Laura breathed sighs of relief, but the voices behind them—at least three or four of them—kept coming.

John edged to the corner. The first two officers were still walking away. It would be safer to wait till they were out of sight, but if they did, the oncoming cops would walk right up to them.

He took Laura's hand. They moved silently toward the stairwell, praying, willing that neither of the men right in front of them turned to look back. John gently opened the heavy door to the stairwell. As they slipped inside, he lost his grip on the door and it closed behind them with a loud, metallic click.

"What the hell was that?"

The two cops wheeled and drew their guns in a mirror-image adrenaline surge.

"Hear that?" a cop shouted from the opposite direction. "Somebody's down there!"

A companion called for backup. "I think we got 'im! We got 'im!"

John and Laura ran for their lives. They were two flights up as the cops drew down on each other, fingers on triggers. All held their fire, shocked at what they'd nearly done.

"Randy! What the hell you doing over here? I almost blew your fucking head off! You and Perez are supposed to be on the other goddamn side of the building!"

"You trying to get yourselves killed?"

"For God's sake!"

"I nearly had a heart attack! No shit!"

They cursed, stomped about, shook their heads, holstered their weapons, and high-fived nervously, as cops all over the building rushed in their direction, guns drawn.

Seconds later the call echoed through halls, stairwells, and John's earpiece.

"Cancel that. We did not sight John Ashley but captured McCall and Perez instead. False alarm."

"QSL," confirmed the unamused SWAT commander. "Nothing in the suspect apartment. But somebody does live there. Food in the fridge and a yappy little dog." Françoise's barking echoed from John's earpiece and police radios all over the building. "Owner's some French broad. Maintenance says her house sitter's a good-looking nurse who's in and out. We need somebody to fix the door before she comes home. K-9's coming in for a floor-by-floor search."

"Shoulda done that to begin with," Perez grumbled.

"You'll need a squad of ghostbusters to search this place right," Randy said. "It's a giant haunted house. I swear, I heard that click and it sounded like somebody racked one into the chamber. Thought my number was up, that Ashley had a bead on cop number three and he was me."

John and Laura emerged at the penthouse level and dashed across the closed bridge to the parking garage. He was impressed but not surprised that she kept up with his long stride and wasn't winded, she didn't run like a girl at all.

She'd already been to the car, an older model gray Volvo, knew exactly where it was. He increased the volume in his earpiece to monitor the SWAT frequency, slipped the painter's clothes on over his, and started the car. "God bless Robby," he said. The gas tank was full.

They drove down several levels without headlights. Blue police flashers splashed shadows at the exit, but John turned away, to the entrance.

Laura slipped from the car, hit the yellow button, and the wooden arm lifted, as Robby'd said it would.

He pulled out onto the street, turned on the headlights, drove south, then doubled back around the block and headed to a causeway at the north end of the county.

John whistled in relief. "That's as close as I want to get."

"It was scary," she said. "But looking back, it was fun."

"Uh-oh. What are you, an adrenaline junkie? Once we settle down, what do I do to keep you from being bored?"

"We will never be bored."

He knew she was right as they drove across the moonlit bay. The lights of boats on the water and planes in the sky seemed so much brighter than they ever had been before. He reached for her hand. "Tell me the truth," he said.

"I always do, always will."

"When you walked across that scaffold five floors up, you visualized yourself as a supermodel on a Paris runway. You did, didn't you?"

"Hell, no. I visualized myself as a great tightrope walker, the one who made it across Niagara Falls from Canada to the U.S. I was so him that I had to restrain myself from doing a double somersault halfway across."

"Glad you did. I woulda had a double heart attack."

She studied the paperwork Robby had left in the glove compartment, and they cobbled together a story in case they were stopped.

"Okay, my name is Danny Ryan, you're my wife, Isabelle, and this is your daddy's car. His name is Eric Alan Brighton. He'll be fifty-one in January and lives on Flamingo Drive in Miami Beach. Our car's in the shop, so you borrowed his to pick me up from my painting job and drive across state to Tampa, where your only sister has gone into labor. It's her first child; we're the godparents and want to be there when he arrives."

"She. I love little girls."

"Okay."

"Good," she said. "What's my sister's name? I want to say Katie, but that might not be smart."

"You're right. How about Faith?"

"Faith is perfect," she said. "How appropriate."

He called Katie, said they were safe and had left Françoise in the apartment wearing her collar, tags, and leash.

They arrived at the fishing camp in the dark hours before dawn. Laura had fallen asleep. He parked some distance away. They got out to walk and were nearly there when the three-quarter moon broke free from a sea of clouds and illuminated their destination in a silvery splash of light.

She clung tight to John's arm in the dark. "Is that it?" she gasped.

"It's not much," he said, "but only for a week or two . . ."

"No." She stepped back, trembling, as though she could see something he didn't.

"What's wrong, darlin'?"

"It creeps me out, John. I have a bad feeling about this place."

"You won't when you see it in the light of day." He kissed her. "It's not so bad. You'll see."

Chilled to the core, despite the heat of the night, she still trembled.

CHAPTER FIFTY-ONE

He groped for and found the key, hidden above the door. The Coleman lantern just inside still worked. Hard to believe he had left it there only six months ago. His world had changed so much since that last visit to watch a meteor shower. No place is darker than the heart of the 'Glades and no better vantage point for seeing heavenly light shows, the constellations, and millions of stars.

Nothing had been disturbed. As always, things needed to be fixed, cleaned, or upgraded. He and Robby intended to tackle those projects in the fall. Now they never would. The reality wrenched his heart.

He shook the dust from a blanket and a few pillows and did his best to make the bed comfortable. Laura said little. They'd both been ravenous on the road, but she had no appetite now. He brought in granola bars from the car, boiled water on a small Sterno camp grill, fixed tea for her and coffee for himself, then poured them each a shot of whiskey from a bottle in the kitchen cabinet.

He cranked up a battery-operated radio on which he managed to hear sporadic news mixed with static and interference, then tried to call Katie to see if she had met with the bail bondsman. As he'd feared, he had no signal. He could charge their cell phones in the car but would have to drive a distance to use them.

"It's dark here, so dark," Laura kept repeating. He adjusted the lantern for her several times before he realized that the darkness that frightened her was far more than a mere absence of light.

"Such a dark and lonely place . . ." She hugged her body and wished aloud that Françoise was with them.

"Dogs are fun out here," he agreed. "They love it. They're good company, a real comfort, but you have to watch out that the 'gators or pythons don't get 'em. We had a close call last year with Robby's dog, Spirit . . ." He stopped, a painful catch in his throat. How impossible it seemed that they would never again spend time here, that his brother was gone forever, with no chance to say goodbye.

"Would've been nice to bring her," he said bleakly. "But she's not our dog. It just wouldn't be right to take her. The owner expects her dog to be there when she comes home."

Laura shivered in his arms that night. He thought she was cold despite the damp heat, but bad dreams kept waking her and her visions then seemed even more terrifying.

"I'm afraid," she finally whispered.

"Of what?" he asked in sleepy disbelief. "You're cool. Today we bought ourselves a little more time, enough to focus on how to fight back." He rose up on one elbow to study her face. "How strong were you tonight? I never wanted a female partner on the job. Didn't trust any of them enough to watch my back. But I'd never hesitate with you. You don't cave under stress. You saved my life when I got shot, then you and Robby"—he swallowed—"did it again. So tell me, what could possibly scare a girl like you?"

"This place is so dark. I've never been here before. But I knew the moment I saw it that terrible things happened here. It's as though I can hear sad echoes from the past. It scares me," she whispered.

She asked for another whiskey to help her sleep. When he brought it, her eyes looked huge and haunted in the lantern's glow. He turned the light down when she finally dozed. But she woke, in a nightmare, before dawn.

The thick night closed in on her, alive with snarls, savage cries, and something slithering in the walls. *Oh God, we're really here. It's real, not a nightmare. How long is this night? Will the sun ever rise?*

He rocked her. "I know what's wrong," he murmured. He kissed her and folded her into his arms. "The problem is all of it. Eagle, Summer, and Cheryl. Strangers stalking you. The shooting in your room. Then I got shot. Lonstein killed. Robby gone. And last night would unnerve anybody."

He rubbed her back, kissed her shoulders, turned her over, and ran his tongue around her nipples. "Those things never happen to most people. The lucky ones don't face even one of them in a lifetime. But we can survive this together."

He gasped as she clutched his hair and roughly pulled his mouth to hers.

The sun rose as always. Her neck felt stiff, her head throbbed, even her teeth ached. What's wrong with me? she wondered.

She had prayed her spirits would rise with the sun, that its forgiving rays would burn away her fears, but what she saw in its first weak, pale light multiplied her misgivings. Before any details in the room around her—such as the rusted, old nail on which John's shirt now hung—were visible, she knew exactly where they were and what they looked like. Panic overtook her.

Who was that pale, distorted face in the old shaving mirror? She scarcely recognized it as her own. She fought a morbid fascination with the ancient straight razor that seemed to await her on a dusty shelf. Old boots stood in a corner. Who had worn them? And when? Why were they so important?

The pantry was exactly where she knew it would be. She found a few supplies: Pringles, pickles, pork rinds, and peanut butter, catsup, canned stew, and coffee, along with dried fruit and several ancient, dust-covered mason jars.

She did not unpack or stock the shelves with the few supplies they'd brought. That would send a false signal, that she was willing to stay, when all she desperately wanted was to leave now.

She found a well-stocked first-aid kit. A rifle, several boxes of ammo, several yards of rope, which strangely fascinated her, and enough whiskey to numb herself if needed. She had always tried to remain alert, senses acute, a single swimmer in a sea of sharks, a drinker who nursed a single margarita or apple martini for an entire evening. But here, in this place, she felt the need to numb the pain of heartbreak, loneliness, and death. She was grateful for the whiskey despite how it burned her throat. Physical pain, she thought, is so much easier to bear.

John was all that kept her there. Since they'd met, she had dreamed of short nights, full of music, love, and laughter. Where had the dream gone? What was happening to her now?

His voice startled her. He was still there.

"See, not so bad in daylight, is it?" He towered naked in the doorway, flashing the grin she loved. When had she first seen it?

"Let's leave. I hate it here."

He was startled. "It's the safest place to be now, darlin'. On the radio last night, they said they think we're still in Miami, but the manhunt's now nationwide. We can stay here while I try to reach that FBI contact, call Joel, and keep in touch with our Miami friends."

She shook her head. "Trust me. Please. We can't stay here."

"Just for a few days, darlin'."

"Not even a few minutes." Her voice shook. "Let's go up home to my gram's. I want to go home."

He pulled on his painter's clothes. "What would you like me to bring back for your breakfast?"

"Bring back? I won't stay here alone."

"They're looking for us together. Our faces are all over the news. I have to make some calls, buy gas, and pick up the newspapers, more Sterno, and groceries. Look how cranky you get when I don't feed you." He winked.

"Don't leave me." She threw her arms around him.

"I won't," he said. "Be right back. I promise."

"I'm afraid I'll never see you again." She began to weep.

"You will. Don't cry, Laura." He sighed. "I can't stand it. I'll be back in an hour or two at the most."

"What if something happens to you?"

"If it did, I wouldn't want you there."

"We're safer together." Her voice kept rising as the room and all its secrets overwhelmed her. "What if I hadn't gone with you to meet Lonstein? Or wasn't at the top of that exit ramp?"

"You saved my ass both times. But right now, I need to find a cell signal, a gas station, and a store. People will be in all those places. Some read newspapers or watch TV. I want us to survive long enough to have a life together."

Despair in her eyes, she turned away.

"Kiss me goodbye."

She ignored him, her profile etched in stone.

He left.

When she heard the car start, she rushed out, raced after him. He stopped and lowered his window. She leaned in and kissed him hard and hungrily on the mouth. "Please?" The word resonated between them like an echo.

"I'll be back quick as I can," he said. "Stay inside, and don't worry." He drove away.

CHAPTER FIFTY-TWO

She steeled herself to step back inside.

If he doesn't come back? she thought. What will I do? Where can I go? I'd be better off dead.

The day was bright but it was shadowy inside. She tried to nap but found it impossible, then caught movement out of the corner of her eye. She was not alone. Something—someone—was in the kitchen. She heard a moan. "Who's there?" she cried out.

She stepped quickly into the room. A woman was hanging by her neck, her body gently swaying above the big kitchen table. Laura heard the creak of the rope, gasped and stepped closer. The light changed as a low-hanging cloud blocked the sun, and the half-naked figure vanished. But if the angle, the movement of the sun, the drift of cloud and shadow had created an illusion, why did the woman she saw, dead eyes staring, look like her? Is this how it feels to be insane? she wondered.

She suddenly heard Katie pounding on the old wooden door, calling her name. Laura rushed to the door and threw it open. But no one was there.

She tried to pray but choked on the words. *If there is a God*, she wondered, *how did He let this happen?*

She felt weak, frail, and foolish and sipped some whiskey to allay her fears. What did they call it? Liquid courage.

John sat with the car door open, just off a main road. He'd finally found a phone signal and the man he wanted to reach.

"John, for God's sake! What the hell's going on?"

"Finally tracked you down, Doug. So you're the top man in Atlanta. Always knew you'd go places."

"John, where are you?"

"I need your help."

"No way I can help you now, John. If you don't arrange a safe surrender, you stand a good chance of being killed when they catch up to you. I can make some calls right now to arrange your surrender to agents in Miami if that's where you are."

"That would increase my chances of being killed to a hundred percent. They will kill me, Doug. It's complicated. But somebody with the Bureau, somebody I trust, and that's you, has to know what really happened, what's going on. You know me. We played ball in school, served together in the military, had each other's backs, worked cases together in Miami. You know who I am, man. All I need is a few minutes to give you the *Reader's Digest* version."

In the silence after he finished his story, John added, "There are documents, photos, witnesses, the works, to back it all up. Which is why they have to kill me. Do you know Joel Hirschhorn?"

"Sure. Who doesn't?"

"He's my lawyer. Call him. Make that one call. That's all I ask. It's huge, major corruption involving two big law enforcement agencies—homicides, cover-ups, big bucks, drugs, money laundering, civil rights violations, and more. It's yours, if you want it. If you don't, I'm screwed, and you're not the man I always believed you were."

"John, you know what I'm legally bound to say. Surrender."

"Sorry, Doug, you're my last hope. Call Hirschhorn."

John returned after two and a half hours. He brought Sterno, news from home, and food, including warm fish chowder and freshly made roast beef sandwiches. Shocked by Laura's state of mind, he reluctantly agreed to leave. He believed it was a mistake, but she was intractable, at the point of hysteria.

"You said my gut instincts were good," she reminded him, her face pale. "You told me I should never ignore them. Right now they are screaming at me to get away from this place. So I am, even if I need to walk all the way to Gram's alone."

He insisted she sip some warm soup and eat something before they left. They ate in the car after she adamantly refused, eyes red, to eat inside, at the big wooden kitchen table.

He filled her in on the news as he drove. His family was about to be released on bond and seemed close to having all the charges dropped. The children, released to their aunt Katie, were enjoying the beach and the pool at the Sea Spray until they could go home. They—and Françoise, still hoarse from barking—would spend nights at her town house, which had an extra bedroom and a daybed in the den. So far, Katie, the dog, and the children, all the siblings and cousins, were fine and excited about the big sleepover at Aunt Katie's.

"Kids are so resilient," Laura said, as she drank in the sunshine and scenery. "They bounce back faster than we do."

The adults, still humiliated, and furious, mourned Robby and feared for John.

Jeff Burnside's story on the treatment of John's family by police had gone viral on the Internet, infuriated viewers and enraged editorial writers. In their "clumsy, heavy-handed attempts" to find John, police had smashed down doors at a nearly empty condo complex, trashed his parents' home, and seized time sheets, logs, and records from cab companies, all to no avail, after unconfirmed sightings.

Miami police swore they had missed Ashley by minutes at an expensive steakhouse after he and his entourage fled through a restroom window, a Victoria's Secret lingerie store at the Dolphin Mall, and at the downtown Miami Public Library, where he had been seen perusing books on explosives. He was still in South Florida, they believed, possibly accompanied by Laura, also a fugitive, and other unidentified accomplices in his escape.

"That," the police chief announced at a press conference, "was no one-man operation. Ashley's escape from custody was clearly engineered and carefully choreographed by his brother and a number of dangerous criminals directly responsible, along with Ashley, for the shooting death of veteran police officer Frank Miguel, who was outgunned and outnumbered by Ashley's gang."

"Steakhouse? Victoria's Secret? Gang?" Laura lifted her eyebrows as she read the news stories aloud.

John looked sheepish. "Two women, a homeless man, and my brother," he said. "That's my gang of dangerous criminals."

"Never underestimate a woman, or Leon," Laura said.

Leon had called to tell John that police, under increasing pressure to make an arrest, were using outrageous tactics, stepping farther and farther out of bounds.

"They're gonna step in it, big time, if they don't watch it," Leon had said. "You know how quick things blow up down here, Johnny." The split in the department had widened, he said, with scores of disillusioned and dedicated young officers now saying openly that John was framed.

Several times, John reached for his phone to tell Robby. Each time he remembered that his brother would never answer shocked him anew with the stark reality and permanence of loss. Death is so final.

"I can't wait for you to meet Gram," Laura said, taking his hand. "She's wonderful. She'll love you."

Laura drove for a time, while he dozed. "Remember . . ." he said, before pulling the painter's cap down over his face.

"I know, I know. Stay in the middle of the pack, don't tailgate, and be courteous."

"If there is no pack, find a rabbit," he said, "a lone car traveling at the speed you want. Follow discreetly from a hundred yards back. If there's a speed trap ahead, the rabbit trips the trap and he's caught, not you. When you see his brakelights flash, that's your clue. Stay sharp."

"Yes, sir." She winked. "Relax and rest your eyes, darlin'. We're almost there."

CHAPTER FIFTY-THREE

When they were twenty miles away, they stopped at the side of the road. Laura's hands trembled as she punched in the number. The phone rang, then rang some more.

"She's not home," John said.

"It takes her a little bit of time," Laura said. "She claims to be ninety-eight but lies about her age. I think she's actually a hundred and one."

Three more rings and Gram answered. Laura squealed in excitement. "Gram!" she shouted. "It's me. Coming home, at last."

"About time! Where you been, girl?"

"Busy working. You okay? Had any company? Anybody been poking around, calling, or asking for me?"

Gram was fine, she said, and home alone. The young woman who helped with housekeeping and cooking had left for the day, and Gram had seen no one else since Sunday.

"Put the water on for tea. We'll be there before it boils. Bye, Grammy." She turned to John and lowered the volume. "You need to speak up when you talk to Gram. She's a little bit hard of hearing."

The golden afternoon sun slanted through the pines and huge live oaks as Laura dropped John off, then drove slowly down the wooded lane to the house. When first built, the place stood alone and remote in the wilderness. The house was still relatively isolated, but civilization and urban sprawl had crept constantly closer, and now one could find a strip mall, a McDonald's, or a Burger King only a few miles away. When she saw no sign of intruders or strange cars, she drove back to the end of the lane. John stepped out from the trees when he heard the car. He'd changed out of his spattered house-painter clothes.

"All clear!" Laura sang out. "It's so good to be home!"

They drove up to the house and around behind it, where she parked among the trees. She rang the brass bell at the front door. They waited, then waited some more, until a tiny, gray-haired woman appeared. She wore a black dress, silver-rimmed spectacles, and a faded facsimile of Laura's smile.

"Lawd, child, where've you been hiding?" she said, her hand over her heart, as though her great-granddaughter's arrival had answered her fondest prayers. "You shore are a sight for these tired old eyes. Pretty as ever, let me have a good look at you, girl. Turn around now."

Laura stretched out her arms and pirouetted for her.

John loved seeing them together, Laura and the small, frail woman. They say look at the mother, he thought, and you will see what your girl will look like in twenty years. Does that also apply to great-grandmothers? he wondered. See what your girl will look like in seventy-five years? He could live with that, if he could just live long enough.

Gram was shorter, shrunken from the physical stature she had once achieved, but behind skin like ancient parchment, a fire still burned. He could see what a beauty she must have been, a young woman to be reckoned with, formidable in her prime and a force even now, in the twilight of her life. What had she seen, experienced, and lost in a century on the planet? World wars, the great Depression, and the chaos since, in a life span that stretched back to the Harding administration. So much history, he thought.

He didn't know the half of it.

The tiny, birdlike centenarian must have read his mind. She turned and cut her eyes at him from behind the spectacles. "Who is this handsome young man, Laura?"

"The love of my life, Gram. 'Member, you said I'd meet him one day?"

Laura took John's hand and drew him closer to the old woman whose stare penetrated his soul.

"John, this is my great-grandma, Arlie Tillman Pickett.

"Gram, this is John Ashley."

"Who?" Arlie's voice rose shrilly. "Who?" Her mouth gaped open.

"John Ashley, ma'am." He spoke softly, but his voice carried like an echo to every corner of the little house.

She fell back, stunned. "John Ashley?" she whispered. "*That* John Ashley?"

"Yes, ma'am," he said, and wondered what she thought of him, dragging Laura into jeopardy and worse all over the state.

Arlie reacted as though slapped, her hands flew to her throat. Laura caught her, or she might have fallen.

"Gram, let's sit down. I'll help you." Laura led her to a comfortable chair, as the old woman mouthed his name and craned her neck to stare at John.

"You might have seen something in the newspaper," John said earnestly, "or on TV." He stepped closer. "You know how it is. If you don't read the newspapers, you are uninformed; if you do, you are misinformed," he said, hoping to comfort her.

She nodded vigorously. "I know. I know. Saw all those terrible newspaper stories. Saved 'em all." Her eyes skipped around the room like those of a disoriented stranger. "John Ashley," she murmured again. "They said you were killed years ago." She frowned, rocked back and forth, and scrutinized his profile with a puzzled expression as he looked to Laura for help.

None there. She'd run into the kitchen to take the boiling water off the burner. "I'll fix the tea," she called. "Will you two be all right, John?"

"Sure, darlin'," he said, hoping Gram wasn't having a stroke.

Her eyes had grown sly. "Where did you say your people are from?"

"Florida natives," he said. "From up here, somewhere around the Caloosahatchee River, then southeast Florida, Palm Beach, and now Miami."

She smiled and nodded, as though he'd given the correct answer. "You come from a big family?"

"Yes, ma'am. Nine of us, five boys, four girls."

She nodded again, eyes wet. "My mama was so in love with you," she murmured. "She gave me and my little brother up to go off with you."

Laura caught that last line as she emerged from the kitchen carrying a steaming teapot, china cups, cream, and sugar on a tray. "Gram? I think you've mixed John up with someone else."

"No, darlin'. My mama loved this man so. He built a fishing camp way out in the 'Glades. She used to go to meet him there."

John made a startled sound and exchanged a look with Laura. "My family's had a fishing camp deep in the 'Glades forever," he said. "Laura and I were just there."

"That's where my mother's heart broke." Arlie sighed. "Her name was Laura too. Laura here was named for her, but never knew 'er. Neither did I. But it was a bad and ugly time in . . ." Her voice trailed off and she looked up like a child. "Laura, honey? Can you hand me that wrap over there? I'm so cold."

Laura brought the black cardigan, helped her put it on despite the oppressive heat, then held her withered hand. "Gram, I do think you have John confused with someone else."

"No!" Arlie said sharply. "I'd know him anywhere, so good-looking. When I last saw 'im I was just a little girl. But later their pictures were everywhere. I'll show you. Come on." Her words were a challenge. "You can help me."

"Rest for a while, sip your tea," Laura said gently. "We shouldn't have burst in on you the way we did. Shoulda called hours and hours ahead. I think the surprise just confused you for a minute there."

"The tea's too hot, needs to cool, anyhow," Arlie said peevishly. "I want to show you." She struggled to her feet.

"Now I know who you take after," John said, as Laura tried and failed to keep Arlie in her chair.

She and Laura proceeded slowly down the hall until Gram turned. "Come along, John. You'll want to see this too."

He followed, as Gram's cane tapped on the original hardwood floor constructed of Dade County pine. She and Laura made their way into her sewing room but lost John. Laura found him in front of a framed, faded black-and-white sketch of a young girl on the riverbank, her skirt whipping in the wind as a storm threatened. The paper had begun to yellow around the edge.

"Is that you?" John said, unable to tear his eyes away. He loved how the artist had caught Laura's posture, attitude, and spirit in just a few spare lines.

"No," she said, "I'm told that was the original Laura, the mother Arlie didn't really know. The legend is that it was sketched by Winslow Homer, the famous artist. He did visit this part of Florida several times, so it may be true. Gram insists that she's seen her mother in several of his major paintings, some with the boy she ran off with, abandoning her, her baby brother, and their father."

"How did Gram come by it?"

Laura frowned. "I'm not sure. We've had it as long as I remember. I must have heard at some point but don't recall. Come on, let's ask her."

Arlie stood impatiently over an old trunk she had unlocked. She lifted the lid. "In here, Laura, they're at the bottom."

Inside were keepsakes, photos, and family scrapbooks. At the very bottom she found two thick black scrapbooks and a white one. "Ah, there they are." Arlie nodded. "I knew this was where I hid 'em. Haven't looked at 'em in years. Was a time I'd take 'em out to read, but the pain was too hard to take, so I put 'em away. But I could never throw 'em out or destroy 'em. Because this," she said proudly, "is Florida history, part of our family's past."

"I've never seen them before, Gram." Laura frowned as she dusted one off with her sleeve. "Why didn't I?"

"Most people wanted 'em gone," Arlie said. "They want to rewrite history, forget these people ever lived. But why? They were pioneers, lived hard lives, loved with a passion, and died hard, and I, for one, who was a motherless child as a result, don't ever want to forget them. They say those who forget history are doomed to repeat it." She sat down hard in a wicker chair, as though her knees had given out. Her voice dropped until they strained to hear. "I'd never want to see such sad times repeat," she whispered. "Too much heartbreak, too much killing.

"So many were ashamed to be blood kin and changed their names. Not me. I was proud of 'em."

Laura carried the scrapbooks into the living room, set them on the coffee table, made Gram comfortable, then opened the first big, black book. "The Ashley Family" was handwritten in black ink and beautiful script across the top of the first page.

"How is it that you have Ashley family scrapbooks?" Laura asked. "How'd you come by them?"

"You see," Gram said, "I grew up without a mother but never lost my connection to her. Neither did my father. When I was young, whenever we heard stories about John Ashley and my mother . . ." She frowned at John for a moment, then went on, "My father wouldn't speak for days. But I'd hear him cry in the night. When he finally realized she was never coming back, he divorced my mother. He remarried, a nice-enough woman, I guess. But we kids never connected. That woman was colorless, as gray and as quiet as a mouse. Meant well, I guess. But she wasn't Laura, and we all wanted Laura. My daddy did, and so did I. Even my baby brother, God rest his soul, who surely could not remember her except as a picture under a newspaper headline. But he always dreamed about our mama. Sure wasn't fair to the mouse, who wiped our noses, nursed us through the flu, washed our clothes, and cooked our meals." She shook her head.

"But how did you get the Ashley family scrapbooks?"

"I'm getting to that," she said impatiently. "From Leugenia, John Ashley's mother. That good woman kept up those books for years, in chronological order as the articles or pictures appeared. Good, bad, or disaster, she clipped and kept 'em all. God bless 'er, she valued history like I do. Over the years, after Laura and John were both gone, I went to see her, to ask questions about my mother. I was curious, and Leugenia was far closer to her than me or my father. He would never discuss her at all 'cept to say she loved us, which made no sense to me. If she loved us, where the hell was she? First time I knocked on Leugenia's door, her snotty daughter-in-law ran me off. But the next time, Leugenia was alone. As sweet as peach pie to me, but bitter about all that had happened.

"Another of her children, John's sister Daisy, died early too." Arlie shook her head. "The girl drank poison. Leugenia took out the scrapbooks and the family Bible with all the handwritten records, and we spent a long afternoon going through 'em together. She'd written lots of notes in the margins. I was fascinated. She saw they meant as much to me as they did to her. We both cried when I left, but I was so happy to finally know my mother better. She explained why Laura did a lot of the things she did and said she had not given us up lightly but had done it to prevent bloodshed.

"Leugenia outlived most all her family, lived into the nineteen forties, I think. But long before that, she couldn't live alone anymore and was going to stay with her last surviving son, Bill, and that uppity daughter-in-law. They wouldn't allow reminders of the past in their home, wanted them burned—the scrapbooks, the Bible, even that lovely sketch that Winslow Homer, the famous artist, did of young Laura down by the river. Leugenia said her daughter, Daisy, brought it home after Laura left it behind at John's fishing camp.

"Leugenia called, said she wanted to see me. When I went, she gave 'em all to me. Cried her eyes out, said she wanted to leave the past in good hands and I was the only one who still cared.

"Hard to believe"—Arlie's eyes brimmed with tears—"how many Ashleys changed their names, moved away, ashamed to be related. That white scrapbook is one I kept since I was a girl. But Leugenia's are far more complete and thorough. There was so much my little brother and me never heard about because our father shielded us from anything he thought might make us think less of our mother.

"I never saw Leugenia again. But there was one thing." Her eyes flashed like a girl's and she smiled. "A few years after I last saw her, that snotty daughter-in-law heard that Winslow Homer was a famous artist whose work was valuable, especially after he passed away. She got Leugenia to tell what she'd done with that sketch, and that woman, Lucy, had the nerve to come knocking at my door. Said Leugenia gave it to me by mistake, that it belonged to her family, and she had to have it back. Did you ever?"

"What did you do?" Laura asked.

"Ran her off, what else?" Arlie's eyes twinkled at the memory.

Laura made more tea and fixed sandwiches. After they finished, she cleaned up, then took the Homer sketch of her grandmother off the wall and propped it up on the kitchen table where they were reading. The scrapbook pages were yellowed and crumbling. But the newspaper articles had held up surprisingly well over the years due to the better-quality paper, with a high rag content, used at the time.

Arlie went to take her nap but promised to answer questions and fill in the gaps when she awoke. John and Laura settled in to read about love, death, and how more than a hundred years earlier their family histories had entwined forever in one of the most colorful, violent, and little-known chapters in Florida's history.

PART EIGHT

CHAPTER FIFTY-FOUR

Wooden planks rumbled beneath the tires as John drove onto the narrow Sebastian Bridge. "What the hell's that?"

Red tail lights glowed up ahead. A Model T Ford had stopped at a barrier on the span.

"Why'd they stop?" Hanford asked.

"A lantern." John slowed down. The big car's headlights pierced the dark like lances.

"The bridge must be out," Clarence said in disgust.

Ray cursed.

"Nobody mentioned it back in Fort Pierce." John cut the engine and opened the driver's side door.

"Storm musta damaged it," Hanford said.

"Could be." John glanced at the backseat passengers as he slid out of the car. "Ray, didn't I ask you to stay outta that food hamper? That has to last us till we get to Daisy's place."

"Sorry, John, only took a biscuit. Your mama's cooking is sure hard to resist." He flicked crumbs from his mustache and shirt front as they all climbed out, stretched, and yawned.

Hanford squinted across the shadowy span. "Nothin' seems wrong. Water don't look high."

"Planks sound solid." John lifted his face to the starry sky and inhaled deeply. "Listen," he whispered.

"Don't hear nothing," his nephew said.

"That's what's wrong!" John dove for the door handle. Too late.

"Move and we shoot! We got the drop on you, Ashley! Hands up high! Everybody! Now!"

John exhaled slowly and raised his hands. "It's an ambush, boys. Do what they say."

Seven shadowy figures emerged from the darkness, one by one. All wore sidearms and held high-powered rifles in the firing position.

Young Hanford tensed, eyes darting, about to run for the car and his gun.

"Don't!" John warned. "Don't give 'em a reason to shoot. That's what they want you to do."

"He's right! Do what he says," a narrow-eyed deputy warned from behind his Winchester.

"They gonna take us to jail," Ray whined.

"So?" John shrugged. "No jail can hold us long."

Sorry, darlin', he thought. I should have listened. Is she thinking of me? he wondered. Or is she asleep and dreaming? He could see Laura's hair, as black and shiny as a raven's wing, spread across her pillow.

The deputies advanced cautiously, the barrels of their long guns trained on the four prisoners. John recognized three as Bob Baker's deputies. The other four were strangers.

"T. W. and Clyde. You too, Dan. Didn't expect to see you up here."

"Shut up, Ashley!" T. W. said sharply. His face glistened and his shirt was sweat-stained, though the night had grown cool.

A shrill high-pitched scream suddenly shattered the silent night. The deputies, already edgy, exchanged frightened glances.

John saw their eyes and felt the first sharp stab of fear. "Take it easy, boys," he said calmly. "That's just a big cat. A panther. We saw it back there on the road." He stood stock still, his words reassuring. "We're unarmed. Just passing through. Nobody here wants a fight."

He saw how they looked at each other, knew what they were thinking, and remembered the fear in Laura's voice. *I'll never see you again.*

"We shoulda ate the ham and the chicken when we had the chance," Ray said, his eyes hungry, his hands high.

"Don't talk," John said.

Two of Merritt's deputies warned John not to move, gingerly approached, handcuffed him first, then marched him away from the others. He did not resist. Resigned to their capture, Hanford Mobley, Ray Lynn, and Clarence Middleton submitted as well.

Once all were handcuffed, T. W. drew his pistol, strode up to John, and slammed it across his face, drawing blood. John staggered, knocked off balance by the blow. Another deputy caught his cuffed hands to keep him on his feet.

"Sheriff Bob Baker sends his regards." T. W. grinned and stood taller. "Not so tough now, are you, Ashley?" He drew the weapon back to strike another blow but was interrupted.

"That's enough!" A tall, broad-shouldered stranger emerged from the woods at the side of the road. He had a high forehead, iron-gray hair, and sharp features beneath a wide-brimmed Stetson. He wore two pistols and a pair of handcuffs in his gun belt, and carried a rifle. "Hello, Ashley."

Blood dripped into his good eye and blurred John's vision. "Merritt?"

The man nodded.

"I knew we'd meet someday, Sheriff."

"So did I, John. I been waiting."

"We have no quarrel, Sheriff. We've done nothing illegal here in your jurisdiction and have no plans to. We're just headed north."

"Sorry." Merritt shook his head. "I don't allow outlaws in my county."

"Where's Baker?" John expected the Palm Beach sheriff to appear next.

"Home in Palm Beach, asleep in his own bed, most likely. Saint Lucie's my jurisdiction. I'm just showing Baker a little professional courtesy."

"Sorry he missed the party," John said. "I been wanting to talk to him."

"I'll tell 'im you said that." Merritt's lips parted in a menacing smile.

When shadowy gunmen confronted the occupants of the car behind them, the two teenaged boys in the Model T on the bridge feared it was a robbery and they were next. They stashed their watches and billfolds beneath the seats and waited, hearts pounding.

After several minutes Ted Miller, the driver, grew impatient. "I'm going back there to see what's going on," he said, and stepped boldly out onto the bridge.

"Don't!" his passenger, Sam Davis, shouted in panic. "Are you crazy? They'll kill us both! They've got guns!"

Miller heeded his warning, scrambled back into the car, and slammed the door.

Sheriff Merritt heard the commotion, glanced up, then stepped away from the prisoner. "So long, John." He sounded cheerful.

"Don't go, Merritt." John willed him to stay, but the veteran lawman ignored him, nodded to his deputies, then turned, still smiling, to walk across the bridge to the Model T.

To their immense relief, the boys in the car recognized the approaching gunman as their local sheriff. Merritt greeted them warmly and chuckled as they shared their fears and how they'd hidden their valuables.

"You've got nothing to worry about here," he assured them. "Those are my men back there. We just captured John Ashley and his gang."

"You sure it's him?" Miller exclaimed.

"Sure as the sun'll come up in the mornin'." Merritt unhooked the chain that blocked the bridge, removed the lantern, then, still holding it, hopped onto their running board for a lift to his car on the far side. As they began to move, he glanced back and smiled again at John Ashley.

The boys dropped off the sheriff, drove back across the span, and slowed down to stare at the three handcuffed men near the Ford touring car. The fourth prisoner stood alone a short distance away, hands cuffed behind him, his face and shirt bloody.

"It's him!" Miller said. "That's really John Ashley!"

"They got 'im! They got 'im!" Davis hollered. "Don't that beat all! Looks just like his picture."

"Think they'll hang 'im?" Miller asked, as a burly, mustachioed deputy tersely waved them on.

"Probably will," Davis said cheerfully.

The boys rushed back to town to spread the news.

John Ashley watched their tail lights disappear into the dark. He listened to the sound of the car's engine fade, along with any hope of surviving the night.

A cold wind in the trees raised the hair on the back of his neck. This time, he knew, was different. A bright quarter moon reigned over a star-studded night made for love, fresh starts, and new beginnings, not bad endings. How did this go so wrong? He closed his eyes, felt

Laura's hands on his shoulders, saw how she looked when he loved her and the sunlight in her hair when he last saw her, so very long ago that morning.

He opened his eyes, took a deep breath, and spoke up for his sister's child. "Clyde. Deputy Padgett, you know my nephew, Hanford, here. He's just a boy . . ."

"Uncle John?" Hanford looked bewildered, then saw what was happening. "Oh, Lord. God, no!"

T. W. Stone fired the first shot. The others immediately followed with a barrage of gunfire.

"Oh, Jesus! No! God!" Ray wet himself as he staggered through muzzle flashes that lit up the night. The sound was deafening. The acrid smell of gunpowder hung in the air. Prisoners twitched and kicked as high-powered bullets slammed into flesh and bone, again and again, until the lawmen's rifles were empty.

Ashley tried to speak as he hit the ground. But no one listened as he choked on gun smoke and his own blood.

He was thirty-six.

The killers stood like shadowy statues in the smoky aftermath. Their ears rang.

T. W. was the first to speak. "Go git it," he told Clyde Padgett. "We got to bring it back."

Padgett's only response was to vomit into the high weeds at the side of the road.

T. W. turned to Dan.

"Not me," he said, and slowly shook his head.

"Damn!" T. W. blurted impatiently. "Okay, I'll git it myself." He reloaded, tried to keep his hands steady, then stepped carefully, so as not to bloody his boots. He stood astride the body, stared down and tried hard to remember which eye this goddamn dead outlaw had lost. He couldn't hesitate. The others were watching.

"Oops." He guffawed in a show of bravado. "My mistake. That there's the eye God gave him." The smells of blood, gunpowder, and death filled his nostrils as he plucked out John Ashley's glass eye with his thumb and index finger. He wiped it off, made a show of polishing it with his handkerchief, then wrapped and tucked it into his vest pocket.

"Trophy," he explained gruffly, as Merritt's men stared. "Baker plans to wear it on his watch fob."

The silence was deafening.

"It's a local thing," T. W. said, weakly. "Bad blood. You'd need to live in Palm Beach and know everybody involved to appreciate it."

CHAPTER FIFTY-FIVE

B ack in town, the teenagers quickly spread the news that John Ashley and his gang had been captured. A rowdy crowd gathered at the jail to see the notorious outlaws arrive in handcuffs.

But the men in handcuffs arrived instead at the local hardware store, which doubled as a mortuary. "We've got the Ashleys here!" Deputy T. W. Stone shouted jubilantly.

"Dead or alive?" Lester Lewis, a nervous part-time employee, called down from an upstairs window.

"Dead as hell!" the deputy bellowed.

Lewis took delivery of the four bodies, still handcuffed and stacked like cordwood atop one another in the back of a car.

Word traveled like wildfire. The crowd deserted the jail and rushed to the mortuary. They didn't have a long wait. The bodies were carried out a short time later for display on the grass. By then the handcuffs had been removed.

Sheriff Merritt issued a proud statement to the press. His deputies, he said, had won a wild gun battle with outlaw John Ashley and his notorious gang, who'd fought to the death. "John Ashley died like he lived, with a smoking gun in each hand," he said, and added that not a single lawman was lost or injured, not even a scratch.

Palm Beach Sheriff Bob Baker quickly followed with his own press release. "I learned," he said, "that John Ashley and his men intended to travel upstate to rob a bank, hide out with relatives until after the election, and then come back to Palm Beach to assassinate me." He said he'd shared the information and his three best men with Sheriff Merritt, who had offered his help.

The newspapers printed the lawmen's statements verbatim.

The crowd continued to grow. Strangers and tourists, reporters and photographers, some from as far away as Miami, came to see the dead outlaws, who were brought out again the next day and displayed, like trophy animals, on a cold slab of sidewalk in front of Fee's Hardware Store and Mortuary.

Spectators hoisted little children to their shoulders to better view "the wages of sin," a reporter noted.

"I remember one body in particular," a young man later told another reporter. "He looked real young, late teens or early twenties, uncovered on the cement sidewalk. He was real pale because all his blood had settled. They were all uncovered, laid out flat on their backs, arms at their sides. It scared the tar out of me."

"John Ashley always looked bigger than life," explained Arlo Harmond, a young harness maker, "so everybody wanted to see what he looked like dead."

Fifty years later, a curious Miami newspaper reporter would ask him to recall his most unforgettable moment in a nearly extinct occupation. Harmond's reply had little to do with the art of harness making. Without hesitation, he confessed that he'd never forgotten what he saw on the sidewalk outside that mortuary, particularly the handcuff marks on the wrists of the dead.

"Wish I never had seen them," he said poignantly, still haunted in old age, half a century later.

Laura, Leugenia, and John's brother, Bill, arrived later that day to claim the bodies of John and his nephew, Hanford. Though hundreds of morbidly curious strangers had leered close up at John's corpse in a sideshow atmosphere, the undertaker barred Laura, refused to let her see him. Not proper, he said, since she was not John's wife and he had already been stripped naked for embalming.

The undertaker changed his mind when she began to scream.

Loved ones also came for Clarence Middleton. Only Ray Lynn remained unclaimed. "We can't let him go alone to an unmarked grave in Potters Field," Laura insisted, "after he died beside John and Hanford."

Leugenia and Bill agreed. They took Lynn to rest with John and Hanford in the tiny family cemetery near the Ashley home.

As the families grieved, Sheriff Merritt was hailed in the national press as a hero and bombarded by congratulatory telegrams. Railroad tycoons, bankers, politicians, clergymen, and postal inspectors praised the little-known sheriff as "brave and brilliant."

New York City's postal inspector urged other lawmen to adopt Merritt's philosophy of "Do to others as they do to you, and do it first!"

Bank presidents sent Merritt and the deputies reward checks. Three days later he was reelected sheriff by a landslide. Palm Beach sheriff Bob Baker won election as well.

No cash or valuables were returned to the families with the embalmed bodies, or ever. John had left home with a large amount of cash in a money belt, his family said. But Merritt and the deputies swore that the dead outlaws didn't have two nickels to rub together, not so much as a pocket watch, among them.

Devastated that John's glass eye had been taken and aware of Baker's plans, Laura dispatched a note:

"Return John Ashley's eye to me. Now! If you don't, I will crawl through hell if I have to, and take it away from you myself."

Never a man to take threats lightly, Sheriff Baker had John's eye delivered to the Ashley home in time for the funeral service.

"If I'd known he'd do that," Deputy T. W. Stone raged to fellow deputies, "I'da smashed it under my foot on the bridge that night."

The Ashley family disputed Merritt's version of the killings even before they saw the cuts and bruises left by handcuffs on the dead mens' wrists.

"They're lying," Leugenia told everyone. "It's all lies. Don't believe 'em. That was no gang. Just John's nephew and two friends. Hanford came home from out of state to persuade John and the others to go with him to find work in a place where they could start new lives. John didn't want no more killing. He didn't plan to hurt no one or rob no bank. He left home wearing a money belt stuffed with cash. They stole it. There was no gunfight. They robbed, handcuffed, and murdered John, Hanford, and the others," she swore.

Three white pine coffins were built, but funeral plans hit a snag when no clergyman would agree to officiate, not even those friendly with John and his family. All feared retaliation from lawmen or relatives of those killed or injured by the gang. Hollow-eyed and desperate, Laura sought help from the Salvation Army commander in Miami. "Who are we to make the final judgment on a man's life?" he told her, and agreed to help. "That's up to God, not us."

John Ashley was laid to rest on Tuesday, November 4, 1924, the day Americans elected Calvin Coolidge president, and Sheriffs Baker and Merritt celebrated their wins at the polls.

The Salvation Army commander brought a woman with an angelic voice with him. She sang two hymns. Laura wept quietly through the service, which ended in prayer.

Leugenia choked back bitter sobs as the coffins were lowered into the ground. "Look there, at all three of them!" she cried. "Killed for nothing. And here's the old man." She lovingly caressed her husband's headstone. "Dead too soon, like the others. My Joe was a good man who never harmed a soul."

"Never mind, Mama," Daisy said, holding her mother. "We'll see them all again someday soon."

But Leugenia was inconsolable. "It's all Bob Baker's fault!" she wailed, as the few mourners dispersed. "We didn't do a thing to him. I wish he'd fall, be paralyzed, and have to be spoon-fed for the rest of his life."

"Doesn't do any good to talk like that, Ma," Bill said, as his wife, Lucy, dabbed at her eyes with a lacy handkerchief.

Rumors that the dead were handcuffed first and then shot spread quickly. Whispers grew into questions asked out loud. Judge Angus Sumner empaneled a coroner's jury for an inquest into whether the shootings were justifiable or murder.

The two groups of deputies each hired a lawyer. A young Fort Pierce attorney, Alto L. Adams, who would later become chief justice of the Florida Supreme Court, was hired by the Ashley family. The inquest began the day after the funerals. The undertaker, who owned the hardware store/mortuary, testified that he'd attended to the bodies and saw no evidence that they'd been handcuffed.

The two young Sebastian men in the other car on the bridge that night, testified for four hours. Ted Miller and Sam Davis swore they initially saw the prisoners standing in the road, hands in the air, surrounded by deputies. They saw Sheriff Merritt as well, they said. When they returned across the bridge, they said three of the men were now handcuffed together while Ashley stood off to the side, also handcuffed. They passed slowly for a good look and plainly saw cuffs on all four, they said, then rushed into town and told a number of people that the gang had been captured. Shortly after, they said, Sheriff Merritt arrived in Sebastian by another route to report the "wild gun battle."

Adams, the Ashley attorney, asked the judge to have the bodies exhumed for an unbiased examination of their wrists and to determine exactly how they had died. When jury members appeared enthusiastically in favor of the move, the judge denied the request and disqualified the jurors on the grounds that they could not be impartial. He quickly empaneled a new, handpicked jury for an inquest on the following Saturday. The carefully selected jurors listened intently to testimony from Sheriff Merritt and the seven deputies and reached immediate verdicts of justifiable homicide in all four deaths.

Lester Lewis, the part-time hardware/mortuary worker who took delivery of the dead and had always said that they'd arrived in handcuffs and stacked like cordwood, was never asked to testify. The two young men at the bridge were not called to appear at the new inquest either.

Each day Leugenia trudged wearily down the path to the little family graveyard to mourn. Laura went alone at night or just before sunrise, carrying fresh flowers and a loaded gun. Twice in the two days after the funeral she had run off vandals and would-be grave robbers she caught creeping into the tiny cemetery after dark. Rumors had spread that more than $100,000 in missing loot had been buried with the dead men.

Ten days later, at midmorning on a Friday, Bill and Lucy arrived unexpectedly. He tooted the horn as they pulled up, and Leugenia dropped her darning to greet them. Lucy's eyes burned bright as she flounced inside. Bill exuded icy anger. Laura first assumed that they had quarreled, but it quickly became apparent that their anger was shared, directed at something—or someone—else.

They totally ignored her and spoke only to Leugenia, who looked confused. What now? Laura wondered, her heart sinking.

"Mama," Lucy said dramatically, "we would never want to be the ones to have to tell you, not ever. But like I told Billy this mornin', you're bound to find out since the whole world knows." The eagerness in her eyes betrayed her words.

"What it is, Lucy?" Leugenia frowned into the pale freckled face of her daughter-in-law.

Lucy nodded at Bill who, with a flourish, dropped a newspaper onto the kitchen table. He stood there, arms crossed, eyes hard.

"Oh, Lord." Leugenia waved it away in disgust. "What are they saying about us now?"

"Not us," Bill said. "Laura."

Still ignored, as though she weren't even in the room, Laura stepped up and read the front-page headline. "What . . . ?" She gasped, then snatched the paper up in both hands.

"Scorned Everglades Queen Betrayed Ashley Gang," the headline screamed over the same photo of them that had convinced John it was too dangerous to travel together. The story reported that Laura Upthegrove, Ashley's rejected lover, was furious when he left her, and in retaliation had tipped off Sheriff Baker about his travel plans, setting in motion the fatal ambush.

"Lying trash! How can they say such a thing?" She hurled the paper to the floor, kicked at it, and burst into angry tears.

Leugenia picked it up, took her reading glasses from the shelf, and sat down at the table. Lips moving, she read a few paragraphs, then lifted her eyes, now flooded by tears, to Bill and Lucy. "Laura wouldn't do that. Ever." She looked bewildered. "This isn't true."

"Now, Mama, how can you say that?" Lucy's sulky, syrupy words were patronizing. "When it's all right there in front of you, spelled out in black and white. Read it again. Better yet, why not ask her?" For the first time since they'd arrived, Lucy, her eyes glittery, turned to look accusingly at Laura.

Leugenia opened her mouth but couldn't utter a word.

"It's a lie!" Laura said sharply.

"You were mad as a red-ass dog 'cuz he left," Bill snarled. "I know. I was right here. You wouldn't even say goodbye to him that morning, and he was dead that night!"

Laura and Leugenia shook their heads in unison.

"Answer me a simple question, Ma," Bill said. "Did Laura go out in the car that day after John and the boys drove off?"

"Laura would never . . ." Leugenia's voice trailed off. "She . . . she loved Johnny."

"Answer the question," Bill demanded.

Leugenia's eyes widened. "*No*," she moaned. Her mouth opened in a look of horror. "Oh, God, Laura, did you do it?"

"No. Don't you believe it," Laura said.

"John was my brother," Bill said, "and I loved 'im, but he was no saint, Ma."

"Billy!" Leugenia stared in shock at her sole surviving son.

"I found out a few things." He glanced to Lucy for confirmation. She looked strangely pleased and nodded.

"Didn't want to tell you this either, Mama, but John tried to force himself on Lucy the night before our weddin'. She didn't tell then, 'cuz she didn't want to upset the family."

"You tramp! You lying bitch!" Laura lunged, caught Lucy's hair, and slammed her face against the heavy wooden tabletop.

Lucy fought back, clawed, bit, and howled for her husband. Leugenia shrieked. John's old hound dog woke from his nap behind his master's empty chair, lurched stiffly to his feet, barked ferociously, and bared his teeth.

Laura and Lucy stumbled against the table. Crockery crashed to the floor. Stunned at first, Bill rushed forward, pulled Laura off his wife, and slammed his right fist into her face with a punch so explosive that he painfully bruised his knuckles.

Lifted off her feet by the blow, she crumpled to the floor like a broken doll. The old dog padded to her side and whimpered.

"Don't care what you say about me," Laura mumbled through bloodied lips already puffy. "But don't you dare lie about John!" She looked up at Leugenia, pleadingly. "He was your best child, everything you believed him to be."

Bill spat at her. "John got Pa and Bobby kilt," he shouted. "Ed and Frank died too, because a him. But remember what started it all? Our family never had a bad word or a bit of trouble in this world till John brought her home. Tell me the truth, bitch." He towered over Laura, his face red and threatening, his voice ragged. "When you ratted them out to Sheriff Baker, did you know they'd be killed? Did you even give a goddamn about what would happen to them?"

"Don't believe it, Lu," she gasped. The left side of Laura's face had begun to swell.

"I loved you like a daughter . . ." Leugenia's pain had turned to shock and anger. "I thought you loved Johnny with all . . ."

Bill stomped from the room, returned quickly with a few garments ripped from John and Laura's closet, and flung them to the floor near her. "Get up and get your ass out of here, Laura. You ain't welcome. Get out! Now!"

"Don't let her take nothing, after all the shit she's done, all the damage she's caused." Lucy patted her hair, torn askew in the scuffle. "Look, Bill," she whimpered. "She tore the pocket and the sleeve right offa my new store-bought dress! Scratched my face too."

Laura struggled to stand, but the room spun and her knees buckled. Using a chair back for support, she finally fought to her feet and gazed imploringly at Leugenia.

"I can't look at your face," Leugenia muttered, and turned away.

Laura picked the few garments up off the floor and walked out the door, shoulders straight, chin up. No one watching knew the physical effort it took. Her last words before she closed the door behind her sounded slurred. "I'm sorry for you, Bill."

"Don't ever come back here," he snarled.

She clutched the handrail as she struggled down the porch steps and went straight to the barn, now a garage. She sat in the car, rested her forehead on the steering wheel for a long moment, took a deep shuddering breath, sobbed aloud once, then backed slowly out of the barn and drove away.

"Why did you let her take that car?" Lucy angrily demanded.

"It *is* hers." Bill no longer sounded bitter, only weary. "And it's the fastest way to get that woman out of our sight for good."

CHAPTER FIFTY-SIX

Laura arrived just after sunset at the remote fishing camp John had built. She needed to recover, rest, and think. Where else could she go? No one had been there since she and John had left for the last time. She loved to be there with him, safe together, hiding out in the heart of the great swamp. But without him, it was a dark and lonely place.

His scent still clung to the shirt that hung from a nail in the wall and to the covering on their bed. She found a few supplies: a tin of crackers, dried apples, a bit of salt pork, and several mason jars—corn, snap beans, and tomatoes—she and Leugenia had put up last season. There was water in the rain barrel and more than enough whiskey to numb the throb of her injuries and allow her some sleep. Several of her teeth had been knocked loose. Her neck felt stiff. Her head ached.

She was grateful for the whiskey, even though it burned her mouth like a hot poker where Bill's fist had split her lip and slammed her teeth through the soft flesh inside her cheek.

She drank herself to sleep but awoke terrified, in a nightmare, before dawn. The long, cold night was alive with snarls, high-pitched cries, and slithering sounds in the walls. With John the nights were short, filled with music, love, and laughter. But the terrible truth was all too real. The man she had loved since childhood was lost to her forever, along with the family she had adopted as her own. They despised her now, all because of Lucy and her lies.

How long is this night? Will the sun ever rise?

It did, as always. In its first pale light she found his straight razor and his boots. She studied her battered face in his shaving mirror and wished to be the way she looked so long ago when she and John were young and Winslow Homer was alive. His sketch of her still hung in the Ashley home, where she would never be welcome again.

She gingerly touched her tender tongue to her swollen lips. What can I do? she wondered. *Where can I go? How can I live?*

She tried to pray but choked on the familiar words. *If God exists,* she wondered, *how could He have let this happen?* If only God was alive and John was with Him in a better place, instead of eternally earthbound, beneath South Florida's fertile black soil like all those before him whose blood had nourished this hungry outlaw peninsula at the bottom of the map.

She yearned for the comfort of another beating heart. If only she had thought to bring John's old dog here with her. They'd both loved him.

She tried to envision a future. She had always hoped to know her children again but was a total stranger, a notorious and alien stranger to them now. Her mother and stepfather had sided with Edgar from the start. No surprise there. Even bad mothers crave access to their grand-children. They might take her in, but could she bear their recrimina-tions, allegations, and reminders of all her misdeeds too numerous to count?

"I'd be better off dead," she murmured, then cocked her head and slowly repeated the words, as though hearing them for the first time.

How inviting, she thought. Freedom from pain. Forever. The good news? A pearly gates reunion with John and all the others who'd gone ahead. The bad news? Hellfire and damnation for all she had done and not done.

Edgar had warned her when she left with John. She never forgot the moment, when he shook his fist and cried out, "You'll burn in hellfire for this, Laura! You'll both burn!"

Reverend Hasley had shouted, "Fall down on your knees . . . Repent! Pray for forgiveness."

Too late now, she thought, exhausted as she recalled her husband's final words to her, "You'll go straight to hell with John Ashley." I'd be in good company, she thought.

There was an appealing third possibility. Nothing. Eternal sleep. What she needed more than anything was sleep.

For three days she drank only water and whiskey and ate nothing but a few stale crackers from a tin. She felt no hunger, a blessing since it hurt like hell to chew.

I will not endure a fourth night in this dark and lonely place. She knew precisely what to do instead.

She felt serene, though sleepless, almost happy. A positive energy welled up from deep inside her and buoyed her spirits.

Most people will be relieved to hear the news, others pleased, even elated, she thought, as she stripped off the clothes she'd worn for days. She felt free, though chilly. It had seemed appropriate to be naked, the way she'd come into the world, but she decided instead to wear John's shirt. She plucked it from the nail where it hung, slipped it on, and was glad she did. Too large, of course—it hung nearly to her knees—but it felt warm, like his arms around her.

Lucy had won but not forever. She was a stranger to the truth, which would be her undoing. Laura took great comfort in knowing that the truth would out. She knew it would. It didn't matter if she wasn't there to see it happen.

Smiling, she cut and ripped a pair of his old long johns into strips and braided them tightly together. Suddenly strong, energetic, and beyond pain, she dragged the wooden table into position below the sturdy crossbeam of rock-hard Dade County pine. She remembered how John grinned at her protests that he had squandered his building and carpentry skills on such painstaking construction of a fishing camp.

"This place," she had said, "will survive anything and still stand like the pyramids long after we're gone."

He'd laughed and insisted it was only practice for the house he planned to build her on Miami's Ocean Beach.

She carried the heavy breadbox to the wooden table, then used a chair to climb up onto it, then onto the box. Cheerfully, she looped the makeshift noose around her throat, fastened the rope tightly around the beam, and pulled it taut.

She gathered herself together for a final quiet moment, took a deep breath, and began to sing a hymn the Salvation Army woman had sung at John's funeral.

"I've wandered far away from God, now I'm coming home. The paths of sin too long I've trod; Lord, I'm coming home. Coming home, coming home . . ." She repeated the verse, her voice shaky as she realized that in her excitement she could no longer remember the familiar refrain.

With tears in her eyes and a smile on her face, she lustily kicked the breadbox out from beneath her. The last sound she heard was not exactly what she expected. Was that the breadbox crashing to the floor? she wondered, as she plunged into empty space. Her feet twitched in a deadly dance more than a foot above the tabletop, then stopped, and she no longer cared.

CHAPTER FIFTY-SEVEN

Daisy laughed aloud, elated to see Laura's car hidden in the pines on high ground near the fishing camp. "Ah knew it!" She slapped the steering wheel. "Ah just knew it! Where else would that girl go?"

Furious at Bill and Lucy, Daisy had fired a piece of her mind like a shotgun blast at her mother, packed up Laura's things, stocked up on food, blankets, and toiletries, and loaded them into her car. As an afterthought, she dashed back inside to snatch off the wall that sketch of Laura that John had liked so well. She paused to look around the room, then took his guitar and a patchwork quilt in which to wrap it.

She'd come in the nick of time. Leugenia said Lucy had promised to come early the next morning to "clear out and dispose of John and Laura's possessions."

"*Loot* would be a more accurate description," Daisy sniped, as she flew out the door, arms full, her car loaded.

Her hunch proved right. They were so like sisters that she found Laura in the first place she looked, John's fishing camp. She rapped at the rugged wooden door. No answer. She knocked louder, then heard a crash inside, as though something heavy had fallen to the floor. "Open up! Ah tracked you down, girl!"

Silence.

She tried the door. Locked. "Laura, it's me! I'm alone."

Nothing.

Daisy rattled the knob, stepped back, and frowned. On tiptoe, she reached up over the door frame to grope for the extra key. She felt it at the tip of her fingers, but it dropped into the weeds around the stoop.

"Laura!"

Dead silence.

"There better not be poison oak out heah." Daisy angrily stamped her foot. "If there is, I'll git you for this, Laura." Then she dropped down on all fours to search for the key.

She finally found it, got up, fumbled, then managed to unlock the door and shove it open.

"Laura?" Brow furrowed, Daisy stepped into the dimly lit interior. Something wasn't right.

It was Laura. Swaying gently above the table, half-naked, wearing only John's favorite flannel shirt. Her face was blue; her hands hung limply at her sides.

"*No!*" Daisy shrieked. She dropped the parcel she carried.

Eyes averted, she scrambled past the horrifying tableau to the shelf where John kept his shaving gear. She seized his straight razor, ran back, lifted the bulky breadbox off the floor, and slid it back onto the table.

Laura stared, eyes wide open. No sign of life.

Daisy climbed onto the chair, then onto the table. The razor in her right hand, she stepped onto the breadbox, caught Laura around the hips with her left arm, and struggled to lift her enough to relieve the pressure on her throat. Staggered by the dead weight, she slashed frantically at the makeshift rope.

"No!" she gasped. "It's not sharp enough!"

Sobbing under her breath, she looked wildly around the room for a sharper blade. John's fishing rods stood in the corner near the stove. His razor-sharp fish-gutting knife hung beside them in a leather sheath on the wall.

She looked up at Laura, then gently released her. Daisy jumped down from the table whimpering. "Oh, dear God, don't let her die!" She ran headlong for the knife on the wall, slid it from the sheath, and rushed back to the table.

"Help me, John," she prayed. "Help me save her!"

Back on the table, she jumped, grunted, slashed savagely at the braided rope. The blade nearly severed it. The strands unraveled at lightning speed. Laura's full weight toppled toward Daisy, who was unable to hold her and lost her footing. She teetered on the breadbox, which toppled to the floor. So did she.

Laura landed with a resounding thud, flat on her back on the hard wooden table top.

Daisy dragged herself to her feet a moment later, wide-eyed and whimpering. Her jaw dropped as a deep sigh came from Laura's open mouth. Did she really hear that? Yes! The impact from the fall had re-started her breathing.

Daisy splashed water on Laura's face and pleaded, called to her, then rubbed her pale lips with whiskey. Laura grimaced. Her eyelids fluttered. Her color began to flood back.

Laura finally focused on Daisy's tearstained face.

"Oh, Daisy," she gasped painfully. "Are you dead too?"

CHAPTER FIFTY-EIGHT

Ostracized by the community, abandoned by the Ashleys except for Daisy, who now had a family of her own in Jacksonville, Laura turned to whiskey to numb her pain and loneliness.

It tormented her that she could not visit John's grave and that he and the others could not rest in peace. Frequent news stories reported how their graves were being vandalized and desecrated by thieves and treasure hunters in search of the rumored money. The publicity only drew more grave robbers and souvenir seekers, until not a single bone was left in their coffins.

Laura drifted from place to place, unwanted by the public and targeted by police, who frequently arrested her. The offenses probably would have been ignored had she not been the notorious former Queen of the Everglades. In and out of jail, she was charged with traffic violations, drinking, gambling, and selling moonshine.

Shunned by half the public for her outlaw past, she was despised by the other half for setting up John and the others for a fatal ambush by police.

No one believed her, and one day, pushed too far by her arrest on another minor charge, she struggled fiercely with the deputies until she was beaten, scratched, and bruised. At the jail she asked for iodine to treat her injuries. When a jailer handed her the bottle, she drank it all before he could stop her. Another failed suicide attempt. The iodine used for prisoners at the jail had been heavily diluted with water as a cost-cutting measure. All it did was make her sick.

She settled in Okeechobee, but police arrested her time after time for drunk driving. Those who knew her said "she looked all used up." Local authorities finally told her she wasn't wanted and had to leave town.

With nowhere left to go, she moved in with her mother, who operated a gas station that sold fuel and bootleg liquor in Canal Point.

At the gas station on Saturday, August 6, 1927, Laura sold a pint of liquor. The customer, already drunk, counted his change and accused her of cheating him. She denied it. He became loud, made threats, and slapped her. They scuffled, and when he knocked her down, she pulled a gun from beneath the counter. Her mother intervened and wrestled the weapon away. As her mother screamed and struck her and the customer shouted threats, Laura snatched a bottle of acid off a shelf and drank it.

Gagging and choking, the acid burning away the soft tissue in her mouth and throat, she fell to the floor, writhing in agony.

Shocked sober, the drunken customer and his friend shouted frantically for someone to get a doctor.

Her mother intervened again. "No," she said. "Don't." She locked the door. "Let her be. She's better off dead."

After twenty terrible minutes, she was.

She was thirty-seven years old.

PART NINE

T hat was my great, great-grandmother." Tears streaked Laura's mournful face, and fell from her chin. "Oh my God. Gram never told me. How sad. How terribly, terribly sad."

John had called his father shortly after they began to read the old scrapbooks. He'd always known he shared the name of an ancestor, a Prohibition-era bootlegger, but knew little more. His father who once traced the family tree, had proudly mentioned ancestors who fought for the South in the Civil War.

But when John's father and grandfather were young, older family members never spoke of the Ashley Gang. They were an embarrassment. Their kin shunned the press, even changed their names and moved away, to escape the shame and notoriety.

John's father consulted his grandmother's family Bible, with its handwritten birth, death, and marriage records, then called back. John, he confirmed, was a direct descendant of Frank Ashley, lost at sea with his brother Ed during a rum-running trip to the Bahamas during Prohibition.

"They are us." Laura wiped her eyes. "And we are them. We share their DNA. Our lives even parallel theirs. It's as though destiny has brought us back together after all these years." She blew her nose and turned another page. "Look! Listen to this." She cleared her throat and read a news story carefully clipped and saved by Leugenia long after her son John and his Laura were dead and gone.

The article reported that Sheriff James R. Merritt, briefly famous for eradicating the Ashley Gang, saw his dreams of higher state or national office fade with time. After dispatching the outlaws, the hard-nosed sheriff became highly successful and increasingly heavy-handed in his pursuit and arrests of bootleggers and rumrunners. As a result, his popularity waned among free-spirited Floridians. And the controversy about what really happened that night at the Sebastian bridge never faded.

Political opponents raised the issue during Merritt's next campaign. His fame had worn thin by then and he was soundly defeated, ousted as high sheriff of Saint Lucie County. He later managed to be elected as a county commissioner despite political mudslingers who resurrected the issue in every campaign.

John Ashley had become the skeleton in Merritt's closet, the reason his political career did not flourish as he'd hoped.

"Could be written today," John said. "That's Florida politics."

"Oh, no!" Laura gasped in heartfelt dismay at another story published years after the fact. "Officer Riblet," she exclaimed, with a fresh rush of tears. "Remember the police officer shot by John's younger brother Bobby?"

John nodded. "The first to be killed in the line of duty. His name's on the plaque in the lobby," he said, recalling the recent stray bullet that had scored Riblet's name.

"He and his wife, Madge, had a little boy, a toddler at the time." She read the story. The grief-stricken widow was so afraid of guns that she vowed at her husband's funeral that their only child would never own, handle, or touch a firearm. He didn't, until he grew into a headstrong teenager who sneaked off to hunt with friends and was accidentally shot in the foot. The wound festered, did not heal, and he died of blood poisoning.

"It killed him, at sixteen!" Laura exclaimed. "She never got over it, it says. Who would? Oh, John, no wonder Gram hid these books away. All those poor, tragic people."

She lifted her eyes to his. "And they are us."

He held her, kissed her, and whispered in her ear, "This time, it's different." Or is it? he wondered.

His cell phone rang. "Johnny," Leon said. "We got trouble in Miami."

"What happened?"

"The cops swear you're still in town. For all I know, you are. They keep checking tips, armed for bear. They stepped in it. Knew they would. It was just a matter of time."

"How?" John leaned forward. He heard sirens in the background. Lots of them.

"Wrong-house raid. Tipster dropped a dime, said you and the little lady were holed up with an old buddy, your high school football coach."

"Reggie? Hell, yeah. Haven't seen him in years."

"They hit the right house on the wrong street. The address they wanted was eleven twenty-four Northwest Twenty-third; they went to eleven twenty-four Northwest Twenty-fourth. Made a classic wrong house raid."

"What's wrong with them?"

"Happens," Leon said.

"All the time," John said. "How bad?"

"Ugly. Shut off the power, smashed windows, and busted down the doors as three sisters, ages seventy-nine, eighty-one, and eighty-seven, was sitting down to supper. The son of one of 'em was visiting to celebrate winning the title of county schoolteacher of the year. They bashed him acrost the head with a billy club, kicked him in the kidneys, and tased him. Twice. His mother had a heart attack and stopped breathing. All of 'em were cuffed, tear-gassed, and roughed up. Trashed that little house. Showed it on TV. I've seen plenty, but nothing worse. Tore the bottoms outta all the furniture—the couch, the chairs, the mattresses. Thought you was hiding inside 'em, I guess. A fat cop crawled through the attic and fell, crashed right through the ceiling into a bedroom. Emptied all the drawers, yanked clothes racks outta the closets, and tossed everything. Pulled down the drop ceiling in the kitchen and chased Sparky, the family cat those ladies loved like a child, out the back door. Got backed over by a fire truck brought in to blow the tear gas outta the house and light up the neighborhood in case you was hiding in the bushes. Then they turned loose a K-9 dog to track you, but it bit a pregnant woman taking out the garbage next door."

"For God's sake!" John said.

"You wore the badge too," Leon said. "You were one of 'em."

"Not me. I never did that."

"Glad to hear it, Johnny. Whole damn neighborhood turned out. Those little ladies work hard in the community and their church. Everybody loves 'em. Twenty minutes later, rocks and bottles are bouncing off police cars, and the grocery store on the next block is being looted and set afire. Motorists are being attacked, robbed, carjacked. And it's spreading, Johnny, just like the bad ol' days."

"Damn. Did the chief, the mayor, or city manager step up to do a public mea culpa, suspend the bad guys, and promise to investigate how it happened, to calm things down?"

"Nope. Some sergeant's the only one to speak up so far. Backed up the cops, said their info was good and they nearly had you, missed you by minutes. The little ladies are in the hospital; the one with the heart attack's critical. The schoolteacher of the year got locked up for resisting arrest, said more charges are pending. He just bonded out. Had 'im on Channel Six, head bandaged, lip split. The poor man cried on camera. Swore the cops never knocked, never identified themselves as police, just busted in like a mob, demolished the place, threw the old ladies to the floor, cuffed 'em, then beat the crap out of him, trying to make him tell where you were. The man didn't know. Gonna be a bad night here, Johnny."

"Be careful," John said. "Watch yourself."

"People in that department are guilty of so much," Leon said. "You're not their only victim, Johnny. Tell me where you're at so I can come lend a hand."

John paused. "It's not that I don't trust you, Leon. I do. But I'm not sure how to handle this. I'm responsible now for other people whose safety I can't compromise. My family's in a bad position because of me. Maybe I'll just run."

"Don't be foolish, Johnny. Keep your cool. Tell me where you are so I can help protect you and them."

"Thanks for the offer, Leon, but your resources are limited and their reach is so long." He glanced at Laura, who was half listening but more focused on the scrapbook in front of her. She had moved a table lamp closer in order to read the sometimes faded old newsprint. "This whole thing is beginning to take on a life of its own," John said. "You have no idea."

"You may be right, but I'm in touch with folks who can help you. Getting some details tonight, directly from the source. We need to meet, sit down face-to-face."

"Let me think on it overnight, Leon. I don't want to risk security where I am now. I'm running out of places to hide. Let's talk in the morning."

"Okay, Johnny, but don't wait too long, they're pulling out all the stops. They tell the press they're sure you're still in Miami. Don't believe they really think that for a minute. It's all a smoke screen. Keep looking over your shoulder. Later."

CHAPTER SIXTY

The late TV news covered rioting in Miami. Shopping centers, police substations, and motorists attacked, performances canceled at the Center for the Performing Arts, and classes suspended at Miami-Dade College, both downtown.

Residents stripped supermarket shelves of food and emergency supplies. Businesses were shuttered, locked down, and curfews declared. Trigger-happy Miamians were heavily armed and, in most cases, drunk and angry enough to open fire if provoked.

John watched the coverage, then roamed restlessly through the dark outside Gram's house. He made sure their car was out of sight, watched for lights, and checked the lane from the main road for fresh tire tracks. He considered stretching a chain across it where it reached Gram's property but decided against it. No chain would deter gunmen on foot.

Night birds called, crickets chirped, dogs barked in the distance. The bright quarter moon reigned over a star studded night made for love, fresh starts, and new beginnings, not bad endings. The night seemed peaceful, unlike chaotic Miami, hundreds of miles to the southeast. Yet the sweet-smelling night air in this place stirred memories John knew he never had and raised the hair on the back of his neck. How, and where, did this all go so wrong?

He closed his eyes for a long moment, took a deep breath, then went inside.

"Does Gram have an alarm system?"

"Didn't need it when Grandpa was alive." Laura shook her head. "Dogs are the best alarms. But hers got old. The last one died six months ago. Gram cried so. She said, 'At my age, you realize you will never have all the dogs you wanted in your life.' I was away, working a lot, and thought it would be easier on her if she didn't have a puppy. They're so much work."

"Yeah, you can't beat 'em for cute, but in Gram's case," John said, "it's probably best to adopt one or two healthy, mature dogs given up by people who can't afford 'em. Can't beat 'em for loyalty. They know instinctively that you saved their lives and they'd give theirs for you. You were right about Françoise. She's got heart."

"Wouldn't scare a soul who saw her," Laura said, "but she was the best early warning system."

"Soon as I get the equipment," John said, "I'll install motion sensor lights outside."

"You can do that yourself?"

"Of course. You have no idea how handy I am." He hugged her.

"I'd keep you even if you weren't."

"How right are we for each other?"

"Perfect," she said. "Always have been, always will be."

He sighed. "Leon wants to meet, says he can help."

"I trust him," Laura said. "He was so committed to the mission the day I picked you up at the overpass. No way he or anyone could have foreseen that it would end the way it did. We can't hold it against him."

John nodded. "You're right. But we don't know exactly what's happening in Miami, what duress Leon may be under."

"He's been there for us at every turn," Laura said. "We have no choice. If he can get here, this is the safest place to meet."

"We're sitting ducks." He frowned. "We have to protect Gram. This address is on your driver's license, gun permit, and voter's registration. They must have checked here early on and found you hadn't come home. Gram either doesn't remember or they talked to the woman who comes in to help her every day. They probably asked her to tip off the local police if you show your face. Either way, they're coming for us, Laura. I can feel it." He roamed through the house, turned off all but one light.

"Don't even think about leaving without me," she said. "Promise me you won't."

He said nothing.

She stared at him in silence, then checked on Gram, who was sleeping peacefully. When Laura joined John in her bedroom, she found him watching the night from her window. He'd put together an escape plan, but there was only one way in and out by car, and a successful escape through the woods was doubtful at best. Laura had an ATV, a three-wheeler, in the barn, which was now a garage, along with her dark-blue Mustang and Gram's Oldsmobile. The gas tanks were all full. He had checked them.

Her hair spilled across the pillow as black and shiny as a raven's wing. She sat up as he came to bed. Silver moonlight filtered through the trees and the sheer curtains in her windows. She took his face in her hands.

"Let's learn from the past, darlin'. We can't ignore those who've gone before, John," she said softly. "I feel so close to them. But I know now that if we carry the seeds of disaster in our genes, we have to outsmart that reckless death wish that took them to the brink. I want us to marry, have children, and live the life the first John and Laura never had but always wanted.

"The first John and Laura," she repeated dreamily as he held her. "What if they weren't the first? What if it was possible to dig deeper into the vast tapestry of the past and find others? What if this is something that happens every hundred years or so until we finally get it right?"

"If the pattern's in our DNA, can we break it? Can we change our own destiny? Or does it always have to end the same way?" he wondered aloud.

"I don't, I won't, believe that," she said, her arms around him. "Learning from the mistakes of the past helps us change the future. Otherwise, what's the point?"

"I know how this sounds," he said, "but years ago a friend told me I had flashbacks and symptoms of post-traumatic stress disorder. I laughed it off, then. That was years before I ever picked up a gun and went to war—or pinned on a badge and patrolled Miami. But even then, violence was never a stranger. And when it came, I was ready, knew what to do, and had no fear. But now I do. My biggest fear is losing you. I can feel it. The end is coming. It's real."

"I wish we had met sooner and had more time together," she said wistfully. "I feel cheated." She rested her head on his shoulder. "When I was young, I'd dream of Seattle, New Orleans, and a man. I could never quite see his face, but now I know it was you. When I saw those cities years later, I recognized them, knew the landmarks. Some were gone, others not exactly the way I'd seen them in my dreams. And you weren't there either, but I felt your presence. Remember what your mother said about us?"

"She was right," he said. "We were meant to be together, but the day we met, our lives took a downward spiral. The question is, how strong is the past? You think we have a chance? Does anybody?"

"We can change the end," she whispered with absolute certainty, and gently raked her teeth across his ear. "But just in case, let's make love now as if it's for the last time."

"We always do," he whispered, and reached for her.

CHAPTER SIXTY-ONE

"T hings have simmered down some," Leon reported in an early call the next morning. Sporadic violence still flared, he said, which wasn't unusual in Miami.

"But the hotel and tourism groups are afraid the press coverage might hurt business. They're still demanding that the mayor ask the governor to send in the National Guard to keep the peace.

"The politicians are against it, say the police can handle it themselves. Hell, it was the police who started it."

John agreed to meet, but before revealing his location, he asked Leon to dispose of the pre-paid cell phone he was using and call him back on a new one.

John, Laura, and Gram discussed the new echoes from the past at breakfast. Gram knew the story. So did they, now. In 1915, after John Ashley was sentenced to hang, his younger brother, Bobby, tried to save him. In a daring daylight attempt to break John out of jail, Bobby killed the jailer, then fought a gun battle in the street with Police Officer J. R. Riblet. The exchange fatally wounded both. Miamians, afraid that Ashley's gang would raid the city, demanded that the mayor ask the governor to send in the National Guard to keep the peace.

"The more things change, the more they stay the same," Gram said. She winked and sipped her tea, as she rocked in her favorite chair, a colorful, hand-knit afghan draped across the arm.

"We think it's best," Laura said eagerly, "to learn all we can from the past, then take a different path."

Gram's eyes grew sad as she listened and watched them together.

John was relieved when she said her home helper had the day off. They could decide what to do about the woman tomorrow.

Leon rang back on his new phone. "You won't regret this, Johnny," he said as he took down the address and directions. "I think things are looking up. We'll be there as quick as we can."

"We?" John asked, suddenly wary.

"A colleague's coming along," Leon said.

"Anybody I know?" John paced.

"Nope."

"Should I be worried?"

"Not about him. You've got lotsa other things to worry about. Focus on them. This is somebody you want to see."

"We trust you, man," John said. "Don't give us away."

"Later, Johnny."

It would take all day to reach Gram's by car.

John and Laura spent hours deciphering Leugenia's notes from the scrapbook margins and her Bible and talking with Gram. Sharp and clever, Gram had a quicker recall of events from eighty years ago than those that happened last week.

At four o'clock John and Laura had tea and biscuits, while Gram sipped her daily scotch and soda. "I'm younger than most people my age," she said at one point. They agreed.

Laura raided the freezer, thawed a roast, and popped it into the oven with herbs from Gram's garden, then scrubbed potatoes for baking. John savored the aroma and the atmosphere of comfortable domesticity, keenly aware that it might be only a brief and tantalizing taste, all they'd ever have, as the past closed in on them.

He heard nothing from Leon, though Gram seemed pleased that they expected company. They ate dinner and chatted. She puttered with Laura in the kitchen for a bit, then returned to her favorite chair. They watched the news and part of a Marlins game, as John cleaned their guns and reloaded them with fresh ammunition. He wore his in a shoulder holster he'd worn on the job and covered it with a loose sports shirt over his T-shirt. Just after dark, he thought he saw a flash of light in the woods between the house and the road. He doused the living room lights, drew his gun, and nudged the front door open with his foot.

"Is this how you normally greet visitors, John?" Gram asked from her chair in the dark.

"No, ma'am," he said.

"Good," she said. "If it was, I expect you wouldn't have many."

He heard the car before he saw it. A white Ford Crown Vic, the same model used by Miami police, other law enforcement agencies, and cab companies, emerged like a ghost from the dark and crunched slowly across the gravel toward the house. This was no cab. Gun in hand, John hit Leon's number on the cell phone.

"Where you at, buddy?"

"If we're at the right place, we should be closing in on your front door," Leon said. "Wanted to stay under the radar, so we killed the lights as we left the main road. Dark as hell out here. I miss downtown already."

"How many of you?"

"Just us two, Johnny. We're getting outta the car now. We'd appreciate it if you don't shoot at us. Guns give us the jitters." He and his companion laughed.

John watched Leon and a tall, lean, middle-aged man exit the car. The stranger wore blue jeans and a Cubavera. He carried a briefcase.

John turned the house lights back on, reholstered his gun, and greeted them at the door. Leon hugged him for the first time, his grip surprisingly strong. "Sorry about your brother, Johnny. Robby was a good man. A true warrior. Somebody you always want on your side."

Leon kissed Laura's upturned cheek, then turned to introduce his companion. "This here's my colleague, Arthur Bass."

"Colleague?" John extended his hand. He liked Bass on sight, something about his clear gray eyes, his body language, and his command of the room. Bass had a strong jaw and a firm handshake. They reminded him of someone he couldn't remember.

"Heard lots about you, John. Thought you were gonna mess up our operation for a while. Turns out we have more in common than I thought."

"Place smells great." Leon sniffed the air with a hungry look.

Gram gave Laura a stare that asked if she'd forgotten her southern hospitality. "Have you eaten?" Laura asked the visitors.

"Not really," Art said. "We're on serious business and had to get here in a hurry."

"How's a roast beef sandwich sound?" Their eyes lit up.

"Mayo or red horseradish?"

"Bless you, girl," Leon said with a sigh. "Both, please."

"Exactly what I was gonna say," Art told her.

As Laura toasted onion rolls in the kitchen, John asked, "What business, Leon? Exactly what business are you in?"

"I'm his boss," Art said. "His name isn't Leon, and he's been working undercover for us for more than eighteen months investigating gunrunning and money laundering in South Florida."

"And who is us?" John's eyebrows rose.

Art shrugged. "ATF—Alcohol, Tobacco, Firearms and Explosives. Leon's good. We thought he'd wandered off track with you, but he was right on the mark, as usual. He recently gave us a fella in Miami with warehouses full of sophisticated weaponry he's desperate to unload. His original buyer, from the Middle East, didn't show. Ron Jon Eagle was the broker. His murder killed the deal. He'd guaranteed the buyer Miami Police protection. The buyer backed off when he read the newspapers and saw that Eagle couldn't even protect himself.

"Eagle and the cops, both city and county, that he participated with in all sorts of illegal operations, had a falling out." Bass paused, took a bite from the sandwich Laura had placed in front of him, closed his eyes, and sighed aloud.

Leon had already worked his way through half his own sandwich.

"The cops were fine," Bass said, "with protecting and assisting in the smuggling and sale of counterfeit cigarettes and luxury watches, using the bank accounts and facilities of the tribe's gambling operation to launder money for drug cartels in Colombia and Mexico, running prostitution rings with underage girls, and the delivery and distribution of illegal drugs, but, God bless America, they drew the line at selling weapons to terrorists. When they opted out, Eagle threatened them. The man had a thing about getting even. They'd done too much business together, and he knew too much.

"From the get-go, Leon identified you as the only Miami cop he knew for sure was not in Eagle's pocket. You see where I'm going with this, John? While some of us thought you'd distracted Leon from his mission, you actually accelerated the case we wanted to make all along." He patted his mouth with a napkin and drank some of his sweet tea.

"Leon says you've got documentation that'll back up your case." The ATF supervisor nodded toward his briefcase. "We have enough to back up ours. If you show us yours, we'll show you ours and combine forces. We can broaden the hell outta this thing. You'll be our star witness for the prosecution, and we'll clean out that rat's nest of a department once and for all."

"It's never once and for all." John sighed and smiled at Laura. "It's cyclical; it'll happen again."

"Well," Art said, "hopefully not in our lifetime."

John glanced at Gram, nodding in her chair. "She just said this morning that the more things change, the more they remain the same. That's true."

"We can offer you protection—"

Gram's eyes suddenly opened, fixed like arrows on the door. Startled, John turned to look. Too late. In that instant he realized that he had never asked Gram why the woman who came to help her each day happened to take this one off.

The locked door burst open with such force that it ripped out half the wooden door frame. A man stepped through it wearing a ski mask and carrying a MAC-10 automatic weapon. Despite the mask, he looked familiar.

"Freeze!" he demanded. "Nobody move, or I'll waste you all right here, right now. Be my guest. Hello, Ashley," he said.

"Myerson," John said.

"Who are these jokers?" Lt. Mac Myerson gestured with his gun and looked surprised. Clearly he hadn't expected Leon and Art. He squinted at Leon. "Do I know you?"

Leon shook his head.

"I know I've seen you around someplace. Doesn't matter," the lieutenant said. He brandished the weapon, his finger on the trigger, and demanded they drop their guns onto the carpet.

When John hesitated, Myerson swung the weapon toward Laura's head. She and John exchanged an anguished look as he and Bass slowly complied. Myerson kicked both guns into a corner.

"Who are you?" Gram rose half out of her chair. "Look what you did to my front door! Put that gun away and get out of my house!"

"Sit down and shut up, old lady!" He waved the gun in her direction.

She sat down stiffly in her rocker, her eyes angry.

"Leave her alone!" Laura shouted and moved toward her.

"Stop right there!" the gunman said. "Don't move! You either," he told John.

"She's more than a hundred years old!" Laura said. "She doesn't know anything about all this!"

"Too bad, pretty girl. Too bad for all of you. I don't care who the hell, or how old, you are. You're in the wrong place with the wrong person." He turned to John. "Any hired gun coulda been sent to waste you. But you caused us so much grief, you self-righteous son of a bitch, we decided you had to know who killed you, that it was us.

"So okay, there's five of ya." He shrugged. "So what? Wouldn't cause a ripple in Miami. When they hear it was you, it'll be a relief." He leveled his gun at John.

"*No*," Laura cried.

"It's all right," John said.

"Or"—Myerson grinned and aimed the gun at Laura—"wanna see the girlfriend go first? Sounds like a plan to me."

The boom shook the room like an explosion. It rattled dishes on the table. The muzzle flash blinded them. The concussion made their ears ring. And the force of the blast hurled the lieutenant against the wall amid a shower of blood. He slowly slid down to the floor, leaving parts of his internal organs stuck to the wallpaper.

Gram's favorite chair still rocked gently. It was empty. She stood in front of it, holding her late husband's smoking twelve-gauge Remington shotgun.

"Another John Ashley is not gonna die on my watch," she said, "not if I can help it." She tottered a bit, took a deep breath, stood up straight, then sat back down in her rocker and surveyed the room.

"Now, look at that mess," she said, annoyed.

"It's okay," Laura said. "It'll be okay."

"Nice shooting, Gram." John gently took the shotgun from her hands.

"No kidding," Bass said, as they all breathed a collective sigh of relief.

"It runs in the family," Gram said.

"I love these women!" Leon said passionately.

Bass and John had already retrieved their own weapons. "Let's see who else is here," John said. "Laura, take Gram into the pantry and close the door."

Before she even helped Gram to her feet, the broken door, half-hanging from its hinges, was kicked open by one of the two marginal homicide detectives who had planted evidence to frame John after the motel shooting.

"Everybody freeze," he cried, his Glock automatic in both hands, eyes darting. He took in the mess, including what appeared to be his lieutenant's liver slowly dripping down to the carpet. His eyes widened and focused on John. "Drop it!" he shouted.

John obliged, dropped the shotgun, and came up with his revolver. "Drop your weapon now," John said, "or I will kill you."

The detective, eyes still wide, swallowed hard, dropped his weapon, raised his hands, turned around, and dropped to his knees. He knew the drill.

John handed the detective's gun to Leon. "Shoot him if he moves," he said.

"With pleasure," Leon said enthusiastically.

John and Art hit the porch in time to see two men in a black Chevrolet Suburban back down the lane at high speed.

"Don't chase 'em!" Art stopped John and punched 911 into his phone. "Let the locals get 'em."

And they did. Both were in custody in less than twenty minutes.

"Did you know that Gram had the shotgun?" John asked Laura.

She shrugged. "She's always kept it right there, under the afghan. It belonged to my great-granddaddy."

"He had a still in the woods back behind the house," Gram explained. "That runs in the family too, darlin'."

"I guess it does," Laura whispered tearfully.

John called Joel Hirschhorn an hour later.

"Hey, John. Doug McCann, FBI, is trying to reach you," the lawyer said. "Nice guy. We had a long conversation. They want you to come in; they're talking immunity. They need you to testify. And my guy at Justice wants to meet you. They're interested in a long list of civil rights violations by the local police, including the deaths of prisoners and suspects. The feds are fighting over you, John. They want to clean up the mess down here and need your help. Any deals we make include Laura, of course."

"I'll have to think about it and talk to her," John said.

"You're in demand, John. Big changes are coming to this city. Thanks to you, they're putting it all together," his lawyer said. "Jeff Burnside, the Channel Six reporter, says you owe him an exclusive. He taped an interview with me a few hours ago. They're airing a major exposé tomorrow night. How quick," Joel asked, "can you get to my office? The US attorney for the Southern District is on the other line. Wants to shake your hand."

"We were here first, John," said Art Bass of the ATF.

"Your lawyer's right," Leon said later. "This is gonna be big. Bigger than anything Miami's ever seen before and ever will again."

John and Laura exchanged a secret smile. "I wouldn't be too sure about that," he said.

ACKNOWLEDGMENTS

I am grateful, as always, for all the heroes present and past: Miami assistant police chief Philip Doherty, Miami-Dade Police homicide major Raul Diaz, Miami sergeant and marine law enforcement officer Art Scrig, all now retired, and fallen hero Miami police officer John Rhinehart Riblet, killed in the line of duty on Wednesday, June 2, 1915.

Special thanks to another hero, Dr. Sander Dubovy, associate professor of ophthalmology and pathology at Miami's Bascom Palmer Eye Institute, and as usual to criminal defense attorney Joel Hirshhorn, and my pastor, the Rev. Garth R. Thompson, who try their best to keep me on the straight and narrow. When they can't, my getaway drivers, the redheads: Marilyn Lane, Joy Gellately, and Mimi Gadinsky save the day.

I will always be indebted to Dr. Stephen J. Nelson, one of the world's best pathologists and chief medical examiner for the 10th District of Florida. The usual suspects include the ever creative and inspirational Miami Beach Community Church Writers Group: the romantic Bill and Mitzi Richardson, the elusive Edgar Bryant, poet and ace photographer Robert Williams, the astonishing Jeffrey Rand, and the ever-evolving T. W. Stone. I could not have written this without the generous help of Jorge Zamanillo, who specializes in yesterday, today, and tomorrow as vice president of expansion at HistoryMiami.

I owe a special debt to writers Ada Coats Williams and the late Hix C. Stuart, who explored the notorious, bullet-riddled exploits of Florida's best-known outlaws. Stuart actually interviewed John Ashley live, in the 1920s. Wish I could have been there! The hero of Morningside, Elvis Cruz, was generous with his time and expertise, and thank you, as always, to *The Miami Herald*, especially Monica Leal, keeper of the morgue, and Andrea Torres, ace reporter, friend, and true sister. Master musicians Rick and Ann Stewart and that most stirring of all tenors, Dale Kitchell, played major roles, as did computer geniuses Bill Swift and Mike Haines. My editor Mitchell Ivers; my agent Michael Congdon; the gloriously brilliant Katie Grimm; Mara Lurie and James Walsh; and my longtime conspirators, Ann Lee Hughes, Sesquipedalians Patricia Keen, Dr. Ferdie Pacheco, Luisita Pacheco, Al Alschuler, and friend Robert M. Wasserman, who shares my love of history and justice, and last, but by no means least, T. Michael Smith, my partner in crime.

What a sterling cast of characters. Friends are the family we choose.

ABOUT THE AUTHOR

Edna Buchanan worked the *Miami Herald* police beat for eighteen years, during which she covered five thousand violent deaths, three thousand of them homicides. She won scores of awards, including the Pulitzer Prize and the George Polk Award for Career Achievement in Journalism, and attracted international acclaim for her classic true-crime memoirs, *The Corpse Has a Familiar Face* and *Never Let Them See You Cry*. Her first novel of suspense, *Nobody Lives Forever*, was nominated for an Edgar Award.

She brings exotic and steamy Miami to vivid life in all her novels. Edna captures both the heartbeat and the hot breath of this restless, dynamic, and mercurial city. In addition to eighteen books, she has written numerous short stories, articles, essays, and book reviews. She lives in Miami with her husband, two dogs, and too many cats.